To Jennifer and to Mum.

For believing, even when I couldn't.

Hope is the worst of evils, for it prolongs the torment of man.

- Friedrich Nietzsche

Prologue

I stood in the hotel corridor, staring at the door to room 134 and I knew this was the end. I stared at that door as though it alone was responsible for the pain and fear and death that had contaminated my life. My body was raw and my soul bruised and torn, as if I'd been infected by a new, virulent strain of an ancient disease that would always find ways to evolve and mutate.

The disease was poisonous and malevolent, as it always had been, and would always remain. People had died because of it. And others had killed. Still others lived, yet bore scars that ran deep and permanent.

I knew which I was at the moment. But which would I be by nightfall?

Even through the blood pounding in my ears I could hear movement from within the room. They were hurried movements, urgent and clumsy. I knew who it was and I wondered if they too knew that this was the end.

I had followed a broken and bloodied path to this door, this room, this instant. A path paved with lies, half-truths, whispered manipulations and self-serving justifications. Some of those hung round my own neck like tainted medals – too many to bear, if truth be told – and every mistake I had made lay before me like a panel of judges poised ready to don their black caps.

I had taken the Bell case thinking it would be simple, thinking I would walk away from it untainted and unchanged from the person I had been. I should have known better. After all, I, more than most, know what the disease is capable of. It had passed close by me once before and had cast its shadow over my life and the lives of those I loved.

And now, evil had found me once more. I had felt its presence as it brushed past me and I had smelt its venom as it breathed on my neck. It had called to me from its dark shadows, called to me in a voice I was too scared to refuse, and I had turned away from the sun and looked it in the eye.

I thought I was ready.

I was wrong.

But I had stood there. I had stood before it and tried not to weep as my soul shattered and bodies fell around me.

And as time passed I felt something dark grow within me and I knew the disease had entered my blood.

And I would never be whole again.

My eyes focused on the door once more as the sounds within the room stopped. I would not knock. This last, final act would be played out my way, on my terms, and justice would be done.

I took a step back and lunged forward, driving my foot into the lock with every ounce of rage in my body.

The lock broke. The door crashed against the inner wall.

I went in and slammed the door behind me.

This was the end.

One

'How long has she been missing?'
'Two weeks.'
'And how old is she?'

Archie Bell looked somewhere between forty-five and fifty, so I could hope we weren't dealing with a kid. Missing kids get to me like nothing else.

'Janet? She's twenty. Twenty last August.'

I relaxed a little. With young adults there could be a number of explanations. With children there were only a few. And none of them were good.

'Have you contacted the police?' I asked.

Archie Bell looked off to the side, out of the window as though something had caught his interest. What it might be I wasn't sure, since all either of us could see was the blank face of the building opposite. Maybe he had a keen interest in slowly crumbling brickwork.

I took the opportunity to study him more closely. He was a skinny man and everything about him was dull, from the drab, neutral tones he wore, to the thin brown hair pasted around his bald crown with nervous sweat. His watery blue eyes spoke of apology and his downtrodden demeanour suggested he constantly expected the world to tell him off.

When he had walked into my office ten minutes ago, he had been stooped over, his shoulders hunched as if protecting himself from attack. He was taller than I was but his posture brought him down to my height, making him look, as my mum would have said, like a half-shut knife. When I had clasped his hand in greeting his palm had smeared across mine and I barely resisted the urge to reach for a tissue.

Archie was still looking through the window when he spoke. 'Well, no. I'm not sure there's any need, really.'

'But you want a private investigator to find her?'

'I just want to know she's alright.'

'Do you think she's run away?' I asked. 'Why would she do that?'

He looked at me sharply, then swallowed something hard as his eyes dropped and skittered across the floor. 'I don't know,' he finally said.

It was so clearly a lie that I almost told him to leave. Had I had any other clients, or even potential clients, I'd have sent him on his way. It was getting to the point I'd forgotten what a client looked like. Maybe they all lied.

So I let him stay. Because I needed the work.

And because I knew fear when I saw it.

There was more to this than a girl becoming tired of living with her father. I wasn't going to risk throwing him out, not when his daughter could be in trouble. And if a young woman was in trouble I needed the truth.

'What's she running from, Archie?'

Archie turned slightly in his chair and adopted a defensive posture, his legs crossed, his mouth unconsciously chewing on his left thumbnail. 'Maybe,' he said through a mouthful of thumb, 'this is a bad idea. She's probably with some friends anyway. I don't want to waste your time.' He didn't seem to notice the latest trickle of sweat that had started to run from his hairline.

I leaned back in my chair and spread my hands, making my posture as non-threatening as possible. 'Archie, I'm not going to fight to make you hire me, I've got plenty of clients to keep me busy.' *Little white lie, who's to know?* 'But you wouldn't be here if you weren't concerned for your daughter.' I let that sink in for a moment before I carried on. 'Finding people is what I do. It's my bread and butter and I'm very good at it. If you hire me to find your daughter I will find her. But you're going to have to tell me what danger she may be in.'

I sat back and looked at him, leaving the ball in his court. I thought for a second I had pushed too far, but then he seemed to relax a little.

'I love my daughter Mr Harper. You need to understand that.'

'I do.'

'I'd do anything for her.' He paused as though that wasn't quite what he had expected to come out of his mouth. 'She's my life. Her mother left us when Janet was four. It's been the two of us since then. I don't know what I'd do if anything happened to her.'

I said nothing, simply looked him in the eye and waited for him to trust me.

'I think she may be running away from someone,' Archie said. 'I think she's scared.'

Now we were getting somewhere. And I hadn't even had to pull any teeth yet.

'Who?'

He took a deep breath and plunged in. 'It's her boyfriend. Well, not anymore, she split up with him.'

That old chestnut.

'I suppose he didn't take the split too well.'

'He's trying to find her. He tried to make me tell him where she was. But I couldn't, I don't know. She didn't tell me.' Something dark crossed his eyes and they drifted back to the floor.

'Tell me about him. About their relationship.'

'There isn't much I can tell you, to be honest.' Archie glanced over his shoulder at the door, checking that we were really alone, before moving his chair a little closer to my desk. 'She met him a few months ago. Around October. He came to the house once to pick her up. Didn't say much but I got a bad feeling about him. Janet didn't really tell me anything about him, just mentioned that she had met a boy. I say, boy, but he was about the same age as her, maybe a year or two older. I still think of Janet as my little girl though, you know?'

I didn't have kids, so maybe I didn't know exactly what he meant. But he was on a roll now so I nodded that I did.

'I know she's not perfect. We've had our ups and downs over the years, like any family. But she's my family. She's all I have.' His voice tailed off and I waited. He was working up to telling me something. Something he wasn't comfortable sharing.

'I thought we were past the worst of it. I hoped it was just her being young, that maybe she was acting up a bit, reacting to her mother walking out?' He said it like a question, as though I may be able to give him the answer. I doubted anyone could have.

Archie let out a long breath, the kind you release just before you do something you really don't want to. 'Janet has had a lot of boyfriends Mr Harper. Truth be told, you wouldn't call them boyfriends.' He left it at that, letting me draw my own conclusion. He had looked into my eyes as he spoke, and still held my gaze. It was the strongest eye contact he had made yet, as though he was daring me to judge his daughter. For all his apparent weakness I could see Archie was fiercely protective of Janet, and it would be a foolish person who underestimated his devotion to her.

I cleared my throat and asked him, 'A lot?'

'A fair number. As far as I'm aware. I mean, I don't know who they were, she wasn't bringing them home. But I know she was,' he paused as he searched for the right word again, 'intimate... with them.'

I couldn't imagine how painful that had been for Archie to tell me. No father should have to admit to anyone that his daughter was less than discriminating with her sexual partners. But painful or not, I had to keep digging while he was in the mood to be honest 'Is there anything else in Janet's background that I might need to know?'

'Like what?'

'You said she was acting up. Was that confined to her sex life or did she act up in other ways? Drink? Drugs? Fighting, shoplifting... anything.'

Archie looked uncomfortable again, but quickly swallowed it. 'She never got into fights. Never. She was a nice girl, not hugely popular, but she had friends alright. And she didn't really drink'

'What about drugs?'

His glance through the window confirmed it.

'What did she use?'

Archie sighed heavily. 'Just some marijuana.'

'Did she use much?'

'I don't think so.'

'You don't really know though, do you?'

'No,' he admitted.

'Is it possible that she took other drugs?'

'It's possible, I suppose. I don't know what she was doing all the time.'

'Then it's also possible that her drug use could be behind her disappearance,' I told him. 'Or even her promiscuity.'

Archie began to protest, already halfway to his feet. 'But she's not like that anymore!'

'Can you be sure of that?'

That took the wind out of his sails. He slumped back in the chair, deflated, the shoulders hunching up again. Back to his natural protective posture. Then he spoke very quietly. 'I don't think he'd let her do anything like that. He likes to be in control.'

Back to the boyfriend. 'What's his name, Archie?'

'Are you going to talk to him?' Archie looked suddenly petrified.

'I need to know if he had anything to do with Janet's disappearance.'

'But he didn't. He doesn't know where she is. He's trying to find her too.' His voice was now strident with fear.

'What did he do, Archie? Why are you so scared of him?' He mumbled something in response. I pushed harder. 'Why is Janet running from him? Did he threaten her? Hit her?'

Archie finally cracked. 'Yes.' The word was something between a sob and a cough and seemed to have been wrenched from him. He carried on, the words coming fast and abrupt. 'Not at first. He was nice to her. For a while. Then he changed. He beat her. A lot.'

I sat up straighter in my chair, my mouth tight. 'Did Janet tell you or did you see the marks?'

'She never had any marks. At least, not on her face. All the marks he left were in places people couldn't see. He used to punch her in the…' I thought he was about to break down but he forced it out, '…in her private place. He did that so much she peed blood.' Archie screwed his eyes tight shut to stop the tears. His hands were clasped more tightly than I would have thought he had the strength for, the nails on his right hand digging into the back of his left.

A flash of anger erupted at my core, like a petrol can touched by a flame. I had no idea how Archie must be feeling. I was angry enough and I'd never met this girl. Had it been my daughter the guy would be taking his meals through a straw for a long time.

Archie opened his eyes, looked up and caught mine, saw the fire burning there. 'If only I could have helped her. If only I could have stood up to him for her.' He looked as though he wanted to weep. 'But I'm weak. So bloody weak.'

He unclasped his fingers and ran his right hand over the top of his head, flattening the hair even more. The left dropped into his lap and I saw four small, crescent shaped cuts on the back of it. I watched as the blood began to weep slowly from them and I realised a part of me was angry with Archie too, for not protecting his daughter, for not standing up to her violent boyfriend, for not being stronger.

I took a long slow breath and told myself not to judge him. We lived in different worlds. In Archie's world you relied on the law to protect you. You believed in society's conventions and trusted them to keep you safe from harm. In my world I learned a long time ago that the law served those it wanted to and the only protection you could rely on came from yourself. And maybe, if you were lucky, a few good friends who would stand with you.

I was searching the room for a tissue for Archie's bleeding hand when he surprised me by climbing to his feet.

'He thought I knew where she was, that I'd helped her leave him. He said he wasn't going to let her get away with it.' He lifted the hem of his beige jumper, pulled his shirt tail from the waistband of his trousers and lifted that too. I had a brief view of a pasty white stomach before Archie turned his back to me and rolled his jumper and shirt up to his armpits. My eyes widened as I saw the bruises. His entire back was covered in a mass of black and purple bruising that spread around his sides and stood out in stark contrast against his pale white skin.

Archie looked at me over his shoulder. 'That was a week ago. I could barely stand the first couple of days.'

I said nothing but my fists tightened as I looked at the spread of bruises. Archie quickly tugged down his shirt and jumper and sat back down. 'I don't want you to bring her home. I just want to know she's safe. She won't be safe at home.'

'Tell me his name and I'll make sure he never hurts either of you again.'

Archie shook his head softly. 'He knows some bad people. He told me if I went to the police he would come back and break my legs. You might not be the police, but...'

'You have to trust me here,' I told him. 'I need to speak to him to see if he knows anything about where Janet is. It's unlikely. It doesn't sound like he would have any reason to do something to her and then throw in a bluff by visiting you looking for her. But I need to be sure. He won't come near you, I guarantee it.'

Archie looked unconvinced that I could follow through on my promise, but I waited, letting him know this was not negotiable. Eventually he sighed. 'It's Johnny. Johnny D'Arienzo.'

'Do you know where he lives?'

'No, but Janet mentioned he works in a garage in the East End. Near Alexandra Parade. She never told me the name though.'

'That's okay, I'll find it. And I'll find Janet. Then we'll decide how to bring her home. Okay?'

Archie nodded his agreement and I decided to change the subject away from Johnny D'Arienzo and his over-eager fists. I asked Archie to tell me about Janet. He raised his eyes to the ceiling slowly as he thought about where to start. When he did start it came pouring out, as though he had been waiting for someone to ask, someone who would take the burden from him. I sat back and took notes, letting him talk uninterrupted.

As he talked he passed me a recent photo, taken at Christmas. It wasn't a professional picture but it was a nicely taken head and shoulders shot. Janet was quite pretty, with a narrow face, small eyes and a wide smile, and, according to her father, she was around five feet five, and slim. Her hair was blonde and straight to her shoulders, with a fringe that swept down across her eyes. Her blue eyes sparkled in the camera flash as she smiled.

They lived together in a house in Cardonald, a residential suburb about twenty minutes drive from here when the traffic was good. Janet had previously shared a flat in Govan with her best friend Rebecca Davidson, however there had been a fall-out of some sort around a year ago and both had moved back home to live with their parents. Seems the girls' big adventure in self-reliance only lasted six months. The impression I was getting of the Bell household made me wonder if Janet had decided to return home after realising her father was the only one likely to run around after her. Archie dismissed the falling out with *you know what girls are like*. I wasn't sure I did anymore, but I made a note of Rebecca's name, along with those of Janet's other friends and colleagues. With any luck she'd have confided in someone.

Archie last saw her on the morning of Thursday 8th February. They'd had breakfast together, she'd gone off to work as normal, and never come home. Archie started to well up at this point and I tried to give him something to focus on. I asked about transport and he told me that Janet had no car and relied on buses for most of her journeys. That at least limited the options available to her and increased the chances of tracing whatever journey she had made.

He stopped for a moment, raised his eyes to the ceiling again, searching for anything he had neglected to tell me. While he was thinking I asked if Janet had any distinguishing features. Anything that might help me spot her if she had changed her appearance in some way.

Archie seemed surprised. 'Changed her appearance?'

'Nothing drastic, but if she really wants to stay hidden she may have done something to make herself look a wee bit different. Her blonde hair is distinctive. Anyone looking for her would expect to see that blonde hair, so she may have dyed it, or cut it short, or both. She may just cover it with a hat. When someone's afraid they can become surprisingly resourceful.'

Archie seemed uncomfortable with the idea of his little girl looking different from the way he expected her to. Or maybe Janet was vain about her hair and he knew she would be unlikely to cut it.

'Well, she has a scar. Would that help?'

'It might. Where?'

'On the inside of her right forearm, it's about this size, sort of curved,' he said, indicating the location on his own forearm and drawing a three-inch arc. 'She fell off a swing when she was young, and the bone went through the skin.'

I winced as I thought about a little girl playing happily, then falling, and a piece of bone suddenly tearing through the skin of her arm. Archie looked concerned for a second. Was he worried that I didn't believe this was how his daughter had become scarred? Or was he too seeing the scene fresh in his mind?

The scar was a good way of being certain that someone was Janet if I was unsure. But even if it wasn't covered I would have to get pretty close before I would be able to see something that size. I'd just have to cross that particular bridge when I came to it.

'There are a few more things that I need before I can find Janet,' I said. 'I need details of her bank accounts and credit cards and the numbers of any phones that she has access to.'

'What?' Archie asked in surprise. I was used to this. Clients often seemed to expect me to track someone down through telepathy and were reluctant to part with anything they deemed too personal. Particularly bank details. Maybe they thought I had an app on my phone that would spit out the GPS coordinates of anyone whose name I typed in. I could have dispelled that notion immediately by showing Archie the less than state of the art brick I had been lugging around for the last few years. But I didn't want him to think he was hiring a Luddite. Even if he was.

'You don't have any idea where she went, do you Archie?' I asked pointedly.

'Well, no.'

'Neither do I. That's why I need this information. Her phone records may show who she talked to around the time she disappeared. And the bank records will show any billing for travel tickets, or maybe a withdrawal at a cash machine near where she is.'

'I don't have any of that information with me.'

'That's fine. I'll come to your home later today to pick it up. I need to have a look through Janet's things anyway.'

He appeared uncomfortable again but didn't protest.

'I know this is awkward for you Archie. But you have to trust me. I'll respect Janet's privacy, and yours, as much as possible. Unfortunately, I will need to do and ask some things that you may not be very comfortable with. But if I don't I can't find her for you.'

He reluctantly nodded acceptance. I turned to the photocopier and made several colour copies of Janet's photograph to show around and gave the original back to Archie. We took care of the financial side of things and shook hands before I showed him to the door and said goodbye.

I returned to my office and stood at the window looking down at the street. I saw Archie stop outside, look around to get his bearings and set off. He walked with his shoulders hunched and his head down against the chill February wind; a man no longer surprised at the kicks life continued to give him.

And I thought about a young woman. A girl really, scared and alone somewhere, afraid to come home because of a man who thought his desires were all that mattered.

And I thought about another young woman. One who had been taken from us. I owed it to her to find Janet Bell, to bring her home and keep her safe.

One girl had been lost. I would not let it be two.

Two

I called Mack to fill him in. He was, in theory at least, my partner, although he took as little to do with the business as possible, without actually taking out a court injunction to prevent me calling him. He was a smart guy, but he didn't have the patience for the mundane side of my job. I usually only brought him in when his particularly *direct* approach was needed.

'Yeah?' Mack answered.

'We've got a new case.'

'So there are desperate people out there then?'

'Apparently so.'

'What's the deal?' Behind him I could hear the thump of punch bags being pounded and the indistinct shouts of one of Mack's instructors.

'Twenty-year-old girl is missing,' I told him. 'Her dad thinks she's run away from her ex. Guy used to beat her so the dad doesn't want her brought back, just wants to know that she's okay. Reckons she's safer where she is.'

There was silence on the other end for a few seconds. I knew what he was thinking. It was the same thing I'd been thinking, only without the social niceties.

'When you going to see the ex?' he asked eventually.

'This afternoon.'

'Want some company?'

'Not yet.'

'You sure? If I go see him, she can come home, no problem.'

'I'll see if I can sort it out quietly first.'

Mack snorted on the other end. 'Quietly. Right.'

The sound of his disgust was cut short as he disconnected the call.

Maybe I'd leave it a while before I went to visit Mack.

*

I spent the next hour on my computer, running traces on the names Archie had given me. By the time I finished I had basic information and an address for each of Janet's friends and colleagues, as well as Johnny D'Arienzo. I shut down the computer and stuffed all the paperwork into a folder, sat back in my chair and thought about my next move. As I did so I looked around my office and wondered what Archie Bell had thought of it. He may have been too preoccupied to give it any consideration, but had he looked would he have been impressed? Or would he have thought twice about hiring me?

My office was a ground floor flat in a sandstone tenement in Garnethill, perched above Sauchiehall Street and overlooking Charing Cross. The location, in the city centre of Glasgow, made me accessible to clients, and, being so close to the M8 slip roads, allowed me to be on the motorway heading either east or west in a matter of minutes. Mostly though, this was my office because it had become available at a knockdown price. Someone Mack had recently become acquainted with was suddenly leaving town on a prolonged trip and he had decided to pass the property on to Mack. I didn't think he'd be back anytime soon.

I didn't live there – preferring to keep my personal life and my business life separate – but the other flats were residential and I sometimes wondered what they thought of having a private investigator on their doorstep; especially one with a name like Keir Harper. When I was naming my firm I had been self conscious about it. I remembered Mack's reaction when I told him that I had decided on Keir Harper Investigations – something that had obviously taken me all of four seconds to come up with. *'It's shit. But at least it's better than Ogilvie, Laing & Drummond. They sound like a bunch of fuckin' parasite lawyers.'* Mack never did have a lot of time for my former employer.

In the two years since I'd thrown open the doors and waited for the masses to throng to my door business hadn't been exactly booming. I told myself it took time to build a profitable business, though my current progress was at a speed that would make a glacier look energetic. So I took whatever jobs knocked on my door; none of them glamorous. Too many of my days and nights were spent waiting to see if someone's husband was having an affair or dealing with scum like this Johnny D'Arienzo. Both scenarios generally left me feeling like I needed a shower.

The flat itself was in reasonably good condition. The main office, where I sat now, was the only room that clients would see and I kept it looking as professional as I could. A desk, a few chairs, and an old sofa in the corner for the odd power nap in between cases. Throw in a computer, phone, fax machine/copier, a handful of pens and a thick pad of paper and I almost fooled myself.

My thoughts were interrupted by a burst of thrash metal piercing my eardrums, signalling the beginning of another practice session for the student band in the flat above. I didn't grudge them the practice – they were in dire need of it – but I had few enough clients as it was, and I didn't need the rest scared away by a barely coherent Slipknot tribute act. I picked up my coat and headed into the city.

With almost half the country's population living in the Greater Glasgow urban area, Glasgow was a city of many faces, the one on show often depending on who was looking. To some it remained the former European City of Culture, boasting enviable art galleries and museums, and home to architectural delights from Charles Rennie Mackintosh and Alexander 'Greek' Thomson. Others saw the former glories of the shipbuilding years, when Glasgow was renowned as the Second City of the British Empire and sent ships around the world. Still others saw the city as vibrant and exciting, a place where business was good and money was there to be spent. But there were those too, who lived in the wrong parts of the city, who knew it only as a place of deprivation and poverty, a place where life expectance was the lowest of any city in the UK and drugs and alcohol provided a blessed, if temporary, relief from the struggle of that life.

And then there were the ones who walked the darker streets.

The ones who would use a blade to end an argument, like some tainted testimonial to the razor gangs of the twenties and thirties. Like any major city, there were those who would end a life if the mood took them.

It was a city that could be everything you ever wanted, or everything you ever feared.

It all depended on where you stood.

*

Hair Apparent was a small salon on Govan Road, tucked between a bakers and a shop which felt the need to reassure passers-by that yes, everything was in fact just £1. The outside of the salon was painted a vibrant green, making it stand out from its neighbours, and the large windows were stocked with a dizzying array of hair care products. Through the glass it appeared busy, but when I opened the door I stepped into bedlam.

There were half a dozen stations with young women either cutting hair, washing hair, pasting something onto hair, or doing something with tinfoil, all the while calling back and forth to each other. The Friday morning conversation seemed to revolve around who had the worst hangover, debated at a high pitch over the slightly too loud volume of the radio playing in the corner.

The women receiving the treatments remained largely silent, reading magazines, presumably wondering how the proclaimed hangovers were going to affect their hairstyles. I stood there for a full minute, waiting to see if anyone would notice the odd man out. Eventually one of the girls looked up from her shampooing and saw me. She seemed surprised for a second, then turned the tap off and dried her hands on a towel. She said something quietly to the lady whose head she had abandoned in the sink and walked towards me.

'Do you have an appointment, sir?' she asked.

I ran my hand over my short hair and wondered if she was serious. 'No, I was looking for the manager, Ms Grant.'

'Is something wrong?' the girl asked, suddenly concerned.

'I just have a few questions to ask her. Is she around?'

The girl turned without another word and disappeared through a curtain at the back of the salon. While I waited for her to return I took a closer look at the place where Janet Bell had worked for the last two years. The décor was white and minimalist, the fixtures and fittings picked out in chrome. A small glass coffee table bearing an array of magazines stood against one wall between white leather couches for waiting customers. On the surface it seemed very stylish and glossy and profitable, just the image it was trying to portray. When I looked closer however, I spotted the cracks in the façade, like a woman who refused to acknowledge her age; the white leather couches were becoming tatty, the chrome fittings far from shiny, and the walls in need of a lick of paint.

I glanced into one of the large mirrors that ran round the walls, saw my two-day stubble and probably less-than-fashionable short brown hair, and wondered if I was any better.

I turned back as the curtain parted to reveal a woman in her mid-thirties; short, dumpy, and bitter about it. She galumphed towards me and barked, 'Yes?'

'Katrina Grant?' I asked.

'And you are?'

'Harper,' I told her. 'I wanted to ask you a few questions about Janet Bell. In private, if you don't mind.'

'Of course I mind. I've a business to run here.'

'Please,' I said. 'It'll only take five minutes.'

'That's five minutes more than I care to waste on complete strangers.'

'I can ask you them here if you'd prefer.' I walked over to the nearest station and leant against the counter, receiving a wary look from both the stylist and her customer. I gave the half-finished haircut an appraising glance and said, 'Love it. Frames your face. Not sure about the back though.'

Katrina Grant scowled and made a production of looking at her watch before turning and waddling back through the curtain. I took that as an invitation and followed her through to a back room that was little more than a kitchenette. There was a small table in the middle of the room and she sat on the far side, thumped her elbows on its chipped veneer and raised her over-plucked eyebrows at me.

'Well?'

'I'm a private investigator,' I explained. 'I've been hired by Janet's father to find her.'

'Find her?

'He hasn't seen her in two weeks.'

Katrina made a noise that sounded like *humph*, and looked at her watch pointedly. 'She hasn't shown up here in two weeks either. You find her, you tell her to look for work elsewhere.'

'Did you try to contact her?'

'What am I, her babysitter? There's plenty others will turn up and do a shift without needing chased up.'

I had to fight to keep the irritation from my voice. 'Can you tell me the last time you saw her?'

Katrina glared at me for a moment, making some kind of point that was lost on me, then turned on her seat and looked at the wall behind her, eyes narrowed as she studied a large wall planner scrawled with names and dates. 'Wednesday the 7th. Didn't show up the next day.'

So Janet never went to work on the 8th. Had she already decided she was going to run? Or did something happen that morning on her way to work that made the decision for her?

'Was there anything different about her that day? Did she seem worried or anxious? Excited?'

'You expect me to remember that?' Katrina snapped. 'I've got more important things to do than molly-coddle these brats.'

'Were you close?' I asked sarcastically.

'*Humph*. No, we weren't. She was an employee. I don't think she was exactly the life and soul of the party anyway.'

'No?' I thought of the things Archie had told me. 'I thought she was a bit of a party girl.'

'Not that I ever heard. Maybe she just kept it quieter than the rest of these tramps.'

'Any sign of drug use?'

Katrina looked incensed. 'How dare you!'

'I don't mean in here.' I raised my hands in a calming gesture. 'I just need to know about anything that could explain her disappearance.'

'Well, in that case, no. I never heard anything mentioned about drugs and she was certainly never high when she was here.'

'Did you ever meet her boyfriend?'

'Why would I?' Katrina seemed genuinely confused by the idea of taking an interest in any of her staff. I was about to thank her for her time when she carried on talking. 'Didn't need to meet him, anyway; he's a bad one, clear as day.'

'Did she say that?'

'No, but I could tell. There were a few times she was walking very slowly, making little noises when she sat down. No visible marks, but it was obvious to me.' Katrina shrugged disinterestedly as though she was simply telling me that Janet wore a blue jacket some days and a black one on others.

'Did you ask her about it?'

The confused look was back now. 'I'm paying them to put in a shift. As long as they can cut, shampoo and dry I'm happy.'

I bit back a retort, thanked Katrina for her help and asked if Leeann Munro was working today.

'For all the good she does.'

'Could I speak to her for a few minutes?'

'Take as long as you like,' Katrina snorted on her way out. 'You'll be doing me a favour.'

A few moments later the curtain was pushed back hesitantly and a head poked through like a nervous tortoise. Leeann Munro was late teens, short and chubby. She wore a plain black t-shirt that stretched valiantly over a pot-belly and heavy, orange-tinged make-up that left a tide mark along her vaguely visible jaw line yet did nothing to disguise her bad skin. When she sat down her mouth hung slackly open as though the hinge was broken, showing me a well-chewed lump of pink bubblegum that was threatening to fall out onto the table between us.

'I'm looking for Janet Bell, Leeann. I hear you two are friends.'

'Yeah.' Her voice was whiny and seemed to come through her nose. 'So?'

'Do you know where she is?'

'Why should I tell you?' she answered, giving me defiant eyes.

'Because her dad's worried about her. He wants to know she's safe.'

'Pish.'

'What?'

'Pish,' she repeated. 'For all I know you're pals with that arsehole she was seeing.'

Her nasal voice was beginning to grate on my nerves, but I kept calm as I spoke. 'Tell me, Leeann. Do you think Janet's ex is looking for her?'

'Duh!' She looked at me as though that question had qualified me for some sort of remedial class.

'Why?'

'Why?' she repeated. 'Because she's gorgeous. And he can't handle being chucked by her. He's a dickhead and she finally stood up to him and he doesn't like it.'

'Was she in danger from him?'

'Of course she was. He beat her up all the time!' Leeann rolled her eyes with exaggerated annoyance.

'Did you see him hitting her?'

'No.' She folded her arms huffily.

'Did you ever see any marks?'

'Didn't have to. You could tell by the way she walked and stuff.'

Just like Archie and Katrina had already told me. This guy Johnny was sneaky, hitting her where he wouldn't leave visible marks. I really couldn't wait to meet him.

'So, Leeann,' I asked softly, 'what's going to happen if Johnny finds her?'

The look of annoyance disappeared from her face as she thought about this for the first time. I pressed on. 'I'm a private investigator, Leeann. Mr Bell has hired me to find his daughter and make sure she's safe. I can't do that if people won't talk to me.'

She looked unsure now, torn between mistrust and a desire to help her friend. Then the tears came. 'I don't know where she is. Honestly. If I did I'd tell you, because I don't think she's safe. He'll find her. He's a really bad guy.'

'That's why I need to find her first.' I hesitated before continuing. 'From what I've heard, the only reason for Janet to disappear was to get away from Johnny. Is that true?'

'Definitely,' Leeann sobbed. 'She was happy, except for him.'

'So you don't think there could be anything else involved? No other men? Drink? Drugs?'

Leeann shook her head hard. 'No. Johnny's the only guy Janet's been with since I've known her. She doesn't really drink, and she definitely doesn't take drugs.'

'Are you sure?' I asked.

'I've been her closest friend for a year and I would know. We don't go out that much – we're both usually skint – we just sort of hang out at my place. We even stuck our credit cards away in a drawer in case we're tempted. So, yes, I'm sure.'

I didn't believe her.

Maybe Janet had calmed down in the time she had been friends with Leeann, or maybe Leeann was trying to protect her pal. I understood her reluctance to speak ill of her friend, but I believed Archie. To admit that your daughter is a drug-taking slapper must be the hardest thing for a father to do, but he at least had realised that only honesty would help bring her home.

There was nothing else to ask Leeann. I gave her my card and asked her to call if she thought of anything, no matter how trivial it might seem. I got up to leave, but was stopped at the curtain by Leeann's whispered plea. 'Don't let him hurt her anymore. Please.'

'Don't worry,' I told her. 'He won't.'

Three

When someone goes missing it usually takes time to interview everyone they were close to. In this case however, Janet didn't seem to have many close friends. Or not that her father knew of at least. I left Hair Apparent, leaving Janet's current best friend behind sobbing at my back, climbed into my '95 black Honda Civic, and went in search of her former best friend.

Rebecca Davidson, the girl who had shared Janet's ill-fated attempt at independence lived in Craigton, another residential suburb, not far from where I was now. Just off Paisley Road West and only a few minutes drive from Janet and Archie's home in Cardonald. When I arrived at the neat semi-detached and rang the bell, the door was opened by a thin woman in a thick navy cardigan and long charcoal skirt, her eyes magnified by the thick glasses she wore. She was probably mid-forties, but the wardrobe added another twenty years.

'Mrs Davidson?' She gave a tight nod. 'My name is Harper. I'm a Private Investigator, and I was hoping to speak to your daughter, Rebecca. Is she around?'

Her lips pinched tight. 'Perhaps you can tell me why you would like to speak to her?' She stepped out onto the top step and closed the door behind her.

'I've been hired by Archie Bell to find his daughter Janet. I believe Janet and Rebecca were friends, and I'm trying to speak to anyone who may know something.'

'My daughter doesn't know anything about it,' Mrs Davidson said, rather forcefully. Getting an audience with the Pope may well be easier than getting past this woman.

'With all due respect, Mrs Davidson, how can you be sure?'

'With no due respect whatsoever, Mr Harper, my daughter and Janet Bell have not spoken to each other in almost a year. If you have been hired by Mr Bell, I'm sure you know why that is.'

As she pulled her thick cardigan tighter around herself to block the chill wind I checked my back for scars left by that lashing. 'They shared a flat and it didn't work out,' I said.

'No, it didn't work out. And they haven't spoken since, so I'm afraid Rebecca can't help you.'

'Would it be possible to speak with her just to be certain?' I asked, fully expecting another barracking.

'I'm afraid not, Mr Harper. Rebecca is on holiday at the moment. She won't be back for another week.'

'Could I leave my card with you then? Perhaps you could ask Rebecca to give me a call when she returns.'

She gave me a supercilious look, somehow managing to look down her nose at me despite being eight inches shorter. 'Why? Don't you think you'll have found the poor girl by then? Oh dear, that's not very satisfactory, is it?'

I smiled through gritted teeth but kept quiet, took a card from my pocket and held it out with little expectation. Even if she took it I doubted Rebecca would ever see it, or even hear of this conversation.

With a long-suffering sigh she took the card and made a great show of holding it between two fingertips. She grimaced at it as though it were a soiled nappy before turning back to her door and opening it a crack. She looked back over her shoulder as she slipped inside, making sure I wasn't trying to follow her.

'Thanks for your time,' I said to the closed door.

*

It was time to visit Johnny D'Arienzo. It was unlikely he knew where Janet Bell was, but I needed be certain. I also wanted to get a feel for how dangerous he might be.

I got back in the Honda and headed into the city centre, coming off the M8 at the Cathedral Precinct. I joined the western end of

Alexandra Parade and cruised along it and round its adjoining streets as slowly as I could in the mid afternoon traffic, searching for the garage where Johnny worked. By the time I reached the far end of the street I had counted three likely candidates. It had also started raining; the kind of lashing icy rain that seemed capable of stripping the skin from your bones if you were foolish enough to step out into it.

I turned in a side street and headed back along the Parade, managing to find a parking space at the side of the road that wasn't too far from any of the three garages. I waited a moment but the rain seemed to be here for the long haul, so I got out and jogged towards the first garage. I reached the small office and dashed inside. As I stood there shivering and dripping on the carpet the wiry old guy behind the counter looked at me, smirked and said, 'Oh, is the rain on?'

I gave him a thin smile while I wiped water from my eyes and told myself killing him wouldn't be worth it. 'Is Johnny working today?' I asked.

'Johnny?' repeated the guy. 'No Johnny here, pal.'

'No? Damn. I'm trying to catch up with an old friend, I know he works in a garage on Alexandra Parade, but I can't remember the name.'

'Sorry, pal. Not here.'

'I'll keep trying. Thanks anyway,' I said as I headed back into the monsoon.

At the second garage I got the same response. Even down to the comedian behind the counter asking if it was raining. At the third garage I tried the same tactic and the guy behind the counter replied, 'Aye, he is. You a mate?'

'Yeah.'

'Hang on a minute then.' He left through a door behind the counter, returned in a few seconds, gesturing over his shoulder. 'He's busy the now, but you can go through and wait. He'll be done in a few minutes.'

I stepped round the counter and through the door into a large cement floored room, covered in oil stains and a scattering of tyres. Two large rolled shutter doors were open at one end, the rain hammering down outside them in a curtain that blocked any view of the street. At the opposite end were two pits with cars raised above them. Two men were working in the furthest pit beneath a maroon Mitsubishi Charisma, while in the nearest pit one man worked alone below a royal blue Subaru Impreza. Archie had given me a basic description, but in the shadows of the cars it was impossible to see anyone clearly.

'Johnny!' I shouted.

'Who is it?' came a voice from beneath the Impreza.

I remained silent, waiting for him to get curious and come out of the pit.

'Who the fuck is it?' he called again, his temper fraying already. Again I remained silent. He began to clamber out of the pit, muttering profanely under his breath. He got to his feet and stepped away from the car. He saw me and looked me up and down while I did the same to him.

Johnny was a big guy alright. At 6'2" he was three inches taller than me, and he looked around two stones heavier. Everything about him was solid and muscular, from his thick neck to the thighs straining at the seams of his overalls. The rampant acne spreading across his lower face and neck told me his bulk wasn't all hard-earned muscle. He may only have been in his early twenties, but he was already the dictionary definition of a steroid-freak.

Dull eyes glared at me from under heavy brows as he tried to intimidate me. His wide square jaw jutted out, making him look like Spike, the bulldog from the Tom & Jerry cartoons, only less friendly. His blonde hair had been cropped so short I could see pink scalp on his flat, anvil head.

'I know you?' he growled.

'Nope.'

'What you want then?' He folded his big arms across his slab-like chest as though I should be impressed.

'I'm looking for a girl you know. Janet Bell.'

That got a reaction. He unfolded his arms and looked around. He called over to the pit beneath the Charisma, 'Lads, take a break eh?' Two heads appeared from below the car and took one look at

Johnny's face before deciding to do as he said. They climbed out of the pit and left through a door on the far side.

Johnny turned back to me, his face dark, eyes twitching with anger. 'Janet, eh? Why you looking for her?'

'Her dad asked me to find her.'

'Yeah? Thought he knew better.'

I ignored the threat. 'Janet hasn't been home in two weeks. What do you know about it?'

'Nothing. No idea where the little slag is. But when I find her I'm gonna make her sorry. The wee slut's not gonna get away with what she's doing to me.'

He had edged closer to me now, his massive chest heaving up and down, but I wasn't concerned. The anger was still within me, but it was cold now, cool and controlled. I inched forward, my hands hanging loose at my sides.

'You're not going to go anywhere near her,' I said. His jaw jutted out towards me, his eyes narrowing. 'Or her dad.'

'You going to stop me?' he asked, rolling his shoulders as he closed the remaining distance between us and looked down into my face. 'If I want to find her, I will. If I want to go round and see her dad, I will. If I want to smash her dad's face in, I will.' With each sentence he thrust his index finger into my chest, trying to push me off balance. 'And if I want to fuck you up, I will.'

That's when I threw the first punch. I twisted quickly and drove a left hook into Johnny's kidney. He grunted and bent sideways, his face twisting in pain. I followed up with a low kick, my right shin smashing into the outside of his left knee, sending him to the floor with a thud.

So much for quietly.

As he writhed in agony I leant over him. His eyes were clenched tightly shut as he held his knee and rocked back and forward.

'Tell you what, Johnny,' I said, my voice ice, 'How about you stay away from Archie Bell, okay? I'll be watching out for him, and if I see you anywhere near him I'll fuck *you* up. For good. You got me?'

He grunted something unintelligible as I straightened up. 'And don't even think about trying to find Janet either. There's no point.

You're so fucking stupid you couldn't find your way to the end of the alphabet if you started at Y.'

Johnny regained his voice as I turned away from him. 'I'm going to fucking kill you!' he shouted, anger cracking his voice. 'I've got serious connections, you prick. You're a dead man!'

I kept walking, through the open shutter doors and into the cold rain, the thundering of the falling water not quite drowning out Johnny's shouts. 'I'm going to fucking kill you!' he screamed again.

I ignored him as I walked back to my car, the rain hammering down on me, soaking through my clothes and chilling me to the bone. Adrenaline coursed through my body in the aftermath of the confrontation. But at least I knew one thing; Johnny D'Arienzo had no idea where Janet was.

And I knew something else; I didn't blame her for running.

Four

Archie and Janet Bell's home was a small, three-bedroom, semi-detached house tucked away on a cul-de-sac in Cardonald. Its tired, shabby exterior reminded me of Archie. The exterior was grey and looked as though it hadn't been painted in a number of years. An untended garden at the front threatened to overrun the driveway where Archie's old red Volvo estate sulked like a child who wasn't allowed out to play.

I rang the doorbell and after a few moments the door opened a crack. Archie peered out over the security chain, recognised me and closed the door again. There was a rattle as the chain slid off and when the door reopened he forced a watery smile and beckoned me in. The living room had the same air of neglect and disrepair as the exterior of the house. A single armchair and a matching two-seater sofa, both old and worn and sagging, squatted on top of a carpet so faded I couldn't guess what the original colour had been.

Archie went into the kitchen to put the kettle on, giving me an opportunity to indulge my professional nosiness. The sole item that appeared to be of any value was the large television in one corner, currently showing some early morning chat show where the ignorant fool masquerading as the host berated the people moronic enough to come on the programme. I watched briefly, hoping this would be the day someone attacked him.

In another corner of the room was a display cabinet, its shelves filled with framed photographs. Almost all of the pictures were of Janet, from early childhood to the Christmas shot I'd already seen. On the bottom shelf was the exception; a group shot of twelve men and women seated around a rectangular table, some turned awkwardly to face the camera, others raising their glasses in a toast.

The Worst of Evils

At the far end of the table sat Archie, a look of mild embarrassment on his face, as though he was ashamed to be caught enjoying himself.

I turned away from the picture as Archie came through the door with a mug in each hand and pushed one of them towards me. I didn't have the heart to tell him I hated tea. The pallid brew in the chipped mug I was now holding did little to reverse that verdict.

He saw the picture I'd been looking at and felt the need to explain. 'That was Christmas. The year before last. A bunch of the lecturers went out for a curry. I left early, after a couple of glasses of wine. Didn't want to be too late home and wake up Janet.'

Just as in the photo, he seemed worried that anyone may think he had been neglecting his daughter by having fun.

'What do you lecture on?' I asked.

'Physics. At the City of Glasgow University.'

'Been there long?' I didn't really care, but I wanted him to relax.

'Eleven years.'

'Do you all do that sort of thing often?' I asked, pointing at the picture.

'Now and again. Usually every few months. The last one was just last month.'

He looked away awkwardly then, as though he'd revealed too much of himself. I took the opportunity to focus the conversation. 'Do you have the phone bills and bank statements, Archie?'

'Oh, those. Yes.' He went to the mantelpiece and withdrew a handful of sheets of paper from behind a hideous ornament featuring a small clock set into a cheap-looking figurine of a lady holding a sun parasol.

I had a quick look at the first few sheets – Janet's bank statement and visa card bill – and saw nothing out of the ordinary, though the last few weeks weren't covered. I turned to her mobile phone bill and glanced over it, noticing that she used her phone far less than I would have expected a twenty-year-old girl to.

'Did she use the landline as well?' I asked Archie.

'Eh, yes, of course.'

'Then I'll need an old bill for that number too.'

For a second I thought Archie was going to protest, but he went into the kitchen and I heard him open a drawer. He returned with more folded sheets of paper and handed them to me. I took them and asked Archie to show me to Janet's room. He didn't like it, but knew he had no choice. He stepped past me and started up the stairs. I ditched the cup of tea on the coffee table before I followed.

At the top of the stairs Archie opened the door to one of the bedrooms and stood aside to let me walk in. I didn't want to go through Janet's things while he was standing watching me though. 'Can you do something for me Archie? Can you sit down with those phone bills and mark off any numbers that you recognise? Just write down next to them what they are. It'll speed things up if I don't have to go through every number.'

'Yeah, okay. Sure. I can do that.' He seemed relieved to have something constructive to do.

I watched Archie traipse down the stairs, the bills clutched in one hand, the other steadying himself on the banister. As soon as he reached the bottom step I took out my phone and dialled.

'Brownstone,' said a young female voice, answering the call so quickly it hadn't even rung at my end.

'Working on your psychic powers? Or have you hacked into my phone line?' I asked.

'You know I'm not a hacker, Keir,' she sighed.

'Then why do I come to you, when I need some information from a secure source?'

'Secure? I'm not familiar with that term.'

'True,' I conceded. She was right; there was nothing she hadn't been able to access for me yet. She probably read Bill Gate's emails in her spare time. Where some investigators had a contact within a bank that would provide them with information for a fee, I had someone with access to any bank. I had Brownstone.

When she was seventeen I had found her chained to a bedstead in a Manchester crack house; filthy, beaten, and hooked on heroin. I had a chat with the guy who was pimping her out to anything with a pulse and the price of a rock. Then I left him in a puddle of his own blood, piss and vomit, and took her home to her family where she eventually got clean.

Now, six years later that same girl was renowned in certain

circles for the information she could obtain, and charged accordingly. She insisted on helping me for free, as a thank you for what she had escaped. The name she used was a reminder; something to ensure she never slipped back down that poisoned slope. I was one of the few people who knew her real name, even Mack and Jessica had no idea. Although I trusted them with my life, Brownstone had asked me to keep it secret and I would not break my promise to her. And not just because she was my secret weapon.

'Can you check a bank account and a credit card for me?' I asked. 'Last six months.'

'No problem,' she answered, suddenly all business. 'Who's the bad guy?'

'No-one yet. Probably just a runaway.'

'Fire away,' she said.

I recited Janet Bell's name, address, date of birth and account numbers.

'I'll get back to you.'

I hung up and turned my attention back to Janet's room. It was more brightly coloured than the downstairs of the house, but equally untidy. There were dated posters of pop stars on the wall, none of whom had enjoyed a hit within the last five years. The wall above the bed bore numerous shelves of books, CDs and videos that – judging by the thick accumulation of dust – hadn't been disturbed in years. A storage unit in the corner held a television, DVD player, and CD stereo, on top of which sat a small mirror and a hairbrush clustered with long blonde hairs. A pile of unwashed clothes trailed from the laundry bin beneath the window and halfway to the door.

I spent the next hour and a half meticulously looking through Janet's belongings. It was a fruitless endeavour. All I could establish was that her passport was still there – at least she hadn't left the country – and that there appeared to be a few missing toiletries, supporting the theory that she had run away.

I made sure the room was as I had found it and went back downstairs. Archie turned in his seat to face me, his eyebrows raised expectantly.

'How did you get on with the phone bills?' I asked.

He stood up and handed them to me. 'I've marked all the ones I recognise, there aren't many left. Will that help find her?'

He was desperate, hoping that I would be able to tell him he had done something valuable to find his daughter. I had to throw him a lifeline.

'It will. Even if nothing turns up through these phone numbers, you've saved me time that can be spent on something that will find Janet. I'll be in touch, Archie. Remember, anything at all comes to mind, call me. Whatever time it is. Okay?'

I headed for the door, leaving Archie Bell standing behind me in his untidy, dingy living room, his hopes in the hands of a stranger.

*

I had barely pulled away from Archie's house when my phone began to ring in my pocket. I parked around the corner and answered the call. It was Brownstone.

'What've you got?' I asked.

'Very little. Credit card was a waste of time. Only four transactions in the last year, all of them at clothes shops, between fifteen and fifty quid. Most recent was June last year.'

That confirmed Leeann Munro's statement that Janet never used her credit card. 'What about the bank account?'

'Plenty of transactions – most of them ten pound withdrawals from various cash machines. Only credits are her wages going in and the odd top up from an A Bell when she was running a bit low. Most recent activity was 8th February when she cleaned it out.'

'Everything?'

'All £127.36 of it. Withdrawn at the Govan Road branch.'

'No payments for travel tickets or anything like that?'

'Nope. Just run of the mill. Till she emptied the account of course.'

I thanked Brownstone and hung up. So, Janet Bell had withdrawn all her money on the day she went missing, and from the branch closest to her workplace. It was becoming more and more obvious that she had done exactly as her dad suspected; run away from a thug who wouldn't take no for an answer.

I sighed and took out the phone bills Archie had given me, unfolding them on the steering wheel. As I'd asked, he'd given me the most recent ones he had. The last date shown was the 31st January, which left over a week unaccounted for before Janet went missing. If I found nothing else I'd ask Brownstone to get those eight days for me.

On Janet's mobile bill Archie had only managed to rule out four numbers, those of his mobile, his department at the university, Hair Apparent, and the Bell home number. There were five phone numbers unaccounted for.

Archie had been more successful with the bill for the landline. Archie's mobile number appeared again, as did his work number and Hair Apparent. Janet's mobile, the local Chinese takeaway, and three colleagues of Archie's completed the list of identified numbers, leaving only three numbers unidentified.

Combining the two bills gave me a list of all the numbers that Janet may have phoned in the last few months before she disappeared. She may have borrowed a friend's phone or used a payphone, but I doubted it. Janet may have been scared of Johnny, but she would not have expected him to go through her phone bills to try and track her down. I considered the possibility that she could have called from the phone at Hair Apparent, but dismissed it. Katrina Grant didn't strike me as the type to encourage personal calls on her time.

Two of the numbers were listed on both bills, bringing the number of unknown numbers down to six. I dialled the first number, withholding my own number so that it wouldn't show up at the other end.

The call rang out several times before an answering machine kicked in. I recognised Leeann Munro's nasal tone and crossed the number off the list.

I dialled the other number that had appeared on both lists. The call rang out and was again connected to an answering machine. I rolled my eyes as I heard the growled message. 'This is Johnny. Leave a message. Or else.'

I didn't bother.

The rest of the numbers Janet had called from her mobile turned out to be a Pizza Hut, a Showcase Cinema, and a local taxi firm. The call to the taxi firm was irrelevant, having been placed on the 6th January, a month before Janet vanished.

I turned back to the landline bill. There was one number left unidentified on it. A number that had been called only once, on the 30th January, just over a week before Janet was last seen. I'd left this one for last as it seemed the best shot.

I hadn't expected to hit the jackpot though.

'Hotel Caledonia,' said a voice as the call was connected. 'Justin speaking. How can I help?'

After a seconds surprised pause I found my voice. 'Ah, hello, Justin. Can you tell me where you are located?'

'Certainly sir. We're just off the Clydeside Expressway, near the SECC.'

'Great, I know exactly where you are now.'

'Wonderful, sir.' And he actually sounded like he meant it. 'Is there anything else I can assist you with today?'

'No, thank you,' I replied, 'you've been very helpful.' His friendly *cheerio* was cut off as I hung up.

Archie Bell didn't strike me as the type to spontaneously book hotel rooms, whether for an illicit rendezvous or otherwise. So, presumably, Janet Bell called a hotel in the city centre, then, a week later she cleared out her bank account and went missing. However, whether she went to this hotel or not, if all she had was £127.36 she wouldn't have been able to stay there indefinitely. She wouldn't even have been able to stay there this long.

But it was a start. Janet Bell may not be at the Hotel Caledonia any more, but I now had a hold of the thread she had unravelled when she vanished. All I had to do was pull it.

Five

The Hotel Caledonia catered for the lower end of the budget and did it well. It was a Holiday Inn sort of place, but cheaper, aiming at hen nights, stag dos, tourists looking for a cheap bed for the night, and business travellers whose companies kept a tight rein on their expenses.

The car park outside the low, rectangular, red-brick building was surprisingly half-full. I had expected it to be quiet, given that tourism wasn't at its peak in Glasgow during the frigid tail-end of winter. I was wrong. As I walked into the cosy lobby, furnished with a couple of armchairs and a few tables for those waiting for transportation, I realised it wasn't just bustling, it was pandemonium. I was weaving my way through a crowd of well-wrapped up Spanish tourists to the reception when a group of young men in their twenties came barrelling round the corner, singing and manhandling one of their number who sported antlers on his head. It may have been only half past six, but some of this stag party looked as though they'd be lucky to still be vertical by eight o'clock.

If Janet had stayed here, she'd chosen well. As well as being one of the most affordable options, it was busy enough that she would retain some anonymity. No-one on the staff was likely to pay too much attention to her, and would probably struggle to remember her the day after she checked out.

I let the stag group barge past and walked up to the reception counter. The clerk looked up as I approached and gave me a broad, if slightly camp smile. The name tag pinned to the left breast of his maroon waistcoat identified him as Justin.

'Hi,' I said. 'I was due to meet a guest here, but I can't remember her room number.'

The smile didn't waver. 'No problem, sir. If you give me their name I'll ring their room for you.'

'Janet Bell,' I replied.

Justin turned to a computer monitor to his right. It was tilted at such an angle that I couldn't see the screen. His fingers danced over the keyboard hidden beneath the counter. He frowned at the screen for a few seconds, his lips pursed. 'Is that B-E-L-L?'

'Yes.'

'I'm sorry sir, there's no record of a guest under that name.' He looked shamefaced, as though he had somehow let me down.

'Okay, time to come clean, Justin,' I said, watching his eyebrows rise. 'I'm not here to meet anyone. I'm a Private Investigator, looking for a missing girl.' I took a card out of my wallet and passed it to him. He looked at it in confusion.

'So, this Janet Bell…' He tailed off, unsure how to finish the sentence.

'Is missing,' I finished for him. 'Her father has hired me to find her. I think she stayed here. Can you check your computer to see if she has been a guest here anytime within the past two weeks?'

'She hasn't been,' he said decisively. 'I searched for any bookings this year with that surname.'

'She could have checked in under a different name, couldn't she?'

'I suppose,' he conceded. 'But we do need to see a credit card on check-in.'

I reached into my jacket pocket and brought out the photocopies of Janet's picture. I handed one over the counter to Justin and watched his eyes.

I was glad I did. They nearly jumped out of his head.

'You recognise her?' I asked.

He hesitated a second or two, then gathered his thoughts and cleared his throat. 'I… I'm not sure. Maybe. Can I show this to the rest of the staff? Maybe one of them will recognise her.'

'Sure.'

'Please wait here, I'll be five minutes.' He scampered away from me without another word.

He was obviously up to something but I might as well let it play out and see what happened. I wandered over to the armchairs in the lobby and was about to grab a seat when I spied a vending machine down a side corridor. I managed to stop myself running to it, but only just. I returned to the lobby with a couple of chocolate bars and a cold can of Irn-Bru, realising that this looked like being dinner. I sank into the soft armchair, ripped open the first bar of chocolate and savaged it. I popped open the Irn-Bru and took a long swallow, savouring the sugar as it blasted through my bloodstream.

I sat there for fifteen minutes, waiting for Justin to come back. To my relief, the lobby started to empty, leaving me in peace, with only Justin's replacement at the reception desk for company. I was just starting to get impatient when I heard the front door open behind me. Out of curiosity, I turned my head to view the newcomer.

A very tall, very thin man in a cheap suit and a short, sturdy woman in a dark jacket and trousers came through the twin doors together, their eyes fixed on me. It was obvious they were cops, even without the two uniforms behind them.

I heard footsteps from the other direction and turned to see Justin approach with an older man I assumed was the manager. Nice timing. They'd obviously been watching on a security monitor.

As everyone walked towards me I remained seated, finishing the second chocolate bar and draining the Irn-Bru. No point in standing to attention, I'd find out soon enough what this was about. All six of them reached me at the same time, the uniforms standing slightly further back out of deference for the two plainclothes cops.

'That's the man there, officer,' said the manager, his finger thrusting dramatically towards me.

'Thank you for your assistance, Mr Harrold,' said the tall thin man. 'We'll take it from here.'

Harrold started to open his mouth, obviously unhappy at being kept out of any potential drama. The tall man cut him off before he could speak, 'We'll let you know if we need anything else.'

He kept his gaze fixed on Harrold until the other man realised he had been dismissed and scuttled away, taking Justin with him.

The tall thin guy turned to me and said, 'Detective Inspector Stewart, Strathclyde Police. This is Detective Sergeant Taylor.' He gestured towards his female colleague as he introduced her.

'Thank God you're here!' I said, jumping to my feet. The uniforms looked puzzled, but the other two were too experienced to let their stone faces crack. I put my hand to the side of my mouth and told them in a stage whisper, 'I think someone has been stealing towels. Maybe even toilet rolls.'

DS Taylor gave me a look that made me glad Glasgow cops don't carry guns. Before she could beat me to death with one of the uniforms' truncheons DI Stewart spoke calmly in his deep bass voice. 'We'll send someone along later, do a door-to-door. Now, sir, would you mind coming with us?'

'Probably,' I said. 'Where to?'

'We'd like you to come down to the station with us to answer a few questions.'

'Which station?'

'Pitt Street. Does it make a difference?' asked Stewart calmly.

'Pitt Street?' I said, sucking air through my teeth. 'That's Strathclyde Police HQ. Must be serious.'

'It's the closest, that's all,' said Taylor.

'No it's not. Anderston is only round the corner. Pitt Street's right back in the city centre.'

Taylor looked furious, her previously pasty face taking on a dangerously red colour. Guess she didn't like having her bluff called. Stewart stepped between the two of us as though he was used to having to do so. 'It shouldn't take too long,' he said.

I gave him a once over, sizing him up. He had short, light grey hair above small, pinned back ears, and a thin, lived-in face that, despite its deep lines, was strangely unreadable. The suit he wore was black and inexpensive and could have done with a press a week ago. Below that he wore a plain white shirt and a maroon tie, knotted so loosely it may have been thrown there by a passer-by.

He stood before me like a worn out scarecrow. Tall, skinny,

almost gangly in appearance. Despite this, and his bookish, pensive demeanour, I suspected it would be foolish to underestimate him.

'Do I have a choice?' I asked him.

'Of course. But it could be misinterpreted if you don't willingly cooperate.'

'Whereas, if I cooperate, this will all be cleared up in a matter of minutes and we'll all be off home to our beds.'

'Of course.'

I cast a glance past his shoulder to his sergeant standing just behind him, still fuming. Her brown eyes looked accusingly into mine as though I was a serial flasher. Unlike her colleague, she was instantly readable. She was the physical, and apparently emotional, opposite of Stewart. Where he was tall and slim, Taylor was short and stocky, a little over five feet tall and almost square in build. Her wardrobe of unflattering dark jacket over a white shirt and charcoal trousers seemed specifically chosen to nullify her sex. With her plain black hair parted in the middle and cut to the level of her square jaw, her thick eyebrows and faint hairs above her upper lip, she seemed determined to exude as little femininity as possible.

There was no choice, of course. I'd be going with them, one way or another. Truth be told, I was too curious to walk away now, despite my mistrust of the police in general. In my business you have to go where the answers are, whoever that may bring you into contact with.

'Okay, let's go,' I said to Stewart. 'I'm due to meet someone, so if you don't mind I'll just make a quick call, let them know I may be a little late.'

Stewart wasn't happy about it but I already had my mobile in my hand and had pressed the button to put the call through on speed-dial. It wasn't worth losing my cooperation, so he let it go. I noticed though that he held a hand out in front of Taylor. He was subtle about it, but I was watching her, expecting her to react.

The call was picked up at the other end and I quickly said, 'Going to Pitt Street with a DI Stewart. Meet me there.' I hung up the phone and gave the two cops my innocent face. 'What?'

'Who was that?' asked Stewart, more calmly than I expected.

'My solicitor.' Like I said, I didn't have a lot of faith in the police.

'Why did you feel the need to call a solicitor?'

'Call me cagey.'

'Right, let's get this over with,' he sighed, his composure showing the first faint sign of cracking.

'Ladies first,' I said to Taylor, holding out my hand to indicate she should precede me through the door. One of the uniforms smiled in anticipation, then Taylor grabbed me by the arm, spun me towards the door and shoved the heel of her hand between my shoulder blades, propelling me through it.

Bad move, I thought. If I were a criminal I was now in the open with all four police officers still inside and no-one to prevent me from doing a runner. It seemed DS Taylor could be a little hasty when she was annoyed. Worth remembering.

I crossed my arms in the cold night air and waited for them to exit the hotel. Stewart directed me towards a marked Vauxhall Astra that sat in the car park. I climbed into the back and the two uniforms got in the front. Stewart and Taylor then got into a dark blue Vectra parked in front and pulled out into the street. We followed them along darkened streets lit only by amber streetlights and the white wash of passing headlights, and I made a few attempts to engage the two cops in conversation but they remained as silent now as they had been in the Hotel Caledonia.

From the concentration on their faces I guessed DI Stewart had them under orders not to say a word to me. Either he didn't want them tipping me off to what was going on, or he didn't want them to prejudice any forthcoming prosecution.

Neither thought was very comforting.

*

They led me through a series of corridors, taking me deeper into the bowels of the orange-brick and glass building that was the headquarters of Strathclyde Police, the biggest police force in Scotland. Once they had found an empty room to sit me down in they disappeared, leaving me alone. Presumably I should spend some time worrying, then break down and confess at the first opportunity. I wasn't concerned. But those two bars of chocolate seemed like a long time ago already. My stomach was starting to think my throat had been cut.

I sat at a plain, formica-topped table against the wall opposite the closed door, and had chosen the seat nearest the wall where I could lean against it. There were three other chairs around the table and I hoped it wouldn't be much longer before they were occupied. The only other feature in the room was the video camera watching unblinkingly from the corner.

It was a long twenty minutes before the door opened and DI Stewart and DS Taylor came into the room. Stewart appeared as calm as ever, but Taylor seemed surprisingly subdued. I wondered if Stewart had read her the riot act for pushing me through the hotel door.

Stewart sat down opposite me, Taylor taking the seat beside him. I smiled at both of them, 'Thanks for coming. Glad you could make it.'

'Sorry about that. Something urgent came up,' Stewart said.

'What was it? An urgent cup of coffee or an urgent fag?'

Taylor smirked, allowing her yellowish, coffee- and nicotine-stained teeth to confirm my suspicions.

Stewart ignored us both. 'Could you start by telling us your name?'

'Keir Harper,' I replied. I wasn't giving them a reason for my solicitor being unable to find me.

Taylor snorted a laugh. I didn't react.

'Okay, Keir...' Stewart said.

'Just call me Harper,' I interrupted.

Stewart made a dismissive gesture, as though this was irrelevant. 'Fine, Harper it is. You were at the Hotel Caledonia looking for someone named Janet Bell. Would you like to tell us why?'

'Nope,' I replied. 'You asked me to come with you, without giving me much choice, then you left me here alone for twenty minutes while you tried to intimidate me with some kind of mind games. I'm saying nothing else until my solicitor shows up.' I crossed my arms and sat back in my chair.

Taylor looked to Stewart to see how he was going to play this. If it had been her choice she would have had the rubber hoses out by now and be halfway through beating a confession out of me.

'Things have changed,' I reminded them. 'You don't get six hours without a solicitor anymore.'

Taylor muttered something under her breath that sounded like *Bastarding Cadder*.

Stewart had just opened his mouth to speak when the door burst open to my right, slamming against the wall. I looked over, expecting my solicitor, and was surprised to see a short, well-built man with shaved blonde hair stride into the room.

He marched up to us and grabbed the table by its edge, his square face tomato red, veins bulging in his temples above small protruding ears. Although he looked mid-fifties he was strong and powerful, his head merging into his shoulders without need for a neck.

I watched, fascinated, as tiny drops of spittle fell from the corners of his mouth while he fought to control the fury within him. This guy was about thirty seconds from a stroke.

'Sir,' Stewart began, before he was cut off by the angry man holding onto the table.

'Keir Harper, you said?' He was looking directly into my eyes. There was no-one else in the room as far as he was concerned.

'And you are?'

'What's her name, you piece of shit? What's her fucking name?'

I was vaguely aware of Stewart and Taylor getting to their feet, but like the red-faced newcomer it was suddenly just the two of us in the room.

'Who?' I asked.

'Fuck you!' he ranted. 'This time, I'm going to fucking bury you.'

This time?

'I've no idea what you're talking about.'

Stewart placed a hand on the guy's shoulder and was shrugged off. Taylor hung back, probably hoping the well-built guy would attack me.

'Really?' he said, injecting sarcasm into the anger flowing

through his voice. 'I suppose you know nothing about Gemma Sinclair either? Or Siobhan Sutherland? Eh?'

His face was an inch from mine when I heard Stewart say, 'Jesus Christ, sir,' and try to pull him away again. This time he managed to pull him a few feet away.

Now that he was further away I could see him more clearly. And I finally recognised him. It had been a long time since I'd seen him, and he'd changed considerably in those years, but I saw now he was the man I'd grown to hate.

'You're Darroch,' I said, my voice quiet. He just stood there breathing deeply, his shoulders rising and falling, the initial anger fading, while mine was only just beginning to build.

'You worked the Katie Jarvie case.' My voice became harder, accusing. 'You *fucked up* the Katie Jarvie case.'

'Yeah, when they let you and your pal go free,' Darroch growled. 'The two of you got away with murder once, and I will *not* let that happen again.'

Six

I sat stunned for a second. It had been thirteen years since Katie Jarvie had been murdered and yet a few words from the investigating officer who had tried to pin it on Mack and I had hurtled me back into the past with the impact of a car hitting a wall.

The room receded from me. My breathing had quickened and my vision narrowed to focus solely on Darroch. My heart pounded as I tried to control the anger welling within me.

Suddenly a female voice cut through the tension, its tone strident and penetrating. 'What the hell is going on here?'

Darroch whirled around and straightened up. He looked at the small, slim woman standing in the doorway, taking in her expensively styled strawberry blonde hair and her carefully tailored skirt suit. She strode across the room and stopped two inches from him, her blue-green eyes crackling like fireworks.

'Andrea Jarvie. Mr Harper's solicitor. Now get out and let me talk to my client.'

Darroch looked stunned by the name. Stewart was the first to respond. 'I'm sorry, Ms Jarvie, we're under no obligation to let you speak to your client at this time, as I'm sure you know.'

Andrea swivelled her head and zeroed in on him. 'Really?' she hissed. She pointed at Darroch and continued, 'I heard every word this constable screamed at my client. Many of which were words I could not bring myself to repeat.'

'It's Detective Chief Inspector, actually,' Darroch said.

'For the moment,' Andrea replied coldly. She stared at the three officers in turn. 'Now, unless you want my client to sue this police force for harassment and abuse, I suggest you get out of this room and switch off any recording equipment that is in use. If you don't

I'll personally make sure the only police role available to you in the future is cleaning up after the mounted division.'

Stewart moved first, walking to Darroch and taking his elbow, leading him from the room, the other man walking backwards, his eyes locked on mine. Taylor hadn't moved yet. Her voice was like dry ice cracking when she spoke to Andrea. 'How do you sleep at night?'

'On a big pile of money with lots of handsome men, sweetheart. Now out you go,' replied Andrea, waving her towards the door.

Taylor stormed from the room and slammed the door, the bang adding to the headache building behind my eyes.

Andrea sat in the chair opposite me and gave me a look of concern. 'You okay?'

Andrea Jarvie worked for the respected law firm of Melrose McLean and despite her youth was garnering a reputation as one of the best and fiercest solicitors in the country. Having known her since we were in our mid-teens I was fortunate enough to receive free representation of a standard that would otherwise have been out of my reach. Her ferocity and desire to defend the innocent had been born during the police investigation into her twin sister's murder and moulded by their short-sighted attempts to charge either Mack or myself with the killing, while simultaneously failing to pursue any other lines of enquiry.

'Yeah,' I replied. 'Been a bad day though.'

'Tell me.'

So I did. I told her about Archie Bell hiring me to find his missing daughter and the trail that had led me to the Hotel Caledonia, and my subsequent trip here to Pitt Street.

'Did you recognise him?' I asked.

'The screaming buffoon that was about to have an embolism? Oh, yes. He might not be grossly overweight anymore, but it doesn't matter how much weight, or hair, he loses, I couldn't possibly forget him. He's the one who was convinced Mack killed Katie.'

'And that I helped him.' I shook my head in disgust. Darroch had been largely responsible for letting a killer walk free while he persecuted a seventeen-year-old boy. 'I can't believe he still has a job.'

'And he's been promoted. He was only a DS back then.' Andrea obviously felt as strongly about Darroch as I did, but she changed the subject. 'How is Mack?'

'He's fine. Still asks about you now and then.'

'I'd like to see him sometime.'

'I don't know if he'd agree to that. It still hurts him to see you. It's not just the memories, it's the might-have-beens. He cares about you though.'

She smiled sadly. 'Tell him I understand.'

I brought us back to the matter at hand. 'What should I do?'

'You need to talk to DI Stewart. You have no client confidentiality to hide behind, so you'll have to at some point.'

'I might not have the same client confidentiality that solicitors do, but I'm good at forgetting things.'

'That's true. But, there's something going on here we don't know about. Do you want to run the risk that Janet is in some kind of danger while you're stalling?'

I realised that I hadn't been putting either Janet or Archie Bell first, despite them being my clients. I had been content to wallow in my own bitterness and it was time to change that.

'I've dealt with Greig Stewart before,' Andrea continued. 'He's a good guy, pretty straight. And they've got nothing on you. But you want to know what's going on, and the only way you're going to get anything is to cooperate with him. We'll try and get him to compromise. Give a little, get a little.'

'It doesn't come naturally,' I said. 'Talking to the cops.'

'Look, you're *my* client. My only concern is protecting you. And I really don't like that remark Darroch made about you getting away with murder.'

She was right, and we both knew it. I smiled in surrender. 'Bring them in.'

Andrea got up and left the room. She was gone a few minutes, during which I folded my arms on the table and laid my forehead on them, willing the thumping in my head to subside.

The door opened and Andrea strode back in and sat beside me. Stewart and Taylor followed her in and sat down opposite.

'Where's your boss?' I asked Stewart.

'DCI Darroch will not be joining us,' he answered, 'as requested by Ms Jarvie.'

Andrea smiled and tipped an imaginary cap to me.

'I thought you were supposed to be the bad cop?' I said to Taylor. 'What's that make Darroch? Dangerously unstable cop?'

Taylor kept her face calm and made no response. Stewart said, 'We're very sorry about what happened earlier, and we apologise for any upset caused. However, Ms Jarvie has assured us that you do not wish to take the matter any further.'

'*If*,' Andrea said, leaning forward and emphasising the word, 'my client remains satisfied with the outcome of this interview.'

'Of course,' Stewart said, smiling politely. He turned his thin face to me and asked, 'Now, Harper. Would you like to tell us why you were at the Hotel Caledonia?'

This time I did. Though I didn't mention Archie Bell's name or Johnny D'Arienzo's. I was unsure why; they had Janet Bell's name so it would only be a matter of time before they caught up.

'Who's your client?' Taylor asked.

'*My* client has been very cooperative, I think it's time you told us a little about why he's here,' Andrea said. Her tone left little room for disagreement.

Stewart made a face, sucking air in through his teeth as he made a show of wrestling with this idea. I wasn't fooled. He had decided before he re-entered the room exactly how much he was going to tell us.

'We were contacted by the Hotel Caledonia four days ago after they became concerned for one of their guests.'

'Concerned?' Andrea said.

'The room had been booked from Thursday until 11a.m. Sunday, but the guest still had not checked out on Monday. The manager entered the room but it appeared the guest had not been there in several days. The manager became concerned that something had happened to them outwith the hotel.'

'You mean the manager became concerned that the guest had legged it without paying their bill? Worried that the credit card they'd taken the imprint of might have been fake?'

Stewart made a dismissive gesture. 'That doesn't concern me.

Whatever the reason, we were notified. A colleague of mine looked into it, but the guest had left most of her belongings behind, so it seemed unlikely they had done a runner. We assumed that some misfortune had befallen the guest at a separate location.'

Taylor picked up the story. 'We got a description of the guest from the hotel staff and ran that against the descriptions of unidentified hospital admissions from Thursday to Monday. No matches. We had no idea who the guest was, so we had to wait for someone to turn up matching her description, or for someone to turn up at the hotel looking for her.'

'So,' I interrupted, 'you asked the hotel management to call you if anyone showed up asking about someone who matched that description. No wonder the receptionist got jumpy when I showed him that picture.'

'They were very cooperative,' Taylor said, a little smugly.

'I bet they were. I take it you let them rent the room out again?'

'Yes,' Stewart said. 'We took all of the guest's belongings.'

Andrea chimed in then, 'How can you be sure that *some misfortune* didn't befall this guest at the hotel?'

'We did consider that, Ms Jarvie, I can assure you. The room was immaculate, there were no signs that any foul play had occurred in that room.'

Foul play? Somehow I'd stumbled into an Agatha Christie. Maybe there'd be a denouement in the library where Stewart would gather everyone together and unmask the vicar as the killer.

Stewart continued after Andrea's face told him that wasn't a good enough answer. 'We also took DNA and fingerprint samples from the room, in case anything did turn up at a future date.' That seemed to appease her more.

I wasn't so sure. I had a feeling of dread sinking into my stomach, like I'd swallowed something heavy and poisonous. 'You're at it, Stewart. That's far too much hassle to go to for something that might not even involve a crime.'

He shrugged. 'What do you want me to say?'

'Tell me when you found the body.'

He didn't react; he was too good for that. But Taylor wasn't. Her eyes looked everywhere but at me, telling me I was right.

Andrea picked up on it too, leaning forwards and fixing Stewart with the look a predator would give its next meal.

Stewart realised quickly that there was no point in trying to hide it any longer. He sighed and said, 'A week ago. Early Saturday morning.'

'Where?' I pressed.

'In the grounds of a church. St Leonard's, just outside Cardonald.'

I remembered the news reports now, though they had contained little information. 'Murdered?' I asked.

'Yes.'

'How?'

'That's confidential,' he said, his face solemn.

'And you can't identify the victim,' Andrea said.

'No. There was no identification with the body,' Taylor answered.

'Then how did you link this body to the hotel?' Andrea asked, a studied look of puzzlement on her face.

Stewart responded, 'I circulated the description to all the divisions to see if anyone had anything similar. A guy from Anderston called to fill me in on the missing hotel guest. The descriptions matched. That's when we headed down and started taking samples.'

'What about the credit card?' I asked. 'They must have used one to check in.'

'Stolen. But it hadn't been reported stolen, so wasn't flagged when she used it. The girl who owned the card never used it so hadn't realised it was missing.'

A small siren wailed in the back of my head. 'What was the name of the person who owned the card?'

'We've spoken to her,' Taylor said. 'She's fine.'

'Please,' I said quietly, my heartbeat slowing to a crawl.

Stewart nodded his consent.

'Fine,' Taylor sighed, opening the folder and flicking some pages. 'Leeann Munro, eighteen-year-old girl, knows nothing about anything.'

Damn.

The missing guest had used Leeann's credit card; something that a friend would know was safe to do; something that a friend would know would keep her location secret. And Leeann hadn't trusted me enough to tell me the police had visited her.

I forced myself to speak. 'So, you have a body with no name, and I have a name with no body. You think they're one and the same?'

'We're keeping an open mind,' Stewart said. 'But the descriptions fit.'

Andrea turned to me and gave me a very small nod. It was time to tell them what I knew.

My tongue was thick and uncooperative as I spoke. 'Does your victim have any distinguishing features?'

Taylor started to open the folder, but Stewart didn't need that. I suspected he knew the contents of that folder backwards.

'She has a scar,' he said. 'On her arm.'

'Inside of her right forearm. Curved. About three inches long,' I finished.

He nodded as Taylor found the page. Her eyes again confirmed I was right.

I'd found Janet Bell.

Seven

We were certain now that the body found in the churchyard near Cardonald, not far from her home, was that of Janet Bell, but there were still formalities to be taken care of. Stewart wanted a formal identification and I volunteered to bring Archie in to identify her.

'I'm afraid that won't be possible,' Stewart said. 'The victim's face is damaged beyond recognition.'

'Would it be satisfactory for Mr Bell to identify this scar?' Andrea asked.

'I'd like that, as a preliminary identification, to make sure we're not running down the wrong road,' Stewart answered. 'But I'd also like to get some DNA from Janet's home and use that, to be absolutely certain.'

'Would it not be easier to check dental records?' Andrea asked.

'The damage to the face was particularly severe,' Taylor said, her attitude still frosty.

'What about taking fingerprints from her home and matching those to the body? Would that not be quicker than DNA testing?' Andrea persisted.

'I'd rather have the definitive DNA confirmation,' said Stewart, cutting in before Taylor had a chance to answer. 'I'm looking for a cast-iron case here.' There was something in his manner that suggested that wasn't the whole story, but it was certainly the only one we were getting today.

'I want to be the one to tell her dad,' I said.

Taylor looked at me with something that may have been respect. Stewart nodded his agreement. 'But we go with you. I want to be there immediately. He'll have questions you won't be able to answer.'

'Fine,' I said. Even though Janet was dead before Archie had consulted me I felt a duty to him, a responsibility to be the one to tell him what had happened to his daughter. As long as Stewart let me do that I didn't really care what else he insisted on.

'Do you have any leads?' I asked.

'We're pursuing a number of lines of enquiry,' Taylor said in a monotone.

'Very informative.'

Stewart's brow had furrowed as he thought something over. Finally he asked, 'Why was Janet staying in a hotel?'

'She was running away,' I told them. 'From her ex-boyfriend.'

'What?' Taylor demanded loudly. 'When were you planning on telling us this?'

'Whenever you got around to asking,' I replied.

'What's his name?' Stewart asked, refusing to get drawn into petty squabbles.

'Johnny D'Arienzo,' I said, watching him write it down in his little notebook. I told them the name of the garage that he worked at. I then explained the beatings and abuse she had suffered at his hands. To my surprise Stewart didn't seem very interested.

'Thank you, we'll pay him a visit,' Stewart said.

I looked at him, amazed. Andrea was equally taken aback. 'Is that it?' she exclaimed. 'You'll pay him a visit? You've got a murder victim who was in hiding from an abusive ex-spouse, and you'll pay him a visit?'

'As DS Taylor said, we're following a number of lines of enquiry. That will be one of them.' He got to his feet and the rest of us followed suit.

As we left the room I stood in front of him and said, 'You know who did it, don't you? That's the only reason you don't care about Johnny D'Arienzo.'

'Believe me, Harper, if I knew who did it they would be behind bars by now,' he said, pushing his way past me.

I spoke again before he was too far away. 'Who are Gemma Sinclair and Siobhan Sutherland?'

Stewart stopped in his tracks and his head fell forward. He pivoted slowly, shaking his head as he faced me. 'Two completely separate cases. Darroch was ranting, accusing you of anything.'

'So there's no connection to Janet Bell then?'

'None at all. He was just throwing out names. They're two ongoing cases, that's all.'

I couldn't tell if he was telling the truth or not, but there was nothing I could do at that moment anyway. 'Come on,' he sighed, 'let's go and ruin your client's life.'

Taylor pushed past me and fell into step with Stewart as he headed for the exit.

Andrea appeared at my side and put a hand on my arm. 'She was dead before you even heard her name.'

'Doesn't make it any easier.'

'There was nothing you could have done.'

'No,' I said. 'But someone could have done something.'

She shook her head sadly. 'Not always. You know that as well as I do.'

'Yeah. And Archie Bell's about to find it out the hard way. Just like we did.'

*

Archie coped better than I expected, though he was probably insulated by shock. I couldn't imagine what the coming days and weeks held in store for him.

Stewart handled him expertly and with real compassion. Taylor too was professional and courteous, the diametric opposite of the aggressive, argumentative bitch I had seen up till now. She showed Archie a photo of the scar, squeezing his hand as she did so. Tears sprouted as he bit his lip and nodded. It was Janet. DI Stewart spoke softly as he told Archie they would need DNA samples to confirm the identification. He sniffed and told them to help themselves. DS Taylor trudged upstairs and reappeared a few moment's later with Janet's hairbrush in an evidence bag, the tangle of blonde hairs bright within the clear plastic.

There was nothing else I could do, but as I stood to leave Archie gave me a sad look. 'Do you have to go?'

'There's nothing I can do now, Archie. It's up to the police to find who did this.'

'Can't you find them?' he asked through trembling lips.

I had to force myself to hold his gaze. 'I don't track down killers, Archie. The police have the expertise, the experience, the manpower and resources. I'd only be in the way.'

'Please...,' he said, his voice tailing off.

'There's nothing I can do that the police can't do better. You need to trust them, Archie. They'll find him.'

Archie looked at Stewart and Taylor and nodded to himself, resigned to the fact he had no choice in the matter. 'Thank you for trying,' he said, in a voice that damned me for doing so little.

I nodded once, unable to speak and moved towards the door. I let myself out and walked towards the street where a police car waited to take me back to the hotel to collect my car. I heard the door open behind me and stopped. I stood for a second in the darkness and listened to footfalls coming down the drive towards me. DI Stewart stopped beside me, staring straight ahead into the night.

We stood like that for a moment, a light smir of rain falling on us, before Stewart spoke. 'Did you mean that?'

'Mean what?' I asked wearily.

'You'll leave it to us to investigate.'

'Yes.'

'That's a good decision. You should abide by it.' His voice held a note of stern warning.

'Like I said, you guys are the experts.'

'I wish I could believe you meant that.'

'I wish I could too.' I walked away from him, but stopped as he grabbed my arm.

'Here's my mobile number.' He handed me a piece of paper. 'Call me if you think of anything.'

I took the slip of paper and looked at it with indifference.

'I'm not your enemy,' Stewart said. 'And neither is Sam.'

'Sam?'

'DS Taylor. She can be a bit,' he searched for the right words, 'in your face, at first. Particularly if she thinks you're one of the bad guys.'

'What does she think now?'

'She's with me. She knows you're innocent and she'll back me to the hilt.'

'No offence, Stewart, but whoop-de-frigging-do. You want me to get excited because you don't think I'm a murderer?'

He refused to look away. 'I know what happened in the past. I know you don't trust the police. And I know I have no right to ask this, but, trust *me*. Please. I want this killer even more than you do.'

'What about what Darroch wants? He has a way of ignoring alternatives once he's made his mind up.'

'Darroch may be in overall charge, but this is my investigation. And no-one tells me what leads to follow.' His face darkened, and he was suddenly tougher, more formidable looking. 'I go where the evidence takes me. Regardless of what anyone says.'

'Then I'll read about it in the papers,' I said.

I walked to the police car and climbed in. The uniform behind the wheel knew where we were going and pulled smoothly away from the kerb. A short time later he dropped me beside my car and I drove home on autopilot. I stumbled up the stairs to my flat and stripped my clothes off clumsily, falling gratefully into bed as tiredness threatened to overwhelm me.

This hadn't been one of my better days, and all I wanted was to seek solace in sleep – to unplug my brain and my heart and get through the night in sweet soporific stupor.

But sleep wouldn't come.

What did come were fragments of memories and shards of nightmares. The past colliding with the present in a soul-draining miasma of pain and sorrow that kept my eyes wide and my nerves aflame.

For the first time in a long time Katie Jarvie haunted me.

Eight

Lochbridge was a small town, a village really, nestled on country roads, surrounded by hills and rivers and trees. It was a nice place to grow up, or so I had thought, until I was seventeen and someone turned the world on its side.

James Mackie and I had already been friends for years when we met the Jarvie twins. They were fifteen, a year younger than us at that point, though beginning to blossom into the women only one of them would ever become. We were spellbound. I was immediately drawn to Andrea, and Mack to Katie. We spent all our free time together, the four of us an inseparable group.

It was shortly after the girls had celebrated their sixteenth birthday, and Mack and I had turned seventeen that things changed, that the world spun and came to rest in a different position. It was then, in the first early days of a new summer, that Katie discovered she was pregnant.

She confided in her twin sister first, before taking Mack for a walk in the Gledhill Woods that curved around the top end of Lochbridge. When she told him he was to be a father he panicked, as many a young boy has done when faced with such news, and he said things that would forever haunt him. He never truly thought it might be someone else's child within her, but that didn't stop him saying those hateful words.

Katie ran from him, blinded by tears as she dashed headlong into the woods, taking the path that led towards her home. Mack almost followed her, but, in a moment that would define his life, he let his pride intervene and walked in the opposite direction. The last he saw of the girl he loved were her devastated tears as she ran crying from his spiteful tongue.

It didn't take long for him to realise he had been wrong, and to go to the Jarvie home to make amends; to be the man he would need to become to be a father. Katie was not home, but Andrea was, and I was with her. We had been there all day and Katie had not been home since she had left with Mack earlier in the day. We worried that she had suffered an accident, that she was lying somewhere in the Gledhill Woods with a broken ankle.

We imagined nothing worse. Nothing like the truth.

Mack and I went to the woods while Andrea stayed at home in case Katie appeared. We followed the path that Katie should have taken home, starting from the opposite end. As we walked and scanned the undergrowth, calling Katie's name at increasingly short intervals, Mack told me the whole sorry tale. Even as slowly as we walked it would have taken only ten minutes to walk the entire path.

It didn't take that long. After five minutes Mack spotted Katie's purse lying at the side of the path, its bright blue plastic visible beneath a cluster of dock leaves. There were broken branches leading from the path and the two of us charged into the undergrowth, pushing aside the damaged branches and calling Katie's name again, more hoarsely now as though our throats knew what lay ahead. After a few moments we emerged into a less densely wooded area and saw a low stone wall ahead of us, a crumbling relic half-hidden by nature's attempts to reclaim the land.

Mack ran to the wall and looked over it, his hands grasping the wall as his legs buckled beneath him. I reached the wall and stood beside my friend as we both looked upon the lifeless, blood-stained body of Katie Jarvie.

Mack climbed the wall, ran to her and collapsed to his knees, cradling her head in his arms and soaking himself in her blood.

I climbed the wall as soon as I was able to move and crouched down beside him. Slowly I eased him away from her. He held on for a second before letting her head slip back to the earth. I pulled him to his feet and turned him towards me, holding him in my arms as he sobbed.

Those were our mistakes: both of us were now soaked in Katie Jarvie's blood.

I closed my eyes and it came to me for the first time, but far from the last; the image of Katie's corpse – her pulverised face, rendered almost unrecognisable by the blood that coated it; her t-shirt pulled up to her throat, her bra pulled roughly down, exposing her left breast; her jeans undone and partially pulled down – and I prayed to any god that would listen for this to be nothing but a nightmare. The nightmares would come later though; haunted visions in which Katie suffered every dark abuse a tortured imagination could conjure.

The hours after passed in a blur of images; Andrea's reaction as I burst through her door, my ashen face and blood soaked clothes drawing from her a scream that ripped my soul to tattered shreds; calling the police; fighting to stop Andrea entering the woods, trying to prevent her closed eyes being haunted by the same image that had burned itself into mine; leading the police to the spot where Katie lay; Mack watching over Katie, tears mingling with the blood on his face, watching over her, protecting her now as he had failed to do in life; the questions; the looks; the accusations.

Even from that first moment, there were only two suspects in the eyes of the police –James Mackie and Keir Harper.

DS Iain Darroch was in charge and was convinced he had a strong case. Mack was the boyfriend, he had motive – he had admitted to being unhappy with the pregnancy – and he was covered in her blood. He had no alibi for the estimated time of death, and there were no other suspects. Not that the police wasted any time looking for one.

Mack was also the one who had found the body. And the only person with him at that time was his best friend, who also happened to be covered in the victim's blood. The police decided that we were both responsible – that he had been desperate to escape his responsibilities, and that I had helped him.

They never explained how we could both be with Andrea Jarvie, without a trace of blood on us, and then return half an hour later soaked through with it. Particularly as the time of death was estimated at several hours earlier in the afternoon, just a few minutes after Katie had left Mack. Only Andrea's stubborn statement that I had been with her all afternoon made the police eventually discount me as a suspect. They had no such problems with Mack though. No-one was able to account for his whereabouts at the estimated time of death.

The village believed he was the killer. It was easier for them to think that a desperate seventeen-year-old boy had gone to an extreme length to avoid fatherhood than believe that an unknown murderer had been in their midst undetected. Andrea and Katie's parents blamed him too. I understood that, and did not blame them. The police had left them with no option; Mack was their only chance of justice. Their relationship with their surviving daughter became strained as she refused to believe that Mack was the killer and told anyone who would listen that he could not have killed Katie.

It made no difference. Mack became a pariah. No-one in the village would talk to him or his mother. She cracked under the strain and threw him out one night, making him appear even more guilty. So guilty that even his own mother could not shelter him.

But my mother did. She took him in and the three of us lived together, a small fortress surrounded by recrimination, hatred and fear. Until the police charged Mack with Katie's murder.

The trial began a few months later and lasted weeks as the police tried to shore up an increasingly circumstantial case. There were no witnesses and very little evidence, none of which pointed directly and incontrovertibly to Mack. After twenty-seven days of trial the jury retired to consider their verdict.

Most people in the civilised world are familiar with the concept of 'innocent until proven guilty', and correspondingly have either Guilty or Not Guilty verdicts. Scots Law has a third verdict, peculiar entirely to Scotland: Not Proven. A verdict referred to by the poet and writer Sir Walter Scott as *the bastard verdict* in reference to the stigma it attached to those tainted by it.

The case against Mack was found Not Proven. Essentially, the jury had said, *we think you did it, but we don't have enough evidence to put you away.*

The good and sympathetic people of Lochbridge were in uproar, incensed at having justice snatched from them. Darroch told anyone that would listen that he would not let the matter rest, that he would find a way to retry Mack.

What no-one realised was that although the jury had not imposed a custodial sentence, by copping out and opting for the Not Proven verdict, they had condemned Mack to a different form of imprisonment. He could not go out in public without someone shouting *killer* or *murderer* at him. The final straw came one dark night when three young men took their shot at local stardom by attacking Mack. He put the three of them in hospital, but scared himself at how close he came to doing irreparable harm.

The next day he signed up for the army and left Lochbridge for the last time.

Andrea and I tried to make our relationship work, partially out of some skewed idea of responsibility to Katie and Mack. We couldn't do it. Andrea struggled with her parents' hatred of me, and both of us felt some form of survivor's guilt at being the couple who were still together. We lasted a few months after the trial, but eventually decided to try friendship instead. That worked better, and still does.

Andrea became a solicitor to protect people from being railroaded by the police. Her parents still believe Mack, and possibly me as well, got away with murder, and her relationship with them remains irretrievably distant. I still didn't blame the Jarvies; they needed someone to hate, and although they still had one daughter, every time they saw her face they also saw the one they lost.

Mack returned to Scotland eventually and put his life together again. Katie's death haunts him more than anyone else. He blames himself for sending her running into the Gledhill Woods that day and for not protecting her from the evil that claimed her. He will not return to our hometown, and it holds nothing for me either. My mother moved away shortly after I did, forsaking the pointed fingers and whispered spite for a more peaceful life further north.

The events of that day, and the investigation and trial that followed changed all of our lives and have haunted us since. It ripped up the path that each of us was on and re-laid it in new, unmapped directions.

For better or worse, I am the person that I am today because someone murdered my friend. And because the police persecuted a young boy and let a killer go free.

Now, as I lay soaked through with sweat and the first red rays of dawn seeped under the curtains, I had to decide whether I could trust the police to bring another young girl's killer to justice.

Did I have any choice?

Nine

I eventually fell asleep for a couple of hours shortly after full light, as though my body had been waiting for the long shadows of night to pass before allowing itself to rest. It was fitful sleep, sporadic and tormented, but it would at least allow me to function for a few hours.

When I awoke it was to a cold grey day that matched my mood. I dragged myself out of bed and spent the rest of the morning shuffling around, aimless and untethered, my mind unable to focus on any task for long. I forced down some lunch and decided to head out for some fresh air to clear my head.

I opened the close door and stepped outside, bracing myself against the cold wind, when a voice suddenly called, 'Smile!'

I looked up into the lens of a camera as the picture was snapped. The camera was lowered and behind it I saw a young woman, her small, pert lips splitting in a mischievous grin. She wore a vintage-looking bottle green coat, baggy black combats and chunky trainers, and she was perched on the bonnet of a battered old, once-navy VW Golf, legs crossed as though meditating.

'Sorry to keep you waiting,' I said.

'No worries,' the girl said. She reached up and pulled on the end of a strand of jet black hair, examining the pink tip as though she had been waiting for it to show up rather than me.

'You know, if you sign up to my newsletter we can post pictures to you. Save you camping out.'

'Cool,' she said, smiling widely.

I smiled back. She smiled some more. This was fun.

'So, why'd the police have you in at Pitt Street?'

Someone always has to ruin it. I stopped smiling.

'Charlotte MacGregor, Glasgow News,' the girl said.

'Then you've got the wrong person.'

She shook her head happily, still sitting cross legged on the bonnet of her car. At least, I hoped it was hers. 'No I don't. You're Keir Harper, P.I.' She said it like she was doing a voice over for Magnum.

I wondered how long she had been sitting there, and if anyone had noticed. Probably not, my street seemed as quiet as it usually was. I lived on a short cobbled street, lined on one side with three old buildings that had once been accommodation for mill workers, until the sixties saw them converted into flats. The other side was lined with residents cars, parked against a short fence that guarded the river rushing below. On the far side of the river was the mill itself. Once, reputedly, the largest of its kind in the world, and a key part of Paisley's economy, the mill had also been converted into apartments in the last few years as part of an ongoing attempt to reinvigorate the fortunes of the town. A walk through Paisley town centre and its collection of closed storefronts would suggest that had yet to pay off.

I headed towards my car, key in hand, and heard the reporter sliding off the Golf onto her feet.

'Ah, come on,' she called. 'Just a couple of questions.'

'Not for that rag you write for,' I said, opening the car door and climbing in. I started the engine just as she appeared beside the window, rapping her slim fingers on the glass.

'You think I want to work there? Come on, this can be your good deed for the day. You give me a story and help me leave the gutter press behind. I get a better job, you get to feel all warm and fuzzy inside. Everyone's a winner!'

I don't know why – probably because she still wore that infectious smile – but I wound down the window, sighed and raised my eyebrows at her. Now that she was closer, and standing upright, I could see she was both younger and smaller than I had realised. She probably cleared five feet, but there wouldn't be much in it, and I doubted she was much over twenty.

'Sweet!' She cleared her throat and put on her serious face. 'So, did you know the girl?'

'What girl?'

'The dead one, duh!' She smiled again, and I wondered what it would take to make that smile falter.

'Don't know any dead girls, I'm afraid. You must be thinking of someone else.'

'Yeah, Keir Harper's such a common name. Can't turn around without tripping over a Keir Harper. C'mon, spill it.'

I laughed. 'Are you for real? Does this approach ever work with anyone?'

'Nah,' she admitted, studying her hair again. 'But just wait till I start playing bad cop.' She wiggled her eyebrows at me.

I shook my head and shifted the gearstick into first.

'Tell you what,' she said, 'you tell me why the police were interviewing you about a brutal murder and I'll make sure you come across innocent in the story.'

'Are you suggesting you'll make me look guilty if I don't?'

'I didn't say that.' She shrugged exaggeratedly. 'But, if there's only one side of a story… it could be misinterpreted, you know?'

I looked at her for a few more seconds then wound the window back up. I could hear her protesting on the other side of the glass but I ignored it and drove off with a bad taste in my mouth. It tasted like the past.

*

I was unfamiliar with the names and locations of the churches around Cardonald, but a quick check of my tattered old A-Z showed told me there were half a dozen within the area. DI Stewart had commented however that St Leonard's was just outside Cardonald, and I found one situated on the boundary with Mosspark. Surrounded by Woodland on three sides it seemed like a plausible location for a killer to dump a body.

I followed the map and pulled up at the side of the kerb where I saw a sign through the open gates, proclaiming this as St Leonard's Catholic Church. I gave myself a pat on the back, got out of the car and walked through the gate into the churchyard. It had been a week since Janet Bell's body had been found and there was no longer any trace of the hive of police activity that would have thronged around the old grey stone building. I made a slow circuit of the outside of the church, looking for any clue to the exact location where Janet's body had been found. I wasn't sure why – or even why I was here – as it was unlikely that I would derive any great insight from the scene. Perhaps I was here purely as a mark of respect for the dead.

I stood for a few moments behind the church, looking out over the attached cemetery at the rows of tombstones, standing like forgotten legions in the chill wind. As I did I thought about the location. It was quiet, and surely even more so in the darkness of night. There were no neighbours to overlook the grounds, no disturbances or potential witnesses, and yet, as I began to walk back round the church, I wondered if that was enough to have chosen this spot. Janet lived with her father only a mile from this church; was that nothing more than coincidence? Had Janet come back to Cardonald and then been murdered? Or had she fallen victim to her killer nearer the hotel she had run to for safety and then been brought back here by an attacker who knew who she was and where she lived?

I was reflecting on this when I reached the front of the church again. I passed through the gate and turned towards my car, stopping as I noticed a man leaning against it.

'Nice car,' he said, his voice soft and hushed.

He was in his forties, greying dark hair, short, with a gut, and dressed in a long navy wool overcoat, the clothes beneath dark and unremarkable. Everything in his appearance seemed average and everyday. But there was something else, some instinctive response to an unnoticed warning signal that told me to be extremely wary.

'Thanks,' I replied cautiously, looking at my N-reg Honda as though it had turned into something desirable since I had last seen it. Truth was, it may not have looked much on the outside – ideal in my job – but it had been heavily tinkered with by a friend of mine and went like a greased cheetah.

'Think it might have broken down though,' the man said. 'I'll give you a lift.'

I glanced at the Honda again, which looked fine, then at the grey

Toyota Avensis behind it. 'You're alright, thanks. I'm with the RAC.'

'Get in the car please.'

'Why?'

'Because I asked you nicely.' He reached inside his coat and eased out a gun, tapped it on his leg. 'And I won't ask nicely again.'

It may not have been pointed at me – yet – but he didn't look the type to miss from ten feet. He also didn't look the type to hesitate if I didn't cooperate.

'Well, since you asked nicely,' I said and walked past him towards the passenger door of the Avensis.

'Other side,' he said. 'You're going to be my chauffeur for the day.'

I shrugged as though it didn't make any difference. Inside I was cursing; I'd been banking on him lowering the gun to drive. Even worse, after I'd climbed into the driver's seat he got into the back directly behind me, preventing me from seeing him at all.

'Where to?' I asked.

The gun appeared briefly between the gap in the seats, waving at the road ahead. 'Just drive.'

Ten

The man in the back of the car told me to head east on the M8 and after that there was silence in the car. I wanted to say something, to ask where we were going and who he was, but I sensed it would be a waste of breath. The Toyota sped on, edging ever nearer our destination, wherever that may be. We passed Govan and Ibrox and I wondered how much further we would travel before he broke the silence to tell me where to turn off.

When he finally spoke it seemed as though I had been driving forever, though it was well under half an hour. He leant forward slightly and told me to take the Tradeston exit. I did as I was told and left the motorway, following the slip road into an area consisting mainly of warehouses and industrial units. We drove past a furniture warehouse and a company specialising in industrial clothing before he told me to turn into a quieter street. A red light stopped us beside a cash and carry that looked as though it hadn't seen any of the former in some time. Panes of glass were missing in the upper floors and those in the ground floor were protected by rusted metal grilles that clung desperately to the crumbling brickwork. On the other side of the street lay a vacant lot, piled high in places with construction materials that had lain dormant so long weeds had grown high around them. The temporary fence erected around the site bore the logo of a security company but there was no-one in sight.

The light changed and I accelerated, travelling along a row of similarly decrepit warehouses. Finally the man with the gun directed me through the open doors of a warehouse that bore no sign nor indication of its business. He sensed my hesitation and I felt the barrel of the gun press against the upholstery of my seat. I turned the wheel and slid the car into the building.

I parked the Avensis where he indicated and my door was opened even before I had time to switch off the engine. Several hands reached inside and hauled me to my feet, two bulky guys grabbing me under the arms and marching me towards a set of stairs in the back corner of the warehouse, the quiet man a few paces behind.

We reached the first floor and walked past four men seated on boxes around a large crate where their lunches sat beside opened newspapers. A bottle of no-label whisky sat on the floor at one man's feet and a torn-open beer can served as an ash-tray. The four of them were silent as we passed, giving me dead eyes and trying to intimidate me. They needn't have worried; I'd passed intimidated somewhere along the M8.

We walked to the rear of the building, passing empty pallets, stacked boxes and the occasional crate squatting in the darkness. Other than the men I had already seen the building seemed mostly empty, but I could hear the sounds of men at work somewhere in the building. For some reason I was more concerned about those I hadn't seen yet.

We came to a door and the guy on my right rapped his huge knuckles against it, pushing it open after a suitable pause and shoving me inside.

The room was a smallish office, with windows that looked out over the street we had driven in on. The rest of the room was mostly empty, like the rest of the warehouse, except for a large wooden table in the centre of the room. There was a single bare metal chair in front of the desk, and a more comfortable, leather chair behind it.

A man sat in the leather chair, his hands clasped in front of him as he scrutinised me. He was solid, despite pushing seventy, with a thick head of close-cropped, bone-white hair. His broad, flat nose bore a small white moustache at one end and cruel, grey eyes at the other. I recognised him from numerous newspaper photographs, and now, as in those, he was wearing his seemingly standard dress of navy blazer and plain white shirt.

I was pushed hard into the metal chair and the old man flicked his bushy white eyebrows at the two big guys, telling them to leave. The quiet man walked round from behind me and stood with his back to the window, hands clasped in front of him. I couldn't tell where his gun was, but I knew it wouldn't be far from his fingertips.

'You know who I am?' the old man asked.

'You're Innes McKenzie,' I replied.

'I know who I am, smart arse, I don't need you to remind me. What am I, fucking senile? I want to make sure you know who you're dealing with here.'

I said nothing and reminded myself to be careful with my answers. Innes McKenzie had been the biggest gangster in Glasgow since shortly after Arthur Thompson died in 1993, and was responsible for countless deaths and brutal maimings. He had made his mark on the streets of Glasgow with a straight razor in the 1960s and was still rumoured to carry one on him at all times. Even in his advanced years I didn't want to test him.

'And I know who you are, Harper. Now, tell me why you were at Pitt Street on Friday night.'

'What?' That caught me off-guard; I had begun to assume this whole thing was a result of my chat with Johnny D'Arienzo. 'Why?'

He unclasped his hands and that's when I noticed the fingers on his left hand. The pinky and ring finger were fused together, the flesh a shiny mass of scar tissue left by a serious burn. The scarring travelled down the back of his hand and disappeared into the carefully folded double cuff of his shirt. I raised my eyes and noticed a small trace of the scar tissue protruding above the collar of his shirt. I shuddered to think what had caused such severe injury.

He tapped his damaged fingers on the table top, intentionally drawing my attention to them. 'That was one. There won't be a second. Understand?'

I swallowed hard and nodded.

'Well?'

My mind raced as I tried to guess why he was asking me this and what answer would get me out of here in one piece. I wondered how many people had been brought to this warehouse over the years and how many had left in a crate rather than on their own two feet.

'I'm a private investigator,' I began.

'I know.'

'I was hired to find someone. The trail led me to a hotel and when I got there the police were waiting to speak to anyone who showed up at the hotel looking for this person.'

'Why?'

There was no point in not telling him. 'They found a body but couldn't identify it. The hotel had reported a missing guest, and the descriptions matched so they told the hotel to contact them if anyone came looking for their guest.'

'Is it the same person?'

'Yes.'

'What's her name?'

I wondered how he knew it was a female, but decided it was wiser not to ask. 'Janet Bell. Do you know her?'

He ignored my question and turned to the man behind him who gave a short shake of his head. McKenzie turned back to me.

'Why did the police ask you about two other girls?'

'They didn't really ask me about them...' I began, before McKenzie cut me off.

'My sources are very good. Think twice before you lie to me.' His grey eyes seemed paler now, even colder than when I had first entered the room.

'One of the cops has a grudge, he's hated me for years.'

'Why?'

'He tried to frame me for something and he's pissed off that it didn't work.'

'What did he try to get you for?'

'Assault.' I didn't know where this was going, but there was no way I was telling McKenzie it was for the murder of a young woman.

He seemed to accept my answer. 'So you know nothing about either Gemma Sinclair or Siobhan Sutherland?'

'First I heard of them was when the cops mentioned them.'

McKenzie turned to the man at the window who walked the few steps to McKenzie and leaned down to whisper in his ear. McKenzie murmured something back, was given a nod by the other man and turned back to me. The quiet man stepped back to his spot at the window again, a decision apparently reached between the two of them.

'Both girls were murdered. Siobhan, seven months ago. Gemma, fifteen months ago.'

I said nothing. I had assumed as much when Darroch mentioned the names.

'Siobhan Sutherland was my daughter,' McKenzie continued, and for a second I saw something human force itself into his eyes.

'I'm sorry,' I said, and it was true. Despite everything I knew about him no-one deserved to lose a child to murder.

'We weren't close. She disapproved of my,' his good hand waved in the air a couple of times while he searched for the appropriate words, 'means of income. She took her mother's surname as soon as she was old enough.'

'Was she still close to her mother?'

'Her mother died when Siobhan was ten. Something else she blamed me for.'

I waited for him to elaborate. It didn't take long.

'I've been the main man in this city for over a decade, Harper. But I've always had enemies, even before that. Always. Sometimes they get brave, think they can take a shot at me. Idiots. I've survived more attempts on my life than Castro. Every method you could possibly think of, and I've beaten them all.' He looked to the side for a second before he continued. But my wife didn't. Nor did my son. Six years old and burnt to a fucking cinder by a petrol bomb. Both of them were. And I survived – again.'

I knew McKenzie was evil. I knew that he had inflicted pain and fear and degradation on people for decades, knew that the men who had thrown those petrol bombs had almost certainly paid with their lives and the lives of their own families. Maybe this was the world's way of paying him back. Maybe it was karma. Whatever it was, I still felt a measure of empathy. To lose one child to violence was terrible. To lose two must be unbearable.

'Siobhan and I hadn't spoken in four years,' he continued. 'She refused to even acknowledge me. I always had high hopes that we may have been reconciled.' His face showed real pain then. 'I don't have many years left, but someone decided I would have to bury a second child. Some walking corpse decided I would not get to speak to my daughter again, that I would never get to see her smile at me even once more.'

McKenzie lifted his disfigured left hand and jabbed it at the air between us to emphasise his point. 'You need to understand what this means to me. It's not just everything to me; it's the only thing.' He lowered his voice and spoke in an ominous tone that ran along my spine like shards of glass. 'I would bury every man in this city to get one single inch closer to this man.'

I stared at McKenzie, the pain in his face and the raw violence in his voice holding my attention like a wild beast released into the room. Until the man at the window finally spoke.

'You're going to find him,' he said.

'What?' I said, surprised. 'I can't do that. I'm looking for Janet Bell's killer. There's no way I can find two.'

'Are you stupid?'

I just looked at him, a horrible feeling settling in my stomach like a ship sinking to the sea bed. McKenzie's expression did nothing to quell my unease.

'Siobhan Sutherland, Gemma Sinclair, and Janet Bell were all killed by the same person, you moron,' said the quiet man. 'The cops are hunting a serial killer.'

Eleven

'A serial killer?' I said doubtfully.

'What?' The quiet man again looked at me as though I was stupid. 'You think you only get them in the States? You never heard of Ian Brady and Myra Hindley? Fred and Rosemary West?'

And the rest. Harold Shipman, Peter Sutcliffe, Bible John, Peter Manuel, Robert Black... the list was endless.

My head was spinning, the whole situation driving a red hot nail through the centre of my brain.

'Why isn't this in the papers? They should be warning people.'

The quiet man looked away from me in disgust, while McKenzie answered as though it was obvious. 'They're not going to advertise their incompetence. Anyway, two victims isn't a serial killer, and they've only just found the third.'

'Seems strange that it hasn't been uncovered by some enterprising reporter though.' I was thinking of a certain young reporter who had been camped outside my door this morning.

'What's to uncover?' McKenzie said, shrugging his big shoulders. 'Three murders spread out over more than a year. The victims are all young women, but completely unrelated and the details of the killings have all been kept very quiet.'

'How do you know the details?'

'A lot of Strathclyde's finest supplement their income from my pocket, Harper. Don't be surprised if I know more about this than the Chief Constable does.'

The quiet man stepped forward and stood at McKenzie's right elbow. 'How long will it take you to find him?'

'I don't find killers. That's a job for the police.'

'Well they can't, so *now* you find killers. Understand?'

'Why can't you find him?' I said to him.

'This is slightly out of Mason's remit,' McKenzie interrupted. 'Usually the ones he finds are thick as pigshit. They have to be to have crossed me. They're predictable.'

Mason. I knew the name, and it was not one I wanted to hear. Mason had been, according to the rumours, McKenzie's enforcer and hitman for almost twenty years. In all that time, and after all the deaths and disappearances he had been linked to, the police had never managed to get him further than an interview room. It seemed witnesses were in short supply where he was concerned.

'I hear you're good,' McKenzie said.

'I'm the best.'

'Full of yourself, aren't you?' I couldn't tell if he admired that or not.

'I've never been one for false modesty.'

'In that case this is how it's going to work,' McKenzie said. 'You're going to keep investigating, and you're going to find this bastard. You keep me updated on anything and everything you discover. You tell the police nothing. I don't want them getting in my way. Once you find him you call me and you walk away with a nice fat pay cheque. You got it?'

'Then I need something from you,' I said, with more confidence than I felt. 'I need to see what the police have on each of the three murders. If you've got so many cops on your payroll that shouldn't be a problem.'

'I already have copies,' McKenzie said. 'It's a lot of information.'

'I don't need everything.' I rattled off a list of what I wanted.

'Don't ask much, do you?' Mason muttered.

McKenzie nodded however. 'Mason will give you what you need.'

Mason walked round the desk towards the door and held it open. I took that as my cue to leave and stood up. McKenzie spoke as I reached the door.

'If you let me down, leave the country. Not that I won't find you. I will. But I'm due a holiday. Go somewhere warm. Where they speak fucking English.'

McKenzie waved his mangled hand, dismissing me and I followed Mason from the room, neither of us speaking until we were back beside the Avensis.

'Can you find him?' he asked.

'You get me the police files, I'll find him.' What else was I going to say? *No, actually, you might as well just kill me now, save wasting time.*

Mason snorted and climbed into the car. Guess he didn't share my faith in my abilities. I jumped in beside him as he eased the car back onto the street and into the thin winter sunlight.

*

We stopped at an office building in the city centre and Mason disappeared inside while I waited in the car like an inconvenient child. He reappeared twenty minutes later with a cardboard box in his hands, dumping it on the seat behind him. He got back behind the wheel, steering us back onto the M8 and before long he had pulled up behind my car once again. We both got out of the car and he watched me lift the box from the back seat.

'If anyone hears you got that from us, I'll blind you. If I think you're messing us around, I'll blind you. If I'm having a bad day, I'll blind you. Understand?'

'Blind. Got it.' I made a pistol of my fingers and winked as I shot him, pretending my spine hadn't just dissolved.

Mason looked as though he'd like to shoot me for real. He glared at me for a few seconds before getting back into the Toyota and driving off.

By the time I reached Paisley and had lugged the box up the stairs to my first floor flat I was filled with a mixture of burning curiosity and numbing dread. Within this box were the details of how three young women had lost their lives. I looked at it, sitting malevolently on my kitchen table as though it was Pandora's box and opening it would release all the evils of mankind into my life. I shook off the feeling of premonition and opened the box.

Inside the box were three separately bound files, each marked with a name. I pulled the file marked Gemma Sinclair in front of me and took a deep breath as I slipped off the thick elastic bands and opened the folder.

Everything I had asked for seemed to be here: copies of autopsy reports, crime scene reports and photographs, statements from anyone with a connection to the victim, a summary of the investigation so far, along with a number of hand-written notes that revealed the beliefs and assumptions the investigation was working under. That was why I had asked McKenzie for the files rather than asking Brownstone to break into the police computer system and risk missing anything that hadn't been entered on a computer.

Gemma had been murdered fifteen months ago, a fact that made me pause. Strathclyde Police had been on this case for over a year and had apparently come up empty. Why should I fare any better?

Because I care.

I picked up the photo of Gemma as she was in life and looked at it sadly. She was twenty-three when she died, five feet four and a little chubby. Her face was round, her blonde hair tied back in a ponytail. The only obvious similarity between Gemma and Janet Bell, other than their sex, was their blonde hair. Had that been enough to draw the eye of a maniac?

Gemma had lived with her mother in a tenement flat in Maryhill, had no current or recent boyfriend, or indeed, girlfriend, and her mother was her only close relative. She had worked as a play assistant at a place called the Kidz Kastle near her home, one of these giant soft-play areas filled with screaming, hyperactive weans and parents a hair-trigger from a nervous breakdown.

So far, so mundane.

Then I came across something that was a little out of the ordinary.

Gemma Sinclair had given birth to a son when she was only fifteen. Not such a shocker in a country where the teen pregnancy rate is the worst in Europe, but Gemma gave her son up for adoption. As the son would now be only eight years old it was very unlikely he was running around killing people. The father on the other hand, may be worth looking into. I flicked through the file and found the police report on Darryl Dempsey, the fifteen year old father, and saw that he was in the army and had been serving overseas when she was killed. Had I really thought it would be that easy?

I carried on through the rest of the file, reading the statements and the commentary on each line of investigation that was systematically followed up and, almost inevitably, ruled out. I reached the post mortem report and skipped the scientific jargon, going straight to the summary where anything useful would be found. The report listed toxins found in the body and revealed that there were traces of ketamine in Gemma's tissues. I'd come across ketamine before; originally intended as an anaesthetic, but consigned mainly to veterinary medicine due to its unpredictable hallucinogenic properties, it was becoming popular among drug users throughout the country, and, more disturbingly, had been linked to a number of date rapes. There was nothing in the file to suggest Gemma was into illegal drugs and it seemed likely the killer had used the ketamine to subdue and abduct her, the effects leaving her compliant and vulnerable.

The pathologist then listed the wounds Gemma had suffered, presenting them in a factual, unemotional manner that somehow magnified the horror of what had happened to her. Her killer had used a very sharp blade to inflict a total of one-hundred and twenty-seven cuts of various lengths and depths across her entire body. The report stated that these had been delivered over a period of several hours, possibly up to twenty-four.

I blanched when I read that, but forced myself to continue.

Once the killer had grown tired of this game he cut her abdomen open from one side to the other, pulled out her intestines and let her bleed to death.

Then he had removed her uterus.

And, for his final act before dumping the body, he had left a message. I turned in horror to the copied crime scene photographs and gave a sharp intake of breath. A young woman's body lay on grey concrete steps, spread-eagled, her arms and legs thrown to four corners, her face and body smeared with horribly dark red blood that almost pulsed in stark relief against the pale skin beneath. But it was her stomach that drew the eye immediately and made you wish for blindness as the intestines spilled from the opening like a twisted parody of childbirth. Her innards snaked forth from the stomach cavity, spilling between her legs, seeming almost to flow down the steps.

And above that hellish chasm, quite clear in the post mortem photographs once the body had been washed clean of blood, was a message carved into Gemma's chest. Savage, jagged cuts that formed characters; the significance of which must have burned like a neon prayer in the mind of the creature who had laboured over them.

TIM 5/8

I realised it was a bible reference and I flicked quickly and clumsily to the investigative summary, knowing that the interpretation would be there. I found it and my heart sank as I read. Words that had originally been intended as a message of guidance had been twisted beyond recognition and applied to an act so cruel it made a mockery of the concept of God.

Timothy 5:8. But if any provide not for his own, and specially for those of his own house, he hath denied the faith, and is worse than an infidel.

I realised then what I was dealing with, and knew that there would be no reasoning with this man, no appealing to his humanity, no hope that he may be crying out for someone to stop him.

No stopping at all.

I read the rest of the summary. Gemma had apparently been abducted on her way home from work, and had then been taken to a secluded area and held captive for more than twenty-four hours. During that time she had been tortured and disembowelled, her uterus removed after death and the biblical reference carved into her flesh. The body had then been dumped, or, more likely, posed, outside the remnants of St Mary's School, south-west of Glasgow. The body had been found the following morning by a groundskeeper who would probably be lucky to enjoy a peaceful night ever again.

There was meaning in where the killer had chosen to dispose of his victim, just as there was meaning in the message he had carved into her flesh. This man felt a connection to God, perhaps even that he was carrying out God's work. The exact workings of his mind would be unfathomable to all but the darkest of thoughts, and all I was sure of was that he had interpreted Timothy 5:8 to say that anyone refusing to look after their own family had denied God.

And Gemma Sinclair had given up her child for adoption.

The question was; how did the killer know, and why, of all the people who give up their children, did he pick her? The reference he carved into her lifeless body and the fact he removed her womb proved that he did know, and that it had almost certainly been the reason for her murder, yet the police had so far been unable to connect anyone with strong religious feelings to Gemma.

I sat back in my chair and ran my hands through my hair, blowing out a long breath, the first I felt I had taken in over an hour. I then returned all the documents relating to Gemma Sinclair's murder back into the folder and exchanged it for the one on Siobhan Sutherland. I took a deep breath, as though I was diving under water, and opened that file too.

An hour and a half later I knew several things. I had discovered that Siobhan Sutherland was twenty-two when she died, and had long, chestnut brown hair, removing any notion that it was blonde hair the killer was drawn to. It wasn't just hair colour that separated her though. Where Gemma had been short and chubby, Siobhan was a tall five feet nine and undeniably sexy, with the kind of figure that would keep adolescent boys, and a number of grown men, awake at night.

She had been a student at Strathclyde University, having just finished her third year studying Economics, and also worked part-time in a pub near her home called, rather gloomily, The Gibbet. Like Gemma, Siobhan had no current or recent boyfriend. Though in her case that seemed to be more through choice and a desire to have as much casual sex as possible. The background gathered on Siobhan seemed to indicate that she spent most of her free time having as much fun as possible, which in her case consisted mainly of binge-drinking as often as possible and subsequently screwing the nearest guy. I wondered what Innes McKenzie had made of that, and who he took out his rage on.

Siobhan shared a flat in Dennistoun with two friends. I noted the address and their names, as I had done with every other person of note in either file. I wondered what they would tell me about her that was not already in the file. Would they, like Janet's friends deny her promiscuity and drinking, or would they be honest enough to tell the truth about their dead friend?

The file also mentioned her infamous father, though no-one believed that this relationship had played any part in her gruesome demise. The file was strangely sparse on this point and I suspected that Mason had heavily edited this section. When I came to the pathologist's report there was no doubt over these murders being the work of one man. Again, it seemed that she was abducted on her way home from work and subdued with ketamine. Again, the killer had kept her captive for a full day, inflicting ninety-six cuts and slashes. I pondered the significance of Siobhan being cut less than Gemma, but put it to one side for the moment.

The pathologist had this time made an additional comment that the victim had almost certainly passed out several times from shock and been allowed to wake up before being cut again. I shivered at the cruelty I felt I was drowning in. As with Gemma, the fatal wound was the opening of the abdominal cavity, and the inevitable blood loss that occurred when her intestines were torn forth.

This time the killer had removed one of his victim's breasts, presumably to add to his repellent trophy cabinet.

And even though I knew it was coming, that it had to be there, it still stunned me when I saw the picture. More savage cuts spelling out a message from a depraved mind.

JAM 1/15

This time I left the wording of the reference until I finished the rest of the report. I read how the body had been left on the steps of St John's church, north of Glasgow's city centre. The photographs showed another young woman, defiled in the same violent manner, body clothed in blood, face masked in redness. This woman had

The Worst of Evils

been posed differently, positioned so that she was kneeling on dark stone, her head hanging forward, her hands tied behind her back. A short length of rope was visible, leading to a circular iron door handle set into a large wooden door. The weight pulled on the rope and its tautness kept her upright.

Again the real horror was in the way the victim's stomach had been cut open. Again her intestines fell from the vivid red mouth torn into her body, the contents a nest of snakes as they tumbled to the earth.

This was no copycat. Only one man could have been responsible for these glimpses into hell.

Her body had been found the following morning by Father Nicol, the parish priest, the choice of venue making the killer's obsession with religion hauntingly clear.

I turned tentatively to the transcription and was taken aback when I read it.

James 1:15. Then when lust hath conceived, it bringeth forth sin: and sin when it is finished, bringeth forth death.

For want of a better expression; *Jesus Christ Almighty*. I had received a Catholic education, but we had never focused too closely on the bible and now I was glad. I had expected innocuous phrasing, guidance, maybe a stern warning against sin. I had not expected something that, in the mind of a sociopath, could be so easily interpreted as an order to kill. Had Siobhan Sutherland been killed purely because she enjoyed sex? And again, the police had been unable to connect Siobhan to anyone who was strongly religious.

I quickly swapped Siobhan's file for Janet Bell's, determined to get through the rest of this horror show as quickly as possible. This file was slimmer and referred to the victim only as an unidentified white female, since the body hadn't been identified as Janet until the previous day. The bulk of the file was made up of the pathologist's report and I was initially surprised to see a discrepancy, puzzled as to why there was no trace of ketamine in Janet's body. It also appeared that her body had been dumped rather than posed, suggesting that the killer had been disturbed, though no-one had yet come forward.

Otherwise, the killing followed the same pattern. Janet had been cut eighty-five times, her face had been bashed in with a blunt object, as had Siobhan's and Gemma's, and her stomach had been brutally bisected, exposing her intestines to the callous hands of her killer and her eventual death. Both of her hands had been removed, and, along with Gemma's uterus and Siobhan's breast, had yet to be found. That explained why Stewart didn't want to take fingerprint evidence from Janet Bell's home to identify the body.

Then came the bible reference.

REV 2/16

Revelation 2:16. Repent; or else I will come unto thee quickly, and will fight against them with the sword of my mouth.

I read it over again, and failed to see the significance. The previous two had been relatively straightforward, but this last one had me stumped. The killer had, I believed, made reference to Gemma giving up her son for adoption, and to Siobhan's promiscuity. What had Janet's perceived sin been? Had it also been her sexual habits? Or her drug use? Was the reference simply harder to interpret because the killer's already warped mind was beginning to fragment?

The report finished with an explanation of the lack of ketamine in Janet's body, pointing out that there had been a large impact wound on the back of her head, an area which had remained untouched on the other victims, and surmised that the killer had for some reason been unable to administer the ketamine and had been forced to resort to brute strength. A strong blow to the back of the head would achieve his immediate goal as easily as the ketamine would; Janet would still have been unable to resist being bundled into a car or van, and it appeared the drugs effects were only required for the time it took the killer to abduct his victim and take her to wherever he unleashed his nightmarish fantasies.

The last thing in the file was the psychological profile of the killer, prepared by a forensic psychologist named Eric Brandon, and produced after the discovery of Janet's body.

The majority of the profile consisted of the usual cut and paste job, so generic as to be almost worthless. The killer was a white male, aged mid twenties to early forties. Intelligent, but not academic. Sullen and withdrawn. Has difficulty forming relationships, and is almost certainly single. Likely to be employed in a menial job where he has little contact with others and his poor social skills would not be noticed. Has a strong religious background, or a bad experience involving some sort of organised religion – *no shit, Sherlock*. And lastly, the killer would harbour a great deal of resentment towards his parents, his mother in particular, and was projecting his rage against her onto his victims.

He finished the profile by suggesting that the existence of a serial killer in the city should be kept quiet, speculating that exposure in the media may drive him away, sending him to another city where he would start afresh. Now I knew who to blame for keeping this shambles under wraps.

I sighed heavily and returned the sheets of paper to the folder, placed it on top of the other two and returned the pile to the box. I lifted the box from the table and took it into the spare room where I stuck it at the bottom of the cupboard and closed the door on it. It was out of sight, but, just like Pandora's Box, it had been opened and there would be no returning those things which had escaped.

I wandered through my home, feeling unsettled and soiled by those terrible words and pictures. I realised how quiet my home was and I suddenly longed for human contact.

I put on my coat and left the flat, wondering what I'd stumbled into and if I'd ever forget the things I had seen. I had started out searching for an innocent young woman, and now I was hunting a monster made from the darkest shadows.

And if I didn't find him quickly I had no doubt another young girl would pay for my failure.

Twelve

I hadn't entered the offices of Ogilvie, Laing & Drummond in two years, not since I had loosened two of Crawford Laing's teeth and quit the company. As I climbed the steep hill from Woodlands Road towards the blonde sandstone building I wondered how long it would be before I regretted this visit.

I pressed the buzzer beside the imposing black door and waited for a response. After a couple of seconds I heard an unintelligible voice through the intercom. I mumbled something equally incoherent and after a moments pause the door clicked open.

I stepped through the heavy door and was immediately taken back several years, to better times, before Crawford took over. In front of me, on the left wall, a large staircase rose to a half landing before carrying on up to the first floor and the investigators' offices. Both doors on the right hand wall were closed. The furthest one would be piled high with filing cabinets and boxes of disks, holding all of the company records dating back to its foundation in the mid 1970's. The other door was the lair of the company owner, the aforementioned Crawford Laing. As far as I was concerned the door could stay shut. If I had a hammer and some nails I could make sure it didn't open anytime this year.

On my left was an open door leading to the reception. I walked in and saw a familiar face behind the desk.

'What the hell are you doing here?' he cried.

'Nice to see you too, Crawford,' I said.

Laing struggled to his feet, his hand unconsciously rubbing his jaw. He was a big man, red in the face, a few inches taller than me and at least three stones heavier. Those three stones however, all seemed to be in the belly hanging some way over his suit trousers.

He still had the same dishevelled appearance I remembered, his brown hair sticking up in several places, his eyes tinged with pink, bloodshot and watery, as though he was tired or run down. But now there was colour in his cheeks as he glared at me from across the room.

'Get out of here or I'll call the police.'

'And say what? Come on, chill out. I'm just here to see Jessica.'

'She's out on a job. We're all busy, so why don't you sod off.'

I glanced down at the desk, where his copy of Nuts lay open at the picture of a semi-naked woman. 'Yeah, you look real busy. Just as well you don't have any clients if that's the kind of greeting they get.'

'Don't confuse my company with your pathetic little one-man operation,' he retorted smugly, hitching his belt up to try and maintain some semblance of control over his gut. 'We're always busy. I know. I pride myself on doing the initial interview for every client that walks in this door.'

'And some of them hire you?' I put on a look of shock.

'You're an arsehole, Harper. You always were, always will be.'

'Are you this bitter when everyone leaves?'

He glared some more. 'Only the ones who bugger off to set up on their own after we've given them years of training and expertise.'

'Don't kid yourself. There's no *we*, and there never was. John taught me everything, and I'd have stayed out of loyalty to him if you hadn't tried your best to flush this company and his memory both down the pan.'

'Leave my dad out of this. It's got nothing to do with him.' His face had turned deep red and a vein throbbed violently in his temple. I wondered how far he could be from a heart attack.

'It's got everything to do with him. He built this company and left it to you, and you're pissing all over it.'

'The company's fine!' Laing shouted. 'You leaving was the best thing that ever happened to it.'

I was about to retort when we both heard a noise from the back of the building. I stuck my head into the hallway to see if it was Jessica. It wasn't. Two men appeared from behind the stairs, the one in front gesturing wildly with a two-way radio while berating the man behind him.

'I mean, Christ almighty, Tim, how the hell could you not see him getting back in the car?' The first man shook his head in frustration. Like Laing, Phil Biggart was a big man. Unlike Laing, Phil was muscular, tall and broad-shouldered, with the thick neck of a rugby player. He was also a good looking man, strong jawed with thick black wavy hair. He'd had a reputation as a lady killer when I worked with him, and I doubted that had changed.

The man behind him was a physical contrast, short and tubby, with a perfectly round beer belly, sloping shoulders and small hands gripping a heavy looking holdall. The most striking thing about Tim Leach was the complete lack of any hair whatsoever on his head. Even his eyebrows were very pale and fine, giving him a strangely smooth appearance. His emotions were usually carefully hidden behind a blank, nondescript face, but today his expression was angry as he fired back at Phil.

'Piss off, Phil,' he shouted. 'You know fine well that truck blocked my view.'

'Right you are Cueball, it's always someone else's...' Phil stopped as he saw me smiling at them. Some things never changed, the two of them would still be arguing when they were back in nappies and trying to control their drooling.

'Harper!' cried Phil. 'How the hell are you, man? What are you doing back here? Need a reference?' His grin was broad and infectious.

'Hardly. A reference from this place would probably get me as far as Barlinnie.'

I turned to see if Laing would react. He did, but only to push past me and storm across the hallway into his office, slamming the door behind him.

'Ooh, touchy,' I said.

'Ah, you know how it is,' Phil said quietly. 'He's still messed up over his wife leaving him.'

'Oh come on. That was what, three years ago?'

'More like four. He's taken it hard though. Don't think he sees the kids at all anymore.'

'Aye, okay, that's got to be tough. But the man was an arse long before that happened.'

Phil gave me a look that told me he wasn't getting into this again. I relented and changed the subject. 'So, how are things around here?'

Phil rolled his eyes. 'Yeah, well, they're a bit quiet. I figure that's why Slaphead here keeps blowing every surveillance he's on. Just to make sure we've got something to do the next day.'

Tim threw the bag to the ground with a heavy thud. 'Right, listen here you big prick,' he said through teeth gritted, his finger pointed up at Phil's face.

'Okay, okay,' Phil laughed, 'I'm sorry man, just having a wee laugh.' He turned towards me as Tim shook his head and heaved the bag off the floor and trudged up the stairs, muttering under his breath.

'Sorry about that,' Phil said when Tim was out of earshot. 'He's got a very *short* temper.'

We chatted for a few minutes, Phil confiding in me that Ogilvie, Laing and Drummond was struggling. A lot of corporate clients had walked, unimpressed with the service. 'There's just not enough of us,' he said. 'You remember how it used to be better than I do. The place was heaving with investigators, two sharing each office. Now there's only me, Jessica and Chrome Dome. We've all got an office each, the place is that quiet.'

'Crawford still not pitching in?' I asked, knowing the answer.

'You kidding?' Phil looked ready to laugh, then became more circumspect. 'He's required in the office to meet clients. Can't have us all out on the street.'

In return I confided in Phil that business was booming, that I was run off my feet with happy customers flocking to my door to push thick wads of cash through the letterbox. Not the exact truth, but I didn't want my predicament to get back to Laing's ears. I liked Phil, but he and Laing had always got on well and I didn't trust him implicitly.

'Take it you're here to see the delectable Ms Brodie?' he asked after a few more minutes. Phil clearly thought he was the one man on earth who could say a line like that and not sound like a sleazy pervert. He was wrong. No man could.

'Yeah. Any idea when she'll be back in?'

Phil looked at his watch. 'Probably any minute.' He leered at me. 'So, you two, uh, knocking boots yet?'

I just looked at him. 'Knocking boots?'

He shrugged, still waiting for an answer. He'd be waiting a while. Everyone we knew seemed to take an inordinate interest in the fact that we could be close friends and not try to jump each other's bones at every opportunity. The fact that she was a red-hot beauty probably made it harder for other men to understand. I like to think my stunning good looks also made it hard for the ladies to comprehend, but I may have been kidding myself.

I was saved from further scrutiny by a voice from the back door.

'And what if we are, Phil?'

Jessica Brodie came round the back of the stairs, a questioning look on her face. She smiled at me and I felt my stomach shift. I knew she was beautiful but every time I saw her I rethought my previous estimate. Today she was at least a sixteen out of ten.

She was five five, and built like women should be, with the kind of curves that made men believe in God and women curse the devil. She was dressed in tight jeans, black ankle boots and a navy t-shirt under a black leather jacket. Her long, dark brown hair was tied back in a ponytail, sleek and shining in the artificial lighting, and the smile she threw in my direction would have had a priest ripping off his dog collar.

'I don't imagine you're here to see Crawford.'

'Nope,' I replied. 'You got time for a beer.'

Jessica hesitated for a second, then she saw something in my face, some sign that I needed this, and she smiled. 'Sure. You look like you need a beer as much as I do.' She handed the folder she was carrying to Phil. 'Cheers Phil, just stick that in my office will you?'

'Sure thing, m'lady,' Phil said, giving a mock bow before heading up the stairs. 'You two behave yourselves now.'

Jessica headed towards the front door. 'Maybe one of these days we should. Just to give them something new to talk about.' She turned to look at me over her shoulder, her eyebrows doing a little jump, her soft lips pulled back in a smile and she laughed the

throaty, dirty laugh that had always made my heart stutter and my mind wander.
   My knees buckled.
   I managed to stay upright. But only just.

Thirteen

When I had regained the use of my legs Jessica and I headed straight to one of the nearby pubs on Woodlands Road; a drinker's den where people went to get drunk and forget whatever had driven them there in the first place. Today it was just what I needed.

Jessica grabbed a table in the back while I went to the bar for a couple of bottles of lager, two double vodkas and a can of Irn-Bru. I put the drinks on a tray and carried them to where she was sitting. As I approached she raised her eyebrows at the amount of alcohol I carried. She transferred the drinks to the table and I returned the tray to the bar. When I came back I reached out for a beer and upended a third of it into my mouth.

Jessica looked at me for a few long seconds with eyes the deep, rich colour of melted chocolate. She blinked, her lashes so long I was sure I could hear them part the still air between us. 'Tough day?' she asked.

'Not the best.'

'Want to talk about it?'

I took another long swallow. 'Do I have a choice?'

'Yeah. We could just sit here and reinforce the image that we're a nation of binge-drinking alcoholics.'

I nodded thoughtfully, as though this was a suggestion that merited serious consideration. 'Sounds like a plan.' I tilted the bottle back, the remains of the beer trickling down my throat.

She looked pointedly at her own bottle, still two-thirds full. 'Some people might say you've got a problem.'

'Yup. You've got a beer and I don't. That's a problem.' I stood up and went to the bar, came back within a minute with two more beers, placed them on the table. 'Problem solved.'

Jessica looked at me with concern. 'What's wrong?'

And I told her. About a frightened young woman trying to escape a violent and abusive partner, and the evil whose path she had stumbled into. I told her about the other victims and about the demon I had made a deal with to find his daughter's killer.

'So,' Jessica said when I had finished, 'since I last spoke to you, you've been lifted by the cops, abducted at gunpoint, met the most dangerous man in the city, received stolen police files and decided to hunt a serial killer. Any other hobbies you've taken up in your spare time? Like bear-baiting, glass-eating... anything like that?'

I laughed, short and quiet and with no conviction.

'What's your take on it then?' she asked as she poured the Irn-Bru into the two glasses of vodka.

'My take?'

'Well, I know you haven't just read the police files and assumed they've got it bang on. So, how do you see it?'

I took a belt of the vodka and thought about it. Jessica was right; I knew the police weren't infallible, and I'd learned the hard way just how wrong they could be. So what was my take on it?

'These aren't the first,' I began. 'He's killed before.'

'Why aren't any other victims mentioned in the police files.'

'They just haven't connected them. Maybe he's changed his routine. Maybe he was hiding them before, and now he's decided he wants an audience. Whatever, he's killed before. More than once.'

'You're right. He could have stuck to runaways, hookers, illegal immigrants – the ones no-one misses. Hide the bodies well enough, where's the crime?' She took a long swig of beer. 'So what's changed?'

'He wants them to be missed,' I said with conviction.

Jessica gestured with her beer bottle for me to continue.

'He needs a reaction, so he's choosing victims who'll be missed, and he's displaying their bodies for maximum impact.'

'How does he choose them?'

I had thought about this one point for hours, and could come up with nothing. 'I don't know. Somehow, they cross his path, then he stalks them. He doesn't know them; if anyone appeared in all three cases even the thickest plod would have spotted it. But he knows enough about them for him to feel like he does. The fact there are no witnesses whatsoever shows how careful he is and how well he plans the abductions. Plus, the amount of violence in the murders suggests he feels real anger towards his victims. Which, I reckon, means he stalks them for a long time before he abducts them.'

Jessica nodded in agreement and said, 'Then there's the gap between the killings. Gemma was killed a year ago last November, Siobhan last July, and now Janet in February. That's gaps of eight and seven months between murders. Why? Presumably, after he's killed he's satisfied for a while. Then he begins to feel the need again, at which point he begins to look for a victim that fits his fantasy. And once he's found her he spends a while stalking her, figuring out her habits and determining the best time to abduct her. It's the stalking that allows him to maintain the lengthy gaps between killings. It's crucial to him. He enjoys watching them, takes pleasure in the knowledge that they have no idea what he plans to do to them.'

Jessica knew what she was talking about. She rarely mentioned it, but she had graduated from the City of Glasgow University with a degree in psychology, and I was grateful for her input.

'What about the biblical references?' she asked, interrupting my thoughts.

'Well, the psychological profile the cops have says the killer either has a strong religious background or has had a bad experience involving religion.'

'My, that's insightful,' Jessica said, deadpan.

'Exactly what I thought,' I told her. 'I believe the references carved into the bodies explain why the victims were chosen. I think that's the key. Gemma was presumably picked because she gave up her son for adoption, and Siobhan because she was promiscuous.'

'A slut,' Jessica said. 'Stop tiptoeing round it. Nobody says promiscuous except the frothing-at-the-mouth god-botherers who work themselves into a righteous frenzy while conveniently forgetting the prostitute they've just banged.'

Jessica had even more issues with organised religion than I did.

'For Christ's sake, Jessica. The girl's dead.'

'Exactly. She won't be offended. The killer thought of her as a slut, and we need to as well to get into his head. We need to understand how he sees his victims before we can figure out why he picks them and where he comes into contact with them.'

I looked at her, aware of the truth in her words, but still uncomfortable with what she said. I was also struck by her saying *we*.

'Okay, but what I can't figure out yet is why Janet was chosen. That reference is too obscure.'

'There is the possibility that the references mean absolutely nothing.'

'You mean he's doing it to screw with the investigation?'

'He could be trying to focus the cops on some kind of religious nut, when he's just your average, everyday, atheist nut.'

I thought about that before dismissing it. 'If that was the case all the references would be random. Gemma and Siobhan's are too specific, they must be important to him in some way.'

'I agree. Just playing devil's advocate.'

'So, we're back at the reference he left on Janet.'

'It makes sense in his head.'

'Torturing and killing three young women makes sense in his head. He's obviously a nutjob.'

'Yeah, he is. But he still has a train of thought. Okay the rails might be bent out of shape and the train's threatening to derail, but it's still running.'

I almost choked on my vodka. 'Nice analogy,' I said, laughing.

Jessica laughed too, her cheeks turning pink. 'I quite liked it, actually.'

We sat quietly for a moment, the sombre mood lifted slightly. We both sipped on our drinks for a few minutes before she spoke. 'Are you going to try and find him?' she asked.

'I need to.'

'Why?'

'You mean, apart from Innes McKenzie wearing my skin for a suit?'

'Apart from that,' Jessica said.

'I don't know… the police can't find him…McKenzie can't find him…' I shrugged, not even sure myself. 'Maybe I'll find something they've missed…someone needs to…'

There was a pause for a minute before Jessica spoke. When she did her voice was soft, almost inaudible. 'Just be careful, Harper. Not every missing girl is Katie.'

I looked up at her from under my brow, the beer adding a sharper edge to my words than I intended. 'I'm well aware of that Jessica. I'm not trying to bring her back.'

Jessica sat back in her chair and gave me a look that said my tone had not only been sharper than intended, it had been sharper than she would tolerate.

'Sorry,' I said. 'This sort of thing always knocks me off centre a bit.'

Jessica nodded, my apology accepted.

After a moment I spoke again. 'You said *we*.'

'And they said you'd never be a detective.'

'You've got a job. You have your own cases.' I wondered if my protests sounded as weak to Jessica's ears as they did to mine.

'Not that many. O, L & D isn't exactly inundated with calls. And none of my cases are life-threatening. Divorces and repossessed cars can wait.'

'Crawford wouldn't be best pleased if he knew you were helping me out on his time.' What did it say about me that I was more pleased at Laing struggling than I was worried about Jessica's job?

'Sod him,' Jessica said before downing the remains of her vodka and smiling at me. 'So what's the plan, boss?'

I was just about to tell her that I had no plan when a voice spoke beside us.

'So this is where you're hiding.'

I turned round and saw a man standing smiling down at Jessica; a smile that said, *Hi, who the hell's this guy?*

'Aaron, hi, what are you…? God, is that the time?' Jessica checked her watch like a young girl caught out past her bedtime.

'I was waiting outside your office,' Aaron said. 'Phil came out and told me you'd left, said you'd probably be here.' He glanced at me curiously, a little pissed off, a little threatened.

I resisted the urge to tell him to get lost. Jessica stood up awkwardly and gave him a kiss on the cheek, pacifying him a little. He looked back at me more confidently and squared his shoulders. He needn't have bothered; he was tall but thin, with the chest of a twelve-year-old boy, and slightly feminine features. His longish brown hair was tied back in a ponytail, his eyes sharp but wary behind thick-framed glasses.

'Who's this, then?' he asked Jessica, while still looking at me.

'This is Harper, a good friend of mine.

'Harper?' he waved his hand, waiting for the rest.

'Keir Harper,' I told him, and watched as the corners of his mouth turned up.

'That's rather unusual, isn't it?' he smirked.

'Yeah, well, Aaron's a strange name for a girl,' I replied maturely.

His mouth turned down again, the lips tight. He looked pointedly at his watch. 'I'll wait outside, Jessica. Dinner's booked for eight.'

And with that he turned and stalked away. I watched him till he had left and I turned back to Jessica. She didn't look happy.

'You're a real arse at times, you know that? Aaron's a nice guy. You should give him a chance.'

'I am?' I was surprised. 'What about that ponce? He started taking the piss.' Somehow I'd ended up in the playground again. *He started it.*

'Well, you can't blame him for being annoyed. I was supposed to meet him an hour ago, and he finds me in the pub with another bloke. No wonder he was hacked off.'

'Then he should take it out on you, not me. I didn't know. You shouldn't have come for a drink if you had other plans.

'I only came for a drink because you looked like you needed me.' Jessica was getting properly steamed up now.

'Well I'm very fucking sorry. I'll be sure to take my troubles elsewhere next time.'

Jessica grabbed her bag and stood up. 'Don't be such a dick, Harper. Why can't you just be happy for me that I've got a date with a decent guy?'

'Decent guy? He's got a fucking ponytail, Jess!'

Jessica fired me a look that would have burned a hole in Superman's chest and stormed out of the pub, the other drinker's watching her go. The door banged shut behind her and they turned to give me a collective look that said, *You let that walk away? Are you stupid?*

Apparently.

Fourteen

The next morning I woke with a hangover, my brain coated in a thick furry blanket that made coherent thought virtually impossible. After Jessica left I had carried on drinking; drinking to forget her and her new man; drinking to forget three murdered girls; and drinking to forget a man who tortured and killed and collected body parts. I drank till the pub closed and they poured me out into the street and still it wasn't enough. It was only a short walk to my office and I crashed out on the sofa, glad that I had no clients due the following morning. They'd have been drunk on the fumes within five minutes.

I got up and walked down the hill to a small café on Sauchiehall Street where I bought a bottle of Irn-Bru and two rolls and sausage to stave off the worst of the hangover. I felt marginally more human after devouring them and I climbed into my car and headed for the gym, crossing my fingers that I wouldn't draw the eye of any traffic cops.

*

Mack's gym was almost deserted that morning, with only a handful of cars scattered around the car park. I parked the Civic in a shady spot cast by Mack's monstrous Nissan Navara and walked into the gym. It was a small, squat grey building that sat quietly on an industrial estate in Govan, not far from Hair Apparent, and had been some sort of trade warehouse before Mack bought it and turned it into a martial arts studio. It wasn't a luxurious gym. It was a hard place, exposed stone walls and metal girders overhead. Mack liked it that way; it kept the posers away. He taught predominantly

Muay Thai Boxing, and he taught it hard. If you weren't willing to train till you threw up, Mack wasn't willing to train you. He'd trained me for years, and I'd lost count years ago of the number of times I had vomited during his workouts.

I walked in through the small reception and crossed the empty corridor, pushing through the double doors into the large hall where Mack was hammering one of the heavy bags, alone and drenched in sweat. It was just after 9 a.m. and I knew that for him to be this exhausted he must have been here for a few hours already. I watched him as he drove fists and knees, elbows and kicks into the bag, making it buck and jerk on the end of its chain. This was his way; pushing his body to the limit of his endurance, using physical pain to drown the emotional pain he had locked within himself. It may not have been healthy, but it was how he coped; how he kept himself sane. And who was I to judge his coping mechanisms? I feared for him, and yet there had been many times over the years that I'd had reason to be grateful for the power and anger that lurked within him.

Mack stopped abruptly and turned to face me as though he'd known I was there the whole time. He ran a hand through his mop of sandy blonde hair, pushing it back from his forehead where it would soon return. That hair and his smooth face made him appear younger than he was. It was only in the eyes that you saw something older, something more distant, and knew that he had seen and done things you'd rather not know about.

'Well?' he asked, folding his muscular arms. 'Have you found her yet?'

Despite the fact he was a few inches shorter and a stone lighter than me I always felt small beside him. When fully clothed, people sometimes underestimated him, thinking he wasn't particularly big. They soon found out to their cost that it didn't matter. But standing before me now, dressed only in his Thai shorts, his muscles stood out like someone had pushed a series of apples beneath the skin.

'Yeah,' I answered.

'That was quick. You must be getting better.'

'She's dead,' I said, flat and final.

Mack's expression never changed. 'The ex?'

'No. A serial killer. She's the third victim.'
'Tell me.'

I laid it all out for him, just as I had done for Jessica. I was starting to think that writing it down and giving out handouts would be quicker. As I talked he remained motionless, his pale grey eyes focused intently on mine, as mute and inscrutable as a bronze Buddha. I watched his expression throughout. It never altered. Until I mentioned DCI Darroch, when his face darkened, anger and pain roiling beneath the surface like a sea in a storm.

'How did he get promoted?'

I shrugged. We both knew there was little justice in the world, but Darroch's successful career was particularly hard to swallow.

'You going to find him?' Mack asked.

'Doesn't look like I've got a choice, does it?'

'McKenzie, you mean?' Mack scoffed. 'You want to tell him to fuck off, we go tell him to fuck off.'

From anyone else that would have been an idle boast. From Mack it was a worryingly small step from the thought entering his head to him acting on it.

'Not just that,' I said quickly. 'I feel like I owe it to Archie. And to Janet.'

Mack nodded his approval. 'Better that than leaving it to those corrupt bastards.'

'I don't know, Andrea says this DI Stewart's a decent guy.'

'Bollocks,' Mack said. 'As long as Darroch's involved this will get screwed up. He might get someone, but would you bet a scabby fiver on it being the right person?'

'You're right,' I conceded.

'Good. Just don't trust the cops. Remember what Darroch did to us. Don't let him do it to someone else. And don't let this killer walk away.' Usually Mack showed little emotion, but his façade had developed a crack and his pain was threatening to spill out. 'The cops aren't going to find him, so you're going to have to.'

'No pressure then?' I said.

'Call me when you need me,' Mack said, and turned back to the bag. I watched as he began to attack it once more, and I knew whose face he saw beneath his bare knuckles. I turned away and left him to vent his rage.

It was an unspoken understanding. His help was always there when I needed it, but we both knew it was dangerous to bring him into something when we knew so little. Using Mack to find out what had happened would be like trimming a hedge with napalm. I needed to know more before I could risk turning him loose.

*

I drove through the city, heading towards Maryhill in the north-west, glad that it was Sunday and the traffic was light, giving me a chance to think about the man I was looking for. The killer had crossed the paths of each of these young women at some point, and to find out where and when I needed to start at the beginning.

Gemma Sinclair had been the first victim. That we knew off, at least. That's why the first person on my list was Lorna Sinclair; Gemma's mother, and by all accounts the person who knew her best.

Lorna Sinclair lived alone now, in a two bedroom flat in a red sandstone tenement building. Her flat was on the second floor and overlooked a residential street that, save for the small newsagents on the corner, consisted entirely of identical buildings. The street was quiet as I parked between a battered Ford Ka and a reasonably new Matiz. As I sat there I wondered how far away the Kidz Kastle, Gemma's workplace, was, and what route she would have taken between there and here.

I got out of the car and walked past a young girl standing outside the tenement, rocking a pram back and forward as she sucked enthusiastically on a cigarette. The swell of her pregnant belly peeking out from beneath her t-shirt didn't seem to be hampering her enjoyment of the nicotine. She eyeballed me from head to toe as I entered the tenement through the propped open close door. As I climbed the stairs I checked my watch. It was just after ten in the morning and I knew from the file that Lorna Sinclair had worked the twelve till eight shift at a nearby supermarket. I was hoping she was still on the same shift and hadn't yet left for work.

I reached the second floor and knocked on the door marked Sinclair. After a long moment there was a shuffling sound from behind the door and the spy-hole in the door darkened slightly. A disembodied voice said, 'Yes?'

'I'm looking for Lorna Sinclair,' I said in a light tone.

'Why?' the voice asked.

'I need to talk to her about Gemma.'

There was a long silence, then, just as I was about to knock again, the voice spoke again. 'There's nothing to say.'

'Please, Mrs Sinclair,' I said quickly. 'I know you have no reason to trust me, but I really need to speak to you. I'm sorry for your loss, but others are going through the same as you.' I paused, giving her a chance to speak, but there was only silence from the other side of the door. 'I'm a private detective, Mrs Sinclair. I was hired by a man named Archie Bell to find his missing daughter. I did, but she was already dead. Her name was Janet, Mrs Sinclair. Janet Bell. And she was killed by the same man who killed Gemma.'

I stopped then and remained silent, letting her make her decision. A few seconds later I heard a key turn in the lock and the door was opened. I knew from the file that the woman behind the door was forty-one, but she looked fifteen years older. She looked terrified as she invited me in. Not just of me, but of ripping off the scab that had grown over her painful past.

I walked past her along the hallway, stopping when I heard a crackle behind me. I spun round to see Lorna Sinclair standing with her back to the closed door, an electric stun gun in her hand. I stared in shock as she pressed the trigger again and a blue spark jumped between the prongs.

'I'm warning you,' Lorna said. 'If you're lying to me I'll zap you.'

'Where the hell did you get that?'

'Internet. Now why are you really here?'

'Because I need your help. I need to stop him, and to do that I need to know why he chose Gemma. You can help me find him.'

'If the police can't, what makes you think you can?'

'Because I lost someone once. And I know what it does to you.'

The shadow of doubt remained in her eyes. She wanted to believe me, but her past made her cautious. I did the only thing I could that would make her trust me; I told her about Katie. By the time I had finished the stun gun had been placed on a table in the hallway and her eyes had filled with tears for a girl she'd never met, and a girl she'd never see again.

Lorna ushered me into the living room like an old friend, and half an hour later I was ensconced in an armchair with the dregs of a cup of tea in my hand and a plate full of biscuit crumbs on the small table beside me. I may not have liked tea, but that and the Caramel Wafers seemed to be a package deal, and my hangover was now a distant memory. Beside the plate was a half-inch thick pile of photographs, showing Gemma at various stages throughout her life. I had looked carefully at each of these and listened intently to Lorna Sinclair's stories of her daughter, slowly earning her trust.

By the time the photos came to an end I knew far more about Gemma than I would ever need to. I felt as though I had met her, that I knew what her hopes and dreams had been, and I felt all the sadder for this newfound intimacy.

We had established quickly that Lorna had no idea who could have harmed her daughter and that Gemma was not the type of person to attract unwanted attention. 'She was very quiet really, she just liked to spend time at home, or round at her friend Amanda's, and sometimes they went to Pizza Hut. But such a wonderful daughter, I couldn't have been more proud of her.'

'What about Gemma's child?' I asked, choosing my words carefully. I saw Lorna's shoulders sag, and what was left of her spirit seemed to dim a little.

'She never got over giving him up. Never,' she said. 'It was the one thing in her life that made her unhappy.' I nodded sympathetically, though I could not hope to understand how Gemma would have felt. Lorna carried on though, largely oblivious to me now. 'Oh, some might not think she had much of a life. You know, living in a small flat with her mum, working at the kids play area. She never had many friends, just her and Amanda really, and she didn't go out much. Saving all her money to buy a car, so she was. Had her eye on a wee Micra.'

She stopped then, her eyes wet. Maybe it was this simple yet unfulfilled dream that brought it back to Lorna. Or maybe she just never had the chance to talk about her daughter much anymore. Either way I hated myself for intruding into her life and forcing her to face her sorrow again. I stood up and retrieved a tissue from the box on the mantelpiece, then pressed it gently into her hand.

'Who knew about Gemma's son?' I asked.

'Hardly anyone, really. The boy and his family moved away, and I think they'd have kept it as quiet as possible. Other than that, it was just me and Amanda. Gemma wasn't proud of herself. She did the right thing, young as she was, but she always said she would do different if she had that time over again.'

'Why didn't she try to find her son if she felt so strongly?' I asked, knowing there were a hundred answers to this question.

'She wanted to. But she was told it was illegal.'

'That's rubbish,' I said, louder than I intended. Lorna eyes opened wide in surprise and she leaned towards me. I carried on quickly to avoid getting her hopes up. 'Adopted people have the right to try and trace their birth family, but the birth family doesn't have the right to trace them.' Lorna's face fell, the disappointment clear on her face. 'But there are options. The family can put their name on a register, showing that they want to make contact. If the adopted person is on there too then they can receive each other's details.'

'And how likely is it that he'll be on there?' she asked, almost bracing herself for my response.

'Very unlikely. He probably won't be on there until he's over sixteen and it becomes his decision. If he's on it at all.'

'If he even knows he's adopted.'

'It's a chance, Lorna. Nothing more than that. But it's a chance Gemma thought she didn't have.'

She nodded glumly, trying to smile. I took a notepad from my pocket and wrote down a few details I remembered from previous cases, ripped the page off and handing it to her. 'This is the Birthlink register, which covers Scotland. It was set up at the request of birth parents who knew they had no official rights. I think there's a charge for the search though.'

'Don't worry,' Lorna said softly. 'I've got eight years to save up.'

*

I left Lorna Sinclair's flat and followed her directions to the Kidz Kastle. This was the same route that Gemma took and I walked so I would see it as she did. And as her killer did. The streets were reasonably wide and none seemed particularly isolated, nor did they look as though they would be badly lit at night. Each street had a lot of homes on it, and that meant a lot of residents who could open their curtains at the wrong time and become a potential witness.

I stood outside the playhouse and thought about that. Our theory that the killer was stalking the victims for some time was looking more solid. To abduct Gemma from these streets at the back of nine o'clock when she was heading home from work took a lot of nerve. To do it without anyone noticing a thing showed a degree of planning and care that frightened me.

I couldn't help but wonder if the same care was being taken in stalking another victim even now. I shivered and stepped into the Kidz Kastle, straight into a blast of warmth and noise and colour.

It took a couple of hours, but I finally made it out, having gained nothing more than a splitting headache and a shortened temper. I had interviewed everyone I could find, despite constant interruptions from hyperactive children who had clearly been gorging on E numbers, and no-one had been able to provide any useful information, not even Amanda Gray, Gemma's best, and perhaps only, friend. The rest of the girls had known Gemma, but none were particularly close to her.

It was late in the day and I was behind the wheel of my car, contemplating my next move, when my mobile rang. I fished it out of my pocket and answered. It was Jessica.

'Hi,' she said, a little awkwardly.

'Hi,' I replied, more awkwardly.

'Look, Keir,' she said quickly. 'Sorry about last night. I was annoyed at myself, and I shouldn't have taken it out on you.'

'Don't apologise. I was out of order. I'm sorry, I'm sure he's a nice guy.'

Jessica paused for a second and I wondered if she knew how much it had cost me to say that. 'Thanks.' The tone of her voice suggested that she did. We moved on quickly, putting the argument behind us. 'How did you get on?'

'Crap,' I said with feeling. 'I've spoken to Gemma's mum and friends and no-one could tell me anything useful.'

'What about the girl that was supposed to be her best pal?'

'Amanda Gray. She *was* her best pal, she just couldn't tell me anything much, except how nice Gemma was.'

'Depressing, isn't it? How can someone have so little impact on those around them? Makes you wonder if any of us do; if any of us will be remembered for anything other than the way we die.'

There was nothing I could say to that. Jessica sounded as though she felt exactly as I did. 'You doing anything tonight? Fancy a couple more beers?'

'Oh,' she said, hesitantly, 'I can't. I'm seeing Aaron again, sorry.'

'Oh, okay. Have a good time then.' *Don't sleep with him.*

'Listen, Harper. I'll give you a call tomorrow, see what I can do to help you out.

'That'd be good,' I said.

I hung up and dropped the phone on the seat beside me. I thought for a second and decided what my next move should be. I knew it would tell me nothing, but still it seemed the right thing to do.

I drove east, leaving Maryhill behind and eventually arriving in Springburn, a part of the city once dominated by heavy industry, so much so that at one point it produced a quarter of the world's trains. Now though, Springburn consisted mainly of housing schemes, some of which had become notorious in the seventies, and was constantly striving to improve the quality of housing and rid itself of the label from its past.

I pulled the Honda to the kerb outside Springburn Park, twenty yards from a bus shelter whose panes lay on the ground in a pile of shattered plastic. Someone had strung orange ribbon across the gaps so no-one suffered an accident. Moving the broken pieces from the pavement may have been a better idea, but they had obviously been too busy with their ribbon for that.

I turned to my right and looked across the road. Set back behind a high stone wall and a row of trees, was an imposing looking building: St John's Roman Catholic Church.

Perhaps it was because I knew Siobhan Sutherland's body had been left here, but the building seemed devoid of colour and light. The trees on the other side of the wall were bereft of leaves, their great branches dark against the sky as though drawn in charcoal. I left the car and crossed the quiet street, walking through the open wrought iron gates. As I entered the grounds the wind whipped up and blasted across a patch of grass to my right, chilling my face and hands. I jammed my hands deep into my coat pockets and hunched my shoulders as I walked along the concrete path leading away from the street.

I stopped as I reached the entrance to the church and looked up at high, wooden double doors set atop six wide steps. The doors were old, weathered wood, inlaid with large, ornate metal hinges, once painted black and long since rusted. My eyes rested on the large circular iron handles set into each door, one of which had held Siobhan's body upright, awaiting the poor soul who would discover it. There were no signs that anything so horrific had once taken place here, not after seven months. But still, the air seemed dead, despite the gusting wind, and I wondered whether it had always felt this way and that is what attracted the killer to this spot, or if his actions had tainted the very air.

I turned and looked back at the gate and the street beyond, thirty yards from where I now stood. Whatever reason the killer had for choosing this spot, he chose well. Even now, with the trees bare, the grounds were dimly lit, but last July, with the trees covered in leaves the area around the door must have been virtually impossible to see from the street.

To the left of the door was a small notice board, its single sheet of mass times protected by plastic. I stepped forward and read the notice, discovering the priest was still Father Nicol, the man who found Siobhan's ruined body. I thought about contacting him, but decided against it. What could he tell me, other than how badly he now slept?

I walked quickly away from the church and returned to the Honda. Thirty minutes later I reached a much quieter area, between Paisley and Barrhead, and set well back from the road. St Mary's School, or what was left of it, occupied a much larger area than St John's church had. I had followed a winding but well-tarmaced path from the main road, hidden beneath a canopy of overhanging trees, and emerged beside a small church. This was a more modern church than St John's, built from red-brick and understated by comparison.

Ignoring the church for the moment I continued along the now cracked and crumbling path and pulled the car to a stop a hundred yards further on where the shell of a building loomed over me. St Mary's had once been a residential school which housed between thirty and forty boys aged from seven to sixteen. The boys were sometimes orphaned, sometimes abandoned, sometimes taken from their neglectful parents. The Catholic Church ran St Mary's as both an educational centre and a care home, helping these youngsters rebuild their lives.

Or that was the idea. The school was open for over twenty years before rumours of abuse began to leak out. Soon there were calls for a full enquiry, staunchly ignored by the church who were resolute in pretending nothing had happened. They still had their collective heads in the sand when the school was destroyed in a fire over fifteen years ago. There was no doubt about it being arson: the doors to the staff sleeping quarters had been barricaded and the windows had been screwed shut from the outside. It was no surprise to anyone that the fire was discovered to have started there.

Three of the four priests who slept in the building that night died in the fire and no-one was ever convicted of their deaths, though it was clear to all that one of their victims had decided to give them an early taste of the hellfire they promised miscreants.

I looked around me for a moment, wondering at the eerie atmosphere that had once again settled over me. Again, I was forced to wonder, what came first – the killer or the atmosphere of despair? I wasn't superstitious in the least, but somehow I couldn't ignore the fact that scores of young boys had been tormented within the black husk of a building I stood in front of.

Was it merely a coincidence that over a decade later a killer not only disposed off, but displayed his first victim here? Yes, it was a quiet secluded area, but there were plenty of those around. As a man fuelled by evil, was he drawn to a place that had been a source of evil for many years?

I was suddenly angry with myself for coming here. Why had I come to these two sites? What had I expected to find?

I left and tried to forget the heaviness that had settled on my heart. As I drove back towards the small church a man suddenly appeared in the doorway, waving to catch my attention. I slowed as I neared him, lowering the passenger window to allow him to speak.

He leaned down and placed a hand on the inside of the window, looking in at me curiously. 'Hello there. I'm Father Flanagan. Are you lost? Do you need directions?'

I looked at him stonily for a second, at the dog collar appearing as a white stain against his black jacket and shirt.

'No,' I said evenly. 'I found exactly what I was looking for.'

Suspicion crossed his face. 'Really? What business could you have up at the old school?'

Having spent the last several minutes contemplating the casual cruelty of organised religion I was in no mood to be questioned by one of its minions. 'Were you here when the school was still open?'

His voice flicked to friendly and jovial, as though he had decided he had to give a little to get a little back. 'Yes, I worked here for four years before it closed. Of course there were a number of us then. Sadly, now it is only myself to tend the flock.'

'Flock? What flock? The church was for the boys wasn't it?'

'Well, yes.' He became defensive. 'But there are many residents living nearby. I keep the church open for anyone who finds themselves in need.'

'Don't you think the boys in care here were in need?' I felt the anger on my face, the pulse in my temple like a living thing. I wanted suddenly to leave the car and drag Flanagan back to the ruins of the school. To force him to admit what happened here, to acknowledge the harm that was done in the name of trust and faith.

He saw it in my eyes and took a step back. 'Of course,' he spluttered. 'And we gave them what they needed. Faith, prayer, hope for a better future.'

'Hope is the worst of evils, Father,' I said. 'For it prolongs the torment of man.'

Flanagan looked puzzled.

'Nietzsche,' I informed him.

'Ah, well. As a man of faith I prefer to take my guidance from the light of the Lord.'

I put the car in gear and controlled my anger, felt it dim as the sun slipped below the skyline, painting the heavens the colour of dying embers. 'The only guiding light that ever shone from this hellhole was that of the flames, *Father*. Remember that the next time you meet someone in need.'

Fifteen

I pulled up outside a row of tenements in Dennistoun at 10 a.m. on Monday morning, feeling as though I had spent the night in a tumble dryer. My head pounded like a pneumatic drill and my throat seemed to have been stripped down with a metal file. Sleep had once again eluded me for much of the night, kept at bay by images of torture and death flashing through my mind. I was tired and out of sorts, and hardly in a fit state to be hunting a serial killer. However, since there seemed little chance of him accepting a note from my mum excusing me from playing today, I had finally dragged myself from my flat.

The flat was on Roslea Drive in the east end of the city, and was situated on the corner of the second floor. I left the car, leaned heavily on the buzzer and stood there for a few moments, letting the cool breeze waft refreshingly over my face.

That morning I had been awoken at an ungodly hour by Jessica phoning to ask me what I wanted her to do. I hoped she had understood when my first response had been *bugger off*. When I had eventually defrosted I gave her a list of names to interview; friends, acquaintances, ex-lovers, anyone who had been close to Siobhan at some point over the last couple of years.

Another two presses of the buzzer met with no response and I decided to come back later when Siobhan's former flatmates were home. I left and turned the Honda around, hoping I'd have more luck at my next stop.

The Gibbet was hidden away on the corner of a side street off the Gallowgate, a ten minute walk from the flat Siobhan had once lived in. The pub wasn't quite on the corner; that honour belonged to a patch of waste ground that was currently playing host to a bunch of underfed kids kicking a flat football around. They looked around ten years old. It would only be a few years before they ditched the football and spent their time on the other side of The Gibbets walls.

Other than a takeaway place that was so filthy Rab Ha would have turned anorexic before he crossed its threshold, The Gibbet appeared to be the only building in the street that was still open for business, though judging by its fading and peeling paint and its grimy windows business wasn't exactly booming. At this time in the morning I had expected there to be no signs of life, and sure enough, when I tried the front door I found it locked. I heard a creak and looked above me at the metal sign blowing in the breeze above the door.

The sign, as I expected, gave a visual explanation of the pub's name, showing a gallows-type structure from which hung the bodies of three executed criminals. The sign was particularly graphic, with loving care having been taken in depicting the pained expressions on the faces of the three men.

I crossed the waste ground as the kids stared at me with a suspicion that belied their years, the football now forgotten as they assessed my purpose here. I rounded the corner of the pub and came to a lane that ran behind the buildings. The rear door to The Gibbet was wedged open and a grubby white Renault Trafic van was parked outside, facing me with its back doors wide open at the far end.

As I walked towards the van I could hear the sounds of someone moving within. I walked around and looked in the back doors and saw an immensely fat man lifting three crates of bottles from the floor. He turned, stooped inside the van, and saw me. He quickly replaced the crates and thumped down out of the van, making it rise several inches on its suspension in relief.

He straightened up and I saw he was absolutely massive, more than a full head taller than I was and easily over twenty stones in weight. He looked at me through glazed, lifeless eyes. I wasn't sure exactly what drug he was on, but whatever it was he wasn't rationing it.

'I'm looking for Drew Nolan,' I said, jerking my head in the direction of the pub.

He continued staring at me, his fat face covered in a thin sheen of sweat from the drugs. He had no neck to speak of and his round head was home to tufts of unhealthy looking black hair, interspersed with bald patches. Either his obesity or his drug use was making his hair fall out; whichever it was gave the overall impression that his barber had suffered an epileptic fit while he was in the chair.

'Is Mr Nolan around?' I tried again.

The fat guy tried in vain to hitch up his tracksuit trousers, which were fighting a losing battle against his massive gut, and crossed his heavily tattooed arms over his flabby chest.

This was going nowhere fast. 'Sorry,' I said. 'I'd love to stay and chat, but....' I turned away from him and walked through the back door of the pub before he could react. I was in a storeroom, with crates of bottles and cans stacked to the ceiling around the walls and spare kegs of beer piled in the corner. My eyes were adjusting to the dim light when I heard a voice coming through the interior door opposite me.

'For Christ's sake, Big Billy. What's keeping you?'

I stepped through the doorway and spotted the man who had spoken. He was crouched in front of a chilled cabinet at the far end of the bar I was now standing behind. As I entered he looked up and froze.

'Who the fuck are you?' he said.

'My name's Harper, I'm looking for the manager.'

'And?'

'And I want a word with him. Are you Drew Nolan?'

'Do I look like the hired help?' he asked, straightening up.

I took a look, just to check. His hair was an unnatural jet black – long at the back, balding at the top; like a threadbare mullet – and his face was a mess of swollen red drinker's nose, hangdog jowls, and turkey-like neck. His shirt had once been white, the sleeves rolled up and several buttons undone, showing off a carpet of thick grey chest hair, betraying the truth of the dark hairs that clung to his scalp like survivors of a capsized boat. A diseased rag masquerading as a bar towel was slung over his shoulder. I wondered vaguely if every pint came with a penicillin chaser.

'I guess you're the manager then,' I said amicably.

'And owner.'

'I asked the big guy outside if you were around. He didn't say much, so I thought I'd stick my head in and check.'

'Big Billy's not a talker. Are you, Big Billy?'

There was a grunt behind me and I turned in time to see the mountain lumber in behind the bar as well. Standing behind this bar with one of them either side of me was not something I was comfortable with. I lifted the hatch in the bar and stepped round to the other side. The pub was dimly lit, but I was sure a look of disappointment crossed Big Billy's face.

'I want to talk to you about a former employee of yours.'

'Lot of people come through here, Mr Harper. Some are never heard of again.'

I ignored the threat. 'This one was named Siobhan Sutherland. And she was murdered. Ring any bells?'

'Oh, aye. Siobhan,' Nolan said, following me into the main part of the pub. 'Now she was special.' His eyes glinted with a lecherous glee.

I took a few casual steps around the pub, putting a little more distance between myself and Nolan, and regretted it as the sticky carpet nearly pulled one of my trainers off. It was a dingy place, and the low lighting may have been its best asset. The mismatched tables and chairs were chipped and scarred and covered in long, thin cigarette burns. With her looks Siobhan could have had a job in any city centre bar, regardless of whether or not she could pour a pint. So why had she chosen to work here?

'What can you tell me about her?' I asked.

'You going to give me a reason to tell you?' Nolan asked.

'I'm an investigator. Her family have hired me to find her killer.' This was essentially true, though I wasn't sure I could call my arrangement with Innes McKenzie a normal business agreement.

Nolan shrugged his narrow shoulders. 'Nice girl. Turned up, did her job, went home. End of story. Hardly knew her.'

'You said she was special,' I reminded him.

''Course she was,' he laughed, as though I was stupid. 'She was a ride! She had a body you'd have paid to fuck.'

I stared at him, trying to remain calm.

'Blokes would pay to watch somebody else fuck her she was that tasty. Tits you could just *eat*!' Nolan declared with relish. 'I bet a lot of guys left here and went straight home to crack one off, know what I mean?'

I tried to ignore the fact that Nolan was pawing absently at the front of his trousers. 'Did Siobhan ever have any bother with the punters? Anyone that couldn't take no for an answer, that sort of thing?'

Nolan laughed. 'Bother? In here?' He hooked a thumb over his shoulder. 'Have you seen my bouncer?'

'Yeah, Billy, of course.'

There was a loud slap from the bar as a meaty hand was slammed down on top of the hatch. 'That's *Big* Billy,' said a voice, as slow and thick as honey, but with none of the warmth.

'Big Billy it is then.' I looked at the monster who was now glowering at me from across the room. He would be slow, I was sure of that, but he would be hard to put down, and he would pack a punch. It was time to finish up here, before a confrontation became inevitable.

'So,' I said to Nolan again, 'no trouble in here as far as Siobhan was concerned?'

'None at all.'

'Did she mention any trouble outside of work?'

'Not to me. But I just paid her wages and enjoyed looking at her tits.' His smile was a perverted smirk and I wanted to ram it down his throat. I wondered what he would say if he knew the killer had cut off one of those breasts and taken it with him for his own sick purposes. Then I realised; he wouldn't even blink.

'Did she have any friends here?'

'It was just me, her, Big Billy and the old bird that comes in to clean the place. Doubt she ever met old Jean.'

There was something Nolan knew, something he was enjoying keeping to himself, but before I could decide what to ask, he spoke again. 'Maybe you should try investigating somewhere else. You could start by investigating why her family are paying you. Looks to me like you'd be lucky to find your dick with both hands and a torch.'

Big Billy laughed along with his boss, though I wasn't sure he had even understood the jibe.

I ignored Nolan and walked to the bar where I stood face to chest with Big Billy. I eyeballed him, showing him I wasn't intimidated, and eventually he lumbered to the side. I backed through the store room and into the lane, keeping my eyes on them both.

I had taken a few steps down the lane when a voice called after me. 'Hurry back now, won't you?'

I glanced at the patch of waste ground and saw it was empty. The kids with the football, responding to some instinct for trouble, were nowhere to be seen. I doubted they would have volunteered as witnesses even if something did happen here today.

I turned and saw Nolan leaning against the van, dirtying a pint glass with the cloth. 'Why did she work here?' I asked.

'Must be my natural charm and winning smile.' He showed yellowed and rotten teeth as he said it; teeth that I figured would look a lot better scattered on the ground at his feet.

'Yeah, must have been.'

'What else could it be?' He was taunting me now, telling me there was something he was keeping from me. I knew I wouldn't get it out of him. Not today at any rate, and probably not without violence.

'Did she have a choice?' I replied.

'Oh yeah, she had a choice.' His smile was a cruel thing. 'There's always a choice. Just like the one you've got.'

'What's my choice?'

'Stay away, stay healthy. Come back here again… well, maybe you'll find out why people don't walk away from me.'

He laughed to himself as I turned away, the sound following me as I left the lane, reverberating through my brain. As I walked my head buzzed with questions.

Why did Siobhan work there? What hold did Nolan have over her? Did she try to walk away, and is that why she was killed?

Then all the other questions faded, leaving me with just one; the most important one of all.

Was Drew Nolan a serial killer?

Sixteen

My mind whirled and throbbed as I replayed and analysed my meeting with Drew Nolan and his sub-human bouncer. It had been several hours now since I had left that alleyway and driven away from them; time I had spent waiting for Siobhan's flatmates to return home. I was parked forty yards away on the opposite side of the road with a clear view of the entrance to their close.

I finished the last of the sandwiches I had bought on my way back to Roslea Drive and crumpled up the paper bag, throwing it over my shoulder into the backseat. I took a small sip of Irn-Bru and returned the bottle to the shade under the passenger seat. Though this was not technically surveillance, the same rules applied; do not eat or drink more than is absolutely necessary. The last thing you want when you're waiting for someone to either turn up or to do something is to be pissing in a bottle or hunting for a toilet.

Jessica had called some time ago to let me know how little success she'd had. She had spoken to a number of people who had known Siobhan, most of them through university, and yet it turned out that none of them actually knew her at all. Jessica was deflated and dispirited and I could offer her no consolation. She told me she'd help me out again tomorrow and hung up.

Since then I had thought of little other than Drew Nolan and I had convinced myself that he wasn't the man I was searching for. He was obviously a human cockroach, and, even after meeting him once, I sensed he was capable of murder, but his reaction to me had been all wrong; too aggressive, too confrontational. I doubted he was devious enough to kill three young women without leaving a single witness or shred of evidence.

But why then had he reacted as he did? Was he simply a petty thug, playing the hard man and trying to intimidate me? Or was he trying to keep me from something in particular.

I was eventually disturbed from my thoughts by two young women appearing on the street and letting themselves into the building. I let a few minutes pass before crossing the road and pressing the buzzer.

There was a click and a muffled, 'Hello?'

'Hi. I'm looking for Erin Douglas and Louise Ross.'

'Yes,' said the voice confidently. 'Who is this?'

'My name's Harper, I'm a private investigator. I need to ask you a few questions. It'll only take a minute.'

'What's it about?'

'I need to talk to you about Siobhan Sutherland.'

There was a buzz as the door lock was released and I entered the close. I climbed the stairs to the second floor and was greeted by a young woman standing in a doorway, leaning nonchalantly against the frame.

She was average height and very skinny, clad in designer clothes, her face thin with a long narrow nose, and her blonde hair cut in a short bob. Her lips were set on *pout*, a setting I guessed was as good as permanent, and her head was cocked to one side, her eyes half-closed in a study of cool boredom, waiting for someone to impress her.

I smiled and said, 'Erin or Louise?'

'Neither,' smirked the girl, putting the tin lid on my instinctive dislike. 'Fiona. Matheson. I replaced Siobhan.' *Replaced?* Obviously Fiona Matheson wasn't acquainted with tact.

'Are Erin and Louise around?' I asked, ignoring her self-satisfied demeanour.

She eased herself off the doorframe and turned her back on me, leaving the door open as she walked away from me along the hallway, sashaying in a manner that would have had more effect had she possessed an arse. She disappeared through a doorway and I assumed that was an invitation to enter. I stepped inside and closed the door behind me.

A head appeared through the doorway that Fiona had walked through and said, 'Come on in,' before vanishing again.

I walked into the room and looked around. It was large, but slightly bare. Other than the relatively new three-piece suite, the large television in the corner, and the expensive looking stereo underneath the window, there was nothing within the room that revealed any personality whatsoever. Having glimpsed Fiona Matheson's personality I decided that was no bad thing.

She had thrown herself down in an armchair beside the bay window, her body carefully arranged in a pose that said she was a martyr for enduring all of this. She may have been in her early twenties but she had the sulky attitude of a fourteen-year-old in dire need of a good smack.

The other girl was seated at the far end of a sofa pushed against the right hand wall, her legs curled up beside her. She was heavier than Fiona and dressed in jeans and a bright orange vest top that, while not cheap, would probably have received a look of scorn from her friend. She had a piggy nose and the vibrant orange skin of a tanorexic. She tossed her hair and said, 'I'm Erin Douglas. I think it's me you want.'

There was something unnerving in the way she said that last line.

'Is Louise around?'

'No, Erin said, frowning, 'she's not home yet.' There was a small trace of annoyance in her voice, as though she and Louise weren't quite as close as I had expected. Fiona remained slumped in her chair, her mobile in her hand as her thumb darted expertly across the buttons, firing text messages at some lucky minion.

'So,' Erin said, 'what do you want to know about Siobhan?'

'I want to know what she was like in the weeks leading up to her murder. I want to know if she seemed any different, if there was anything bothering her, anything strange that she mentioned.'

There was a little huffing noise from beside the window. 'The police *did* ask us, you know,' Fiona said, reigniting my urge to slap the snooty cow.

I looked from Erin to Fiona, who looked away from me as her phone chimed to signal the receipt of a text message. 'I appreciate that the police will have asked you a lot of questions, but sometimes they can get focused on one thing, and not necessarily the right thing. If you could just spare a couple of minutes, you never know, it might help find the man who killed your friend.'

Fiona snorted, obviously not impressed. Her phone was hanging limply in her hand now, having just replied to the message she had received. 'So you think you can find this guy?' Her mouth was twisted in an expression that conspired only to make her appear very ugly.

Erin turned to look at me, her head on a swivel, her attention rapt, as though she were watching the final at Wimbledon.

'It can't do any harm, can it?' I asked them both, trying to remain reasonable. 'What harm can come from giving up a few minutes of your day?'

There was another loud sigh, interrupted by the beeping arrival of a text message. My anger flared briefly, but was interrupted by the sound of the front door opening.

'That'll be Louise,' Erin said.

I turned to the door, and caught the look of surprise on the face of the young girl who entered the room a moment later. She was small and slight and looked to be closer to her mid-teens than twenty. Her skin was pale, her features small and delicate. She looked warily at me through dull blue eyes that were almost hidden behind the mousy brown hair hanging either side of her face.

I waited a moment for one of her friends to introduce me, but neither did. The stress had obviously overcome Fiona, who had produced a pack of cigarettes from somewhere and lit one before returning to her phone. Erin, meanwhile, was sitting with her mouth open, defining the word *glaikit*.

'My name is Harper, Louise. I'm here to ask a few questions about your friend Siobhan.'

As I said the name a tremor ran through Louise, and I was relieved to see someone show some humanity. I pulled a kitchen chair out from under the table that was pushed into the far corner, keeping a good distance between myself and the nervous newcomer.

I sat there silently until Louise felt she had no choice but to sit.

She pushed herself right back into the armchair and drew her knees up in front of herself, wrapping her arms around them and keeping her small shoulder bag close at hand. Where her flatmates were dressed in either designer, or wannabe-designer, clothing, Louise was smothered in a baggy pair of combat trousers and a big, thick red GAP hoody, from which her head poked like that of a tortoise.

Fiona leaned to one side and tapped her cigarette on the rim of a wine glass sitting on the floor, adding to the collection of ash already floating in a small amount of white wine.

'Look,' I began, 'I'll get out of your way as soon as I can. I just need to know a little about Siobhan. Okay?' I looked around the room, getting two nods from Erin and Louise, and nothing more than the sound of frantic button pushing and an exhalation of smoke from Fiona. I ignored her and pressed on with the other two. 'What was Siobhan like in the weeks before she died?'

Erin tried to catch Fiona's eye, but gave up when she heard another text message arriving. Instead she exchanged eye contact with Louise.

'Fine, I suppose,' she said eventually.

'Was she acting differently at all? Did she seem worried about anything?'

'No,' said Erin, looking at Louise, who agreed by shaking her head quickly.

'Did she mention anything strange? Anything out of the ordinary?'

Again, two head shakes. And again, Fiona was glued to her phone.

'How was she getting on at uni?'

'Fine,' said Erin.

Louise simply shrugged.

Fiona carried on texting.

This was like getting blood out of a stone.

'What about work? Any problems at the bar? What about the guy she works for?'

'No, nothing,' said a quiet voice. It took me a second to realise Louise had spoken. The other two girls seemed surprised as well;

Fiona even looked up briefly. I looked at Louise, surprised, but slightly suspicious too. Her answer had been surprisingly abrupt.

'Look,' Erin said. 'It's pretty obvious none of us know anything that can help you. Maybe you should leave.'

I looked around the room. Louise looked scared, even more so than when she had first entered the room. Fiona still had not torn her attention away from her phone. She had however, produced an iPod and switched it on, placing the small white buds in her ears.

Suddenly anger welled up inside me. I jumped to my feet and strode across the room, wrenching the phone from one hand and the iPod from the other, the headphones popping from her ears and dropping to the wooden floor. I pointed the phone at her like a weapon.

'Do you even give a damn that your friend was murdered?' I yelled at her. 'Can't you get your head out of your arse for five seconds and help me find who did this?'

I turned and threw the phone and the iPod onto the sofa beside Erin, almost daring her to pick them up. I turned back to Fiona and saw a sneer slide across her thin face.

'She wasn't a friend of mine,' she hissed. 'I don't know where you got that ridiculous idea. She was a dirty little tart and it's really no surprise what happened to her.'

I stared at her, momentarily lost for words. I was incredulous at her lack of empathy and stunned to see her lounging back in her armchair as though we were discussing the plot of a rather mundane film.

'Oh, come on!' she continued. 'She'd been ridden more times than the Glasgow Underground! You put out like that, you're going to attract some unsavoury people. She swam in a very shallow gene pool, Mr Harper.' The smirk on her face was something I had not expected to see in this room. I had expected sympathy and sorrow, not righteousness and sanctimonious preaching. I wanted desperately to wipe the smile off of her face, to remove it by whatever means necessary, and I lashed out.

'So she deserved it?' I shouted as I stepped closer, towering over her. 'You think sleeping around means she deserved to have her face smashed to an unrecognisable pulp? That she deserved to have her body cut ninety-six times? You think she somehow deserved to be disembowelled and left to bleed to death?'

I stopped shouting and stood in front of her, my chest heaving as I tried to slow my breathing. To my surprise Fiona appeared untroubled by my outburst, though I could hear Louise crying behind me, and from the corner of my eye I could see Erin's lip trembling.

'She made her choices and they came back to haunt her,' Fiona said calmly. 'If she hadn't been so busy running around playing Little Miss Gorgeous, getting coked out of her mind and trying to be everybody's fuck buddy, maybe she wouldn't have become a target.'

And that's when I realised where this animosity came from and why Fiona Matheson showed no empathy for a young woman's death. 'You were jealous of her.' I said it simply and quietly, and yet it hit the mark, even as she tried to protest. Where the gruesome details of a murder had failed to unsettle her, the simple truth that she was jealous of Siobhan had rattled her.

'You were jealous of her because she was what you wanted to be. She was gorgeous, she had a body *you* would have killed for, and you know that it doesn't matter how much money you spend on clothes and make-up and beauty treatments – you'll never look that good.'

'That's not true,' she said, rising to her feet. Her voice shook as she tried to convince herself.

'Yes it is. You don't care who she screwed, or how many of them there were. If you could find enough guys who were interested in you you'd do the same. You hated her because she reminded you of what you'd never be.'

I turned in disgust and walked towards the door, ignoring Erin and Louise as I went. As I reached the door I turned to face them one last time.

'This could have been any one of you. Remember that when you judge Siobhan.'

Fiona stood in the middle of the room, staring back at me, her face hard and defiant and ugly. Erin sat shamefaced on the sofa, her teeth worrying at her lower lip, unable to look me in the eye. Louise had once more pulled her knees up in front of her and had her arms wrapped tightly around them, her fingers clawing at the skin on her arm.

Before I left I took a last look at Louise and wondered why she had been so on edge since she returned home and saw me. She appeared upset over her friend's death – certainly more so than Fiona or Erin did – but there was more to it than that, though there was no chance of getting her to open up while the other two girls were there. I took one last roll of the dice and took one of my cards from my pocket and threw it on the arm of the sofa.

'If any of you think of anything and realise you're still human, give me a call.'

I looked at Louise as I said it, but she would not meet my eyes. Before I turned and left I saw that her scratching had become faster and that her previously flickering gaze had become a steady stare focused on nothing.

I recognised the signs.

This was a girl with a dark secret.

And the secret wanted out.

Seventeen

I left the flat in Dennistoun and got into the Honda, took a long breath and swallowed the bile that had risen in my throat. Louise Ross was the only one of the three girls who seemed remotely upset, and even that may not have been due to her friend's death. Seeing the indifference of the other girls to the death of someone close to them, I knew where my next stop had to be.

A few minutes later I turned off the motorway into Cardonald and pulled up outside Archie Bell's home. I owed it to him to tell him I was working the case again. Especially as I had turned him down when he asked me to stay on it.

I rang the doorbell and after a minute I heard Archie's voice from the other side, nervously asking who was there.

'It's Harper, Archie. Can I come in?'

The door flew open, then bounced back as the security chain was jerked taut. Archie fumbled with the chain and opened the door wide. 'What's happened?'

'Nothing, Archie. I just wanted to talk to you for a few minutes. Can I come in?'

He stepped aside and let me squeeze past him through the tiny porch. I entered the living room and sat down on the sofa as Archie sank into the armchair and stared at me with a haunted look in his eye.

'I'm investigating Janet's death again,' I said abruptly.

He looked stunned. It was a few moments before he could speak. 'But why? You said the police were the experts. You said there was nothing you could do that they couldn't. Didn't you?'

'That's true, I did.'

'Has something changed?'

'I owe it to Janet, and to you.' I didn't mention Katie Jarvie and the shadow her murder cast over my decision. 'And the police haven't been entirely honest with you, Archie. They were doing what they thought was best, but I don't agree with them. You have a right to know.'

'Know what?'

'Janet wasn't the first victim.' I said, as gently as possible.

'Not the first? But, why didn't the police tell me that?' His voice was choked, his face ashen.

'They don't want to create a panic by telling the public there's been a killer on the loose for over a year.'

'Over a year!' Archie cried. 'People should be warned. We've got a right to know, to be protected....' His voice tailed off. I knew what he was thinking: would Janet still be alive if the police had gone public?

'I agree. But a forensic psychologist told them the killer could disappear if they went public. He'd start again somewhere else. They don't want that, Archie, they want to catch him.'

I had expected Archie to scream and shout; to rage that he wouldn't have cared if the killer had started elsewhere, as long as his daughter still lived. But he did none of that. It didn't even seem to have crossed his mind. Instead he looked at me with eyes that were fearful, and I wondered what other hurt he could possibly experience now.

'You're going to find him then?' he asked me.

'Yes. I am.'

'You said they were the experts.'

'I was wrong,' I said with conviction. I looked into his eyes, urging him to believe in me, to see how important this was to me. 'I'm the expert. I find people. And I have never wanted to find anyone more than the person who killed Janet. I will not stop till this man's in jail.'

Archie swallowed deeply, he seemed intimidated by my desire to find the killer, and the lengths to which I seemed prepared to go. 'But... he could be dangerous. He is dangerous! He killed Janet. And two other girls.'

'He murders young women. Young women who are unprepared,

who don't know what sort of evil might be standing beside them at a bar or sitting next to them on the bus. Yes, he's a killer, but I'm not walking into this blind, like Janet and the others were. I'm going to hit him head on, and he's the one who's going to get a fright.'

'I... I can't afford to pay you anymore.' He looked away, embarrassed.

'This isn't about money. It's about being able to sleep at night.'

*

It was dark by the time I arrived home, the heavy clouds above helping the night to smother daylight. My street was quiet and dim, and, though it may have been a reflection of my mood, the streetlights no longer seemed so bright, and the shadows around their amber pools of light seemed longer and deeper. I walked across the slick cobblestones towards my building, my footfalls the only sound other than the soft rush of the river as it continued its steady march past.

Until a man spoke behind me, his voice rough and gravelled.

'I thought you were the best.'

I turned and looked at Mason, standing ten feet from me, his face hidden in shadow. He was dressed in similar clothes again, dark, plain and unremarkable. Even in those clothes I was annoyed with myself that I had not spotted him. He came closer, his expression neutral, though the gleam in his eye told me how he hoped this would develop.

'I told you it would be a few days,' I replied. 'You think I'm going to find him overnight?'

'Overnight? No. Over two nights? I would expect something. A less charitable man might think you were pushing the limits of Mr McKenzie's generosity.'

'Generosity?' I laughed. 'Oh yeah, he's a real humanitarian.'

Mason gave me a hard look. 'Don't make the mistake of thinking you're hard because you're still alive.' He took another step towards me. Just two feet separated us now. 'That status is under constant review, and I'll be happy to amend it.'

I swallowed, but held his gaze. Despite his threats, I didn't feel in any immediate physical danger. Mason was standing in front of me with both hands in his pockets – hardly a fighting stance. True, he was probably armed, and probably with a gun, and I've no doubt he wanted to shoot me, but I doubted that a man who'd made a career of killing people and getting away with it would be stupid enough to shoot me in the street over my big mouth. But there was a look on his face that told me the bill would be paid somewhere down the line.

Mason walked to the fence that overlooked the river and leant with his back to it, the top railing meeting the small of his back. He brought his right hand from his coat, sending a momentary surge of adrenaline through me. All that appeared however was a pack of Benson & Hedges. He opened the pack with his thumb and nudged a cigarette clear of the rest before pulling it free with his lips. His left hand emerged from his coat with a cheap, disposable plastic lighter whose flame he touched to the end of the cigarette held between his gloved fingers.

'Have you made *any* progress?' he asked, without turning to look in my direction.

'It's going to take time. The cops have been hunting this guy for over a year.'

'The cops aren't very well paid. Really, who can blame them if they take the odd bung? Or if they put their feet up from time to time and let a case slide past them? You, however, have more of an incentive.'

'I don't know if you've seen my rates, but I'm not all that well paid either.'

'I was talking about maintaining the use of your eyes.'

Mason's cheeks drew in as he took a deep pull on the cigarette, and the small ember glowed in the darkness, casting a shadowy light and giving his features the appearance of a skull.

'I thought the blinding thing was if I messed you around?' I said weakly. *What was it with this guy and eyes?*

'You are messing me around,' he said. 'And Mr McKenzie too. So I suggest you find this man before he loses his patience. Don't misunderstand me – I'll happily kill you. But Mr McKenzie would be very disappointed if he was unable to meet the man who murdered his daughter.'

He took a long draw from the cigarette and threw it behind him into the river. 'Remember; you call me as soon as you find him, no-one else. Do that and we'll all walk away happy.'

I doubted happiness would be making any kind of appearance when Mason was in the vicinity.

'And don't get any daft ideas, like calling the cops. I've checked you out, Harper, so I shouldn't have to tell you this, but the cops screw things up. They make things more complicated than they need to be. Guilty people walk free, and innocent people go to jail. Keep it simple. Find him, call me, walk away, forget we met.'

'Doesn't seem like I have a choice does it?'

'You don't,' Mason said as he turned to walk away. 'Remember that.'

*

The ringing of the phone cut through my sleep like a surgical blade. It seemed mere minutes since I had managed to finally clear Mason and McKenzie and Drew Nolan and all the others from my mind, and yet, as I untangled myself from the covers and reached for the phone on the bedside table the clock read 04:27.

No good ever came from a phone call this early.

'Yeah?' I grunted as I answered the call.

There was a second of silence, then a couple of clicks before I heard a voice.

'Hello, Harper.' The voice was husky, deliberately hushed and throaty, impossible to identify.

I knew instinctively why this call was being made and I gulped as a sick feeling spread through my stomach like spilled paint, thick and viscous and tainting everything it came in contact with. 'Who's this?'

'I'm what you are looking for.'

'Really? How do I know you're not just some crank?'

'Because I took the sinners. Because I bled them till they repented. Because I opened their shell and freed their sins. I took their humanity and gave them eternity. I gave them forgiveness and sent them to their judgement with untarnished souls.'

Okay, I thought, *he certainly ticks the lunatic box.*

'That's quite a service you provide. You sound like just who I'm after.'

'I am not *who* you seek. I am *what* you seek.'

'Right,' I said slowly, drawing the word out. I was stalling for time as I stood up and quickly crept to my spare room. In the darkness I opened the top drawer in my desk, took out a dictaphone and held it beside the earpiece. He knew there was no way I could trace the call, but I wanted to keep him talking. I hoped that he might at least give something away if only I asked the right question. 'And what am I seeking exactly?'

'You won't know until you find it, Harper. But when you find it… it will know you too.' The voice chuckled darkly.

'Very cryptic. Don't suppose you fancy coming round to clarify that, do you?'

'What makes you think I'm not already there?'

For a second my blood stopped moving and a sliver of ice slid along my nerve endings. I moved to the window and parted the curtains, looking down into a street being lashed by torrential rain. I scanned the area and saw nothing unusual, though the heavy rain reduced visibility so much I couldn't be sure. I breathed deeply and decided he was bluffing. Why would he be outside my home, other than to attack me? And if that was his intention, why would he call to warn me?

I realised then that he was completely in control of the situation, and had been since he started taking lives. It was time someone knocked him off his stride. I needed to make him less comfortable than he was at the moment. If I made him uncomfortable enough, maybe he'd reveal something – anything – that might take me a step closer to finding him.

'Yeah, sure, sure. I bet you're in the close right now. Or, wait… was that a noise I heard in my cupboard? Or, I know – you're the monster under the bed!'

'I'm the monster under *everyone's* bed, Harper.'

'Yeah, I bet you'd be right at home under someone's bed. You sound like a wee pervert. I can picture you now - all wild eyes and two-inch stiffy, slavers running down your chin while you sniff the skidmarks on some poor sod's pants.'

'Do you think it wise to mock me?' the voice screamed.

That one hit the back of the net.

'Don't call me up and try to come across like some bad-ass super-psycho,' I said, forcing amusement into my voice when all I could feel was revulsion. 'You're not outside my home. You're not Ted Bundy, you're not Jeffrey Dahmer, and you're not Jack the fucking Ripper. You want everyone to think you're some shadowy killer who can flit in and out of people's lives at will, when you're really just some insecure, impotent, unremarkable wee prick who's killed three people and thinks it makes him a big shot.'

'Three, you say?' the voice asked, in control once more.

'Yeah, three. You going to try and convince me you've got more notches on your belt? Want me to tell all the girls you're a big bad psycho killer, see if it'll impress them so much you get laid for the first time?'

'Don't you dare!'

'Come on, you know all that wanking will make you go blind eventually.'

I knew this wasn't the smartest move, but I was determined to provoke him into making a mistake.

'I will gut you like a fish, Harper! I will come to you in the night and I will take you from your home and I will show you pain such as you have never imagined. You will beg me for death before an hour has passed. After a week I will own your soul!'

'Yeah, yeah. You're the man,' I said, as my skin crawled and the back of my neck began to itch.

'You're making a big mistake. You have no idea what I am.'

'Oh, I'm making a big mistake?' I paced the room. 'You're the one who called me up and you're the coward hiding behind a phone call. You want to act the big man, come on round. Stick your head up out of your god-forsaken hole in the ground and I'll knock it off your fucking shoulders.'

When the voice spoke again it had regained its composure.

'Soon enough, Harper. Soon enough. In the meantime, perhaps you could help the police with their enquiries.'

'What?'

'They have found another penitent. Another who has confessed their sins and embraced that which I offered.'

My heart sank. I was too late.

'Go to your car, Harper. There you will find the sinner's offering, the prayer that let him embrace his judgement. He listened to me and he grew wings. As you shall all listen. Take it to the police and let them analyse me, let them *profile* me. Let them try to comprehend what I am.'

A cold chill swept through me as though every window in my flat had suddenly blown open in high winds.

'And what are you?'

'I am Redemption,' the voice said, and the line went dead.

I looked at the phone in my hand as though it were a snake poised to strike. My hand shook as I placed the phone and the dictaphone on the bedside table and returned to the window. I parted the curtains again and looked down at my car. It was parked across the cobbled street, facing me, the orange glow of the streetlights shimmering in the flow of water that ran along and around it. My breath caught as I realised there was something there, something that caught the light and diverted the smooth flow of the water.

I left the flat cautiously, my nerves aflame, my senses alert for danger hiding within the curtain of rain. I crossed quickly to the Honda, my eyes darting across every shadow, my ears attuned to every breath of wind, drenched by the time I covered that short distance. I reached the car and stopped abruptly as I saw what he had left for me.

There was a transparent freezer bag lying on the bonnet, its upper edge trapped beneath the windscreen wipers, rainwater running across it in thick rivulets. The inside surface of the bag was smeared dark and red. I reached out with trembling fingers and lifted the bag, felt something move inside. The bag twisted in my fingers and caught the light as it spun, and I saw an ear beneath the blood.

He listened to me and he grew wings. As you shall all listen.

Eighteen

'Look, Clouseau,' I said, 'I want to see Detective Inspector Stewart, and I want to see him now. I've got urgent information for him.'

The desk sergeant was a big fat guy, with arms like bags of sand and the finest moustache I'd seen outside of The Broons. I'd spent the last five minutes explaining who I was and why I wanted to see Stewart, and he'd spent the last five minutes stonewalling me. We'd reached the stage where he looked as though he could happily pull me over the counter and drag me through the back before breaking out the rubber hoses. What a way to go; beaten to death by Paw Broon. I'd be black affronted.

'And I've told you,' he said, his voice fizzing, 'if it's that important, give it to me and I'll pass it on.'

'Fat chance,' I said with a glance at his gut.

His eyes narrowed and he pointed to a small group of plastic chairs on the other side of the foyer, barely controlling his temper. 'In that case, take a seat.'

I thought about taking the freezer bag from my jacket pocket and slapping it down on the counter, seeing if that would speed things up any. It had been a few hours now since I had found the severed ear on my car bonnet, hours that I had spent asking myself questions that remained unanswered. I had known straight away that I had no option but to go to the police with this. What else could I do, keep it in the freezer? But I had known also that it would not be easy. They had been looking for a killer for a long time now, and I knew from experience what desperation could drive them to.

The sergeant was still staring at me, waiting for me to leave. I turned away from him, muttering under my breath. He picked up the phone beneath the counter as I walked away. I sat on one of the hard chairs and checked the clock on the wall, saw it was ten to eight, and settled back for a wait. My gaze wandered around the reception area, lingering on flyers promoting the latest initiative to tackle knife crime and the usual, generally unheeded, warnings on the dire punishments faced by drink-drivers.

After ten minutes the door to the street opened and a woman walked in, stalking directly towards the reception desk. The slump in Paw Broon's shoulders suggested he knew her. I watched in delight as she began to harangue him, cutting him off every time he tried to open his mouth. All he could manage was a repeated shake of the head and a *what can I do* gesture with his huge arms.

Her tone was hushed, her voice hissing at him like an angry snake, and I was unable to make out why she was so angry. That didn't detract from my enjoyment. All I needed now was some popcorn.

After a time the sergeant stopped listening and began to look around for an escape route. His eyes rolled across my face and I could almost see the light bulb ping above his head. He leaned conspiratorially towards the woman and whispered to her, his swollen belly pushing against the counter as he did so. As he whispered he inclined his head in my direction and the woman looked at me as though I was a lifebelt she wasn't sure would stay afloat.

A smug grin split his features as the woman stepped away from the counter and walked towards me. She was average height, thin and haggard, her face sharp and angular, with a pronounced chin and cheekbones that could cut cheese. Dressed in tight black jeans, and a brown imitation-leather bomber jacket, her hair was peroxide blonde, long and stiff, hairsprayed to within an inch of its life. She looked not far short of fifty, but something told me she was ten years younger and had served an extremely hard paper round

'The clown on the desk says you're a private eye.'

'Yes,' I said, my voice stilted.

'Kim Kennedy,' she said, her hand thrusting out like an attack. I stood up and shook the hand she had offered, noticing that the other hand remained at her side clutching a piece of paper. 'I need your help.'

I tried to think of the right words, a way to tell her that I couldn't, but nothing came. I wasn't used to turning people down when they said they needed me.

'It's my friend,' Kim said. 'I think something might have happened to her, and the police don't care. They think she's just buggered off, but she wouldn't do that.'

I motioned to her to take a seat and sat down beside her, averting my gaze from the still-smirking desk sergeant. 'Why wouldn't they care?' I asked.

'I'm a prostitute,' Kim said, and looked hard into my eyes.

I looked back at her, my face neutral, refusing to give her the reaction she expected.

'So is my friend,' she continued. 'So they won't bother looking for her. They tell me she's a hooker, she's probably run off to a new patch and she'll turn up. Aye, probably in a ditch, raped and strangled.'

I thought about the ear in my pocket and knew that at least this had not belonged to Kim's friend. There was still hope for this girl. 'When did you last see her?' I asked, almost automatically.

'Just over two weeks ago. It was Saturday night so we were working. We always keep an eye out for each other, but she must have gone away with a punter while I was away too.' Her voice caught. 'I waited for her to come back but she didn't.'

'Have you filed a missing person report?'

'Aye, for all the good that'll do.' Kim sneered at me. 'All that means is they'll let me know if some old biddy walking her dog falls over her. They won't actually bother looking for her.'

'I can't help you…' I started to say, but she cut me off as hope died in her eyes.

'Please. I don't want to beg…' There was a desperation in her voice that made me feel like I'd taken her last chance and thrown it in the Clyde.

'I'm sorry, I'm in the middle of a case…'

'Her name's Diane. Diane Hill. She's only nineteen, but we look out for each other, make sure we're both alright, you know?'

'Normally I'd help you,' I said, knowing how weak and pathetic it sounded, 'but I have a case...'

'I've got money,' she said desperately. 'I can pay you.'

'It's not the money.'

Kim brought up her arm then, and held out the folded piece of paper to me. It was a colour copy of a photograph. 'Just look at her. Look at her and tell me you won't help.'

I reluctantly took the picture and looked down at it. I saw a young woman smiling and raising a bottle, toasting the camera. She was blonde, her hair shoulder length and parted in the middle, her eyes blue and sparkling. I looked again and was struck by the similarity to Janet Bell, felt a twinge in my heart as I realised even if we found and stopped this killer there would always be more. More girls who went missing, more who were beaten and tortured and raped and murdered. And young men too. And children, and parents, the elderly and middle-aged; a never-ending flood of death and violence.

I felt a weariness in my soul as I thought of the world around me. I was focused on finding one killer, but I'd forgotten that he was only one of many. He may be worse than some in many ways, but was the end result any different? I closed my eyes and a montage of newspaper headlines and grim-faced newsreaders flashed before my eyes, a subconscious slide-show of cruelty and despair, and I realised there was no end to the capacity humans had for inflicting pain on one another.

I opened my eyes and I looked again at the picture of Diane Hill, young and lively, and knew that the only difference her profession made was that she was more likely to have been a victim of violence than most girls of her age.

I felt low and pathetic and ashamed of myself, knowing that I had let both of these women down; the one who was missing and the one who only wanted someone to stand up for her friend, to say to the world that she mattered.

I looked back at Kim Kennedy and I slowly shook my head. 'I'm sorry. I can't help.'

Anger flashed in her eyes and she stood up quickly, backing away from me.

'You're just as useless as they are. You won't help, just because she's a prossie. You think you're better than us, so you'll turn your back and pretend nothing's happened, just like the rest of them.'

There was nothing I could say. Nothing that wouldn't have sounded self-serving and defensive. I held out Diane Hill's picture.

'Keep it,' she said, her voice dripping fire. 'Maybe you'll take a look at it sometime and see who she really is. She's not just a prostitute, – she's my friend.'

Kim Kennedy stormed away from me and banged through the doors into the street. I looked at the desk sergeant, but he had his head down, realising that discretion was indeed the better part of valour.

I folded up the photo of Diane Hill and put it in the inside pocket of my coat, unsure of what else to do with it. To let these women down had left an acid taste in my mouth; to throw the photo away would have felt like the worst kind of betrayal.

Turning your back on someone in need is never easy, but I thought of the phone call I had received and the fact that a killer had taken an interest in me. I needed to stay focused on him if I was to find him before he visited me again in the night – this time without the phone call.

The interior door squeaked open and DS Taylor stepped through, her fierce glare telling me exactly how much she resented having to come down here to escort me into the building. She crooked her finger at me and I got up and walked towards her.

'Why are you here?'

'To help,' I replied.

'Yeah? Well, we'll give you a call when we need someone's bins raked through.'

'Have you identified him yet?'

She crossed her arms and scowled. 'Who?'

'The body you found.'

'What body?' She tried to cover it, but her eyebrows had jumped when I'd mentioned a body, and her mouth still hung open a little in surprise. I doubted she'd be any good at cards.

'The one that's missing an ear,' I said. 'I know who he is. Now cut the crap and let me speak to Stewart.

Taylor reluctantly stood to one side and let me pass through the door. Her eyes were scrunched up and her forehead had developed a deep groove as she glared at me. She maintained the look as she guided me to a lift and pressed the button for the second floor. She stood opposite and tried to drill holes in me with her eyes. The lift was slow and the atmosphere thicker than a welder's glove.

'If you're fucking with me, Harper,' Taylor warned as the doors pinged open, 'I'll personally have your balls.'

'I wouldn't bother, Sam,' I said, stepping out. 'I think yours are bigger.'

Nineteen

'This better be good, and it better be quick,' Stewart said. 'I'm a bit busy at the moment.'

Taylor had led me to this room and Stewart had spoken before I'd even had time to take a seat, giving Taylor no time to fill him in on the few words we had exchanged.

The room was smallish, with one large desk at the front and a row of smaller desks along the back wall. In the middle of the floor were several rows of chairs, all facing the front where a flipchart stood beside the desk and a pull down projector screen hung on the wall behind them.

Stewart sat on the big desk at the front of the room, his trousers hitched up slightly to avoid his knees ruining their shape. He needn't have bothered; this suit was navy, but just as worn as the black one I'd seen him in previously. His shirt was light blue and neatly pressed, and his dark- and light-blue checked tie was neatly knotted around his throat, but it was still early and I doubted that would last long.

Taylor pulled a chair from the front row and carried it over to where Stewart sat, placing it down beside the desk, its back towards us. She sat down with her legs astride the chair and leant her elbows on the backrest. Very ladylike. Thank God she was wearing a trouser suit.

I dragged my attention back to Stewart who seemed oblivious to his colleague's display of classy femininity. 'I'm not surprised you're busy. Hunting a serial killer must be hard work. Especially now he's killed a fourth victim.'

Stewart stared at me for a second, deciding whether or not to lie. Eventually he said, 'How do you know?'

The Worst of Evils

I ignored the question. I doubted he had expected me to tell him anyway. 'Was Janet Bell killed by the same person?'

'Yes,' confirmed Stewart. 'The only details ever released were the victim's names and that they had been stabbed to death. There are a lot of aspects of the killings that match up almost perfectly. Too many for them to be the work of different people.'

'Why do you think he killed a man this time?'

Even Stewart struggled to maintain his poker face when I said that. 'What do you know?' he asked slowly.

'I know he's killed again. I know this time it's a man. And I know the victim's name is Keith Lamont.'

I reached into my pocket and withdrew a freezer bag of my own, stood up and held it out for Stewart, facing him so he could see the killer's freezer bag within it and read the name KEITH LAMONT that had been printed there in block capitals. His eyes widened as he realised what I held. 'Sam,' he said urgently. 'Get that in an evidence bag and get it to the lab.'

Taylor slipped on a pair of latex gloves and took the bag from me, placing it inside a larger bag she took from her pocket. She left the room as Stewart looked sternly at me. 'You realise you've contaminated evidence?'

'I doubt it. It was hammering down last night. It would've been washed clean. Plus, this guy's far too careful to make such a stupid mistake. You won't get anything from the bag or the ear, except a name for your victim.'

Stewart knew that was true and didn't push it any further. Then I told him about the phone call. When I had finished I took out the dictaphone and pressed play. His eyes remained half closed throughout the recorded conversation, as though he would be better able to see the face behind those deranged words.

'Why you?' he asked when the recording finished.

'I wish I knew.'

'You'll need to make a full statement, get everything you've told me on record. We also need that tape.'

'Fine, but I want a copy,' I told him.

Stewart agreed, knowing it would be the easiest way of getting the tape from me. He looked at his watch. 'Can you wait here for a few minutes? There's someone I want to run this past.'

I shrugged and Stewart left, promising he'd be right back.

Ten minutes later Stewart returned, apologising for the delay. 'Took me a while to find him.'

The *him* he referred to followed Stewart through the door; a thin, bookish looking man, a little shorter than me, but slightly hunched, taking another couple of inches from his height. His lack of a chin was almost disguised by his full beard, which, like the hair around his bald crown, had once been dark brown but was losing the battle with grey as he entered his sixties. The eyes were small behind half-moon glasses that perched precariously close to the end of his prominent nose.

His clothing screamed *academic*, from the grey tweed jacket to the dark green waistcoat and paisley-patterned bow-tie to the mustard-coloured corduroy trousers. The man looked as though he had found a bag of clothing outside a Salvation Army recycling bin and decided it was a winning ensemble.

'Harper, this is Eric Brandon,' Stewart said, introducing the man. 'He's a forensic psychologist that does some consulting work for us. He's been involved in this case since we found Gemma Sinclair.' He sighed. 'Seemed fairly obvious we were dealing with a lunatic, right from the start.'

Brandon stuck out his hand and I shook it, introducing myself. I was interested to meet him, given how unimpressed I had been with his profile. Now that a man had been killed I wondered if he would revise his opinion that the killer was projecting his anger at his mother onto his victims.

'Ah, Harper, eh?' he said, his head tilted slightly back, his voice hazy, nostalgic almost – though for what I wasn't sure. 'That tells me a lot.'

'It tells you my name,' I said, puzzled.

'It says to me,' Brandon said, with the air of a man addressing an auditorium, 'that you feel inadequate. That you feel the need to assert your authority, and using only your surname makes you feel stronger, bolder, less susceptible, perhaps, to the small failings that permeate your life. In essence, you're creating a new persona, one you feel free to mould to the image you desire.'

'Oh, he's got you there, Harper,' Stewart said, smiling broadly.

'Does that sound about right?' Brandon asked. His voice oozed with so much smug certainty that he might just have asked a small boy if he liked Christmas.

'Or maybe it's because my first name's Keir.'

'Oh,' Brandon said, flummoxed.

Stewart saved him. 'I've given Mr Brandon a brief overview of the events of last night,' he began. 'He is extremely interested in this development.'

'Quite, quite,' interrupted Brandon. 'We haven't had any communication from this perpetrator since the investigation began fifteen months ago, and now, not only has he contacted the police and the media with the location of a body, he's contacted you – a nobody!'

I was too surprised to hear that the killer had also contacted the police to be offended by this remark. Not that Brandon would have noticed. He carried on undeterred. 'It's really quite fascinating.'

I looked at him in the same way some people examined their tissues after blowing their noses – with a mixture of curiosity and revulsion. 'Four people are dead,' I said. 'Perhaps you could explain why that is fascinating?'

'Oh, certainly,' he responded with glee, my sarcasm drifting harmlessly over his head. He got to his feet and Stewart rolled his eyes a little as he clasped his hands behind his back and rocked back and forward slightly, from his toes to his heels and back again. His eyelids were slightly lowered, his lips pursed in thought, as though he hadn't rehearsed this speech and didn't deliver it at any and every opportunity.

'What I do, Mr Harper, is quite simple in essence, but incredibly detailed and complex in its execution. In truth it is more art than science. And, like all great art, infinitely fascinating when you are aware of the nuances and you have the mental capacity to fully understand what has been laid in front of you.'

Great art?

There was no stopping him now; he was in a lecture theatre, unaware that his audience were waiting for the bell to ring signalling the end of class.

'In simple terms, I reach into the shadowy parts of the human mind to determine why people are compelled to commit crime, particularly violent crime. But make no mistake; this is far from a simple task.' He shook an admonitory finger at us to ensure we jotted that point down for exam day. 'I have spent decades studying the human mind and all its fascinating quirks. I like to think of myself as an explorer – an adventurer if you will – trekking across the vast wilderness that is the human mind, plotting compass points and mapping routes that will enable others to follow my path.

'I have saved countless souls from their tragic backgrounds and the prisons of their own selves, and sadly, to my deepest regret, have lost others to the depths of their own despair. This wealth of knowledge and experience has combined to give me an unparalleled understanding of what makes someone a criminal, and has proven invaluable to the police in solving many of their most difficult cases.'

Nothing like blowing your own trumpet. I glanced sideways and saw Stewart was struggling to keep his face straight. I doubted this was the first time he'd heard this spiel.

'That's some CV,' I said. 'What do you do for a hobby? Cure cancer and put an end to war?'

Brandon eyed me through his glasses as though I was a specimen he wasn't sure was worthy of being examined.

'Harper, play the tape, please?' Stewart asked quickly, before Brandon could react to my sarcasm.

Brandon seemed almost surprised to find himself standing and took his seat as I pressed play. I watched him as he took in every word, waiting for some sign of distaste from him. None came. Presumably this was the sort of thing he had to stomach on a daily basis. Maybe this was tame in comparison to some of the headcases he dealt with.

When the tape finished we both looked at Brandon, waiting for the adventurer to don his pith helmet and ride into action. We waited for a minute before he finally spoke.

'This man seems to have an unusual interest in you, Harper. Any thoughts on why that is?'

'I've got a nice smile?' I suggested.

Brandon looked annoyed for a second, miffed that I was not taking his questions seriously.

'I'll take that as a no,' he said. 'I believe this man is starting to crave some sort of recognition.'

'Really? What tipped you off? Would it be when he called the police to tell them where to find a body?' Brandon pursed his lips in distaste. I turned to Stewart. 'When did he call?'

Stewart sighed, resigned to telling me the rest of it. 'He called last night, at midnight – very dramatic – and told us there was a body in the cemetery behind St Anthony's church in Shettleston. I've heard the call, he was calm, told us exactly where to find it. That's not something an innocent person who stumbled across a body would have been able to do. Not with the… appearance… of the body.'

'So it was definitely him,' I said.

'Definitely. And he called the papers at the same time. There was quite a crowd of them there this morning.' He turned his attention to Brandon, 'What's changed? You said that publicity would drive him away, make him move on to another hunting ground.'

'I appreciate that, Detective Inspector.' Brandon's voice was frosty, unused to being second-guessed. 'However, we are dealing with a complicated predator. We must use all of the information at our disposal. Unfortunately, one is sometimes required to make recommendations based on less information than is ideal. And sometimes, regrettably, new information is discovered which means we must accept previous statements were erroneous.'

Erroneous? Does that mean you ballsed it up?

'Will going public with this help the investigation?' I asked.

'I believe so,' Brandon said. 'This man – Redemption, as he calls himself – seems upset that he has not been credited with his first three victims. This has led to him selecting and killing his fourth victim much more quickly, to him contacting the police to tell them where the body was, and also to him contacting the media to ensure the police were forced to reveal his existence. Not to mention the ear that he left you. He's saying *listen to me.*'

'Are the police going to confirm there's a serial killer on the loose?' I asked.

'That's not been decided yet.' Stewart was unable to hold my eyes and I knew this was out of his hands.

'Then you *will* have another body on your hands. Sooner rather than later,' Brandon told him.

As Stewart rubbed his hands over his face I felt sorry for him, knowing that he was bound by red-tape and bureaucracy, handcuffed by decisions made by men behind thick doors whose windows looked onto a different world from the rest of us.

'What's your take on the killings?' I asked Brandon.

'Well, the first killing is crucial, as it so often is. The vast majority of murders are committed by someone close to the victim. In the case of Gemma Sinclair, we have examined her acquaintances extremely closely and found no likely candidate.' He held one finger in the air. 'However, the first killing is certainly the most savage. The victim was cut one-hundred-and-twenty-seven times, considerably more than either of the others. I don't yet have the report from the latest murder, but I would expect it to be less than that.

'Given that Gemma's killing was the most vicious, and that no-one close to her can be considered a viable suspect, I found myself asking what it was about her that caused such a vicious assault. Normally I would expect the killings to become more vicious as the killer found it harder to gain satisfaction from his deeds, but not in this case.'

'You think it was because she put her kid up for adoption,' I said.

Brandon's mouth pinched in annoyance as I stole his thunder.

'Oh, come on,' I said. 'It's obvious. If it wasn't someone close to Gemma who killed her, there must have been something about her that pissed this guy off. She was a quiet girl, so the most likely trigger is the adoption. This Redemption guy's got parental issues. Maybe he's adopted.'

'Not necessarily,' Brandon replied, a little huffily. 'He may be, but he may as easily feel abandoned by his parents in some other way. Perhaps they weren't there to prevent him from being abused, or they died when he was young, leaving him alone to face a difficult life. There are a number of possibilities.'

Whatever the cause of the killer's hatred, I knew that the adoption was the reason Gemma had died. It fit the bible reference carved into her chest too neatly to be coincidence. I was interested to hear Brandon pontificate on the religious aspects of the murders, but, as far as Stewart knew, I was unaware of our psychopathic friend's biblical graffiti. It was no great loss however. I doubted Brandon would tell me anything I couldn't have picked up from watching Robbie Coltrane in Cracker.

'What about the other victims?' I asked. 'How would they fit into that?'

Stewart looked unsure whether or not to let Brandon answer. He was uneasy about revealing information to me, but had to weigh that against the fact the killer had called me and, for whatever reason, had brought me into this.

Brandon took the decision out of his hands by immediately trying to reassert himself as the expert. 'It would appear that each killing was a variation on a theme. Each victim fits the general theme, but Gemma Sinclair also fit a more personal category that led to a higher level of violence.'

'What theme?' I asked, as though I didn't already know.

'So, where does that leave us?' Stewart interrupted, ensuring Brandon wouldn't reveal the biblical references.

'Unfortunately, Detective Inspector, it doesn't take you much further forward at the moment. I'll prepare a report for you, taking this recording into account, as well as the calls to the police and the media. Of course, you'll need to give me details on the latest victim too. I'm sure I'll be able to provide a few areas to concentrate on once I have a look at this Keith Lamont fellow.'

Yeah, I'm sure you'll be a lot of help.

'Why has he chosen a male victim this time?' I asked.

Brandon looked smug and self-satisfied as he leant back in his chair and stroked his beard. 'I don't really think I should elaborate on that, Harper. Perhaps some things are better kept among the professionals.'

'Aye, you're doing a bang-up job so far,' I replied. 'Tell me, when he gets to ten does he get a commemorative plaque?'

Stewart rose to his feet and towered over me, his neck colouring as I saw him angry for the first time. 'Listen to me. I've been after this man for a long time, and other than the victims' families, no-one – *no-one* – feels the passing of time more than I do. You think I don't care when he kills again? You think it doesn't tear my heart out when we find another body? Don't you dare sit there and question me when you can walk away from this.'

I stared up at him, feeling a little guilty, but refusing to back down. The truth was, I didn't envy Stewart his task and it hadn't been him I had been trying to needle.

'I'm walking away from nothing,' I told him.

'Really?' Stewart said sarcastically. His voice became sharp. 'You think you're tough? You think you're ready for this? Ready to face real, true, evil as it howls in your face and tears at your soul?'

I looked back and saw there was no exaggeration in his face, no hyperbole in his words. This man that had seen so much in his years as a police officer was deadly serious in his warning. His eyes softened, saddened. 'You don't need this in your life, Harper. No-one does, but at least we get paid for it.'

'He called me, remember. I might not have a choice.'

'It's a game to him,' Brandon butted in.

'He was pretty serious in that call,' Stewart pointed out.

'Oh, a serious game, yes. But a game nonetheless.' Brandon smiled, pleased that he was able to explain something to us mere mortals. 'You see, in this game, he sees the police as his opponent. Not the victims, they are merely playing pieces to him. Pawns, if you like. But you, Harper, are not part of the game. You shouldn't even be on the board. I suspect he is insulted that an amateur believes he can catch him. I'm sure he sees you as unworthy of playing against him.'

'He brought me into this.'

'No, he didn't,' Stewart said. 'You brought yourself into it when you started looking for Janet Bell. He only contacted you after that.'

'In his eyes,' Brandon continued, 'you interrupted the game. You're an unwelcome addition to the game, an unnecessary playing piece. He expects the police to be involved, needs them even. You, he does not need, or want.'

'He seems to want me to be involved now.'

'Well, once you're on the board I rather think the only way you can leave it is to be removed from the game.'

'Meaning?'

'Why, isn't it obvious? I'm afraid he won't be satisfied until he's killed you, my dear fellow.'

Twenty

It was well after lunchtime before they finished taking my statement and let me go. I was under no illusions that they hadn't also been testing me, checking and re-checking my story for any inconsistencies, wondering if I had invented the whole thing and somehow fabricated the call. Darroch didn't appear, but there were others cut from the same cloth, and I could see the question in their eyes: *Is he the killer?*

I stepped back onto Pitt Street and was momentarily blinded by the cold winter sunlight. I turned in the direction of my office, eager to get away from here before they thought of something else to ask me.

Suddenly an obscenely cheery voice cut through my thoughts.

'Hello, sunshine!'

I turned towards the voice, blinking against the light, and saw Charlotte MacGregor standing before me, still wearing the same bottle-green coat and brilliant smile.

'How you doing, Scoop?' I replied. I was somehow unable to be angry with her, despite how our last meeting had ended. 'Hot on the trail of an exclusive?'

'Nah. I was looking for you actually. You must be hungry by now. Fancy grabbing something?'

'I think I'll pass. Who knows what you'll slip in my drink to get me to talk.'

Charlotte put on an expression of deep hurt and held her hand to her chest. I looked at that hand more than I probably should have. 'I'm off duty when I'm eating, Harper. You'll be lucky to get two words out of me. Go on, I'm buying.'

I thought about it and realised I was absolutely starving. 'Sure, why not. But no shop talk.'

'Cool. We'll just eat. No talking. We'll pretend we're married.' She smiled mischievously and strolled off towards Sauchiehall Street.

We found a bar that was reasonably quiet and placed our order in virtual silence, Charlotte concentrating on the menu like it was written in hieroglyphics. True to her word we engaged only in small talk until the food arrived, and from then until her plate was clear all I heard were small mumbles of contentment as she devoured a portion of macaroni and chips that would have fed a lion.

She sat back and wiped her lips with a napkin. I watched in amusement as she patted her stomach and proclaimed that she could now die happy. There was a companionable silence for a few minutes, broken only by the barmaid clearing our plates away, and then I asked the question.

'You weren't here by chance, were you?'

'Of course not. I went to your place this morning, saw you leaving and tagged along.'

'Why?'

Charlotte looked away awkwardly. 'Listen, Harper. I'm sorry about the other day; that was the bitch in me trying to get a story. I didn't mean that about putting you in a bad light, I wouldn't do that. I wanted to apologise.' She smiled again. 'And then I saw you going into Pitt Street and thought it might be worth hanging around.'

I believed her. 'So, no threats this time?'

She blushed. 'No threats.'

'But you want to know why I was in there, right?'

'Hell, yeah!' she said excitedly. 'Was it to do with your dead girl? Or was it this new body? The one where the perp called the cops and the papers.'

'Perp?'

She shrugged. 'Too many US cop shows. So, which was it?'

'Both,' I said. And then I told her.

*

When I had finished Charlotte scribbled down her contact details, threw them at me and left quickly, anxious to get a head start on her rivals. There was a lot I hadn't told her – details of the killings, the biblical references – but it was enough that this story was coming out whether the police wanted it to or not. I wondered if that had been Stewart's aim as soon as I told him I knew; his only way of doing what he knew to be necessary while his hands were tied.

I left the pub and walked up the hill to my office. I had switched off my phone when I entered police headquarters and I realised I had not yet turned it back on. I switched it on and after a few seconds it beeped to tell me I had several missed calls. One from a number that looked vaguely familiar, but had left no message, and three from Jessica, whose messages became steadily more irate as time passed. I called her back first.

'Where the hell have you been?' she demanded. 'I've been trying to get in touch. I thought we were working again today.'

'I've been at Pitt Street.'

'Really?' That stopped her. She knew how I felt about the police. 'What's wrong?'

'I got a call last night. And a present.' I told her everything then, from the killer's call to Keith Lamont's ear being left on my car, to my meeting with DI Stewart and his pompous profiler. When I mentioned Brandon Jessica interrupted.

'I see he's not changed then.'

'You know him?'

'Yeah, he was one of the lecturers when I was at uni.'

'Brandon lectured at the City of Glasgow Uni?' I was surprised. 'Seems beneath the great man, does it not?'

'He taught a few lectures on criminal psychology, that sort of thing. He was a pretentious arse.'

'He still is.'

We discussed the case for a few more minutes and I asked her to find out what she could about Keith Lamont while I took care of another matter. Hopefully by the time I'd finished that she'd have something for us to work with.

*

I parked a little down the street from the flat and took my phone from my pocket. I brought up the number that had called me that morning and dialled it. It rang six times before it was picked up with a tentative, 'Hello?'

'Hi Louise,' I said.

'Who... who's this?' Louise Ross asked.

'This is Keir Harper, returning your call.'

'I didn't... I never...'

'Don't worry, Louise. I'll be there in ten minutes, we can talk about why you called.'

I hung up and waited.

Two minutes and twenty-three seconds passed before Louise Ross burst through the door to her close like she was coming out of the traps at Shawfield. I got out of the car and followed as she headed down a side street. Rather than approaching from behind and scaring her, I cut down a parallel street and jogged to the end, turning onto the main street well before she did. When she did turn onto the street she walked in my direction, arms folded across her chest, head tilted towards the pavement.

She started when she saw me and caught her breath, her eyes flitting across mine in fear.

'You forgot to leave a message, Louise.'

'What? When?'

'You got time for a coffee?'

'I should really get going,' Louise said with a cursory look at her watch.

'Please, Louise. I need your help. Siobhan needs your help.'

I could see conflicting emotions war across her face and I felt low for playing the emotional blackmail card. The next few minutes would determine whether it was justified.

After a moment's indecision Louise consented and we walked to a small cafe nearby. The place was empty when we entered, just one young girl behind the counter, leaning on a Daily Record with a bored expression on her face and headphones in her ears.

We waited until she sulkily removed her headphones, then

placed our orders – some bizarre coffee concoction for Louise and a can of Irn-Bru for me – and I paid before leading Louise to a table in the furthest corner of the small room. The waitress had already replaced her headphones and I hoped that no more customers would come in to either overhear us or make Louise clam up.

'Why did you phone?' I asked as soon as we were seated.

'I… I just dialled the wrong number.'

'You picked up my card, dialled the number on it, and thought you were calling someone else?'

Her eyes dropped to the table. She seemed even smaller, even more fragile than she had when we had first met. I still found it hard to believe she was twenty years old. The way she looked now fifteen would have been a stretch.

'There's something going on here, Louise. Something you know about and Fiona and Erin don't, isn't there? Maybe if they knew what you know they'd be a bit nicer about your friend.'

'You're wrong,' Louise fired back, suddenly angry. 'You think she's perfect and it's Fiona and Erin that are just being bitches, but you're wrong. Siobhan was a bitch as well. She didn't stick up for her friends either.'

'What did she do?' I asked gently, hiding my surprise.

Tears suddenly erupted and Louise brought her hands to her face, the sleeves of her thick jumper covering her fingers and muffling her words. 'She left me behind.'

Just then the waitress appeared with our drinks. She put the mutant coffee down gently in front of Louise and slammed my can in front of me. She glared at me, having decided that I was the source of Louise's torment. I didn't bother explaining. 'What happened?' I asked Louise when the waitress had returned to her perch and I could hear tinny music once more.

'I thought she'd stay with me. She said she would. It's all her fault. She said it was easy money.'

Easy money. Two words guaranteed to lead to trouble.

'Louise. You need to let go of this. It's causing you too much pain. What was easy money?'

Louise took a deep breath and plucked a tissue from her pocket, began wiping her streaming nose. 'The films.'

I tried to hide my surprise. 'What kind of films?' There was only one type of film that could cause this kind of trouble, but I needed to hear it from Louise.

'Dirty ones,' she sniffed, sounding for all the world like an ashamed ten-year-old.

'How did Siobhan get into that?' The porn industry may have been growing rapidly in this country, but it was still hidden away behind closed doors.

'The guy she worked for. He gave her a loan a while back. She was desperate. She had no money to go out, and Siobhan hated staying in.'

I knew why. The ghosts of her past couldn't touch her when she was drunk or high or rolling around with the nearest guy. And her desperation had forced her to turn to Drew Nolan.

'How much did he give her?'

'I'm not sure. A few thousand, I think.'

A few thousand from a guy like Nolan could take forever to pay off once he'd applied his exorbitant interest rates.

'She couldn't pay it back though.' Louise hiked her shoulders. 'I'm not sure she ever intended to. She just kept asking for more, said she'd pay it back when she could.'

'And Nolan made a suggestion, right?'

'Yes,' Louise said, unable to look me in the eye. 'He said he knew a guy who made some movies, said she'd get paid for being in them.'

'Did he tell her what kind of films they were?'

'Yes. Siobhan told me later she didn't even think twice. She figured she was doing it anyway, and she didn't care who with, so she might as well get paid for it.'

I felt a deep sadness take root inside me at the thought of a young woman who was so unhappy in her own skin that she would treat herself with such little respect.

'When did this start?'

Louise thought about it. 'Maybe a year and a half ago.'

'How did she get you involved?'

Fresh tears spilled forth, rolling unabated down her face. Louise shook her head, unable to form the words.

'It's the only way to make it better, Louise,' I said softly. 'You need to face it.'

I expected her to say that she couldn't, that it was too painful, but she surprised me. She squared her shoulders and swallowed. 'Nine months ago,' she began. I remained motionless, scared of breaking her resolve. 'Siobhan and I were in the flat one night, just the two of us. We had a couple of bottles of wine between us. Siobhan had most; I've never been a big drinker. Anyway, after a few drinks Siobhan told me how she'd been making extra money.' Louise took a long gulp of her coffee. 'She seemed to really enjoy it. She made it sound glamorous, like she was a star. She asked if I fancied doing it, and I said no. I couldn't imagine doing it in front of a camera. But then she told me Mr Nolan had asked for me specifically.'

'Had he?' I had a horrible suspicion I knew why.

'He said he'd seen us all with Siobhan once and thought I was the prettiest. He said I'd be gorgeous on camera. He really wanted Siobhan to get me to do it. And I believed it. I'm so stupid.'

I looked sadly at Louise and at that moment I felt a surge of anger at Siobhan Sutherland. Louise had looked at her friend and had not seen the sorrow and loneliness she carried; she had seen popularity and fun, a young woman possessed with self-confidence and the ability to take what she wanted from life. Louise had seen everything she was not, and she wanted it. And Siobhan knew that. Siobhan had manipulated her friend into taking part in these home movies. She knew that Louise was unused to flattery and desperate for a compliment. To tell her she had been asked for specifically, and that she was the prettiest one of the flatmates was exactly what Louise needed to hear.

And I was sure that Drew Nolan had taken a nice chunk off Siobhan's loan repayments for recruiting a friend. Especially Louise Ross. Although I would never tell Louise, I believed that Drew Nolan had specifically requested her. Not because he thought she was pretty, but because her small stature and young features made her appear under sixteen. Nolan knew there was a market for underage sex videos and I would bet the house he knew exactly where that market was.

'You're not stupid, Louise,' I told her. 'You trusted people, and they let you down. That's not your fault.'

Her lip trembled and I watched as a shockwave rippled through her. Despite what she had already told me she seemed to only now be approaching the real root of her pain.

'What happened, Louise?'

It took a few minutes, but eventually she composed herself and began to speak. Her words were sometimes halting, sometimes rushed, as though she was desperate to hurry through the story but her mind kept erecting barricades.

I sat there in silence as her heart bled and mine wept alongside, the pain in her voice destroying what emotional distance I had managed to keep between myself and her tale.

She told me how she went to The Gibbet with Siobhan one night, how Nolan drove them to a house in a suburb of the city. They were separated on arrival, and Siobhan disappeared. Louise was led to a basement where spot lights lined the walls and a variety of strange structures lined the floor, none of them the bed or sofa that she had expected. She became immediately uneasy, having expected her friend to stay with her.

Louise turned to the grotesquely fat man who had introduced himself as The Director, and asked to leave. He gave her a smile that almost made her lose bladder control and told her that was impossible. He then ordered four men to repeatedly rape her, while he gave directions to the cameraman. She was unsure how long it lasted, only that it felt like hours.

Eventually The Director announced that the shoot was a wrap – he actually used that term – and allowed Louise to get dressed. He then gave her the money that she had been promised and told the other men to take her somewhere and drop her off. Siobhan had already left. Louise wasn't sure where she was pushed from the car. All she knew was that a taxi had eventually pulled over and offered her a lift. She must've given her address because she ended up at home, but it was the following day before she began to process what had happened to her. Then she shut down for a week, locking herself in her room and speaking to no-one.

'Siobhan never mentioned it. But she never looked at me

again. She knew what had happened. What she had let happen.'

I opened my mouth but no words came. What could I say to this young woman who had not only been abused by strangers but abandoned by someone she had called a friend. My instinct was to reach out to her, but I stopped myself: the last thing Louise would want was a man she barely knew touching her.

'You know the strange thing?' Louise said. 'I can't remember the faces of the men who raped me. But every time I close my eyes I can see the face of The Director. He didn't lay a finger on me, but I blame him. He was the one who ordered them to… to… do what they did. He was the one who refused to let me leave.' She shook her head, as though trying to dislodge something that refused to be cast aside. 'Every time I close my eyes.'

'Describe him for me,' I said.

'He was fat, really fat. And he had this long, thick, curly black hair, and a horrible goatee. He had a big nose too, and scars, like he'd been in loads of fights.'

'That's a good description, Louise. Have you been to the police?'

She shook her head, and her eyes welled up again. 'No,' she croaked. 'How can I? They paid me! I still don't know why I took that money. And the worst thing is the look he gave me when he handed me the money. Like I'd enjoyed it and was just playing a part. He made me want to die.'

My eyes stung as I looked at her, and even though I knew it was necessary, I felt guilty for ripping off the scab that she had grown over this trauma. I looked at her and saw a mirror that I had shattered with a hammer. And in her broken pieces I could see myself reflected, and I looked away before I too broke into shards.

'It's not your fault, Louise,' I said, my jaw tight. 'You took the money because you were in shock. Not because you enjoyed it. Your mind had shut down to protect itself. You're not responsible for what you did under those circumstances. He knew giving you the money would make it difficult for you. That's why he did it, to manipulate you into keeping quiet.'

'It's too late now.'

'It's not too late. You can still report it, if that's what you want.

But whatever you decide to do, you need to speak to someone about this. You need to talk to someone who knows how to help you.'

'It won't do any good.'

'It can, Louise. Don't let this define you. You have to fight it, and the way to do that is to speak to someone and move on as best you can.'

I tore a page from my pad and wrote a name and phone number down on it, then passed it to her. It was the number of a woman I had met a couple of years ago when a young girl had gone missing from her home after suffering a brutal rape. This woman had helped the girl piece her life back together.

'Call her, Louise. She can help. Don't let him win.'

She nodded, still more tears leaking from her eyes, and I stood up. I was reluctant to leave her in this state, but I could feel a redness descending on my mind and a current of violence flowing through my skin like electricity. I took one last look at her devastation and left, ignoring the glare of the waitress as I went.

Outside the café I took my phone from my pocket and dialled as I walked back to my car.

'Yeah?' Mack answered.

'I'm going to pay Drew Nolan a visit. You interested?'

'A friendly visit?'

I thought of the agony etched on Louise's face. 'Not exactly.'

Twenty-One

We pulled up a few doors down from The Gibbet, stopping outside the takeaway place that had turned my stomach the last time I was in this street. Night had fallen but even under cover of darkness the shop still looked as though each dish came with a side order of E Coli. It was no surprise to see it was empty, but the absence of any staff made it look as though the bacteria in their dishes may well have been the only life around.

The street was deserted, the shadows stretching long between the lone streetlamp at the far end of the block and what faint light had managed to penetrate the grime of the takeaway shop's window. At the darker end of the street a single jaundiced bulb hung above the door to Nolan's pub.

As we stepped out of the car Mack looked over the roof at me.

'You sure?'

'Definitely,' I told him. 'He knew Siobhan better than he let on, and I want to know what else he knows.'

'And then there's Louise Ross,' Mack said. I had told him the full story after I picked him up. It was like pouring petrol on a bonfire.

'Yeah. I'd really like him to regret that.'

'He will,' Mack said. 'And his fat pal.'

'He's a big lad.'

'Yeah, well. The bigger they are...'

'The harder they fall?'

'No. The harder I hit them.' He walked through the door of the pub, his smile as loose and relaxed as the jeans and t-shirt he wore beneath his long black coat.

There were five men in the bar, four of them huddled over pints and whiskies. They fell into silence and turned to look at us, a silence that thickened as something in our faces betrayed our purpose. We'd need to account for them too; this was the kind of place where most of the punters thought they were hard men.

The fifth man was Big Billy. He sat on a stool with his back to the bar, his gut spilling over the waistband of his jeans as he looked at us through clouded eyes. I could almost hear the gears turning as he tried to place me.

Before he could make the connection Drew Nolan appeared from the storeroom, carrying a fresh bottle of whisky. He glanced over in our direction and his face twisted in fury. 'What the fuck are you doing back here? I told you what would happen if you showed your face again.'

'I'm going to ask you a few more questions,' I said.

'Big Billy,' Nolan said. 'Get these arseholes out of here. And don't be gentle about it.'

'Is that Big Billy?' Mack asked as the giant lumbered down from his stool. 'He's not big. He's just a fat fuck.'

It took a few seconds for the insult to register, then Big Billy charged at Mack, surprisingly quickly for the bulk he carried. Mack stepped to one side, picked up a stool from beside an empty table and smashed it into the outside of Big Billy's knee. He howled and staggered sideways. Mack followed up with a front kick, driving the sole of his foot into Big Billy's chest and knocking him completely off balance. He bounced off the fruit machine and landed in a heap on the floor. Mack moved in and swung the stool above his head, bringing it thudding down on Big Billy's head, his back, his shoulders, four times, five, six, until he was motionless and blood oozed thickly along the stained carpet.

Drew Nolan watched in shock as Mack incapacitated his bouncer in seconds. It may not have been Muay Thai, or any other martial art, but it was brutally effective.

'You bastards,' Nolan roared. He put down the bottle of whisky and leant forward to retrieve something from under the bar.

As he leant forward I moved quickly to the other side of the bar and grabbed his head in both hands, bringing it down sharply on top of the bar. His nose broke with a wet splat. On the second impact he screamed in pain and dropped whatever he had picked up. Before he hit the bar for a third time I moved his head a little to my left, aiming for a glass ashtray full of stubbed-out cigarettes. His face connected with a crunch of teeth and a crack of glass as the ashtray split in half.

I adjusted my grip so one hand was under his chin and the other cradled the base of his skull. Then I heaved with all my strength, dragging him across the bar and hurling him to the floor.

The four drinkers were on their feet now. I reached across the bar for the bottle of whisky that Nolan had put down. I lifted it by the neck and smashed the base on the edge of the bar, took two steps towards the man nearest me and thrust the jagged edge in his direction.

'We're enforcing the smoking ban. Now sit the fuck down.'

He quickly retreated and sat back down. The other three looked from me with my broken bottle to Mack with his blood-stained stool and swiftly took their seats.

So much for the hard men.

I took a quick look over the bar to see what Nolan had been reaching for. Lying there was a mini baseball bat. Easier to swing in the confined space of the bar but still capable of causing damage given the chance.

'He's gubbed,' Mack said, gesturing towards Big Billy. Then he looked to where Nolan lay motionless on the floor. 'Did you kill him?'

'He's at it. Probably thinks we'll go away if he's unconscious.'

We put down our weapons and moved towards Nolan. He still didn't move, not until Mack pulled his right arm up towards the ceiling and rotated it, threatening to rip it off at the shoulder. Then he screamed like someone had scraped a razor blade across his eyeballs.

'Get up,' I told him.

Mack let go of Nolan's arm and the barman struggled to his feet. He stood unsteadily before me and I felt a grim satisfaction as I saw the damage I had done. His nose was smashed, his jaw hung loose and swollen and one eye would be fully closed in minutes. There were gaps inside his mouth where yellowed teeth had been uprooted and blood and ash painted red and black streaks across his face.

'I'm going to ask you about Siobhan Sutherland again,' I said. 'And this time you're going to tell the truth.'

'I've already told you. She was just some tart that pulled pints, that's it. I hardly knew her.'

'Except for her sideline in porno movies, of course.'

Nolan looked off to the side while he chose a lie. 'News to me, pal. Not my business if the slut wants to make some extra money getting shafted on camera.'

I beat Mack to the punch for once, jabbing Nolan's ruined nose. He screeched and would have slid to the floor had Mack not held him upright. He propped Nolan against the bar and wandered off to make sure none of his customers were getting any braver.

I dug my fingers into Nolan's throat and squeezed. 'You loaned her money and you got her into the porn films to pay you back. How much did she borrow?'

'A grand,' he croaked.

I let go. 'That's it? A grand?'

'Yeah. But she came back and wanted more. All I did was suggest a way to make some more money. She was a big girl, she made her own decisions.'

As much as I hated Nolan at this moment, he was right. Siobhan had made her own choices. She had chosen a lifestyle she couldn't afford and she had borrowed money and appeared in pornographic films to maintain that lifestyle. No-one had forced her into it, unlike Louise Ross.

'What do you know about her murder?'

'Bugger all. I wouldn't have killed her, not with those tits.' I clenched my fist again and Nolan flinched. 'For Christ's sake, I don't know! Probably some guy she turned down. Couldn't handle not having her and done her in.'

'Who?'

'How the hell would I know? Everybody wanted a piece of her.'

'Why did you tell me you didn't know her?'

Nolan laughed, a wet gurgle through the blood in his mouth

and nose. 'Because you're a nobody. Fuck do you think you are, coming in here and demanding answers? Lucky we didn't kill you first time round.'

I looked at his ruined face and I laughed. 'Luck had nothing to do with it. You're not a hard man, Nolan. You're barely a parasite.'

He looked at me through a mask of slowly drying blood, his eyes burning with contempt and hatred.

Mack appeared by my side. 'What's he saying?'

'Nothing much.'

'Really?'

'I don't know anything!'

'We'll see,' Mack said. He grabbed Nolan, spun him round and kicked the back of his knees, dropping his head to the height of the bar. Nolan's mouth fell open in fright and Mack forced it onto the edge of the bar, his teeth wedged apart by the thick wooden counter.

Mack held Nolan's head firmly in place and whispered in his ear, his voice as hard and final as a judge's gavel. 'Here's how it works, Drew, my boy. You tell me what you know about this girl's murder, or my mate holds you while I kick you in the back of the head. And I'll tell you now, I kick like a fucking horse.'

'I swear to God, I don't know anything!' Nolan's words were muffled by the bar between his teeth, but the desperation in his voice was unmistakeable. 'Please! Don't! I'd tell you!'

'You know, Drew, I almost believe you,' Mack said. 'Almost.'

I rounded the bar and grabbed hold of Nolan's head, pulling it towards me and into the wood. From here I could see the four drinkers clearly. They were motionless, their faces white with shock and fear.

'Glad you're wearing dark clothes, mate,' Mack said to me. 'This could be messy.'

'Just mind my fingers,' I replied.

As Mack removed his coat and folded it over the back of a chair, Nolan whimpered and I saw tears leak from his tightly shut eyes. I almost felt sorry for him. Then I saw Louise Ross's face as she told me of her nightmare.

I pulled him down harder.

'Please! God! I don't know anything!'

Mack took a run up, lifted his right knee, slammed the heel of his boot into the bar an inch from Nolan's head.

I let him go and he slumped to the floor, gasping for air, his tears cutting pale tracks through the blood on his face. A sudden acrid smell told me he'd lost control of his bladder. He lay whimpering on the floor and I wondered if I'd feel guilt and shame at some point. For the moment, I felt nothing but gladness that he had suffered.

'I spoke to Louise Ross.' I prodded him with my foot. He looked blankly at me, waiting for an explanation. 'She was Siobhan's flatmate. The one you wanted because she looked underage.'

A look of recognition crossed Nolan's face, followed by a glimpse of fear. 'I had nothing to do with that. That was a sin, what happened to that wee lassie.'

'You're damn right it was. And you knew all about it. You gave her to the men who raped her. That makes you every bit as guilty. Now, tell me and we'll leave. Who is The Director?'

'No idea.'

'You take the girls to him.'

'I just hand them over,' Nolan said. 'I don't know who makes the movies. Don't give a toss as long as I get paid.'

'That's all you care about?'

'Long as I get paid, it doesn't worry me.' Nolan was regaining some of his cockiness now that he'd become convinced we'd reached a line we wouldn't cross.

'You're a real humanitarian. Who do you take them to?'

'Why? You going over there to smash the place up?'

'If that's what it takes to find him.'

'Good luck then. You'll need it. I hand the girls over to Ruby Volta.'

I felt my stomach drop like I was on a rollercoaster. I had not anticipated Nolan having such a heavyweight connection, and I had not expected The Director to be involved with a major gangster.

'Aye, you're not so tough now, are you?' Nolan sneered.

'You're pretty mouthy for a guy that's pissed himself, aren't you?' Mack said as he put his coat back on.

It was time to go. Nolan knew nothing about Siobhan's murder and staying longer would only lead to more violence. We walked to the door, past the still prone form of Big Billy, and stopped when Nolan shouted to us. We turned and saw him leaning against the bar.

'Watch your backs, boys. You'll be getting a visit soon.' His smile was a foul thing, made still uglier by the red stain across the lips and gums, and the absence of the teeth I had knocked out.

'Know where we're going now, Drew?' I asked conversationally. 'We're going to see Siobhan's dad, tell him what you got her into.'

'Do I look like I give a fuck?'

'You should. Her dad's Innes McKenzie.'

Nolan's smile slipped from his face like it had been sliced off and I knew his stomach had just experienced that rollercoaster drop. Everything Mack and I had done here today was nothing to what Innes McKenzie was capable of, and Nolan knew it.

I smiled at him. 'Don't worry about it, Drew, at least you got paid. You've probably got enough for a real nice headstone.'

Twenty-Two

'You alright?' Mack asked as The Gibbet faded away behind us, my adrenaline subsiding with every turn we made. My face was set in stone and I had not yet spoken since we left Nolan's pub.

'Yeah.'

'Your Catholic guilt complex giving you a hard time yet?'

'Not yet.'

'Good. He deserved all of that. And more.'

'I'm more concerned about Ruby Volta being involved in this,' I said. 'I didn't expect that.'

'Doesn't change anything though, does it?'

I glanced at Mack and saw he was completely unperturbed by this new development.

'Of course it does. We can't exactly walk up to Ruby Volta and beat the crap out of him, can we?'

'Why not?' Mack sounded genuinely puzzled.

'I can think of about a hundred reasons. Mainly the bullet holes they'd find in our bodies whenever they washed ashore.'

'Look, I know Volta's place. It looks well-protected, but you know there's going to be a way in. We go in, take out a few of his guards, take him out, make it look like a hit. Volta's been nipping at McKenzie's heels for ages now. The cops would reckon it was McKenzie that topped him. Volta gets what he deserves, McKenzie walks as usual, it goes down as an unsolved, and the cops don't pursue it.'

'I'm not going to kill someone, Mack. Even someone like Volta. Even if it was possible, which it isn't.'

'Then what did we just do in there? What was the point?' He

was getting angry now. 'If someone smaller-time had been behind these movies would we let it go? No, we'd be round there giving them the same as Nolan just got.'

'But we wouldn't kill them! And we can't go after someone like Volta and leave him to come back at us.'

'So we make sure he can't,' Mack said, the logic obvious to him. 'He's not exactly going to be a loss to society, is he?'

I thought about the pain and suffering a man like Volta caused. If we did nothing how many more girls would suffer as Louise Ross did? But if we did act, it would have to be lethal, and I wasn't sure my soul could cope with that.

I thought about it and realised there was another answer. Mack saw my mouth tighten as I made my decision. 'Well?' he asked. 'What are we doing?'

'We're going to see Siobhan's dad.'

*

I stopped the car outside Breakers, a somewhat dingy pool and snooker hall in the south side of the city, trapped between a drycleaner and an estate agent. I had never been here before but this was where Mason had directed me to when I had phoned to arrange a meeting with McKenzie.

We entered the building and climbed the stairs to the first floor under the watchful eye of a security camera. As we reached the landing we came to a sealed booth where a fat man sat collecting entrance fees. I gave my name and he waved us through with sleepy eyes. As we walked past I noticed there were no CCTV monitors in the booth, though I suspected they were watched by someone altogether more alert. And altogether more dangerous.

The hall was smallish, with twelve pool tables laid out in four rows of three to our right, and four snooker tables beyond them. The room was in semi-darkness, small puddles of light cast over the five occupied tables scattered at random, a haze of cigarette smoke hovering around each one. The click of cues and the crack of colliding balls were the only sounds within the room. It didn't seem the kind of place people came to chat.

To our left was a small bar area, a lone barmaid pouring a whisky from the optic for the solitary customer. The man turned on his stool and I saw it was Mason. He looked at us coldly, examining Mack with calculating eyes.

'Where's McKenzie?' I asked him.

'What have you found?'

'I need to talk to McKenzie.'

Mason took a sip from the glass the barmaid had placed before him. He took his time savouring the peaty warmth of the whisky before he spoke. 'That's not how it works, remember? You find anything, you tell me. If it's worthwhile, I tell Mr McKenzie. So what is it?'

'This is for McKenzie's ears only. And it's not negotiable.'

Mason looked at me with reptilian eyes. 'Tell me.'

'You don't want to let me speak to him, fine. But if he learns about this from someone else you can tell him why.'

'Did you forget who you're dealing with?' Mason asked, standing up and stepping towards me.

Mack stepped in between us and shoved Mason back onto his stool. 'We know who you are. We're just not impressed.'

They stayed like that for a few moments, Mason on his stool, Mack in front of him, staring into each other's eyes. I had tensed and forgotten to breathe, wondering how this would end, when a voice came from behind me.

'Mr Harper. You have something for me?'

I turned and saw Innes McKenzie standing at the open door of an office at the back of the room. He stood there, hands on hips, the spotlights glinting off the brass buttons on his blazer.

Neither Mack nor Mason had yet broken their eye contact.

'I think you'd rather hear it in private,' I said to McKenzie.

'I have no secrets from Mason.'

'I'm giving you the option of having one. You might want to take it.'

'You're telling me what to do?' McKenzie asked, his voice hard.

'A suggestion, that's all.'

McKenzie thought about it for a moment then spoke to Mason. 'Check them.'

Mason stood, still maintaining eye contact with Mack. Mack stood with his legs apart and his arms extended at shoulder height, allowing Mason to pat him down. Mason satisfied himself that Mack carried no weapons then walked over to frisk me.

When he was satisfied I followed McKenzie into his office. Mack stayed behind and took a seat at the bar. Mason followed me before McKenzie whispered softly in his ear, sending him back to the bar. The look of malevolence in Mason's eyes as McKenzie shut the door told me we'd made a bad enemy.

McKenzie sat in a large leather swivel chair and gestured to the single chair on my side of the desk. As I took it he tapped on the desk three times with his damaged left hand, as though bringing a meeting to order.

'Well?' he asked.

'It's about your daughter,' I began. Suddenly I was unsure how to tell this man that his only daughter had been involved in home-made porn films. This would have been a difficult enough conversation with any father, but given McKenzie's propensity for violence I needed to choose my words with extreme care.

'Have you found her killer?'

'No. Not yet.'

A look of anger flashed through McKenzie's grey eyes. 'Then you're wasting time.'

'I've found out something about Siobhan. It's not the sort of thing a father wants to hear, but it'll probably come out sooner or later.'

'I'm well aware of Siobhan's drinking. And her drug use. And, sadly, I'm also aware of her reputation amongst her peers.'

I doubted that knowing all that would make it any easier to take, but I cleared my throat and told him about the porn films, about Drew Nolan, and about Ruby Volta.

When I had finished McKenzie closed his eyes momentarily. Then they sprang open, as sharp and probing as drill bits, his face a mask of concentration as though he was barely controlling his emotions. 'Are you certain?'

I thought of Nolan, smeared with blood and stinking of urine, and I thought of Louise Ross, her face streaked with tears, her body racked with sorrow.

'Absolutely.'

He looked away awkwardly, unsure of the words he sought. He nodded absently a couple of times and I knew that was as close as I would get to gratitude. 'Why did you refuse to tell Mason?' he asked

'You're her father, I had to tell you. But it's nothing to do with him.'

'Most people find themselves very eager to do what he says.'

'I'm becoming harder to impress.'

McKenzie nodded, and I saw a darkness cross his face. It was raw and painful and I was glad that it was not directed at me. 'If you'll excuse me,' he said, standing up, 'I have graves to fill.'

McKenzie gestured towards the door and I stood and opened it, stepping out into the bar where Mack and Mason were locked in eye contact like two wild dogs who had somehow found themselves tethered too far apart to savage each other.

Mack followed me as I left, his eyes never leaving Mason's until we had turned the corner and started down the stairs to the pavement. As we stepped out into the cold night air neither of us spoke. We climbed into the car and sat in silence for a moment.

'Well?' Mack asked.

'He's hurting. And he's angry. He'll take them out. Nolan, Volta, all of them.'

'Result,' Mack said.

He held out his right hand, clenched in a fist. I made a fist of my left hand and bumped it against his. Result indeed.

If my plan worked it would mean no more girls suffered as Louise Ross did – at least not at the hands of Nolan and Volta – but still I wondered what I had done, and at the consequences that surely lay in wait.

Did McKenzie know the real reason I had told him about Siobhan's involvement in these films? Did he suspect that my intention all along was to turn him loose on Ruby Volta?

Did the ends we aimed for justify the means we used to shoot them down?

And if the weapon I used was the devil himself did that damn me as surely as it did him?

Twenty-Three

I dropped Mack off at his gym and drove aimlessly around for a while. My mind was in turmoil, and so was my heart, thoughts and emotions tumbling within me like soiled clothes on a spin cycle.

The guilt and shame over the beating I had given Drew Nolan had crept up and taken root. I had known as I drove to The Gibbet, known even as I picked up the phone to call Mack, that my conscience would not let me forget this easily.

But despite knowing this I had chosen to proceed with a course of action that would, at best, lead me into physical danger, and at worst, scar my soul. As the street lights flooded the car with intermittent amber beams I became sure that knowing somehow made it worse.

And yet, when I thought of Louise Ross and the abuse she had suffered, and of the other faceless, nameless – countless – girls who had been violated in the same way, I knew that I would make the same decision again, even if it tore fragments from my being in the process.

I pushed the Honda onto the motorway and pressed down on the accelerator, heading for nowhere.

Traffic was sparse and I weaved in and out, slowing down, speeding up, slow lane, fast lane, all the time trying to keep my thoughts from sinking in a morass of human stupidity and cruelty.

I thought of the people I had come across since Archie Bell had asked me to find his missing daughter, and I thought of what they represented. A cross-section of humanity, of the people we share the world with, and a damning indictment of who we are and what we have become.

I thought of Drew Nolan and Big Billy, men of cruelty and

violence who had been visited by the same in recompense for acts they had committed; of Innes McKenzie, a man with an immeasurable capacity for inflicting pain, motivated solely by the desire to inflict inhuman torture on the man who murdered his daughter; of Mason, a man who has made a career of violence, intimidation and death; of Ruby Volta and Johnny D'Arienzo and others cut from the same cloth.

And I thought of less obvious evils: Of Siobhan Sutherland, abandoning her friend to be repeatedly raped by men she had led her to; of Fiona Matheson whose self-absorption was so deep she shed no tears over the brutal murder of a young woman she had known; and of everyone, myself included, refusing to help a distraught woman find her missing friend.

I thought too of the victims. Of those who were dead – of Gemma Sinclair and Siobhan Sutherland and Janet Bell and Keith Lamont. And of those who remained – of Louise Ross, and Archie Bell, and Lorna Sinclair, and Kim Kennedy and Diane Hill, and of those whose names I didn't know, and those whose faces I would never see.

And I thought of the man whose face I had not yet seen. I knew, without doubt, that soon I would see him as he truly was, his evil unmasked, and I wondered if I would be ready.

I found myself shaking, the weight of my thoughts overpowering me. I realised I had pulled off the motorway some time ago and I had stopped the car without conscious thought. I looked out of the window at the building I was parked in front of, and part of me asked what I was doing here. The other part – the part that needed contact, that needed reassurance, that demanded my brain be allowed to disconnect – knew why I was here and led me from the car and up the pathway to the door of the close. It was unlocked and I let myself in, stopped at the left hand flat on the ground floor and rang the bell.

She answered a few moments later, surprised at first, and then her smile spread across her face and she leaned against the edge of the door. 'You found me then? My, my, you *are* a detective.'

'Hi, Charlotte,' I said.

'Not the best opening line, Harper, but still… come on in.'

Charlotte stepped aside and waved me into her home, guiding me into her living room. I looked at the place where she had been sitting on the sofa, a blanket pushed to one side when she had risen to answer the door, a glass of white wine on the side table, the television showing the frozen image of a paused film. The room was cosy, filled with lit candles and the tension in my shoulders began to melt in the warmth.

Charlotte locked the front door and entered the room, giving me a look that said she knew exactly why I was there. She came towards me as though she knew how badly I needed human contact and I opened my mouth to speak, to attempt some sort of explanation. The words were lost as she stood on her tiptoes and pressed her lips to mine. She pulled my head down towards her and I felt her fingers tug at my clothes with a desperation I quickly matched.

After that we didn't talk.

*

Later, as Charlotte snored softly beside me on the sofa, tangled in the blanket, I looked around the room at our scattered clothes, hidden in the flickering shadows cast by the last of the candles. Her head lay on my shoulder and I glanced down at her black hair shining in the same dim light that made the pink tips of her hair flame orange. I could feel her breasts pressed against my side, her rhythmic breaths on my neck and her left hand resting on my chest, the fingers contracting slightly as she dreamed.

It was long past midnight and I had lain watching Charlotte sleep for the best part of an hour, unable to sleep for the thoughts crashing through my head. I was calmer now, and more in touch with the world than I had been earlier, and yet I still could not close my mind. I now realised that I didn't want to. I needed to stay focused to find a killer.

I slid out from beneath Charlotte's sleeping form and rose from the sofa. I walked softly to the window and parted the blind with one finger. The street outside was dark and silent. There was no movement and the only sound was that of Charlotte's breathing. I

The Worst of Evils

couldn't stay here, not with the thoughts that were churning in my mind. I needed time to think about the case, and, equally, after what I had done today, I felt unworthy of Charlotte's company.

I crept round the room and collected my clothes. I was half-dressed when the sofa creaked as Charlotte rolled over and propped herself up on one elbow. She sat with the blanket around her waist, unashamed of her nakedness. Her eyes were puffy with sleep and her mouth hung slightly open as though she was unsure whether this was a dream or reality.

She looked up at me and blinked a couple of times to waken herself.

'Sneaking out?' she asked, a sleepy smile on her lips.

'No,' I whispered. 'Just didn't want to wake you.'

'Why are you leaving?'

'I'm sorry, Charlotte. I shouldn't have come here tonight.'

'Why?'

'I came here for the wrong reasons... I just needed someone...'

Charlotte smiled, a thing of beauty in the soft light. 'It's cool. I'm not looking for a relationship. I like you, you seem to like me too, so there's nothing wrong with messing around now and again. You want to stay, you're welcome. You want to go, that's fine too.' She hiked her small shoulders. 'Whatever.'

I looked at her in surprise as she reached out and squeezed my fingers in understanding. 'We all need to grab onto something – someone – now and again. Sometimes it's the only thing that stops you spinning off the earth.'

'You feel that too?'

'Sometimes.' She smiled again, more sadly this time. 'Don't let this drag you down. You're a good guy, hang in there.'

'How do you know I'm a good guy?' I didn't especially feel like one today.

'Because you don't take the easy road. Not many people would take this on. They'd leave it to the police. It says a lot about you.'

I stood and pulled my t-shirt over my head, picked up my jacket from the floor. 'I'm not sure about that. You ever feel like you do more harm than good?'

Charlotte looked at me with eyes wiser than her years, eyes that looked deep within me. 'You fight the bad shit for long enough it's going to start affecting you. At some point it'll really hurt you, or someone close to you. When that happens you need to remind yourself why you fight it, because bad shit's still going to happen. So what you going to do? Let it?'

I nodded 'You're very deep.'

Charlotte held up a finger. 'Don't forget *meaningful*.'

I leant down and kissed her lips. She responded, her hand caressing the back of my neck. After a few moments I pulled away and headed for the door, knowing that if I stayed much longer I'd be there for the night. 'Thanks, doc. You're quite the shrink.'

Charlotte smiled at me over the back of the sofa as I left. 'Give them hell. And make sure you call me when you find him. I'm only fucking you for the story, you know.'

Twenty-Four

I awoke early the following morning, refreshed and invigorated, my head feeling clearer than it had in days. I showered and dressed quickly before heading out to the car. I stopped off at a bakers to pick up some croissants for breakfast, and a newsagents where I bought a copy of the Glasgow News, with Charlotte's serial killer article on the front page, and headed for Charlotte's flat in Partick. I felt that there had been a connection between us the night before. I had been fragile and adrift and my faith in humanity had been shaken, and yet Charlotte had convinced me that there was more to the world than badness. The least I could do was take her breakfast to say thank you.

I pulled up outside her flat and stepped out of the car into a brightly chill morning. I smiled at the colourful window boxes perched on the sills of her ground floor flat as I walked briskly up the three steps to the close door. It was again unlocked and I pushed it open and rapped my knuckles on Charlotte's door. There was no answer and I wondered if she was still asleep. I checked my watch and saw it was only eight-fifteen. Perhaps I had jumped the gun by coming so early. I decided since I was here I might as well knock again – hopefully providing breakfast would mitigate the damage if I did wake her.

There was no response again and I wondered if she had already left. But her Golf was still outside and I guessed she wouldn't go far without transport in case a story broke elsewhere. A strange, unsettled feeling blossomed in my stomach. I walked back outside and looked at the downstairs windows. Both had their curtains closed and there were no gaps at the edges to see inside. The flowers in the window boxes seemed to have lost some of their vibrancy.

I took my phone from my pocket and dialled Charlotte's number as I walked back inside. The phone began to ring on the other end and when I took my mobile from my ear I could hear a faint ringing from beyond the close door. I left the close through the back door and studied the two rear windows. Both of these were covered too, this time with Venetian blinds, and again I could see nothing.

The phone was still ringing as I returned to the close and stood before Charlotte's door once more. I placed the croissants and the newspaper beside the door, crouched and flipped up the letterbox, and peered into the dimness of the flat. At first I saw nothing but the vague shape of two doorways on either side of the hallway, the darkness deeper within each. Then as my eyes adjusted I noticed something at the far end of the hallway, on the wall about five feet above the wooden floor. It was dark and irregular shaped and looked like blood.

I dropped the flap of the letterbox and stepped back. I didn't hesitate. I threw myself forward and kicked beneath the lock with everything I had. It was a sturdy door, solid and unyielding, but my desperation lent me strength and it took only two more kicks before the wood cracked. One more and the door fired open like a gunshot.

I charged into the hallway and flicked on the light with my elbow.

It was blood.

At exactly the height that Charlotte's head would have been had she been standing upright. I turned left into the living room, the only room I had entered the previous night, and saw that, other than the blanket and Charlotte's wine glass being absent, nothing had changed. I crossed the hallway and entered the next room – the kitchen – and found nothing unusual. The wine glass sat beside the sink, suggesting Charlotte had put it there when she went to bed.

Back in the hallway I looked at the two remaining doors and knew would be the bathroom and one the bedroom. The bedroom was probably the one at the front and I checked that first, throwing the door wide as I entered. The double bed sat in the middle of the room against the right hand wall and the duvet was thrown back as though Charlotte had got out of bed in a hurry. I scanned the room quickly and noticed nothing else out of place. I stepped back into

The Worst of Evils

the hallway and looked at the closed bathroom door. Beside it was the red stain on the cream wall and I tried to stem the flow of images conjured by my imagination.

My fingers stretched out before me and I saw them tremble as they took hold of the door handle. I pushed down and the handle turned slowly, the door easing away from me as it did so. The bathroom door yawned wide and I saw hell before me.

The shower curtain was pushed to one end and Charlotte hung from the sagging pole by her wrists, the cord that held her biting deeply into her flesh. She was naked and her head hung forward, a piece of material visible within her mouth where the killer had forced it to muffle the screams drawn forth by the dozens of cuts across her body and limbs. The blood had flowed down her body, painting her scarlet, before pooling beneath her on the floor, following the grouting to mark red borders around the few tiles that remained unblemished.

But it was her intestines that were truly horrific. The killer had cut her stomach open and pulled them forth as he had done with the other victims. This time though he had weaved them around her body and legs in a twisted embrace, as though she were captured in the coils of a snake.

My eyes were drawn to her chest where I expected a biblical reference, but there was none. In its place the killer had used a large knife to pin a glossy piece of paper to her chest. I steeled myself to look more closely and when I did I spun to my side, vomit burning its way up my throat and splattering on the hallway floor. My body shuddered as I threw up again, the bile scorching my insides like hellfire.

When the heaving had subsided I turned back to Charlotte and the 8x10 photo that had been pinned to her chest so viciously the knife was embedded up to its hilt. I hadn't seen it before, but I knew when it had been taken. It was the photo Charlotte had taken as I left my office last Saturday.

The photo was of me, and the message was clearer than any biblical reference could ever be.

Charlotte had died because of me.

*

I sat on the stairs inside Charlotte's close with my head in my hands, my blood humming as it thundered through my veins. DI Stewart and DS Taylor had arrived shortly after I called them, and Stewart had swiftly taken charge of the scene after seeing the horrors that lurked in the bathroom. Taylor had escorted me from the flat – surprisingly gently – and had stayed with me until support arrived. Now that it had she was back in the flat with Stewart while a uniform kept an eye on me. I knew it was more from concern that I was the killer and might leg it than any worry over my wellbeing. I had told Stewart and Taylor what had happened but I knew we'd have to go over it again once they had the situation under control.

The crime scene was buzzing now, with uniforms stationed at the door to the flat as well as the front and back doors of the close. More officers were canvassing the other occupants of the building and still others were talking to neighbours in adjacent buildings. White-suited Scene of Crime Officers flitted around like ghosts, and I caught the occasional sound of Taylor bawling someone out. The doctor had shown up briefly for the formality of pronouncing death, allowing the medical examiner to start work on Charlotte's body, and the Procurator Fiscal had shown up for a few minutes before turning white and scuttling off.

At least you never knew her.

Stewart appeared before me, his eyes concerned. He put his hands on his hips and blew out a long breath. 'Did you touch anything other than the door handles and the letterbox?'

I unclenched my teeth and replied. 'Not this morning.' *Apart from the carpet I spewed on.* 'I probably touched a fair few things in the living room last night.'

'But you didn't go into any other room?'

'No.'

'And you had sex with the victim?'

'Charlotte,' I said. 'Her name is Charlotte.'

Stewart didn't reply, just waited for my answer.

'Yes,' I finally said. 'We had sex.'

'We'll need to take some samples. For elimination purposes.'

'Why? He doesn't rape them.'

'Come on, Harper. You know how it is. When we catch him this case needs to be watertight.'

I sighed, knowing he was right. 'Fine. Whatever you need. Just catch him.'

'We will.'

'When? He's attacking people in their homes, Stewart. He's getting more daring.'

'And taking more risks. Which will help us catch him.'

'Not a lot of consolation if you've just been carved open.'

Stewart took a deep sigh and said, 'Harper, I want you to accept our help. I know you don't like us, and I know you don't trust us, but it's time to look past that. This guy is becoming increasingly obsessed with you. It's only a matter of time before he makes his move. You need our protection. You and anyone else close to you.'

I thought about Stewart's offer and I knew he was right, just as I knew more innocent people would be hurt before this monster made his move on me. I knew what my decision had to be.

'No.'

'What? Are you fucking stupid?' Taylor stood in the flat doorway, looking at me as though I had just confirmed her suspicions that I was mentally sub-normal.

'Why?' Stewart was equally puzzled. 'He's obsessed with you. He wants to kill you, and he's not going to just stop. Can't you see that?'

'Exactly. He's not going to stop. It doesn't matter if I go into hiding. He'll just wait until I eventually come back out. Or worse – and more likely – he'll continue to kill innocent people until I do.' I shook my head. 'I'm not having that on my hands.'

Stewart sighed and said, 'You're not bulletproof, Harper. He'll find you, and he'll kill you.'

'What will you do when someone else dies?' Taylor asked bluntly.

'Fuck you, Sam.'

'Sam, cut that out,' Stewart said. He turned back to me, rubbing his hand across his chin, the light stubble scratching like sandpaper. 'Would you agree to us giving you protection while we use you to draw the killer out?'

'Bait?' I asked.

Stewart shrugged. 'It could work.'

I looked from one to the other. Taylor looked interested again, while Stewart looked nonchalant, as though he hadn't just asked me to risk my life.

'Do you really think you can protect me?' I asked. 'Who are you protecting me from? You've been on this case for over a year and you've got nothing.' I laughed humourlessly. 'I'll take my chances.'

'This could be our best chance to catch this guy,' Taylor said. 'You said you didn't want any more blood on your hands.'

'Don't try to manipulate me.' I shot her a look of disgust. 'If I believed for a second that you clowns could organise it properly and make it work I'd agree without a second thought. But you'll screw it up and someone will die.'

'Someone will die regardless,' Taylor said.

'Nobody's going to die,' Stewart said forcefully. 'What if we just put a couple of officers on you to follow you, look out for you? It won't be for long, just until we find him.'

'No.'

'For Christ's sake, Harper.' Stewart was getting frustrated now. 'I don't want another bloody death.'

'If you're protecting me, he'll just kill someone else.' I looked them both in the eyes, and they saw the truth in my words. 'If he comes for me... at least I'll be prepared.'

'And you think you can take him out?' Taylor asked.

'I've got a better shot than someone who doesn't know he's coming.'

'You're a fucking idiot,' Taylor said. She turned on her heel and stormed out of the close, barging past the uniform on her way.

'I'll get someone to take you to the station for those samples,' Stewart said.

'Tell me one thing. And don't mess about. Just tell me.'

Stewart looked at me warily. 'What?'

I threw the dice, banking on Stewart's increasing desperation stopping him from pressing me too hard on my sources. 'There was no message with Charlotte's body – I guess the photo is the new message – but what was the message left on Keith Lamont's body.'

He kept his expression neutral, as I'd expected, but I knew I'd shocked him. 'What makes you think there was a message?'

'Gemma, Siobhan and Janet were all left with a biblical reference carved into their chests. Timothy 5:8, James 1:15, Revelation 2:16. Unless our boy was fed up with that particular party piece, I'd expect him to have done the same with Keith. What was it?'

'How do you know?' Stewart asked.

'I can't tell you that. Look, I know three anyway, one more won't make any difference.'

'Can't your source tell you?' Stewart asked bitterly.

'Yeah, but it'll take longer.'

Stewart sighed and I could almost see him weigh up the pros and cons, balance the potential benefits against the possible repercussions. I had no idea which way he would go until he spoke.

'If you tell anyone I'll deny it.'

'I don't tell.'

'Leviticus 20:13.'

'I must have missed that day at school. What's the passage?'

Stewart looked sickened as he recited it. *'If a man also lie with mankind, as he lieth with a woman, both of them have committed an abomination.'*

'Nice,' I said. 'I do love the Christian spirit.'

'You think that's bad? That's the nicer half. It ends; *they shall surely be put to death; their blood shall be upon them.*'

A sick feeling flowed through me, settling heavily in my stomach and leaving me stunned at the inherent cruelty in these words. 'So he was gay,' I said more to myself than Stewart. 'And that's why he was killed.'

There was a pause for several seconds before Stewart spoke again. 'I know why you've refused protection.'

'I told you, I don't believe you can protect me.'

'That's only part of it.' Stewart's eyes bored into mine. 'I want this man as much as you do, Harper.'

'Nobody does.'

'I can't condone vigilantism.'

'I don't need you to.'

He looked at me sadly. 'Don't cross a line you can't come back from.'

Then Stewart turned and walked back into Charlotte's flat, leaving me alone with my thoughts. I thought about the previous night and the last image I had of Charlotte; the smile she had given me as she told me to call her when I found the killer. I thought too of the words she had spoken; words that, with hindsight, had the ring of premonition.

At some point it'll really hurt you, or someone close to you.

And it had. We may not have been close yet, but Charlotte had been kind to me when I needed it, and she had been killed because of that kindness.

When that happens you need to remind yourself why you fight it, because bad shit's still going to happen. What are you going to do? Let it?

No chance.

I had told Mack yesterday that I could not kill someone, even a man such as Ruby Volta. Today, I knew I had been wrong. Today my blood sizzled with the certainty that I could kill.

And when I found this man he was going to die.

Twenty-Five

I spent the next few hours at Pitt Street giving my statement and having fingerprint and DNA samples taken, then giving another statement, and another. A less charitable man would have called it an interrogation. Eventually they let me go and a constable took me back to Charlotte's flat to retrieve my car. There was no activity visible from the street now, but a uniform still stood sentry outside the close door and he watched me with a beady eye until I had driven from his view.

I had been driving for a few minutes when my mobile rang. I fished it from my pocket and checked the screen, saw it was a withheld number and pulled the car to the side of the road to answer it.

'Do you think she's in heaven yet, Harper?' The voice was hushed once more and again it sent a shockwave through my body like the aftermath of a bomb blast.

I fought the urge to scream down the phone and tried to calm myself before I replied. *He wants to rattle you. Don't let him take control.*

He spoke again before I regained my composure. 'I believe she is, Harper. She repented her sins and her soul was freed. Our Father will welcome her cleansed soul back to his arms.'

'And what do you think he'll do with the diseased rag you call a soul?' I asked. 'You have heard *thou shalt not kill*, right?'

There was silence for a few seconds and I suspected the caller was trying to maintain his calm in the same way I had. Finally he spoke. 'I would not expect your mortal mind to understand the magnitude of my calling. It is the Lord who guides me, and he who forgives me, and I shall be seated at his right hand when the time comes.'

'I'll see what I can do to bring that time closer.'

The voice laughed. 'There is nothing you can do to me, Harper. Nothing. You think you are tough, you think you are brave, but I am filled with the power of the Lord. My hand is but an extension of his.'

'You seriously think God's telling you to kill people, or you just flying that one to see if a jury will buy it?'

'No jury will ever see my face. I shall finish my work with the sinners and I shall disappear like fog.'

'You can't disappear,' I told him. 'Not from me. I'll hunt you with every breath in my body and I'll find you.'

'You would be well advised to expend your breath on more pressing matters. Such as protecting your women.'

'What?' I asked as my temperature plummeted.

'You have lost one already,' the voice gloated. 'Just as your friend did. But what if you were to lose another? Miss Brodie, perhaps? I have to wonder, Harper. How much can you stand to lose before you beg for Redemption?'

The call ended abruptly and I threw the phone down on the passenger seat. I opened my mouth and bellowed to the heavens, pounding my fists against the steering wheel in rage. A minute passed, then two, until finally I was able to control my anger and terror and put the car in gear.

*

I pressed the buzzer and waited for a response, hoping Jessica was here since I didn't want to do this over the phone. Telling someone that a sociopathic serial killer may want to kill them should really be done in person.

After a few seconds the intercom garbled something and I rapped my knuckles against the microphone in response. The lock clicked open and I entered Ogilvie, Laing and Drummond. I was met in the hallway by an irate Crawford Laing, hitching his belt up and demanding to know what the hell I was playing at.

'I need to see Jessica,' I told him.

'Tough, she's busy. She's got plenty of paperwork to catch up on.'

'So she's here? Thanks.' I headed towards the stairs, stopping only when Laing grabbed my arm. I gave him a look that told him what kind of day I'd been having and he let go.

'I want you out of here in five minutes,' he said, trying to reassert his authority.

'I'll leave when I'm done.'

I climbed the stairs slowly, just to annoy him, and met Phil Biggart coming the other way.

'Harper,' he said in surprise. 'You just can't get enough of this place, can you?'

'Just like to keep Crawford's blood pressure topped up.'

Phil looked at me strangely, as though he sensed there was a more serious reason for my presence. 'Everything alright, mate?'

'Yeah, fine. Just need a word with Jessica. Same office?'

Phil confirmed that Jessica still used the same office I'd once shared with her, pointing it out in case I didn't remember. I thanked him and knocked on the white gloss door. There was a sound from within and I opened the door and stepped inside, stopping in my tracks as I saw a man sitting across the desk from Jessica, sipping coffee and looking very much at home. The same man who'd found us in the pub. He looked even less pleased to see me than I was to see him. He carefully placed his coffee mug on the desk and looked at me from behind his thick glasses.

'Harper,' he said, his voice stilted.

'Aaron.'

Jessica looked awkward and embarrassed, and a little worried. 'What's wrong?'

So I told her. I wanted Aaron to leave but once I'd started Jessica decided it was fairer for him to know what he was getting into.

When I finished I waited for the inevitable reaction. Aaron didn't disappoint. 'You turned down protective custody?'

'Yes.'

'Are you insane?' His face was bright red as he jumped to his feet. 'Seriously, what made you think that was a good idea? Are you retarded?'

'Don't push it,' I told him. 'I'm having a really bad week and punching you could only improve it.'

Aaron looked to Jessica in outrage. She didn't respond. At least someone appreciated there were more important matters to deal with.

'You're going after him, aren't you?' Jessica said. 'That's why you turned it down.'

'Mainly.'

'Oh, great!' Aaron exclaimed, throwing his hands up in the air. 'You're *going after* him. A serial killer, and you're going to challenge him to a square go. Wonderful idea.'

'Aaron,' Jessica said calmly. 'Shut up.'

I brightened. *Get that one up you, Aaron.*

Jessica turned to me. 'I don't know why, but he's got it in for you. He's even abandoned the biblical references in order to kill someone close to you. He's changing, and it's because of you. He's coming after you. Or someone you know.'

'That's what I figured,' I said.

'Fantastic,' Aaron sneered in the background.

'Maybe you should reconsider Stewart's offer,' Jessica asked.

'I can't. If I go into hiding, someone else will die. I can't live with that.' I hesitated a second. 'But that doesn't mean other people can't take protection.'

Jessica spoke with a voice like frozen acid. 'You think I'm going to run off and hide somewhere till this is all over?'

'I'd be happier if I didn't have to worry about you.'

'Don't be so bloody selfish. Do you think I wouldn't worry about you? I'd be going out of my mind.'

'It would just be until I find him.'

'Actually,' Aaron said timidly, 'I think it's a good idea.'

Jessica ignored him and was silent for a moment. 'Tell me, what did Mack say when you asked him to leave?'

I sighed heavily. 'I didn't ask him.'

'When are you going to?'

'Alright, alright, I'm not going to ask him.'

'Because he'd tell you to piss off, same as I'm doing. There's no difference between me and Mack. So drop it.'

As selfish as it may have been, the knowledge that Jessica was willing to risk everything by standing by me was an injection of hope, a belief that I could stop this killer.

Aaron leaned forward and cleared his throat. 'Eh, Jessica? Can we talk about this?'

'There's nothing to discuss,' Jessica said flatly. 'Harper's my friend and I'm not abandoning him.'

'What about us? I don't want to wake up some night and find a maniac standing over the bed with a kitchen knife. I want to be with you, and I want us to be safe.'

'I can't leave Harper,' Jessica told him. 'I *won't* leave him.'

'But you expect me to stay? You expect me to put my life on the line?'

'No.' Jessica looked away. 'I won't ask you to do that.'

'Okay then, we need to make plans, decide where we're going.' Aaron had misunderstood.

I watched Jessica get to her feet and looked away, uncomfortable at being in the middle of this. She lifted a thin folder from the table and held it out to me. 'This is everything I found out about Keith Lamont. It's not much, and there's nothing promising there, but...'

I took the folder and recognised my cue to leave. She'd call when she was ready. I left the room and found Laing standing at the top of the stairs with a face full of storm clouds. I ignored him, listening instead to Aaron's wheedling tone through the door. 'Come with me, Jessica. He's making a mistake and he's going to get you killed. If he wants to die that's his choice, but don't let him make that choice for you. You don't owe him anything, just walk away. Please. I don't want to lose you.'

Laing started to speak but I shoved him aside and started down the stairs. From above I could hear Jessica's response, her voice as flat and cold as a frozen lake.

'You lost me as soon as you asked me to abandon my friend.'

Twenty-Six

Jessica had found a reasonable amount of information, but none of it provided any clues as to how Keith Lamont had met his killer. I remained convinced that this was the key; if I could establish how the victims crossed his path I could identify him. My only option now was to speak to those who had known Keith.

Keith had shared a flat just off Great Western Road, in the prosperous Kelvinside area of the city, with a man named Gordon Tierney, and it was him I needed to speak to, though I didn't hold out much hope that he would provide any more clues than the friends and relatives of the other victims had.

The rain was lashing down as I exited the car and even in the short distance between the car and the front door I was soaked. I made my way upstairs and knocked on the door of flat 2/2, dripping heavily on the carpet as I waited for a reply. After a minute I knocked a second time and heard movement within. The door opened halfway and a large man stared out at me, his eyes red-rimmed and shadowy.

'Gordon Tierney?' I asked. It was a redundant question. Grief came off him in waves, leaving me in no doubt that this man had been Keith Lamont's lover.

He nodded, a shallow dip of the chin, then stood motionless in the doorway.

'I understand Detective Inspector Stewart has been out to speak to you?' I said. 'My name's Harper. I just need to ask you a few more questions. May I come in?'

Tierney made a half-hearted attempt at a shrug then shuffled backwards and opened the door wide for me to enter. He trudged away in a daze as I closed the door behind me. I squelched after him, feeling a sliver of guilt work its way under my skin. I may be able to argue the case with the authorities that I hadn't told him I was a police officer, but I'd deliberately let him believe it. I told myself it was the only way and wondered why that didn't make me feel any better.

Gordon Tierney slumped into a well-cushioned sofa and avoided my eyes for a minute or so. I sized him up while he composed himself. He was a big man, a few years older than me, his shoulders telling me he had played a lot of rugby in his younger days, his gut telling me he had not yet stopped drinking like he was still in a rugby team. His face was dominated by a Tom Selleck moustache, his hair black, short and untidy.

The room we sat in was large and spoke of money. The floor was rich wood under a thick, soft rug. The rest of the furnishings were sparse yet tasteful, with even the flat-screen television on the wall bucking the current trend of bigger being better. All around the room were pictures that showed Tierney and another man I assumed was Keith Lamont. Keith was the physical opposite of his partner, a slight and petite man, who, without the spiky hair and trim goatee, may have appeared almost feminine. He looked at least five years younger than Tierney and at least ten years trendier, his clothes fashionable and expensive looking. There were pictures from summer holidays, weddings, house parties, nights out – snapshots of a life together. In each one they looked happy and in love and I was reminded again of the ripples this killer cast into the world, the damage that snaked through the lives of those on the periphery of his violence.

Tierney looked up suddenly and seemed surprised to see me sitting there. He gave himself a small shake and tried in vain to smooth the creases out of his shirt. 'I'm sorry. How can I help?'

I began by asking him gentle questions about himself and about Keith, based on the information Jessica had given me. He answered in a soft monotone, telling me about their life together. They had been a couple for five years, both openly gay, and they had lived together in this flat for the last four years and were as friendly with their neighbours as anyone was nowadays. I asked about Keith's job, his friends, his habits, his hobbies, everything I could think of – and learned nothing of any use.

Eventually I asked, 'Did you ever get any hassle because you're gay?'

Tierney simply shrugged. 'We'd get some funny looks occasionally. You know how it is.'

'Nothing more than that?'

'No. We were pretty circumspect when we were together. If we were out we'd act like mates. Keith was always more inclined to put his hand on my knee or something like that. Then he'd laugh as I shrugged it off.' He paused to shake his head angrily. Angry at himself and angry at everyone. 'I should have let him. I should have held his hand. Why couldn't we? Why did I let them dictate how we acted?'

I didn't know what to say. We may have lived in an apparently liberal, cosmopolitan society, but two men together still received looks that betrayed the prejudices of those around them. And there were still moronic thugs who took matters further in an effort to rid their environment of anything that could be deemed different, hoping it would make themselves feel part of something they never realised wanted nothing to do with them.

'Imagine being out for dinner with a woman you love,' Tierney said. 'And imagine not being able to do something as simple as reach across the table and hold her hand.' His eyes were fiery now, the anger momentarily smothering the grief. 'Imagine that one small act caused the rest of the restaurant to look at you like some kind of pervert. Imagine that kissing the woman you love in a bar might make someone follow you when you leave, shout abuse at you, maybe even attack you.'

There was nothing I could say, and nothing that Tierney wanted to hear. He knew the double standards that existed in our society, and he knew there would be no resolution to them in his lifetime.

'I should have handled it better. Keith came here to get away from that crap and I let it run our lives. He deserved better than me.' He slumped back in the sofa, his head tilting back until he looked at the ceiling as fresh tears leaked from angry eyes.

'What do you mean, Keith came here to get away from that?'

'Keith moved here from Ireland when he was eighteen. His parents were strict Catholic. You know the kind – it's fine to beat your weans and spread spiteful bile about people as long as you go to mass on Sundays and eat fish on Fridays.'

I knew the type.

'He came out when he was sixteen, and put up with them for two years before he moved here.'

'That was brave,' I said.

'It was. They were horrible people.'

'Have you met them?'

Now he looked at me. 'Are you kidding? I'd throttle them. Keith had no interest in them, anyway. They were nothing to him anymore.'

'I guess he didn't need them.' I gestured at the photos around us. 'You two seem to have been very close. Not many people are that lucky.'

Tierney looked at them and quickly looked away, his eyes drifting towards the window where the rain formed vertical rivers on the glass. He turned back to speak then looked away again, his mouth clamped shut. He clasped his arms around himself, his whole body shuddering, and I watched helplessly as tears began to flow down his cheeks as freely as the rainwater in the streets outside.

He tried one more time to speak before his mouth dissolved into anguished sobs. I stood to go to him but he waved me away. Through the tears he asked me to leave and like a coward I did.

I left the building and stepped back into the rain. It stung as the wind whipped it into my face and it felt deserved. I thought of my conversation with Louise Ross. Now, as then, I had forced someone to look at things they were not ready to and had torn them into an emotional wreck. And in the process had learned nothing that brought me any closer to the killer.

You ever feel like you do more harm than good?

I felt the bite of the icy rain and wondered how much more pain I would have to cause before I found the man I sought. The case was getting to me and I knew I needed help. Professional help.

Twenty-Seven

Hillhead Library was nearby and I found what I was looking for in one of their yellow pages. Maybe my luck was changing; the address was located on Highburgh Road, just a short walk along Byres Road from where I stood. Within ten minutes I was looking at an imposing tenement building that had long since been converted into a series of flats above a ground floor business.

The business in this case was psychology. I pressed the button beside a brass plaque that read *E. Brandon*, and carried more letters after the name than an episode of Countdown. There was a buzz as the door unlocked.

As I entered I was faced with several doors, only one of which was open. This led to a small waiting area, currently empty apart from the customary barely-alive pot plant and table full of dog-eared copies of Good Housekeeping and OK. I was about to take a seat when a door opened opposite and Brandon's bespectacled face appeared.

'Oh,' he said, as he saw me. 'Mr Harper. To what do I owe the pleasure? You don't have an appointment, I assume?'

'No. But I need to speak to you.'

'Yes, quite. But so does my patient.' He made a small gesture to the room behind him.

'I understand that. But things are getting out of hand and I'd like your help.'

Brandon glanced at his watch and sighed. 'Okay. Give me ten minutes, I should be able to squeeze you in before my next patient.'

He scurried back into the room and closed the door firmly behind him before I could speak. I took a seat in the waiting room and tried to clear my mind. After exactly ten minutes of flipping through a copy of Hello and counting my brain cells as they slowly died, I heard the door to Brandon's office open and him say goodbye to his patient. Ten minutes exactly. Time was obviously money where Brandon was concerned.

He called my name and I left the waiting room and followed him into his office. He took a seat on the far side of a dark wooden desk, straightened the edges of the blotter and steepled his fingers. He didn't invite me to, but I took a seat anyway, occupying a black leather chair opposite him. He pursed his lips in thought, his eyes half closed as he analysed me.

'Well? You wanted to see me, Mr Harper?'

And yet I wasn't sure why, since I hadn't respected his opinion previously. Perhaps visiting Brandon was a sign of desperation, an acknowledgement that I was rapidly running out of ideas. I glanced around the room as I tried to find the right words, my gaze coming to rest on a framed photograph a few inches from Brandon's elbow. It was tilted towards him, but the angle of my seat allowed me to see the woman and young child in the photograph, smiling in anoraks on a wind blown beach.

'Your family?' I asked, more to be saying something than out of genuine interest.

Brandon's eyes dipped sharply to the photograph, his shoulders sagging almost imperceptibly. He looked at it for a few seconds, during which I realised the photo was at least twenty years old. And then I found myself wondering why he hadn't replaced it with something more recent.

Brandon looked back up at me with a sadness that answered my unspoken question, and made me regret the one I had voiced.

'How can I help you, Mr Harper?'

I accepted his help out of the hole I had dug myself into and returned to the reason I had come here. 'There's been another killing.'

'Yes. Another young woman.' He nodded importantly, but for the first time I wondered if his motives were perhaps more than personal aggrandisement. If that nod of importance was for the need to see justice done, where, perhaps, it had not been done in the past.

Brandon was sitting forward now, his mind focused once more. 'Detective Chief Inspector Darroch called me this morning to give me some details. Iain was keen for me to get to work immediately. Especially now the press know there is a serial killer at work.'

I still had not read Charlotte's article, and doubted I ever would. By the end of the day there would be a hundred articles about the murders, and yet, what could any of them tell me?

Brandon was still talking. 'Obviously, I can't discuss the case with someone outside the official investigation.'

'Do you know who the victim is?' I asked

'Actually, I know very little thus far. I have a duty to my patients to honour my appointments before I begin to look at this latest case.'

'There was no biblical reference carved into the victim,' I told him. 'What does that mean?'

Brandon tilted his head back and examined me. 'My, my. You are well-informed. Inspector Stewart certainly seems to be keeping you up to date.'

'I found the body.'

He sat up, interested now. 'I assume this was not coincidence then?'

'I knew the victim. He killed her because of me. He wanted me to find her.'

'You seem very sure of that.'

'He used a kitchen knife to pin a photo of me to her chest. A photo she had taken. So yes, I'm fairly certain.'

My anger didn't seem to trouble Brandon. He merely sucked in his cheeks as he thought about what I had said. He also seemed to have forgotten any misgivings he had about discussing the case with me.

'Then that's why there was no reference left. The reference is his way of telling us why the victim was chosen. In this case the photograph provides that information. You say this girl took the photograph of you? Were you close?'

'We'd only just met. But he obviously thought we were close.'

'Why? Because he killed her?'

'Yeah.'

'That doesn't necessarily follow,' Brandon said, frowning. 'We could be looking at a hierarchical selection of victims.'

'You've lost me.'

Brandon picked up a gleaming silver pen from his desk, pulled a notepad towards him and began to scribble. 'Imagine an archery target.' He held up the pad and showed me the four concentric circles he had drawn. 'Each circle represents a step closer to you, with you being the bullseye. Each ring has a different value to him, depending on how close it is to you. The latest victim…'

'Charlotte MacGregor,' I interjected.

'Ms MacGregor,' Brandon acknowledged, 'may be the outer ring. He may kill others from there, or he may now move in a level.' He pointed at the second largest circle.

'Someone closer to me.'

'It may be someone very close. But he may wish to take his time. He may wish to utilise another layer before he comes to those closest to you.' Brandon's pen now pointed to the next smallest circle. Then he moved it to rest on the bullseye. 'And finally you.'

'Why has he changed his pattern?'

'You mean, forgoing the biblical reference?' Brandon pursed his lips and considered. Had he been standing I knew he would now be rocking back and forth on his heels. 'It's possible that the biblical references were not what they seemed.'

'He was trying to throw us off the scent?'

'Not exactly. The biblical aspect may have been a rationalisation he clung to. Something to convince himself that he was not to blame. A way of passing the blame onto the victims.'

'So you think he's found another way of doing that now?'

'Perhaps. He may still come back to the biblical messages; he may take strength from them. He could also have convinced himself that you are evil in some way, and that those around you deserve to die for protecting you. Therefore he does not need to label them in the same way. Their connection to you is reason enough.'

'You think?'

Brandon waved a dismissive hand. 'It's a theory. I wouldn't say at this juncture that it's definitive. Remember, I don't have all the facts yet.'

I knew exactly how he felt. The more facts I gathered the less useful any of them appeared to be. I realised I had wasted my time by coming here and I stood up to leave.

'I merely suggest,' Brandon added, 'that you don't become too focused on people with religious backgrounds.'

'Well, the only strongly religious people connected to the case so far are the previous victim's parents who couldn't handle him being gay. I can't see them being responsible for four deaths.'

Brandon nodded. 'Well, I wish you luck. I suspect this is more troublesome than the cases you're used to. We're a long way from lurking in the shadows watching husbands and wives having affairs or looking for runaways.'

I stood up to leave and my hand was on the door handle when Brandon spoke again. 'Do come and see me again if you wish to discuss any more aspects of your investigation. I'm afraid I can't give you any confidential information, but I'm always happy to offer guidance when it comes to matters of the mind.'

'I'll bear that in mind. Thanks for your time.' I paused before I left. 'Shouldn't you be worried about being seen with me? That could qualify you for the outer circle.'

Brandon gave me a thin, humourless smile. 'I suspect your admirer has already moved beyond that circle. Ask yourself why Charlotte MacGregor in particular was chosen first. Could it be because she was a young, pretty female? Because she would remind you of Katie Jarvie? Because he knows what effect that would have on you?'

I was stunned and for a second could find no words to speak. 'How do you know about Katie?' I eventually asked.

Brandon gave me an apologetic look. 'You know, the police didn't necessarily take your word for it that you were not involved in these killings. They asked me to give them my opinion, and of course, before I could do that, they needed to give me your background.'

'And what was your opinion?' I asked through gritted teeth.

'That you are completely innocent, of course.' Brandon slid his glasses to the end of his nose and looked at me over them. 'However, I'm glad I know about Ms Jarvie. It tells me something about how this killer is operating. He's manipulating you, making you dance to his tune, destroying you from the inside out. He knows you. He knows how you think, how you act, and how to pull your strings. The longer you avoid him, the more people around you will suffer. More people will die before you do.'

I wanted to tell him he was wrong. I wanted to tell him that I would protect those close to me, that no-one else would have to die. I wanted to tell him that I would find this man and stop him before he could wreak any more havoc.

But no words would come. The empty platitudes and pointless bravado died in my throat and I turned from him in silence, pulling my coat tight around me as I stepped into the street. The wind buffeted me and the rain began to slant in from the north, driving into my face as I trudged along Byres Road, sure that the trail of contamination I left in my wake was visible to those I passed.

I got back into my car and sat there without turning on the ignition, my eyes closed as the world spun around me. The rain continued to hammer down on the metal and glass around me, reminding me of the countless times I had been on surveillance in weather like this, the rain obscuring the target. Normally though, when I was on surveillance it wasn't a matter of life and death. I had never been charged with protecting someone from a psychopathic serial killer, and I was thankful for that. For all that I sometimes found my day-to-day work dull and unchallenging, it was relatively safe and it paid the bills. I was now in a position where I was risking my life – and a great many others – with the probability of not getting paid at the end of it. Right now, a cosy little marital dispute would be a relief.

I could hear Brandon's words in my head and knew he was right: This case was nothing like I was used to. *Lurking in the shadows watching husbands and wives having affairs or looking for runaways,* was how he put it, and for the most part that was the truth. I had become involved in this case to essentially search for a missing child. True, Archie Bell's daughter may be twenty, but she was still his only child and he wanted her to come home safely.

My eyes fluttered open again as I thought about that. About what I had been hired to do, and what I do on a daily basis. My mind raced back over the case files and my heart began to accelerate, gathering momentum as a tiny alarm bell rang in the back of my mind.

Twenty-Eight

I called Jessica and told her what I'd found. What I *thought* I'd found. She saw my point but she didn't jump on it with the same excitement I had felt.

'It's thin,' she said.

'Thin?'

'Thin.'

'It's maybe a little undernourished, but thin?'

'Practically anorexic.'

'But it feels right,' I persisted.

'Maybe. Let's see if we can put some meat on those bones first, before we make twats of ourselves with this.'

'When have I ever led you in the wrong direction?' I asked innocently.

There was a pause before Jessica answered. When she did her voice was a little frosty. 'I've told Aaron it's over. He's angry, and I understand why. I've bet on you, Harper, so don't mess this up.'

'I won't.'

*

It had been only a few hours since I had left Gordon Tierney, but he had deteriorated rapidly even in that time. When he answered the door his hair was even more unruly, his untucked shirt more rumpled, his eyes even more bleary and bloodshot. He said nothing, merely looked through me as though he had expected someone else to come knocking on his door.

'Gordon,' I said. 'Can I come in for a few minutes? I just have some follow up questions.'

'Of course,' he said quietly before once more leading me to his lounge.

I felt guilty as I took a seat opposite him. Letting him believe earlier that I was a police officer was one thing, but coming back and being invited into his home, knowing the pain I was about to cause him, was something else entirely. I felt small and vile and knew it was only going to get worse.

Tierney sat and looked out of the window, seemingly unaware that I was there. He wasn't being evasive; he was simply in too much pain to bother with social niceties.

'I'm sorry, Gordon,' I began, awkwardly. 'But this is important.'

That seemed to get his attention, and his eyes cleared a little.

'There's something you're not telling me,' I said softly.

Tierney said nothing, merely turned back towards the window. A tear began to gather at the corner of his eye and I felt like weeping myself.

'Who did you have the affair with, Gordon?'

It was the cruellest of blows and it struck deep. A huge, choking sob escaped his lips and his shoulders shuddered. His head bent forward and he cradled it in his hands as the tears flowed. I wanted to go to him, but I had no idea what to say or how to comfort him and so I sat in awkward silence until the sobs subsided and Tierney lifted his head. His wet, red eyes bored into mine with a new intensity.

'How important is this?'

'Vital,' I said. 'Or I wouldn't ask.'

I saw again the guilty look of a cheating spouse that I had seen earlier. I hadn't been expecting it and I'd missed it. Until Eric Brandon's words had made me think about my usual cases and I had recognised the look I'd seen a hundred times before.

'His name's Fraser Irving. I met him through work,' Tierney said.

'Did Keith know?'

'No.'

'Did he suspect?'

'Yes,' Tierney gasped.

'How do you know?'

'I ended it six months ago. Keith didn't mention it till later though, maybe a month ago. He apologised and blamed himself for being jealous and paranoid.'

'Was he the jealous type?'

'Yes, he was very insecure. But I'd never cheated on him before. I put an end to it after three months. The guilt was tearing me apart.'

'How did Mr Irving take it?'

'He wasn't bothered. I realised afterwards that it had just been about the sex for him.' He shook his head in disgust, and I knew it was with himself. 'I can't believe I risked it all for something so stupid.'

'So he wasn't jealous of Keith at all?' It was unlikely that Fraser Irving was Keith Lamont's killer, but the question had to be asked.

'Not at all,' Tierney answered. 'He probably had some other guy in his bed within an hour of me calling it off.'

'If Keith was the jealous type when there was no reason for him to be suspicious, how did he become convinced that he was wrong when you were actually having an affair?'

Tierney looked at the floor and I could see his shoulders tense. Mine did too: this was the crucial question.

'I don't know,' Tierney said, 'I really don't. It doesn't make sense.' Then he went back to looking out of the window, his eyes momentarily free from tears.

Damn.

I looked at my hands and wondered what to do now. Was I wrong after all?

Then Tierney spoke again. 'I don't know how they missed it.'

Bingo.

'How who missed it?' I asked.

'He hired a private detective. Just like in the movies. He hired a man to spy on me to see if I was being unfaithful.' Another shudder ran through Tierney as he said that last word.

'So why didn't this detective find anything?' I asked. 'Were you being discreet?'

'No, we were stupidly blatant. That's why I can't understand how he didn't find out. We went out together, bars, clubs… anyone following us could have figured it out.'

I wondered about that. I knew that some private detectives were little better than nosey neighbours, but from what Tierney had said, the most incompetent investigator should have been able to uncover his infidelity.

'Do you know the name of the company?' I asked.

'No. Keith never told me. He just told me he'd hired someone. I didn't want to push it in case he started thinking he'd hired a bunch of cowboys and hired someone else to do a more thorough job.'

Tierney broke down again and I looked awkwardly at him as I made my way to the door. My conscience was far from clear at forcing Tierney to face this aspect of his relationship with his dead lover, and I knew leaving him alone now was particularly cruel, but I had a scent to follow for the first time in this case and I had to move quickly.

As I passed Tierney he grabbed my arm and looked at me with haunted eyes. 'I loved him. You have to understand that. I may have been unfaithful, but it doesn't mean I loved him any less.'

'I know,' I said.

And I left.

Because we both knew it did.

*

I prayed that Archie Bell would be at home as I pulled up behind his Volvo. My luck was in; he answered the door on the first ring, as though he had been expecting me.

He led me through to the small living room and I could see that he was his usual defeated self. He flopped awkwardly into his armchair as though he was a robot whose power had been suddenly disconnected. I sat on the sofa against the wall and noticed two tumblers on the coffee table in front of me, a small amber residue at the bottom of each and I wondered if it was the only thing preventing a complete collapse. It was after five o'clock now and I suspected Archie's dinner would consist of more of the same.

Kelvinside wasn't all that far away, not in miles, but it was still a long way from there to here. Archie's home was shabby by comparison with Tierney's luxurious apartment, and yet their grief rendered material objects irrelevant.

'Archie,' I began, 'I need to check something with you. It could be important, but it might be nothing. I don't want to get your hopes up.'

I realised then that Archie hadn't even bothered to ask me if I had found Janet's killer yet, or even if I had made any progress, and I realised just how little cause for optimism anyone had been able to give him.

'Okay,' Archie said.

'This might sound a bit off the wall, but, did Janet ever consult a private investigator, or mention one at all?'

Archie looked at me blankly for a few seconds. 'No. Why would she?'

'I don't know. It could have been anything. Are you sure?'

'Yes, absolutely. She would have told me if she did.'

Damn.

'Why do you ask?' Archie asked.

'I thought we'd found a connection between Janet and some of the other victims, but I must be wrong.' I felt all of the excitement fade and the adrenaline begin to ebb from my system as my theory slid through my fingers like sand.

'Oh, well, maybe if I have a think about it,' Archie said hurriedly. I could see in his face how desperately he wanted to do something, anything, that would help catch his daughter's killer. The awareness that he could do nothing was painful for him. I knew the feeling.

'It's okay, Archie. I got it wrong. I'll let you know when I come up with something concrete.' I stood up and walked to the door, leaving Archie slumped in his armchair, impotent and powerless.

Outside, I climbed into the Honda and drove off. I had another two stops to make, but I suspected they would be as unproductive as this one. I could only hope that Jessica was having better luck than I was.

Twenty-Nine

An hour later I was in the pub. A dim, gloomy bar that matched my mood. The rest of the customers were like me, huddled over their drinks in silence, all but hanging out signs telling the rest of the world to *piss right off*. I sat in a booth in the back, nursing a beer and staring into the distance, my eyes seeing only Charlotte's brutalised body. It was an image that had been hovering in my peripheral vision since I had opened that bathroom door.

Had that really only been this morning?

'Ground control to Major Tom,' called a voice.

I snapped out of it and looked up in time to see Jessica walking towards me, her long legs striding across the pub in jeans that hugged her thighs. She slid in opposite me and placed two beers on the table, pushing one of them towards me.

'You look like you need another.'

I toasted her with the bottle I was holding then finished it off, swapped it for the new one and took a long pull from that.

'So,' Jessica said, 'you going to spill, or am I going to have to beat it out of you?'

'Good and bad,' I told her.

'Oh, stop being so bloody cryptic.'

'Well, Gordon Tierney admitted to having an affair.'

'Bonus points for spotting that.'

I tipped an imaginary hat in Jessica's direction. 'He also confirmed that Keith Lamont was suspicious and hired an investigator to follow him.'

'Excellent. Did he get caught?'

'No. Tierney can't figure that out. Says he and this other guy were so blatant that anyone following him couldn't have failed to figure it out. He's no idea how they got away with it.'

'So Keith never knew?'

'Nope. Must have hired the worst PI around.'

'I thought you didn't know him?' Jessica said with barely disguised glee.

'Hilarious.'

'I thought so,' she said, a low dirty chuckle escaping her lips. 'Did he give you the investigator's name?'

'No. Couldn't tell me anything about them at all.'

'Damn.' Jessica scratched behind her ear in absent frustration, her deep purple nails digging into her skin.

'It gets worse. Archie was certain Janet never mentioned a PI, or would have had any reason to consult one.'

'What about her friends?'

'No luck there either. After speaking to Archie I went to the hairdressers where Janet worked and spoke to her friend Leeann. Janet never mentioned anything to her either.'

'Leeann's the girl whose credit card she pinched to use at the hotel?' Jessica said.

'Yeah.'

'Some pal.'

'Leeann doesn't mind. She says she knows Janet would have paid her back as soon as she'd sorted everything out.'

'Any other friends?' Jessica asked.

'Just one. Rebecca Davidson. But she's still on holiday. Spoke to her mum again, asked her to make sure Rebecca gives me a call as soon as she's back, but that's not for another couple of days. We can't wait that long.'

Jessica looked around the pub for a few seconds, pulling at her lip with two fingers as she thought. There was never any stillness with Jessica when she was thinking. She was always fidgeting in some way, her mannerisms telling you she was deep in thought. I finished the beer while I waited and pushed it to the side. I didn't want another; I needed to stay sharp.

'He wouldn't necessarily have known,' she said finally.

'Archie?' I replied. 'They seem to have been very close.'

'You said her mother left them when she was young, right?'

'She was four.'

'I presume you mean ran out on them, rather than died.'

'Yeah, she legged it.'

'So, what if Janet wanted to find her long lost mammy?'

I nodded, seeing what she was getting at. 'And she wouldn't necessarily want her dad to know.'

'Didn't want to hurt him. He brought her up after all.'

'So she might have consulted a PI, and never told him.'

'We've no way of knowing, but it makes sense.'

'Are we reaching?' I wondered.

'Definitely. But there's a distinct lack of other options, so I say we run with it.'

'For the moment,' I agreed. 'How did you get on?'

Jessica's smile faded abruptly. 'Not very well.'

I raised my eyebrows, waiting for her to elaborate.

'Lorna Sinclair's not at home. Tried the supermarket where she works, she wasn't there and she's not due in till Friday. None of her neighbours or workmates had any idea where she might be, so I sat for a while, hoping she'd turn up. She didn't, and she's not got an answering machine.'

'At least that one's still a possibility,' I said, seeing that Jessica was frustrated.

'And then I went to see the Bitches of Eastwick.'

'Ah, you liked Siobhan's old flatmates, eh?'

'The quiet one's fine. But the other two? What a pair of cows. Don't know how I kept my hands off their throats.'

'Tempting, isn't it?'

'If I'd started I'd never have stopped.' Jessica smiled again. 'Anyway, I asked the question, and once I'd filtered out all the bullshit and bitchiness, got a resounding *dunno*.'

'Can't blame her for not telling them. Did they have any ideas why she might have consulted a PI?'

'None at all. Fiona suggested she'd done it just to get some attention, but that sounds more like something she'd do.'

'I'll need to remind my secretary not to take any calls from a Fiona Matheson,' I said.

'What secretary?'

'Fancy the job?'

Jessica appraised me over the top of her beer. 'What, so you can chase me round the desk?' She put the bottle to her lips, oblivious to the thoughts going through my mind. 'Actually, the way Crawford's running the company, I'll probably be looking for a job soon enough.'

That silenced us both. Jessica was quiet while she contemplated her future career. I looked out of the window as I thought about what Crawford Laing was doing to his father's legacy, as well as the effect it would have on Jessica, Phil and Tim. I shrugged those thoughts off quickly, well aware that there were more pressing issues facing us.

'Think we're on the right track?' I said to Jessica, drawing her back from her own gloomy thoughts.

Jessica began to flick her upper lip with a fingernail as she thought it over.

It seemed much longer than a few hours since the idea had first come to me. It was Eric Brandon's words that had started me thinking, and, as I realised Gordon Tierney had been torn apart by guilt as well as grief, it came to me. What if Keith Lamont had suspected his lover was cheating on him? What if he hired a private investigator to follow him?

And I remembered that Gemma Sinclair had wanted to find the son she had given away. She'd wanted it just as badly as Archie Bell wanted to find his own missing child, and maybe she too had hired a private investigator.

And there it was – a possible link. It seemed thin and tenuous even now, but when the seed had first planted itself in my mind it immediately made a strange kind of sense.

I thought about the other victims and wondered what reasons they could have had for consulting a private investigator. The only way to know for sure was to ask those closest to them and hope they could enlighten us.

'Well,' Jessica said eventually, drawing the word out, 'we agree Charlotte MacGregor was killed for another reason. Of the other four, only Keith contacted an investigator for certain.' She took a slug of her beer. 'Gemma and Janet both had possible reasons for contacting one, but we don't know if they did, and Siobhan may not have had any reason to.'

'Yes or no,' I said. 'Do you believe it?'

'Yes,' Jessica replied, without hesitation. 'We need a couple more confirmations before we take it to Stewart, but I believe it.'

I nodded my agreement as my phone began to vibrate in my pocket. I took it out and looked at the display, mentally bracing myself as I saw a number I didn't recognise.

I pressed the answer button. 'Hello?'

'Mr Harper?' said a man's voice.

'Yes?'

'It's Archie Bell.' His voice sounded strained and I sat up straighter.

'What can I do for you, Archie?' I asked. I leant into the middle of the table and turned the volume up as high as it would go as Jessica leant towards me.

'It's about what you asked earlier.'

'Yes?'

'I'm sorry. I wasn't entirely truthful with you.' He sounded like a man weighed down by shame and regret.

'What do you mean?'

'I'm sorry,' he said again, 'I was too ashamed to tell you, but I know it must be important or you wouldn't ask.'

'It is, Archie. It's crucial.'

'Janet did mention something a few years back,' he said, his voice cracking.

I could feel a jolt of electricity jump between Jessica and I. 'About hiring a detective?'

'Yes. She wanted to find her mother.' For the first time I heard a trace of anger in Archie's voice. Not at his daughter, but at the woman who had left them both. 'She wanted to meet her. She thought a detective would be able to find her.'

'Did she consult one?' I asked.

'Not that I know of. But she might have done. She knew I wasn't keen, so she might not have told me.'

'Did she mention any names? A company? A person?'

'No. Just the general idea. It was years ago though. She never mentioned it again.' Archie almost sobbed. 'I'm sorry I lied. I didn't want you to think I was a bad parent. Janet only wanted to meet her so she could ask her why she left. Not because I wasn't good enough.'

'I know, Archie,' I said softly. 'I know.'

I heard a racking sob from the other end of the line. 'Does it help?'

'I think so, Archie,' I said, choosing my words carefully. 'I'll let you know.'

I told him to look after himself and to call me if he remembered anything else, or if there was anything I could do for him.

Jessica and I looked at one another as I ended the call. 'It's not a confirmation,' Jessica said.

'No, but the idea was in Janet's head,' I replied.

'That's as good as we'll get. We need either Gemma or Siobhan, then we can try to convince Stewart.'

'Lorna Sinclair would probably know. She and Gemma were very close. Plus, Gemma had the more obvious reason to hire a PI.'

'We can't sit around waiting for her to show up though. For all we know she's away on holiday,' Jessica said. 'I don't fancy waiting around for a couple of days till she returns to work, hoping that a sociopath doesn't try to gut us in the meantime.'

'Then we find out about Siobhan.'

'How? Her flatmates are beyond useless and she won't have told her dad anything.'

'No,' I said, 'but I know a man who knows more than he's telling.'

Jessica's eyebrows crept up. 'Drew Nolan?'

'The first time I met him, he knew a lot more than he told me. And I don't think it's anything to do with the porn films she was making. Whether it's useful or not, we'll see. But there's only one way to find out.'

'What, you're just going to stroll in and ask him? After knocking him around the last time?'

'Pretty much.'

'I like your style,' Jessica said with a wicked smile. 'Let's go get him, tiger.'

Thirty

We left the pub and headed to my office to work out a plan. Despite my bravado I wasn't going to stick my head into the bear pit without checking if a few more grizzlies had moved in. I sat behind the desk and put my feet up while Jessica lay on the worn-out couch against the opposite wall, her feet hanging off the end, tapping against the radiator in time to whatever tune was stuck in her head.

I picked up the phone and dialled Mack.

'Yeah?' he answered.

'I'm going to see Drew Nolan again.'

'Count me in. Fiver says he pisses himself again.'

I explained what I wanted to ask him and told Mack that I didn't think we'd catch him cold again.

'Good,' Mack said with enthusiasm. 'Last time was a bit tame.'

Tame?

I told him to meet us at my office and hung up.

'Let me guess,' Jessica said. 'He's already looking out his knuckle dusters.'

'Don't forget the nunchuks.'

We both laughed and Jessica tapped her foot a little too hard against the radiator. It sagged away from the wall and she sat up in a panic before it steadied itself.

'Don't worry, it does that,' I told her.

'And you haven't got it fixed?'

'It's still attached, isn't it?' I said defensively. 'Anyway, it's only if you knock it in the wrong direction.'

Fixing a radiator was low on my list of priorities when the money wasn't exactly rolling in. And it had slipped even further down the list in the last few days. Maybe when I had a paying client I'd get something done about it.

Jessica shrugged, pushed the radiator back against the wall and asked what the plan was. I tapped a pen on the edge of the desk as I thought about it, then said, 'Mack and I go in, ask Nolan if Siobhan ever mentioned a PI, and find out what he's not telling us.'

'You and Mack?' Jessica raised her eyebrows ominously.

'Yeah. He knows what we're capable of.'

'And what? You don't need any help?'

'We managed the last time.' I was getting defensive because I knew where Jessica was going with this. But I wasn't being sexist. She was more than capable of holding her own and I knew it. The truth was; I couldn't stand the thought of her being hurt.

Not that she'd let me off that easily.

'Like you told Mack, you won't catch him off guard again. He could have backup. I'm as much a part of this case as you are, so stop being such an arse and come up with a plan that involves all three of us. Okay?'

I wilted under the heat of her glare and realised there was no way I could stop her coming with us. Fortunately, she had given me an idea.

'You're right, he could have backup. So we can't go in blind. He knows Mack and I, so we can't check it out. You go in, have a look around, then leave and let us know how it looks. If everything's cool, we go in.'

'While I sit in the car?'

'No. You go in, ask for directions, come back out and drive away. We can't take the chance of tipping them off. Most of his customers have more tattoos than they have teeth, whereas you… well, you're not what they expect to see in there. And you're wearing a wire so we know the natives aren't getting restless.'

Jessica sighed, but she knew my plan made sense. She stuck out a petted lip and folded her arms like a child being denied a trip to the zoo. 'You know, I remember when you used to be fun.'

*

The car clock passed nine p.m. as I drove towards the East End of the city, Mack beside me in the passenger seat, his eyes crackling with fire. Jessica would leave a few minutes later, giving us time to find a suitable place to watch her enter The Gibbet.

I finished telling Mack the full story and how we hoped Nolan would confirm our suspicions. I hadn't bothered with a plan for after we entered the pub. I already knew the one that Mack had in mind. *Punch, kick, headbutt. Repeat.*

The takeaway place was closed tonight and we parked opposite with a view of The Gibbet's front door. The street was dark but we slid down in our seats before I called Jessica and gave her the go ahead. I then took two earpieces from my pocket, handed one to Mack and placed the other in my left ear.

A five-year-old maroon Ford Mondeo appeared in the rear-view mirror minutes later and slowed to a crawl before stopping a little past the pub and pulling into the side of the road. Jessica climbed out, looking every inch the wary, lone female, unsure if asking for help around here was preferable to being lost. She looked around nervously then headed reluctantly towards the door of the only lit building in the street.

There was a little burst of static as she neared the door and switched the microphone on. We had tested it in my office but I was still relieved to know it was working when we needed it too. Jessica stopped beneath the sickly yellow bulb above the door, placed her hand on the door and whispered, 'Are you sure you don't want me to just kick all their arses?'

Mack laughed beside me, though he'd be distraught if there was violence and he missed it. The transmission was one-way and we said nothing. I held my breath for a few seconds after Jessica disappeared from view, releasing it only when I heard her voice.

'Em, sorry to bother you,' she said softly, her voice suddenly meek and helpless. I willed her not to overdo it; Drew Nolan might not be able to resist too much vulnerability.

'What?' came a rough, unwelcoming voice I recognised as Nolan's. Then he must have looked in Jessica's direction, for his voice became considerably friendlier, though no more appealing. 'Well, hello. How can I help you, darling?'

I could picture him, eyeing Jessica from top to toe, and I felt a fuse light within me at the thought of his eyes violating her.

'I'm afraid I've taken a wrong turning. Silly me! Would you be able to point me in the right direction?'

'Of course. But surely you'll stay and have one with me first?' Nolan slimed. 'You look like you could do with a stiff one.'

My fingers had already tensed on the door handle when Jessica said, 'I'm afraid I'm already late. I called my friend and told her where I was but she's no good at directions, so I told her I would just pop in here and ask. She didn't even know where The Gibbet was!'

I smiled in the darkness of the car and let go of the door handle. Smart move. She'd just told Nolan that someone would be looking for her if she didn't show up soon. And they'd come here first.

'Right, well,' Nolan said brusquely. 'Where are you looking for?'

'Could you point me in the direction of London Road?' Jessica asked sweetly.

'Aye sure.' Nolan then gave her completely inaccurate directions and told her to drive safely. After a short thanks Jessica appeared outside the door of the pub and safely out of Nolan's clutches. She headed quickly back to the Mondeo and climbed in, remaining silent as she started the car and drove off in the direction Nolan had told her to.

It was only after she disappeared from sight that her voice came through our earpieces. 'Christ, I need a shower.'

There was a small click as she switched off her microphone before leaving range. After a few seconds my mobile began to vibrate. I answered quickly.

'Right,' Jessica said, 'Nolan's there, behind the bar and looking a bit the worse for wear. There are four others. One old boy, sixties, quite small, sitting at the bar talking to him. Two younger guys, thirties, at a table on the far left, both quite big lads. And one big fat guy, Big Billy I'm guessing, sitting at a table on the right, carrying a stick and wearing a knee support. And his face is banged up something rotten. Nice job, Mack.'

Mack smiled and gave a little bow.

'No-one else?' I asked.

'Nope. Unless he's got a bunch of guys hiding in the toilets on the off-chance you show up.'

'Cheers, Jess. I'll give you a call when we're done.'

'Sure you don't want a hand?' Jessica's voice told me how tough it would be for her to sit there and wait for my call.

'I'd rather there was one of us that Nolan didn't know about. You never know when that might come in handy. If you come back and someone sees you we lose that.'

'Fine,' Jessica sighed, knowing I was right. 'Call me as soon as you're out. And remember, Harper; this isn't a Die Hard movie, and you're not John McClane.'

'No. But I think I might be sitting beside him.'

'Yippi ki yay, Jessica!' Mack called.

She hung up. I turned to Mack and asked what he thought.

'No bother,' he replied. 'Fatso isn't going to be an issue if his legs fucked. The old guy at the bar won't be a problem. Leaves us with Nolan – who's a pussy – and the two other guys, who might or might not want to get involved. They're an unknown quantity, but we're good. Three on two, I'd back us.'

'You ready to do this then?'

'Always.'

We left the car and walked to the door. We went in quick and I headed straight for the bar where Nolan had his head bowed talking to the old guy. Mack followed, eyeing the rest of the bar. Nolan looked up and I watched for the surprise spreading across his face as he recognised us.

It never came.

Nolan reached under the bar as I advanced on him, his hands searching for the sawn-off baseball bat. The object he came up with was sawn-off alright, but this time I found myself looking into the twin barrels of a shotgun.

My feet ground to an abrupt halt as malicious intent spread across Nolan's bruised and swollen face. I looked around for a way out and saw the two guys on the left were also on their feet, each pointing a handgun at us.

At a shout from Nolan a door opened in the back and four men poured through. As the door closed behind them I saw the symbol on it and felt sick. Jessica had joked, but Nolan had indeed hidden a bunch of guys in the toilets on the off-chance we turned up.

At three on two I had fancied our chances. At nine on two the fight-or-flight response took hold and adrenaline began to flood my body. It didn't look like flight was going to be an option though. As soon as we turned our backs to make for the door they'd open fire. And they couldn't miss.

'Get those fuckers on the floor!' Nolan shouted.

The four guys from the toilets charged at us and we reacted instinctively, stepping forward to meet them. I launched a front kick at the first one to reach me, his progress stopping abruptly as he folded at the waist. The next one was on me quickly and I felt a fist catch me on the side of the head. It wasn't a solid punch and I rolled with it, bringing my knee up and driving it into the guy's thigh. It slowed him up, but only long enough to let his pal regain his balance and throw a couple of punches at me. None connected with any power, but as I blocked them a gap formed between Mack and I.

Mack was now six feet away, and as I caught a hold of the guy's head and spun him into a table I saw Mack throw four elbows in the time it took me to blink. By the time the last one landed the guy before him was crumpling to the floor, his face ruined and bloodied. The next one looked wary for a second, then, glancing past me, he regained his confidence. I sneaked a quick look as I dodged another punch, now finding myself with my back to a table, and saw the two guys with the guns wade into the fray, the guns tucked into their waistbands.

Despite the uneven numbers I felt a surge of hope. If we could get a hold of one of those guns we had a chance. I drove a straight right into the nearest face and felt his legs go. Mack had floored a second guy, though this one was already struggling to his feet. He turned towards me and as he did so a stick whipped through the air and connected with the back of his head. He stumbled forward, revealing the obese figure of Big Billy behind him, stick in hand, smiling wickedly. The stick cut through the air again and I saw it thud into Mack's back. Big Billy was saying something, but the hammering of my heartbeat drowned it out as I tried to fight off the two men before me.

Suddenly a third was coming at me. The cramped space worked in my favour, preventing them from being able to attack from all sides. Then something hard connected with the side of my head and I stumbled sideways and hit the ground, trying desperately to get back to my feet before they closed in. My hand brushed against something – a beer bottle – and I realised what had been thrown at me, and what had taken me down.

A boot connected with my side and I gasped as pain lanced the length of my body. I barely had time to register that before another boot came down on my shoulder. I lashed out with my feet, making contact with something, and hoped that it was a knee or a groin. A face hovered close to mine as a punch landed on my jaw. I threw one back and missed, the face dancing tantalisingly out of range.

More blows rained in and now I could hear nothing but the blood thundering in my ears. Rage flowed through me but it was impotent against so many attackers. I no longer had any idea how many people were attacking me, or whether Mack was still on his feet. I had lost track of the guns and even who had them. All I could do was lash out and hope I landed lucky blows that might even the odds.

Then I managed to get semi-upright. I threw a hook into the side of someone's knee and knew it had hurt them. I felt a surge of energy with the knowledge that I could still cause them pain. The melee in front of me cleared for a second, and through the blood in my eyes I saw one of the guns, briefly, as it rushed towards my face. The butt crashed into my nose and I began to lose consciousness as blood ran down the back of my throat. Then something connected with the side of my head and blackness rushed forward like an old friend eager to betray me.

I embraced the darkness and let it take me to a place where I felt no pain.

Thirty-One

Time passed. How much, I couldn't say. Events came to me in hazy snatches, floating past the edges of my consciousness in a way that left me unsure if they were reality or nightmare.

I came around slowly and remained still, hoping for a clue to my situation before giving myself away. I was lying on my front, my right cheek in contact with the rough surface beneath me. I felt movement and realised I was in a moving vehicle. Then I realised the rough surface wasn't underneath my head, it was all around it. I tested my wrists and ankles as discreetly as possible and was surprised to find they weren't bound. Then something hard pressed against my temple, pushing my cheek into the floor.

'This is a shotgun.' The metal pushed harder still into my skin, in case I hadn't made the connection. 'Your head's in a sack in case you move. Makes cleaning the van easier. Got it?'

I said nothing. I was in a van, being taken somewhere at gunpoint with a sack over my head. Not a promising development. It was no surprise witty banter had deserted me.

I had no idea how long I had been out, and I had no idea where we were. I thought of all those movies where the kidnapping victim hears something that can identify where he is and almost laughed at how ludicrous that was. What good would it do me if I detected a change in the road surface and knew we'd crossed a bridge?

What a load of bollocks.

Instead I began to take stock of my injuries. I knew already that my nose was broken from the gun butt, though it had at least stopped bleeding and my throat was clear of blood. The side of my head where the beer bottle felled me throbbed painfully and felt like an egg had been pushed under the skin. The back of my head had one to match, and my side and shoulder throbbed in rhythm with my pulse but neither seemed serious. I was lucky to have avoided more lasting damage, yet somehow I didn't feel like buying a lottery ticket just yet.

The van soon slowed to a stop. We idled for a moment and I heard a thin metal shutter rise. Then the van lurched forward and the shutter rattled back down behind us. The van veered slightly left and stopped as the driver yanked on the handbrake.

The engine died and there was movement around me. The back doors popped open and the van rose as bodies climbed out. I was hauled out and carried across the concrete floor of a large room that echoed with the sound of footsteps. My legs were dropped to the floor and I was forced onto a chair. Suddenly a fist crashed into my face. The shock of the unexpected blow made me cry out with pain as my broken nose was crushed again. My arms were wrenched behind me and tied to the chair, then my ankles, and by the time the fireworks had cleared from my eyes I was helplessly bound to the chair. I could flex my toes, but that didn't hold much promise of providing an escape route.

The men stepped away from me now and two new sets of footfalls approached, one of which sounded like it was dragging one leg. Good. Hope it was permanent.

The footsteps stopped beside me and another few seconds passed before the sack was wrenched roughly from my head. I blinked several times at the sudden light. When my vision cleared I saw Drew Nolan standing before me, his jet black hair hanging long beside the victorious smile plastered across his smashed face. Big Billy stood slightly behind him, leaning on his stick. He had been the one dragging his leg, and I took great pleasure in seeing the damage Mack and I had inflicted on them.

'Surprise!' Nolan exclaimed. Then he hit me. I saw it coming but there was nothing I could do to avoid it. It hurt. Really hurt. The only positive thing about it was that he threw a hook, rather than a straight. One more blow to my nose would probably put me out again.

'Think you could just swan back into my bar, did you?' Nolan's face was contorted in outrage. 'Here's a tip, boy. Finish what you start.'

He lifted his knee high and stamped on my groin. Pain rolled across my body like backdraft from an inferno. Then came the sickness and I threw up, a reddish spray of blood and vomit splattering around Nolan's feet.

'Duly noted,' I gasped, as I spat the last of it from my lips.

Nolan looked like he would happily smack me around for the rest of the week, but he turned and led Big Billy away, the fat man looking disappointed that he hadn't been allowed to have any fun. His eyes lingered on me as he limped away. I looked at the stick he was leaning heavily on and noticed it was slick with blood.

'Where's Mack?' I asked. I didn't want to give them the satisfaction, but I had to know.

Nolan turned. 'Now... what was it I told the lads to do with him?' He paused and pretended to think. 'Oh, that's right. *Dig him a shallow fucking grave.* Last time I saw him he was eating the barrels of a shotgun.'

The two of them turned away laughing. My head spun and my stomach fell through the floor. Something inside me cracked and splintered as I realised Mack had rescued me from trouble for the last time, and it had been I who had involved him in this. For all that his restless soul had actively sought trouble and revelled in physical confrontation, many of those occasions had been to either protect me or to help me achieve my goals.

There was no denying the truth; he'd be alive but for me.

I wanted to scream and roar and weep, all at the same time. But this time I would not give them the satisfaction. I vowed to myself, quietly and resolutely, that no matter what else happened today, Drew Nolan would die.

I focused my attention on the room I was in, seeing it now for the first time. I sat on a lone chair in the centre of what appeared to be a disused factory. The room was roughly the size of a football pitch. Fifty yards to my left was the metal shutter where we had entered. It was rusted, with several holes in it, but would still prevent a quick exit. To my right was the back wall, from which projected several bare shelves. Opposite me was the rear of the van, side on to the shuttered entrance, and dotted around the factory floor were small stacks of boxes and piles of oily rags. All around me were armed men; I counted eleven, all stone-faced and flat-eyed, watchful and aware. There were no windows and no other door that I could see. The rusted shutter appeared to be the only way out.

I heard a noise from the opposite wall, twenty yards away, where a large pile of machinery parts obscured part of the wall. The sound was that of a door opening and closing. I now knew there was another exit, but the question remained: How did I get to that door? And how did I make sure that Drew Nolan had breathed his last by the time it closed behind me?

Two men appeared from behind the rusted pile of metal and my breath caught. The man at the front was the fattest man I had ever seen, even larger than Big Billy. He led the second man by an arm as he too had a sack over his head. I felt a brief surge of hope that it was Mack, still alive and merely biding his time before unleashing hell.

My hopes were quickly dashed. The man's build was all wrong. Mack was muscular and athletic. The kind of muscle earned the hard way. The hooded man was much larger and had the muscled bulk of someone who lifted as many steroids as he did weights.

Whoever he was he'd taken a beating already. His white t-shirt was splattered with blood, most of it appearing to have oozed from beneath the sack. He staggered forward, compliant with wherever the fat man led him. Another man appeared from somewhere with a chair and sat it down facing me, a gap of eight feet between us. The hooded figure was pushed into it and I watched as he too was tied to the chair.

The fat man waddled towards me, stopping a few feet away and watching me with a strange intensity. He was in his forties, and so obese I was amazed he could remain standing without his knees collapsing. His hair was thick and curly, a greasy black mullet growing long down his neck. The face was swarthy and marked with long scars that looked the product of knife fights. Sweat glistened on his forehead above a thick monobrow, large Slavic nose and straggly goatee.

But it was the eyes that stood out. Small, dark, piggy eyes. Set deep in his face like half-buried obsidian, they smouldered with something cruel that longed for release. His hands remained behind his back, and if the intention was to make me worry about what was held there, then mission accomplished.

'You are aware of who I am?' he said. His accent was thick, Eastern European.

'Yes,' I said, the accent confirming my fears. 'You're Reuben Volta.'

I had never seen him before. Unlike Innes McKenzie even the newspapers seemed reluctant to print photographs of him; as though doing so would incur his wrath. I had heard him described though. And again recently. I had heard him described in the tortured story of a young woman racked with pain.

'I also know that you call yourself The Director, and that you make cheap porn films.' Anger that had been simmering below my fear began to boil to the surface. 'And I know that you order men to gang-rape young women and film them while they do it.'

Volta studied me for a second, his face curious. Then he smiled. 'But Mr Harper, they sell so well!'

He continued, undeterred by my look of revulsion. 'You may think of me as something cruel and evil, but remember this: there is no supply without demand.' He wagged an admonishing finger in my face. 'You may be surprised just how many men pay to watch a woman being raped. Perhaps they pretend to themselves that the rape is all an act, but they know. They may pretend to be different from me, to be respectable. But the only difference is how we react to society's boundaries. They respect them. I destroy them.'

My stomach churned, not least because I knew he was right. 'Do you remember a girl named Louise Ross?' I asked.

Volta waved an airy paw. 'So many *actresses*,' he laughed.

'She was chosen because she looked about thirteen. Chosen because she looked like a child, but wouldn't bring the heat from the cops that a kid would.'

Volta leaned close and I smelt fetid meat on his breath. 'Do not fool yourself, Mr Harper. If I want a child in my film then I will take one.'

Sickness rose in my throat and I felt the acidic burn of bile as I fought to hold it down. I saw in his face that he was capable of the very worst acts I could imagine

'Do you understand?' he asked. 'Boundaries are for weak men. Men like you. Had you been strong you would have killed Nolan at the first opportunity. You would not now be here, awaiting my mercy.'

Something in his voice told me mercy would be in short supply today.

'Do you know why I wished to speak with you, Mr Harper?' Volta asked.

'Dietary tips?' I suggested. *In for a penny...*

'Hah!' exclaimed Volta. He finally brought his hands round from behind his back and I was relieved to see they were empty. He slapped them against his huge belly and roared with laughter. 'Do you think I would take advice in a nation that will deep-fry chocolate bars? A nation that has the highest rate of heart disease in Europe?'

'You've probably doubled it since you got off the boat,' I said recklessly.

A fat hand cracked across my jaw, the speed of it astonishing. My neck snapped sideways and the chair toppled until it was caught by someone behind me. I shook my head, then decided that was a bad move and kept it still. Volta loomed in front of me.

'A few days ago I did not know who you were, Mr Harper,' he said. 'For you, this was a good thing.'

Given the present circumstances, I'd have to agree.

Volta carried on. 'You have interfered with my business. You have cost me reputation, and you have cost me money. Of course, for that you are going to die.'

Fuck.

'And why would I help you if you're going to kill me anyway?'

Volta took a knife from his pocket. An impossibly sharp knife that glinted in the light like a killer's smile. The kind of knife carried by men who knew how to use one and enjoyed doing so.

'Because, if you do not,' Volta said, 'I shall take your right arm and peel the skin from it. Then I will carve the flesh from it. To the bone. After that I shall begin with your left arm. And you shall watch, Mr Harper. Do you know how I know that? Because the very first thing I shall do is remove your eyelids. Oh yes, Mr Harper, you shall watch me carve the flesh from your bones. And after you are dead I shall make soup from your meat.'

Double fuck.

I fought the urge to vomit again. 'Well, since you ask nicely, what can I help you with?'

'Ah! So eager to please!'

Volta rolled away from me and ripped the sack from the other man's head. His head fell forward groggily until Volta raised his chin, displaying a mask of blood. His face had been beaten beyond recognition, the features swollen and ruined. It was only the cropped blonde hair, now streaked with blood, that identified him

It was Johnny D'Arienzo.

He had warned me that he had serious connections, and now I knew just how serious. But all I could think of at the moment was that I was here because I had been investigating Siobhan, and now I was faced with a link to Janet.

Volta slapped him and the crack echoed in the vast space. Johnny's eyes came alive and darted around the room before locking on Volta, his fear of the fat man so great that he never even noticed me.

'Welcome back, John.' Volta turned back to me. 'John has been lying to me, Mr Harper. The foolish boy.'

'I haven't! I swear to God I haven't!' Johnny's shook his head violently.

Volta didn't even turn round, he simply reached behind him and back-handed Johnny across the face. Johnny's head snapped sideways and his chair tipped until it was caught and then righted again by the man standing behind him.

'Now, Mr Harper,' Volta said conversationally. 'I believe you have been looking for a young lady named Janet Bell. Is that correct?'

'Yes.'

'And John was involved with Miss Bell before she disappeared.'

'Yes.'

'You have found Miss Bell?'

'Yes. She's dead.'

'As I am aware. Now, Mr Harper, this is where the water is muddy.' Volta paused for a moment and returned the knife to his pocket, before reaching inside his grubby white suit jacket for a handkerchief. He mopped his brow with it and returned the now sodden cloth to his pocket. 'What do you know about my business interests?'

'Very little,' I said. I may be daft but I'm not suicidal.

'Then I shall tell you. If you promise not to tell anyone.' He turned and winked at the watching men, who sniggered on cue. Clearly my going home wasn't part of today's agenda. 'I have many interests, Mr Harper. The movies, as you know. Some drugs, some guns, some prostitutes. And some businesses who pay well for my protection. You understand this?'

'Yes.'

'Now, this protection money. Someone must collect this for me. Someone who is not afraid to be a little physical if he must. It is a job for the body, not for the brain. I trusted John with this job.' Volta's head shook with what may have passed for disappointment had he been capable of human emotion.

Oh, Johnny. Tell me you didn't.

'Unfortunately, some of my money has vanished since John collected it.'

You stupid bastard.

Volta continued. 'John of course says he did not take it. He says that Miss Bell took the money from him. Perhaps John is not as stupid as he looks. To blame a dead person is almost clever. But of course, stealing from me is never clever.'

I thought for a second that Johnny was going to butt in – so did Volta by the way his hand raised from his side – but his lips quickly closed.

'What do you want from me?' I asked.

'I have a decision to make, Mr Harper. You will help me make it.' Volta stood beside Johnny and placed his hand on his head. The hand was massive and dwarfed even Johnny's anvil-like skull. 'Am I to believe that this man is innocent? That his girlfriend stole my money and was then coincidentally killed? Is my money now in the possession of a fortunate murderer, or is it lost somewhere?' His hand started to squeeze Johnny's skull. 'Or, am I to believe the more likely explanation that this man stole my money and blamed his dead girlfriend to escape punishment? Perhaps he even killed Janet Bell to create this story and keep my money?'

I looked at Johnny, his eyes bulging as Volta's fingers increased their pressure on his head. 'I think he would tell you if he had it.'

'Ah. But I do not think so. He knows the only thing keeping him alive is the possibility that he is innocent. Once he is found guilty he will be executed.'

A small moan escaped Johnny's lips. Volta glared at him before continuing. 'You searched for this girl. Did you find any trace of this money having been in her possession?'

I stalled. 'How much money?'

'£23,000.'

The amount was loose change to Volta, but this was about power and reputation. I dodged the money issue for the moment. As soon as I told Volta that Janet hadn't had any money I'd be joining Johnny in a shallow grave.

'Johnny didn't kill Janet Bell,' I told him.

'How can you be sure?'

'She was killed by a serial killer. The same man who's killed four other people.'

'Perhaps John is this killer,' Volta said.

'He doesn't have the brains to kill five people and get away with it.'

Volta tilted his head one way then the other, weighing it up. He seemed to agree. 'It is of no concern of mine. I care nothing for what this man does.'

'He has your money,' I said, playing on his greed.

Volta pursed his fat lips in thought. 'So finding this murderer will find my money?'

'Yes.' It was nonsense – Johnny was stupid enough to have stolen the money without considering the consequences – but if I could convince Volta that I was his best shot at getting his money back I might yet walk out of here.

'Do you know who he is?'

Not yet. But I'm close. Another few days, a week at most and I'll find him. And your money.'

'I would like this money back,' Volta mused.

Take the bait, take the bait, take the bait...

'I can find it,' Johnny said desperately. 'That bitch took it from me, but I know her… who her pals are, where she lives… I can find it. Maybe her dad found it after she was killed. I'll make him tell me.'

'Archie Bell doesn't have it,' I said. 'And you'll stay away from him. He's suffered enough.'

'You think he's suffered?' spat Johnny. 'I'll tell you something, and see if you still feel sorry for him. I followed him after Janet fucked off, figured he'd lead me to her. Gave up after the dirty bastard spent every night cruising for hookers. Didn't look to me like he was suffering.'

Volta gave Johnny an impatient look. 'All men have needs, John. Needs that I have made a great deal of money from. The man's wife had left him, what was he to do?'

Johnny's eyes flicked around frantically now that Volta was listening to him, as though he'd spotted the slimmest of chances to survive and was deciding how best to seize it. 'But he obviously wasn't worried about her! He must have known where she was, and if he knew where she was, he knew where the money was. Let me go and I can make him tell me!'

'You're full of shit, Johnny,' I said. I didn't want to condemn him to whatever fate Volta had in mind, but there was no way I was letting him turn the fat man loose on Archie. 'Janet didn't take the money, and Archie didn't go round picking up hookers every night. You've made all this up to try and fool Volta. Do you think he's stupid?'

'Fuck you! You think Archie Bell's a good guy? Then tell me why I saw him pick up a lassie that could have been his daughter. Sick fucker!'

Volta's lips tightened into a thin line. 'John, if you speak one more time without being asked a question I shall cut out your tongue.'

The Worst of Evils

Johnny's mouth snapped shut like a bear-trap.

I shook my head in disgust. Even if Archie had picked up a prostitute – which I doubted – it made no difference; at that point he believed Janet was alive and well, and she may still have been. Whether it was true or not, Archie was my client and I would treat him the same as any other client. And that meant protecting him from Johnny's desperate lies.

'Archie Bell doesn't have your money,' I told Volta. 'There's only one person who could have taken it.'

'As I thought,' Volta replied.

'He's full of shit!' Johnny shouted. 'He's probably in on it with Janet's dad. They've probably split the money between them. I recognise him now, the two of them are pals, I've seen them together.'

Volta looked at Johnny the way a snake might eye a mouse. He seemed as angered by Johnny's lies as I was, yet his voice when he spoke was slivers of ice. 'I told you to remain silent.'

Then he lunged at Johnny. Johnny's mouth dropped open in fright and Volta's fat fingers slithered inside and gripped his tongue. One hand pushed against Johnny's throat as the other yanked on his tongue, trying to wrench it from his head. Volta heaved and grunted. Then he took the knife from his pocket and cut his way into Johnny's mouth. Johnny screamed, the sound muffled by the knife and Volta's fingers.

Volta's arm sawed back and forth while his other hand pulled and blood gushed from Johnny's mouth, great floods of it spilling across the sleeves of Volta's jacket. Finally, with a tearing, squelching sound, Volta ripped free Johnny's tongue and stood panting with it in his hand. Johnny tried to scream but succeeded only in gargling blood. Volta threw the tongue at him, the bloody tissue hitting him in the face. Then he stepped forward again and pulled the knife across Johnny's throat.

Johnny's head fell backwards as muscle and tendon were severed and a torrent of blood splashed down his front.

A look of almost sexual pleasure swept across Volta's face, his eyes riveted on Johnny's face as his life faded. I stared in silence, eyes wide and mouth agape.

The spell held for a few seconds, and then just as suddenly it broke and sound rushed back into the room. I began to thrash wildly in the chair, my muscles straining against the ropes, but I was held firm from behind and could do nothing more than rock the chair. Volta stood before me and I smelt death on him.

'Do you think £23,000 means so much to me that I would let you leave here to find it for me? No. The police will identify this man and then I shall take my payment.'

'They won't find him.'

'Then I lose some money.' Volta looked nonplussed. 'But you will cease to annoy me.' He glanced absently at the knife in his hand. 'I do not believe in reincarnation, Mr Harper. But perhaps I am wrong. If I am, I trust you will remember me, and you will know not to interfere with my business. I would enjoy killing you twice.'

His arm moved with almost tender slowness, the knife turning as though an extension of his fingers.

I saw the hunger in his eyes and my heart stopped. I braced myself, refusing to look away.

Until I heard the bang.

And all hell broke loose.

Thirty-Two

It was a colossal bang. A huge, tearing, screeching bang as metal made furious contact with metal.

My head spun round as the rusted metal shutter buckled and tore, half of it dragged across the factory floor by the van that had powered through it. The van kept coming at full speed until it smashed into the van that had brought me here. There was an ear-shattering boom as the two collided and came to a halt.

For a second there was only the sound of the echoes reverberating around the concrete walls. Then the gunfire started; a dozen firearms, all blasting away at the now stationery van. Holes were punched in the side of the van, in the doors, the windows shattered, and the tyres burst with dull bangs. They took no chances since the sheet of metal had wrapped itself round the front of the van and blocked any view of the cab.

Volta had retreated and was now a good deal nearer the back of the room as he watched to see what threat presented itself. He, along with everyone else, was focused solely on the van which was swiftly beginning to resemble a colander. Even the man who had so far remained behind my chair had stepped around me for a better aim.

I was the only one not watching the van. Because I know a diversion when I see one.

And I was the only person who noticed a figure slip in from the darkness outside, sliding inside the edge of the now gaping front door and along the wall. I couldn't see his face but I knew those movements as well as I knew my own.

Mack wasn't dead after all.

My heart soared briefly before crashing back into the pit of my stomach. He may not be dead yet, but he soon would be. The van would only hold their attention for a short time, and as soon as they turned round he'd be facing a dozen guns armed with nothing but a seriously bad mood.

I silently implored him to see sense, to realise this was a suicide mission. But he would never turn away. Not now. Not ever. I did all I could and faced the van again to avoid drawing attention to his presence.

The gunfire ceased, though no weapons were lowered. A short man in a brown jacket cautiously approached the driver's door and flung it open, his gun darting inside. He paused then stuffed his gun into his waistband and reached into the van. He pulled a body out, dropping it on the concrete floor at his feet, and stared at it uncomprehendingly.

I didn't recognise the driver, but the rag stuffed in his mouth and the two obviously broken arms suggested that crashing the van had not been his own idea. Fortunately, since he now sported more holes than Gleneagles, he was unlikely to tell any tales.

Suddenly it clicked, like a switch had been pressed. Everyone began to turn in synchronised panic, the man in the brown jacket reaching into his waistband for his gun once more.

And then the gunfire started again.

This time it came from outside, muzzle flashes flaring like starbursts in the darkness. The man before me was one of the first to fall, the bullet making a dull thump as it tore into his chest. He crumpled at the same moment Mack tackled me, driving both me and the chair to the floor. Mack grabbed the back of the chair and dragged me behind a stack of crates out of the line of fire as Volta's men began to return fire.

'Jesus Christ,' I panted. 'Who did you bring with you? The SAS?'

'Nah, they were busy,' he grinned, pulling out a knife. 'Had to make do with McKenzie.'

Mack had already severed the rope binding my hands and I flexed my fingers to bring some life back to them. I was stunned. I couldn't even begin to imagine how Mack had freed himself from the overwhelming odds at Nolan's pub, but this wasn't the time.

Not while we were in the middle of a firefight between the two most dangerous criminal gangs in the country.

Mack stuck his head out quickly and looked around. He leapt forward on all fours before scuttling back into cover. He now held a dead man's gun, and checked it, grimacing as he saw it didn't contain a full magazine. For the first time I saw the injuries he had suffered. One eye was puffed up, his nose crusted with dried blood and his lips split. There were scrapes and cuts all over his face, and a vicious-looking swelling on the back of his head from the stick that Big Billy had struck him with. There would be other injuries across his body that I couldn't see, ones that would begin to hurt soon after the adrenaline faded. But for the moment he moved as freely as if he had just nipped out for the morning paper.

'Are you alright?' I asked, knowing that he could have two broken legs and not let on.

'I'll be just peachy as soon as we get a hold of Nolan.'

'Where is he?'

'Him and Fat Billy are edging their way to the back door. Can't get a shot at them from here.'

'What about Volta?'

'Near the door. Just waiting for a clear run at it. Can't hit him from here either.'

At that moment there was a pause in the shooting. Volta took his chance and bolted for the door, his bulk moving surprisingly quickly as he fired blindly behind him, forcing our heads back into cover.

'I really don't like people who try to kill me,' Mack said

'It is rude,' I agreed.

'Can't let that go, can we?'

'Wouldn't want them to think it's acceptable social etiquette.'

Mack popped up and fired four shots in the direction of the front door. He wasn't trying to hit anyone, but his aim was better than most of Volta's goons and the proximity of his shots forced McKenzie's men into cover.

For a few seconds there were no bullets heading towards us. Or Drew Nolan and Big Billy. They both emerged from their hiding place and made for the door, Nolan in front and Big Billy limping along as quickly as he could on his damaged knee.

Mack and I were off too. He tore away from me as my stiff joints protested the sudden demands put on them.

Nolan reached the door and dived through it before Mack could take aim. Big Billy was slower though. Mack aimed as he ran and fired a round into his back. A puff of red exploded from between Big Billy's shoulder blades and he pitched forward onto his face.

Mack passed him, gun at his side, and pulled the trigger again, blowing a hole in the back of Big Billy's head before crashing through the door. I forced the image from my mind and accelerated, reaching the door a second behind him.

We were now in a second factory floor, the space above lined with gantries and high windows. Most of the panes were broken and shards of glass glinted around the edges of the concrete floor. Fifty yards to our right was a wide open gap in the wall where a steel shutter had once hung.

Nolan was twenty yards ahead of us, running as though his life depended on it. After the casual way Mack had disposed of Big Billy I knew that he was.

Suddenly I heard the growl of an engine from the darkness beyond that opening. Volta was making his escape and Nolan was about to follow.

'Shoot him!' I shouted.

Mack dropped to one knee and sighted along the barrel. He squeezed the trigger and the click seemed to echo in the empty space. 'I'm out!' he called as he got back to his feet and began to sprint.

Nolan had a gun but he didn't turn to fire. He must be out of bullets too. He was thirty yards away now and closing on the door, but he was out of shape. If there was a vehicle near the opening it would be close.

I ran as fast as I could but Mack's trainers pounded the concrete floor as though it had personally offended him. Either he'd catch Nolan or he'd die trying.

Nolan ran gasping into the night air, with Mack only seconds behind him. As I reached the opening I saw a gravel area, strewn with holes that would snap an ankle. Nolan had somehow negotiated his way through safely and was at the door of a run down Escort, his hand fumbling with the keys.

It was the age of the car that was his downfall. The seconds he spent trying to insert the key in the lock let Mack catch up, but only just. Nolan was halfway into the car when he heard Mack thundering towards him. He aimed over the car door and dry-fired, hoping his bluff would make Mack duck for cover.

It didn't. Mack kept running and slammed into the door with the side of his body, crushing Nolan between it and the frame of the car.

I heard the wheeze as the air was forced from him and the cry as he slumped to the ground, the empty gun falling to the gravel at his feet. Mack stood over him, breathing deeply but otherwise showing no sign of exertion.

As I reached them there were still intermittent gun shots within the building. It wouldn't be long before McKenzie's men killed the last of Volta's troops, but in the distance I saw the lights of a car turning onto the main road and accelerating away from us. Volta had escaped.

Mack and I stood side by side, looking down at Nolan's gasping form. He looked scared, but not nearly as frightened as he should have been. After the last time we'd met he'd decided we were unable to finish the job.

In his haste to get away he obviously hadn't seen Big Billy's fate.

'You told me my friend was dead,' I said to him, my voice calmer than I felt.

'I thought he was,' he croaked.

'Because that's what you ordered.'

'No,' Nolan shook his head calmly. 'Ruby ordered that. I just do as I'm told.'

I reached down and grabbed hold of Nolan's long, greasy hair and yanked upwards. He came with it, yelping, scrambling to his feet as his hair tore from his scalp. He found his feet and I swung an elbow into his face, knocking him back against the car. I grabbed hold of the back of his neck and drove a knee into his stomach.

'Listen to me,' I growled. 'People are dying, and I don't mean the arseholes back there. People I care about are in danger, so you're going to tell me about Siobhan.'

'Go fuck yourself,' Nolan said. 'You think I'm scared of you? I'm more scared of what Ruby will do to me if he thinks I've talked to you.'

Nolan didn't understand how I had changed since the last time we had met. I had seen a lot since then, not least of which were Charlotte's mutilated body and Johnny's violent death. These things had changed me, and not for the better.

'You need to focus on the here and now, Drew,' I said, pulling him away from the car. 'Mack, open that door.'

'No warnings?' Mack was delighted.

'None.'

'Happy days,' Mack said, swinging the car door wide open.

'What the fuck?' Nolan said as I grabbed his hair again and forced him headfirst into the Escort. Mack climbed in from the other side and looped his arm around Nolan's throat, holding him tight.

I stood upright and held Nolan's left leg outside the car. I ignored his feeble kicking and grabbed hold of the door. Then I hurled it closed with all my strength.

Nolan screamed in agony as the door crushed his leg and bent it at a frightening angle. Even before the scream died I slammed the door a second time, drawing another horrendous cry from him. I opened the door and pulled on his shattered leg, dragging him onto the gravel.

'Ruby may be scary, Drew, but if you don't talk there'll be nothing left for him to play with.' I pressed down on his leg with my foot and he screeched in pain. Finally, I saw real fear on his face. 'So stop messing about. Do you know who killed Siobhan?'

'No,' Nolan sobbed, tears on his face. 'I don't know.'

'You know more than you're telling. What is it?'

'Noth... nothing.'

'Lie to me again, your head goes in the door.'

'Fuck sake,' he cried. 'She was a fucking junkie, alright! She was right into it. Loved a bit of coke. You want to know why she worked at my place? Because I kept her topped up with the best gear, alright? You think she's some innocent wee lassie with the sun shining out her arse. You're wrong, she was just another cock-hungry, junkie slag.'

'I know she took drugs. Tell me something new.'

'There's nothing!'

Mack grabbed Nolan's leg and began to bend it the wrong way. Nolan shrieked and almost fainted before Mack dropped his leg and left him squirming like a landed fish.

I began to doubt what else he could tell me. He wasn't brave enough or mentally strong enough to withhold information from us anymore. Only one question remained. 'When did Siobhan hire a private investigator?'

'What?' Nolan was confused. 'That was ages back. Must be a year, easy.'

And there it was. The connection. It was a second before I could phrase the next question. 'Why did she hire one?'

'She didn't. Couldn't afford it. Was right pissed off about it too.'

Mack and I stared at him, waiting for him to elaborate. This time we didn't have to threaten.

'She wanted someone to get the film back. The one of her pal. She thought some private dick would be able to find it for her – like one of those twats would go up against Ruby Volta. But she couldn't afford them.'

'Who did she speak to?'

'She never said, just went on a rant about how they were robbing bastards.'

'When?'

'Jesus, I don't know. About a year ago.'

'Why did she tell you?' Mack asked in a dangerous voice.

'She wanted me to help her instead. Thought I might be able to have a word with Ruby, get the film pulled.'

'And did you?'

'You think I'm going to tell Ruby how to run his business?'

'Siobhan wouldn't have expected you to help,' I said. 'Not out of the goodness of your heart. So why bother asking you?'

Nolan looked away, his gaze following the road that Volta had taken away from this place, perhaps wondering if he'd make that journey. It was as he avoided my eyes that I figured it out.

'You wouldn't do it just to help her,' I said. 'And she couldn't afford to pay you either. Not in money anyway. She offered to sleep with you if you helped her out, didn't she?'

'So what if she did?'

'And there's no way you'd pass that up. So you did. You fucked her. Then you fucked her again by not even trying to get the film pulled.'

Nolan was suddenly belligerent again. 'And what if I did? She was fucking red hot. You'd have done the same…'

We were interrupted by the sound of footsteps on gravel and I turned to see Mason exiting the building with two other men. Nolan's face turned alabaster white as he recognised Mason.

Mason's face was expressionless, his pulse seemingly no higher than if he'd been soaking in a warm bath. The two men either side of him appeared equally at ease with the carnage that had been wrought inside.

Mason indicated Nolan. 'Did you get what you needed?'

'Yeah.'

'Good.' Then he raised his gun and shot Nolan through the forehead.

I flinched in shock. Mack merely flicked a piece of something damp from the sleeve of his coat, as untroubled as Mason and his two colleagues.

'You realise we didn't come here to help you,' Mason said to me. 'We came here for Volta. Mr McKenzie won't be happy that he got away.'

'That's your problem,' Mack told him. 'We gave you a shot. You're the ones that blew it.'

'We'll see if that's how Mr McKenzie views it.' He walked away, the other two men following him back into the building.

Mack and I walked around the side of the building, eager to avoid more contact with Mason and the rest of McKenzie's goons. As we walked Mack explained what had happened after I passed out at The Gibbet.

'Some of it I only know because Jessica told me,' he said. 'She decided she wasn't going home to wait and find out what happened. She drove a few streets away in case anyone was watching then came back. Seems she got back just in time to see a van driving out of the lane behind the pub. That was the one you were in. Then she saw four guys and a shotgun huckling me out the back door towards another van.

'I'm half out of it, but playing it worse, biding my time, getting my strength back. Next thing I know, this car's flying towards us and the guys holding me let go to try and get out of the way. I dive back into the doorway as she passes and hits three of them. I come back out and the car's sitting there, one on the bonnet, one against the wall looking pretty bad, and one on the deck who's obviously dead.'

'Dead?'

'Oh aye, she ploughed right through them. Killed one of them outright. Another one, well, he's probably dead by now I'd reckon. Looked like he had some internal damage.'

'What about the other two?' I asked.

'Well one of them came at me with a knife. Obviously that ended up in his own back, so he's dead too,' Mack said breezily. 'And the other guy went for Jessica as she got out of the car.'

'What happened? Is she okay?'

'Oh yeah,' Mack laughed. 'She came out of the car with this big steel torch. Nearly caved his head in with it. Beautiful sight. Fair cheered me up.'

I smiled with relief that Jessica had not been hurt.

'We figured you'd been in that first van, so we asked Jessica's new pal where they were heading. He didn't fancy telling us, but she scared him shitless and he coughed it up.'

'Jessica did?' I had expected Mack to be the one doing the threatening.

'She scared me too, man. I'd have told her anything.' I waited for Mack to smile but he didn't and I found myself wondering just how frightening Jessica had been.

Mack continued. 'Soon as we heard Volta's name Jessica called McKenzie on that number you gave her. Told him he had a shot at Volta and the guy who got his daughter into porn. Jessica told him they had to move quickly and they had to play it her way. He agreed, obviously. This was his chance for revenge, and a shot at his biggest rival into the bargain. Mason turned up with the rest of them, armed to the teeth, and tried to take over but Jessica stood her ground. We found the place and kept an eye out through the holes in that shutter, hoping to get a moment when you were on your own. Of course, soon as Fatso started ripping that guy's tongue out we had to move. So, our pal goes in the driver's seat, the accelerator gets wedged down, and we've got a quality diversion.'

As he finished we turned the corner, bringing us to the front of the building. Mack began to walk towards the only vehicle with lit headlights. As we approached a silhouette crossed one of the beams and I knew, somehow, that it was Jessica. My pace quickened and, as I neared the car, I finally saw her. She broke away from the car and rushed towards me, throwing her arms round my neck and hugging me tightly. I responded in kind, my arms around her waist, threatening to squeeze every last molecule of air from her lungs.

We held on tight for a long time, parting only at Mack's not-so-subtle cough. Jessica smiled and shook her head. 'Honestly, I turn my back for five seconds…'

Thirty-Three

We went to Jessica's flat in case Ruby Volta decided to have another go at cutting me up. I didn't think he would, not with McKenzie so close on his heels. I suspected both men would be putting all of their efforts into the war that was sure to erupt between them. Volta would come after me at some point, unless McKenzie killed him first, but it wouldn't be anytime in the immediate future.

Jessica refused to take any chances though, and insisted I spend the night at her flat, since Volta didn't know she existed. I had enough self-awareness to realise that the danger wasn't the only reason I agreed to stay. I had been as close to death today as I had ever been. Perhaps it was this proximity to mortality that had prompted the feelings that soared within me on seeing Jessica, but when she had thrown her arms around me it felt, clichéd as it may seem, like those arms were made for that one embrace. I had to remind myself throughout not to kiss her.

When we reached Jessica's flat Mack led me to the bathroom while Jessica disappeared into the kitchen. The clinking of glasses suggested some much-needed alcohol was on the horizon. Mack stood me in the centre of the room, directly beneath the bright overhead light, and examined my broken nose clinically. He nodded to himself then placed his palms on my face, a thumb either side of my nose.

'Is this necessary?' I asked.

'Don't be a jessie,' he answered.

Then he gave his hands a sharp jerk and I flinched as he reset my nose. Blood flowed instantly and I turned quickly to the sink, letting the red drops fall freely into the peach ceramic basin.

Mack opened the mirrored cabinet and produced a bag of cotton wool balls.

'Get some of that up your beak,' he said before leaving the room.

Say what you like, he's got a wonderful bedside manner.

I tore off some cotton wool and twisted it up my nose to stem the flow of blood. Then I braced myself to look in the mirror.

It wasn't as bad as I had feared. Yes, my nose was swollen and broken, and yes, the lump on the side of my head felt like a small animal had burrowed under my scalp, and yes, my face felt like it had been set on fire and put out with a shovel. But given how close I had come to being filleted I could only feel relief. One thing about bleeding; at least you know you're still alive.

I waited a few minutes before I tentatively removed the cotton wool from my nostrils, waiting for a fresh flow of blood. When none came I stripped off my clothes and stepped awkwardly into the shower as my body began to seize up. I let the warm water soothe my muscles, and took my time washing the blood and grime from my hair and body, wishing only that I could wash it from my mind and my soul as easily.

Eventually I left the shower and dried myself in the steam-filled bathroom, dabbing a fresh trail of blood from my nose before I dressed once more in the same clothes I had almost died in. I walked into the living room and was surprised to see only Jessica, a tall glass of something clear in her hand. The glow in her cheeks suggested that I had been in the bathroom long enough that she'd had a couple of drinks.

'Where's Mack?' I asked.

'Away home. Said they won't come back for him.' Jessica smiled and rolled her eyes. 'He sounded disappointed.'

'He's right. They won't come back for us. They're too busy with McKenzie.'

'Doesn't matter,' she said. 'Mack, I can't argue with. But you're staying here tonight.'

'I don't think that's necessary,' I began, then stopped when I saw the look of determination on Jessica's face. 'Fair enough, whatever's easiest.'

Jessica smiled and held out a second glass, condensation running down it as the ice melted inside. I took the glass from her and took more than a sip. The vodka hit me instantly and I knew, after what I had been through, I could get very drunk very easily. I sat down on the sofa and placed the glass on the table beside me.

'Mack told me about your stock-car driving,' I said, a smile on my lips.

Jessica shrugged, embarrassed.

'And your torch-wielding fury.' My smile broadened.

'Fine, okay, you know everything I did,' Jessica said, her face colouring still more. 'Any chance of filling me in on what happened in there?'

I took another drink before I told her everything that had been said and done inside that disused factory. She listened intently, without interrupting, and I was glad to get it out of my head.

We agreed that there was no possibility of going to the police and reporting the carnage that had taken place today. Apart from anything else, the police – and the courts – would view our involvement in the deaths of several of those who died today as less than innocent. To successfully argue self-defence in all of those cases would require Johnnie Cochran to open a law practice in Scotland.

'You okay?' Jessica asked me for the fourteenth or fifteenth time.

I shook my head as though I could dislodge the images of sudden death from behind my eyes. 'Yeah. Fine.'

Jessica wasn't fooled though, and she knew what I was thinking. 'Drew Nolan would have killed you himself given half a chance,' she said.

'Oh, I know that. Intellectually I know that, and I know the world's better off without him in it. Just as it's probably a better place without Johnny D'Arienzo, Big Billy, and the rest of the men who died today. In my head I know all of that, but I can't help but feel like I left a bit of my soul in that factory today.'

Jessica looked at me for a second before bursting out laughing. 'Away you go, you big drama queen.'

I smiled, suddenly feeling self-conscious. 'Too Hollywood?'

'Worse. More like one of those cheesy flicks your mum watches on that true movie channel.'

'Ouch.'

Look,' Jessica said, the smile now gone. 'Drew, Big Billy, the rest of those guys, they died because of the life they lived. If it wasn't today it would be tomorrow, or next week, or next year. Sooner or later though, those guys were going to die violently. They made their choices and they lived and died by them.'

'That's very black and white.'

'My eyes got opened today.' Jessica was suddenly unable look at me. 'When I knew you had been taken away in that van, and who you were being taken to, I got frightened. I got desperate. If someone had asked for the lives of fifty men like them in exchange for yours... I'd have offered a hundred.'

I swallowed, unsure what to say next. A minute passed and still I didn't speak, afraid to break some spell or upset some fragile balance that may have existed only in my mind.

Jessica spoke hurriedly, covering the awkwardness my silence had caused. 'These people bring it on themselves, Harper. Look at Johnny D'Arienzo. He's onto a good thing – for someone like him – then he screws it up by ripping off someone you'd have to be retarded to steal from. Blaming it on a dead girl was never going to work. Volta might be a lot of things, but stupid isn't one of them.'

'So you think Johnny took the money?' I asked.

'Definitely. Johnny was already beating Janet up. She wouldn't risk stealing a packet of fags from him, never mind twenty grand. Volta was right. He didn't admit it because then he'd be dead for sure. He just didn't realise Volta would kill him anyway.'

I nodded. 'That's what I figured. The money will be sitting wherever Johnny stashed it, and either somebody will stumble across it or they won't. It doesn't change anything. The money's just a sidebar. Something that can be carved on Johnny's headstone. *Here lies a stupid greedy bastard.*'

'At least you got what you needed from Nolan,' she said. 'Now we know you were right. Three of the four original victims consulted a private investigator some time before they were killed. That's a huge coincidence. Too huge. We need to go to Stewart with this.'

'Not yet.'

'Why not?'

'Because they'll screw it up. Or Darroch will use it as an excuse to come after Mack and I again.'

'He can't,' Jessica said. 'That would be ridiculous.'

'That never stopped him before.' I rubbed my palms over my face, wincing as I touched a tender spot.

'We can't do this alone anymore, Harper. We don't have the resources to investigate every PI company in the city. If it's even a city firm.'

'We can at least rule out two companies. Yours and mine.'

'Oh, yeah,' Jessica said sarcastically. 'That'll make a huge difference.'

'Look, Jessica,' I said quietly. 'Let's at least talk to Lorna Sinclair. It would be better if we could link all four victims. And you never know, she might be able to give us a name.'

'Fine.' Jessica drained the rest of her drink and stood up. She took my glass and walked into the kitchen, returning a few moments later with both refilled.

'You know,' she said, 'if it is a private investigator involved in this, it could explain why he's interested in you.'

'You mean he sees me as a rival?'

'Yeah, something like that. Or he's jealous of you.' She shrugged. 'I don't know. It just seems weird that he focused on you so intently all of a sudden.'

'If you listened to Stewart you'd think it was because I instil homicidal tendencies in everyone I meet.'

'That's ridiculous. It's probably no more than three-quarters of the people you meet,' Jessica said with a smile.

'You're all heart,' I yawned.

Jessica realised how tired I was now that the adrenaline had worn off and she declared that it was time for bed, insisting that I have hers as it was more comfortable than the futon in the spare room. 'You'll need a good night's sleep,' she said. 'You've been beaten like a red-headed step-child'.

Despite my tiredness I lay for some time in Jessica's bed, unable to fall asleep. My senses were on high alert again, though not for danger this time. I could smell her scent from the sheets, the faint trace of the perfume she wore and the shampoo she used. I lay very still at first, willing myself to forget where I was and let sleep wash over me.

Eventually I must have relaxed enough to sleep and I slipped into a nightmare world where people were killed and beaten before me and I was powerless to stop it. At some point in the dream a hand reached out to pull me from that world but I was too scared to take hold of it. Instead, I stayed where I was and watched the carnage, unable to cry for those who had gone, and wracked with sorrow for the hand I had not taken.

Thirty-Four

I woke late the next morning, startled by the strange surroundings. After a moment I remembered where I was and crawled out from under the duvet. I looked at the storm-tossed pile of sweat soaked rags I had turned Jessica's bed into and began stripping the covers. I gathered the pile under my arm and took it to the kitchen where I put it straight into the washing machine and started the programme, concealing the evidence of last night's nightmare-induced perspiration.

I made a quick trip to the bathroom to relieve the pressure in my bladder and stole a glance in the mirror. Far from improving during the night, things had taken a turn for the scarier and I wondered if holing up indoors for a few days might be the kindest thing for society. Maybe John Merrick and I could flat-share.

I was about to knock on the door to the spare room when I heard a key turn in the lock and Jessica stepped through the door into the hallway. She had a large cardboard coffee cup in one hand and a paper bag in the other, from which wafted the unmistakeable smell of bacon.

'Damn,' she said. 'Now I'm going to have to share these.'

I realised how hungry I was and almost ripped the bag from her fingers as I freed a bacon roll. I was halfway through a second before I decided starvation had been kept at bay long enough to engage in polite conversation.

'Where you been?' I mumbled through an enormous mouthful.

'Work,' Jessica replied. 'Some of us have to get out of our scratchers of a morning.'

'Did Crawford give you a hard time?'

Jessica rolled her hand, indicating she'd answer when she'd finished the half-pig in her mouth.

'He wasn't even there,' she finally said. 'Phil and Tim were. I spoke to them for a bit, asked how they're feeling about the whole imminent-redundancy thing.'

'And?'

'Tim's not saying much, as usual. Mind you, he could be suicidal with worry and he'd never tell you.'

'What about Phil?'

'As you'd expect. Laughing it off, sticking up for Crawford, refusing to take it seriously.' Jessica shrugged. 'He's probably got something lined up already, maybe that's why he can afford to be magnanimous.'

'Typical Crawford,' I muttered. 'Company's going down the pan and he's nowhere to be seen.'

'Anyway,' Jessica said, eager to change the subject, 'I didn't go in this morning just to chat with the gruesome twosome.'

'No?'

'No. Like you said last night, we can at least rule out two companies. You obviously would have remembered these people if they had been clients, so I wanted to check our computer records, make sure none of the victims were on there.'

'And?' I asked, uneasily.

'No, they're not on there. And if they'd had a consultation they would have been.' Jessica laughed. 'I know how you feel. I was kind of holding my breath too.'

I exhaled, and joined in the relieved laughter. 'I can't imagine what that would have been like, if they'd been on there. If this was a movie they would have been.'

'Thank God this isn't a movie then.'

'At least in the movies we'd still be alive at the end. I'd settle for that.' I tried to smile, but didn't quite pull it off.

'Well, that's two down anyway,' Jessica said. 'And if Lorna Sinclair can't give us a name it's time to bring in the fuzz.'

'I guess so,' I said reluctantly.

The Worst of Evils

*

After we had finished our breakfast and I had showered we got into Jessica's car and drove to Lorna Sinclair's home. We rode most of the way in silence, both of us lost in thought until Jessica pulled up outside Lorna's building. She leant forward over the steering wheel and peered up at the windows. 'Hope she's in this time. And she better not be in her bed.'

'Tough if she is,' I replied. 'She's getting up whether she likes it or not.'

'Yeah, don't suppose she insists on appointments.'

We got out and Jessica pressed the buzzer for Lorna's flat. She responded quickly and unlocked the door. My mind had snagged on something, but I couldn't place it and it swam out of reach as I followed Jessica up the stairs. When we reached the door to the flat Lorna showed us into her living room, where we sat on the sofa. Lorna sat opposite, perched on the edge of the seat, bolt upright and eager for news.

I apologised and told her we didn't have anything to tell her, only more questions to ask. Her shoulders slumped a little but she put on a brave face and told me to ask away. I started with one that I should have asked the very first time I met Lorna.

'Who told Gemma it was illegal to trace her adopted son?'

Lorna looked at me in confusion. 'You said that wasn't true.'

'It's not,' Jessica confirmed. 'But we need to know who told her that.'

'Well, it was that private detective she spoke to,' Lorna said.

Jessica and I exchanged a quick glance, picked up immediately by Lorna.

'What?' she asked. 'What does that mean? Is it important?'

'We might have found a connection between Gemma and some of the other victims,' Jessica told her.

'Do you know the detective's name?' I asked.

There was a long pause as Lorna racked her brain before slapping her thigh in exasperation. 'No, I'm sorry, I can't remember. She only told me afterwards, and I felt so bad for her that I never really took it on board. If I remember right it sounded more like a law firm than a detective agency.'

Law firm?

Lorna Sinclair shook her head sadly. 'She was so disappointed. If I'd known she was going I'd have gone with her. She was ashamed of the adoption, you see. Even with me. She thought it made her a bad person.'

'She's not the bad person here,' Jessica said.

'When did she speak to them?' I asked, trying to ignore the dark, heavy feeling growing in my stomach; a feeling that had the steely ring of inevitable truth.

Lorna thought about it before answering. 'Nearly two years ago.'

'And how long was it before she died?'

Another short pause. 'About six months.'

And there was the pattern. Siobhan, Keith, and now Gemma, had all definitely consulted a private investigator – and Janet almost certainly had – and they had done so around six or seven months before they were killed. It wasn't a smoking gun, but it was a pattern.

And I thought I knew what the pattern showed.

'Do you have a phone book?' I asked, my heart hammering.

'Yes, it's in the hall,' Lorna replied, getting up.

'What's going on?' Jessica hissed as soon as Lorna had left the room.

There was no time to answer as Lorna bustled back into the room and handed me the thick book. I flipped through the book for the section I wanted then stood up and showed the book to Lorna Sinclair. I pointed vaguely to the page, trying not to influence her. 'Do you see the name, Lorna?'

Her eyes scanned the Detective Agencies page methodically, one entry after another. My heart rate increased as she edged closer to the name I thought she would recognise. The name that Mack always said sounded like a bunch of fucking parasite lawyers.

'Yes!' Lorna suddenly said, her finger jabbing at the page.

I looked at the print beneath her chipped nail polish and saw that Mack was right. Parasites indeed.

I looked up at Jessica and felt the ground slip away as I read the name. 'Ogilvie, Laing & Drummond.'

*

We left in a dazed rush, promising Lorna that we would be in touch as soon as we had something solid. She wasn't happy about being left in the dark, but we gave her no option. This was something we needed time to think about. We sat in the Mondeo in silence, staring at the inside of the windscreen, the ignition key still in Jessica's hand.

If this was a movie…

'Pass the popcorn,' Jessica muttered, as though able to read my thoughts.

I said nothing. I was still in shock.

'It's someone I work with?' Jessica said incredulously. 'How the hell could I miss that?'

'I missed it too. I worked with them all. Everyone always says that afterwards: S*uch a nice quiet man. You'd never guess.*'

'But I checked the records…'

'We forgot about something.' I had realised what my mind had caught on as we arrived at Lorna's home. 'You mentioned something earlier about not needing an appointment. If they walked in without one and they were never taken on as clients…'

'There'd be no record of them,' Jessica groaned. She punched the steering wheel, accidentally sounding the horn and making us both jump. 'You know who it is, don't you?'

'Yeah.' We both did.

'Crawford Laing.'

'He does all the initial client interviews,' I agreed. 'None of these cases were ever taken on, so he's the only one that would have spoken to them. He's the only one that would have heard about Gemma's adopted son, about Keith's homosexuality, and about Siobhan's promiscuity. And whatever bullshit sin he pinned on Janet.'

Jessica started the car and pulled into the street. 'It explains why the killer has taken such a dislike to you,' she said. 'He already hated you long before this all started.'

'All because he thought John treated me more like his son.' I shook my head in frustration. 'John was the smartest man I've ever known. How could he not realise his own son was a killer?'

'You know,' Jessica said thoughtfully, 'I bet Crawford started about four years ago. His dad died a few months after his wife ran off with the kids. Add to that the pressure of running the firm when he knows himself he isn't cut out for it... that's a hefty load to carry. If he's already a bit screwed up, could be enough to tip him over the edge.'

It was possible, and it absolved John Laing of blame for failing to see the dark truth in his son. But even then I couldn't understand how the best man I'd ever known could produce a homicidal maniac for a son. I drifted into silence as I watched the traffic flash past. So many people coasting through their lives, never knowing how close they were to evil. I hadn't known, nor had Jessica. Neither of us had seen the madness in Laing's eyes, and neither of us had suspected what he was capable of. Neither of us would be absolved.

'What now?' Jessica finally said. 'Cops?'

'No. We don't have any evidence. And while they're looking for it he'll disappear. We need something solid. Something they can use to bring the bastard in and lock him up.'

'Just us then. Me, you and a violent sociopath. Sounds like a hell of a party.'

'You forgot one last guest,' I said. 'If you're up against a violent sociopath, it's nice to have another one on your side.'

'Well let's go pick him up then.'

*

We met Mack at his gym where he was teaching a class and moving so freely last night may never have happened. Even the cuts and bruises that covered large areas of his exposed skin did nothing to make him appear any more vulnerable. He handed the class over to an assistant and took us through to his office where I explained what we had discovered. When I had finished I sat back and let it sink in, waiting for the questions.

Mack only had one. 'You telling the cops?'

'Not yet,' I said.

'Good.'

'We could speak to everyone again,' Jessica suggested. 'We use the company name, use Crawford's name, maybe someone can give us something we can take to Stewart.'

Mack gave Jessica a sceptical look. 'Even if bringing in the cops would do any good, that'll take too long. And you'll spend all that time wondering who's next on his list.'

'What do you suggest?' Jessica asked.

'We find Crawford Laing, we stick to him like shit on a pig and we catch him in the act.'

'Then we bust him,' Jessica added.

'Bust him, or bust him open?' I asked.

'Oh, I think you know,' Mack said.

Thirty-Five

Mack left the room to shower and change while Jessica and I came up with a plan. Jessica called Ogilvie, Laing & Drummond to determine if Laing was in the office and was told by Phil that he wasn't, and hadn't been since yesterday. This was unusual in itself; Laing was a desk jockey through and through, and unlikely to be out and about on any company business.

I then called Brownstone and asked her to trace any property registered under Crawford's name, and even John Laing's name, in case his father had left him anything when he died and Crawford hadn't changed the ownership deeds. I also asked her to check what vehicles were registered to both. She said she'd call back within half an hour.

Jessica used Mack's computer to find Crawford Laing's home address and read it out to me. I flipped to the appropriate page in Mack's A-Z just as he re-entered the room, pulling a t-shirt over his damp hair.

I showed Mack where Laing's home was on the map and explained that was our only option unless Brownstone came back with any other locations. A few minutes later my phone rang and Brownstone informed me that, other than Crawford Laing's home and the Ogilvie, Laing & Drummond office, there were no properties registered to either Crawford Laing or John Laing. She also told me that the only vehicle registered to Laing was the green Land Rover Discovery we knew about. Before I hung up I asked her to do a full background check on Laing, and as an afterthought, on Phil Biggart and Tim Leach, just in case. Then I told Jessica and Mack we could focus on Laing's home.

'He must have another property,' Jessica said. 'He can't be killing them in his kitchen.'

'He could be,' Mack argued. 'That Austrian guy kept his daughter and three of her kids in his cellar for twenty-odd years.'

'At the moment this is the only place we know about,' I said. 'He doesn't know we're onto him yet, so he'll come home at some point.'

'Okay then,' Mack said, taking charge. 'We'll run a three point surveillance from our cars.' He tapped three locations on the map and allocated one to each of us. Working solely from a two-dimensional map wasn't ideal, and we'd have to be ready to adapt when we arrived, but Mack was the best at this and we deferred to his expertise.

'He'll recognise our cars,' Jessica pointed out.

'I've got a few spares outside that we can use,' Mack told her.

Jessica was puzzled. 'You keep spare cars in your car park? Why?'

Mack gave her a flat look. 'Do you really want to know? Or do you just want one?'

Jessica wisely decided not to ask and Mack left the room for a few minutes before returning and handing us both a car key, a torch, a walkie-talkie and a spare set of batteries. 'Radios are all set to channel three, but keep the chat to a minimum. Remember; he's not the crap investigator you all thought he was, it's always been a cover. He might be listening in, so no real names. Phones on silent, and only used as a last resort. And I want everyone checking in every fifteen minutes, on the quarter hours, okay?'

'What happened to keeping the chat to a minimum?' I asked.

'I'd rather know everyone was still alive.'

'Fair point.'

We stepped outside and Mack said, 'Remember, I go first and check it out. You don't move into position until I say so.'

We nodded and Mack pointed Jessica to an R-reg Renault Laguna, then pointed to the eight-year-old Nissan Primera beside it and said, 'That's mine.'

The two of them stood there waiting for the punchline. 'Okay,' I sighed. 'Where's mine?'

'There,' Mack said, pointing to a child's toy parked against the building.

'That? That's not a car. What is it?'

Mack and Jessica burst out laughing before climbing into their cars and driving off. I was left staring at a severely dinged seven-year-old Fiat Seicento and wondering how I was going to squeeze into it. I opened the door and slithered inside, wondering why the designer had chosen to model the car's dimensions on a coffin.

I winced painfully as my knees were crushed against the steering wheel before I managed to rack the seat back as far as it would go. I eventually achieved a semi-comfortable driving position and started the car, wondering which Oompa Loompa Mack had borrowed this from.

The home Laing still lived in, long after his wife and kids had left, was in Pollokshields, and I'd originally planned to take my time driving there to give Mack enough time to check it out. The way this car drove though, it wasn't going to be an issue: I'd be lucky to be there by sunset.

I was still several minutes from the location when Mack's voice came over the radio. 'Dylan. Target's vehicle is in place. Move in.'

With the knowledge that Laing could be listening in, Mack had allocated us code names for the duration of the surveillance, and for some reason he had chosen characters from The Magic Roundabout. I wanted to go for The Banana Splits but Jessica couldn't say Drooper without sniggering.

Laing was to be referred to only as the target, and Mack's transmission told us that Laing's car was in his driveway. This, however, was no indication that Laing was home. It was unlikely that Laing was using his Land Rover to kidnap his victims, suggesting he had another vehicle somewhere. We could only hope that he was not already out in that vehicle, cruising for his next victim.

A minute later Jessica's voice snapped me away from those thoughts. 'Florence. In position.'

I smiled to myself at the ridiculous names Mack had chosen and finally realised he had done it to relieve the tension. When I eventually reached my destination I announced, 'Zebedee. In position.

I was briefly grateful that Mack had warned us against excessive use of the radio. At least it would prevent Jessica making endless digs about how long it had taken me to get here.

An hour later I was bored out of my mind and wishing the radio embargo could be lifted. My mind wandered to the map we had looked at earlier and I tried again to think of any possibilities we had missed. I came up with nothing, again. Mack had made a careful recce of the streets around Laing's home before he told us to move in, and he was satisfied with the plan.

Laing's home was a large four bedroom detached, the middle one of seven on a side street that curved between two busier roads like a shallow inverted U. The houses were separated from their neighbours by high hedges, but at the front there were only low walls, perhaps three feet high, leaving them visible from the street. Another row of houses backed up against these seven, on a similarly curved street, with decent sized back gardens and more large hedges separating one row of houses from each other.

Mack and I were parked at either end of Laing's street, far enough away that we would not be noticeable but close enough to see any movement. Jessica was on the street behind Laing's and from her position she could see that entire street, in case he tried to leave through the back gardens.

It wasn't ideal – we would need to sleep at some point, and it was unlikely that Laing would be going hunting at two o'clock in the afternoon – but the three of us were all we had and we weren't taking any chances.

I also suspected that Mack did not intend this surveillance to last until Laing made a move. I fully expected him to take a more proactive approach as darkness fell, something I was anticipating and dreading in equal measure.

Time dragged, as it always did on any surveillance. Usually I'm able to enter an almost Zen-like state of inner calm where my mind relaxes to the point of being aware of what is happening around me without really focusing on any of it. That was how I usually coped with the hours of inactivity, but today I couldn't achieve that state of mind. I was too keyed up, too aware of the evil we were trying to capture, and too aware of the consequences should we fail.

I sat there, cramped behind the steering wheel of the tiny car, and wished I could pick up the walkie-talkie and speak. I wanted more contact than the quarter-hourly check-ins, and I longed to hear Jessica make some cutting remark. I remained silent however, save for, 'Zebedee. Check,' every fifteen minutes.

Dusk fell and the streets around us became busier as people returned home from their working day. I envied them as they hurried home to relax, to spend time with their spouses, their partners, their children, their friends, and I wondered how I had reached this point in my life. I tried not to dwell on that, nor on the fact that a man I thought I knew reasonably well had turned out to be a psychopathic killer. But, as the hours passed the roads became quieter and the shadows lengthened until they owned the streets. The houses around me were large and brightly lit, set back in spacious gardens, their occupants well insulated from the murky streets I found myself occupying.

Sitting alone in the dark it became harder and harder to wait for something to happen. I had carried out surveillance countless times and never had it been so difficult to simply wait. But never before had I been watching or waiting for someone who had already murdered five people and was anxious to add me to his tally.

By the time it had been full dark for an hour Mack's voice came over the radio for Jessica's benefit. 'Dylan. Still no lights.'

My inner pessimist told me that meant Laing was either not at home, or he was only too aware that we were out there and he too was watching and waiting. He could, however, just as easily be in a room in the back of the house where none of us could see any lights. It wasn't time to give up just yet.

At seventeen minutes past nine the heavens opened and rain began to rattle the car like God had knocked over his penny jar. Visibility deteriorated as the windows began to run with rainwater. Mack and Jessica would be in the same boat as none of us could risk using our windscreen wipers. If this kept up for long Laing would be able to sneak past one of us with ease.

Mack obviously agreed, as, a few minutes later he asked us all to confirm we still had visibility. None of us had better than partial visibility and with the rain getting heavier I could feel the tension coming through the radio.

Shortly after the ten o'clock check in Mack came back on the radio.

'Dylan. I'm going in,' he announced.

I had been expecting it, and yet when he said it my stomach still lurched. Because I knew what I had to do.

'Zebedee. Me too,' I said.

After a moment Jessica confirmed that she would stay where she was. I knew that had been difficult for her; she wanted to be in there with us, but she knew someone had to make sure Laing didn't slip out of a back door while we were going in the front.

'Dylan. Radio silence except emergencies. Florence, two short clicks means everything's cool. You get one long click, send in the cavalry.'

'Don't take any chances,' Jessica said. 'If he's in there, take him down and take him down hard.'

Thirty-Six

I was about to remove the bulb from the interior light to prevent it giving me away as I opened the door when I remembered this was one of Mack's cars; he'd have done that as soon as the vehicle came into his possession. I placed the radio in my coat pocket, slid the torch inside my left sleeve and slipped out into the rain.

I walked normally to avoid attracting any attention. At least the rain gave me a reason to have my head bowed and my collar turned up. By the time I reached Laing's garden I was completely soaked and the rain was running from my hair in a steady stream. Mack slid into step beside me as I opened the garden gate and we crunched up the gravel driveway without hesitation. If Laing was watching us our cover was blown by now anyway. At the front door Mack scanned the house, the garden, the street, while I made a show of fumbling for a key and surreptitiously tried the door.

The door clicked open.

I raised my eyebrows at Mack and he inclined his head, motioning me inside. I took a silent breath and braced myself.

Did serial killers go out and leave their front doors unlocked? Or was Laing still in the house?

I pushed the door, relieved that it swung open silently, and we slipped inside. Mack closed the door behind us, allowing it to come to rest in the frame before easing the handle up. We stood with our backs to the door and listened for a full minute, letting our eyes adjust to the darkness and our ears to the normal, unthreatening sounds of a house at rest.

As my eyes became used to the gloom I saw we were standing at the end of a hallway. The only light filtered weakly in through the glass panels in the front door and the one window set high above the staircase that started from our immediate right and led up to a first floor shrouded in darkness. A closed door faced us at the far end of the hallway, with two more on the left and one on the right. There were no lights visible around any of the door frames. There could be something incriminating in any of these rooms, but first we had to make sure we were alone. We'd have to check each room in turn.

Mack pointed to the door nearest us, then himself, then me. We crept forwards, waiting for a creaking floorboard to give us away, and stopped either side of the door. Mack was on the hinge side of the door and he placed his left hand on the handle. I stood on the other side, torch held high ready to illuminate the room. Mack counted from three on his fingers then threw the door open and flowed into the room, moving left. I followed him in, moving right, our torch beams casting long shadows around Crawford Laing's living room. We swept the light around the room quickly and it was obvious there was no-one within. The only item of furniture large enough to conceal a person was the floral three piece suite but both sofas and the armchair were pushed against the wall making them impossible to hide behind.

We flicked the torches off as soon as we were sure the room was empty and drifted back into the hallway. The brief flash of light had obliterated our night vision and we waited for it to return before moving to the next door and repeating the process. Behind the next door we found a dining room that looked as though Crawford's wife had still been around the last time it was used. It too was empty. We then checked the door on the opposite side of the hallway and found a small bathroom, with a toilet and sink crammed in under the slope of the stairs.

We turned then to the last door on the ground floor of the house – the kitchen I assumed – and paused before going in. Despite the cold in the house a film of sweat had formed on my forehead and I could feel a trickle run between my shoulder blades. Mack looked as relaxed as if he were merely viewing a show home, pondering whether or not to put in an offer.

Mack pushed the door open and we entered the kitchen. Even

with the large windows there was no more light, the high hedges in the back garden blocking most of the ambient light. The torches flashed round and revealed once more that there was no one else here. My eye was suddenly caught by a flashing red light and I whipped the beam of the torch back to its source. The light halted on a washing machine, the red light flashing to indicate it had finished its program, a load of what looked like white sheets inside, ready to be hung up to dry. I breathed again and reflected that, even if he was not home, that surely indicated he intended to return. But would that be before or after he had claimed another victim?

I glanced at the clock on the microwave and realised we had been in the house almost half an hour. I reached into my pocket and pressed the transmit button on my radio twice quickly to let Jessica know we were still okay.

I flicked off the torch and we moved back into the hallway, pausing again to let our eyes grow accustomed to the darkness once more. We moved to the bottom of the stairs and Mack began to climb, tight to the left hand side to avoid the middle of the steps where creaks were more likely. I waited until he was half a dozen steps up before following, hugging the right hand side of the steps to make us separate targets.

Mack paused a few steps from the top, and I followed suit, dropping into a crouch while I waited for him to carry on. After a few moments he did and I continued up the stairs behind him. As I neared the top I looked for him and saw his outline standing further along the landing. I hurried up the last few steps wondering what was wrong, looking to either side of me and making sure all the doors on this floor were closed.

As I reached the landing I realised what had made Mack stop. In the dim light coming through the hall window I saw the loft hatch at the far end was open. And I saw the rope that hung down through it and the body that swung by its neck at the end of that rope.

Mack turned and crept back towards me.

'Laing?' I whispered.

Mack nodded.

I took the radio from my pocket and was about to transmit when Mack grabbed my forearm in steel fingers. He gave me an angry look and hissed, 'We clear *every* room.'

I nodded, embarrassed at my error, and mentally kicked myself. I had been so relived that it was over that I had forgotten to take the most basic precautions.

Mack led and I followed as we repeated the same process we had downstairs, checking three bedrooms and a bathroom until we had established we were alone in the house. Other than the cold, dangling figure of Crawford Laing, who greeted us like an accusing finger every time we returned to the hallway. It took longer to check upstairs since we had to check inside wardrobes, cupboards, and behind and under beds. Neither of us expected to find anyone, but Mack was right; we had to clear every room, and we had to do it properly.

We came back to the landing after checking the last room and Mack gestured for me to give him a punt into the loft. It was the last place to check and it needed to be done. I laced my fingers and Mack placed a foot in them. I heaved him up towards the ceiling where he gripped the edge of the hatch and flashed his torch around the attic. We were inches from Laing's corpse and I tried not to look at it as Mack finished checking the attic. Finally he clicked off the torch and dropped to the ground with a shake of his head.

Now that the house was clear Mack flicked on the overhead light. The suddenly blinding light made me screw up my eyes. When my vision returned I stood beside Mack and looked up at the man who had caused so much carnage.

There was no doubt that Laing was dead. His eyes bulged, the pupils huge and black. His face was pale, a dark purple tongue protruding from his open mouth. His hands and forearms were deep purple where the blood had stagnated and pooled beneath the skin. His neck was cut deeply by the thin rope that was tied around it and which disappeared into the open loft hatch where it was tied to a roof beam. A step ladder leant against the wall where Laing had pushed it after climbing into the loft.

There was a sheet of A4 paper pinned to the front of Laing's shirt, the characters on it printed in thick black marker pen.

Rev 2:26

I looked at that message and my curiosity at its meaning was washed away by relief that no more victims would have the same self-justifying evil carved into them.

A soft breeze came through the opening and made the rope begin to spin slowly before us. I shuddered slightly as Laing began to rotate. I reached out to steady him but hesitated and stopped myself before making contact, letting him twist in the wind instead.

'Chicken-shit bastard,' Mack said in disgust.

'At least it's over,' I replied.

Mack simply shook his head and rubbed his hand across his jaw, incensed at being cheated of a chance to bring justice to this man. And I knew too that he felt robbed of a chance to atone for Katie Jarvie's killer walking free. Nothing could free Mack from that prison, but finding another killer may have given his soul temporary respite. Crawford Laing had taken that from him too.

I took the walkie-talkie from my pocket and pressed the transmit button.

'Zebedee. Target's dead,' I said heavily, then added, 'Dead when we found him.'

'I'm coming in,' Jessica replied.

I returned the radio to my pocket and looked at Crawford Laing. I thought about all the people he had killed and wondered how any of us could try and explain this to Archie Bell or Lorna Sinclair or Gordon Tierney. Even Innes McKenzie, a man used to violence – and a man who was evil in his own right – even he could not comprehend the kind of deeds that Laing had perpetrated. And I thought too of the death and violence that I had seen since I had taken this case, and I knew that, although it was over, I could never return to the person I had been a week ago.

I leaned against the wall and slid down it until I sat on the floor and could rest my head against the faded paintwork. I stared straight ahead and watched the man in the noose slowly rotate; a man I had known and had worked for and had spoken to many times, and I wondered if I would ever know just how many lives he had corrupted and poisoned. A sharp pain began to pierce my temple and I felt my eyes moisten.

The door opened downstairs and footsteps entered at a rush. Jessica's voice called out, 'Harper, are you alright?'

I don't know, I thought, as Laing and the world spun. *I really don't know anymore.*

Thirty-Seven

Stewart arrived shortly after I called him, Taylor in tow as usual. He took one look at Laing's body hanging through the loft hatch and was on his phone immediately. Soon the house was busier than Sauchiehall Street on a Saturday afternoon and Mack was becoming more and more tense with every police officer that arrived. He stood against the wall in a corner of the upstairs landing, where Jessica and I formed a human barrier between him and the cops.

Stewart took a couple of scene of crime officers aside as soon as they had donned their white paper suits and instructed them to give the kitchen a quick once over. Mack and I had already compromised almost every aspect of the scene, with the exception of the body, but Stewart was playing things by the book from this point on.

It was some time before one of the SOCOs came up the stairs to tell Stewart that the kitchen had been cleared. Stewart thanked her then ushered the three of us into the kitchen, glad to finally get us away from Laing's corpse. Fortunately, from an evidential point of view, this case would never see a courtroom.

I sat in a daze as a steady stream of uniformed officers, plain clothes detectives and crime scene technicians flitted in and out of the downstairs rooms. I'm no expert on crime scenes, but it seemed an awful lot of cops were milling around doing nothing. No-one had touched Laing's body yet and they wouldn't do so until the duty doctor had arrived to pronounce death and the pathologist had conducted a preliminary examination.

At some point someone thought to check if the house had a basement and a door was found at the side of the house. Some of the technicians went down for a look and we could hear them moving about below our feet. Then suddenly there was stillness and a few seconds later one of the techs appeared at the door and called Stewart outside. Stewart spoke to him for a few moments then followed him to the basement.

A long time passed before Stewart appeared upstairs again and when he did he walked past us and called Taylor down. Taylor hurried down the stairs and Stewart spoke quietly to her. She said nothing but her eyes widen as she listened. When Stewart had finished he sat down at the table with us while Taylor hurried through the back door.

'If you're planning a surprise party for us, don't bother,' I said. 'We don't like a fuss.'

Stewart smiled wistfully. 'Well, if any of you had any doubts about Crawford Laing's guilt you can dispense with them now.'

'What have you found?' Jessica asked.

'Human remains.'

'Whose?' I asked.

'It's hard to tell. They're frozen. We'll need to let them defrost then take a look.'

'If you're sure it's human and not just frozen meat then it's recognisable.'

Stewart looked around the kitchen, satisfied himself that we were alone. He seemed to feel we deserved some sort of explanation. 'Keith Lamont's genitals were removed, as well as his ear. They haven't been found yet. Hadn't,' he corrected himself.

I tried not to think about that too much. 'What about the other victims?'

'Nothing yet. When we find where he's killing them we'll find their remains.'

I didn't share his optimism.

The doctor arrived shortly after we'd all turned vegetarian, and confirmed death, as if there had ever been any doubt. If Laing was playing possum he was one hell of an actor. The doctor stayed only until the pathologist arrived and they passed in the hallway like members of a tag team. The pathologist disappeared upstairs and it was a long time before Taylor appeared downstairs.

'Still alive, is he?' Mack asked sarcastically.

'Hanging in there,' Taylor said with a straight face. 'He's been dead twenty-four hours, give or take. Cause of death appears to be hanging alright. They'll get him on the slab tomorrow and let us know what's what.'

'Any doubts about it being suicide?' I asked.

Everyone looked at me in surprise.

'Why do you ask?' Stewart asked.

'Just checking,' I said, shrugging. And that's really all it was: nothing more than the residue of my surprise at such a sadistic, evil killer throwing in the towel.

'Like I say, they'll cut him open tomorrow and we'll find out,' Taylor said. 'Obviously we'll need to see the tox results before we can say if he was drugged, but I can't see any restraint marks, so he wasn't tied up, and the lividity says hanging.' She nodded to herself. 'It looks real.'

'Plus, the contents of his freezer would have Hannibal Lecter licking his lips,' Jessica added.

'Yeah, you're right. Sorry, ignore me. I'm just…' I never finished the sentence and wasn't sure I could, but nobody pressed me on it.

Stewart and Taylor disappeared back up the stairs and we lapsed into silence. Despite the relief that the killer had been found and that he was in no state to harm anyone else, there was a strange sense of anticlimax and none of us felt much like talking. We knew we should be relieved, happy even, but we couldn't be. Not when so many people were dead.

I was staring at the washing machine and its hypnotically flashing light when the front door banged open and a change in atmosphere rode in on a gust of cold air. We looked up and saw Darroch stomping towards us.

Mack crossed his arms tightly, as though he knew he'd have to physically restrain himself.

Darroch arrived and stood silently for a moment, giving the three of us a look that could have boiled lead. Then he erupted. 'What the fuck are you doing here?' he almost screamed.

'Finding a killer,' I replied coolly.

'You've not found a killer, you've found a dead body! I'm going to have the three of you for interfering with an investigation, perverting the course of justice, and any other fucking thing I can think of! You've destroyed a crime scene and I'll nail your fucking balls to the carpet for it!'

'Does that include me?' Jessica asked innocently. Darroch's mouth zipped into a tight line and Jessica took the opportunity to get a word in. She stood up and leaned towards him, both fists on the table between them. 'You listen to me, you little prick. You've been after this sick bastard for over a year and got nothing. We've been looking for him for less than a week and we've found him, so don't give me any of your shite. You come after us and I'll make sure every paper in the country prints how incompetent you and the rest of Strathclyde Police are. We've got nothing to lose by going public. There's not a jury in the country would convict us of anything. They'd probably give us a damn medal. So how about you ditch the empty threats, get your head out of your fat arse and DO YOUR FUCKING JOB!'

Darroch's face turned a worrying shade of crimson as Jessica finished tearing into him. He stood for a few moments, his jaw trembling with rage, before he finally stormed out, banging up the stairs, sending cops and crime scene techs scuttling out of his way. We heard his voice rumble as he began interrogating Stewart and Taylor.

I stared at Jessica with undisguised awe.

'I think I'm in love,' Mack said, making her blush furiously.

*

Another hour passed before we were allowed to leave, and that was only so we could go back to Pitt Street to give our official statements. Stewart found some white paper coveralls for us to wear to throw the press off the scent and we rustled our way into them before trooping out of the front door under the curious gaze of the attendant cops. We found ourselves inside a large blue crime scene tent that had been erected over the entrance to Laing's home. As we pushed through into the early morning darkness cameras began to flash hopefully and they combined with the TV lights to blind us. We found our way to the bottom of the driveway and pushed through the throng of reporters who, despite now ignoring us, made no efforts to get out of our way.

We were taken back to Pitt Street in a marked car driven by a police officer who looked barely old enough to shave but who seemed old enough to realise Jessica's coveralls did nothing to hide her figure. We were separated and interviewed for hours. I was forced to go over not only the events of tonight but everything that had happened over the last week to lead us to Crawford Laing.

Well, not quite everything. We had been given plenty of time to think about our stories and we all knew what was best kept from the police. I spun the story time and again, and watched them carefully to see if they noticed the gaps. If they did they gave nothing away. I suspected everyone was just glad the killer had been found and wouldn't lose too much sleep over how it had happened.

They quizzed me on my injuries a few times, but every time I told them the same thing: Mack and I had been sparring and we had really gone at it. It was plausible – except if it were true I would be in worse shape than Crawford Laing – and, as I was certain Mack would tell them the same thing, there was no way they could disprove it.

Daylight was breaking by the time they let me go and I was shepherded back to the foyer where Jessica and Mack sat waiting for me under the bored gaze of a desk sergeant I didn't recognise. When they saw me they stood up without speaking and the three of us stepped outside into the dawn. The air was already choked with traffic fumes, but it tasted fresh and clean after the cloying intensity of Laing's home and the police interview room.

A voice to our left dragged us all back to the present and we turned to face it.

'I just wanted to say thanks,' Stewart said. His face was drawn and tired but his eyes were clear.

We all nodded but no-one said anything. There was nothing to say now. Death may have passed us by, but it had whispered in our ears, and I doubted any of us were untouched by the experience.

We turned to walk away and Stewart spoke again. 'It was from Revelations.'

Mack kept walking, caring nothing for Laing's last message. Jessica, I think, wouldn't have stopped either, were it not for me. Curiosity got the better of me.

'What did it say?'

Stewart recited the verse, his voice flat and lifeless. '*And he that overcometh, and keepeth my works unto the end, to him I will give power over the nations.*'

I looked at him a second longer, watched as he disappeared into the police station. The door slammed behind him and I felt Jessica's hand on my arm, pulling me away, towards normality. Towards life.

Thirty-Eight

It had been a long night and sleep called to me like a siren's song, but I had one more stop to make before I could go home. I picked up my car from Mack's gym and drove to Cardonald. It was a couple of minutes before Archie answered the knock on his door, his bleary eyes and dishevelled hair telling me I had woken him. He pulled his dressing gown tighter around himself and let me in.

I sat him down in his living room and explained what had happened and when I had finished he sat before me like his insides had been replaced with sand. He sagged so much I thought he may slide onto the floor and I braced myself to catch him. His mouth opened and closed as though he was testing his ability to speak and wasn't happy with the results.

'This man killed my daughter?'

'Yes.'

'You're sure?'

'Yes. It will be announced later. The police will be in touch with you soon, but I wanted to tell you myself.'

Archie shook his head in disbelief, as though he couldn't believe his daughter had become one of those tragic people whose killers' names will be remembered long after theirs are forgotten. He stood up and suddenly hugged me tightly, thanking me for everything I had done. I said nothing, inordinately ashamed that I had been unable to save his daughter, even though she had been dead before Archie had ever entered my office.

At the door I warned him about the press coverage that would erupt and told him to contact me if he needed me. I also asked him to let me know when the funeral was. He couldn't look me in the face then and I wondered if I'd overstepped the mark. I decided to let it go and see if he contacted me. If he didn't I'd assume he didn't want me there. Perhaps I only served to remind him of a world he'd rather forget.

I left Archie and returned to my own home where I slept much of the day, letting my body recover from the damage it had suffered. Jessica would be in her flat doing the same now that she was no longer employed. I wondered briefly if anyone had told Phil and Tim yet.

Mack, I knew, would not be at home. He'd returned to the gym as soon as we left Pitt Street, seemingly unfazed by everything. But I knew he'd be venting his anger on the heavy bags, pushing himself until exhaustion finally claimed him.

I had tried to call Innes McKenzie several times but received no response. I left it at that. There was no way I was going anywhere near him in the middle of a gang war. He'd find out soon enough.

A news conference appeared in the afternoon but I slept right through it, finally catching it that night on the six-thirty news. Darroch was clearly a man who enjoyed the cameras and he played his part to perfection; a pained expression for the loss of life; a serious face as he explained the killer had taken his own life as the police closed in; a look of regret that the case had ended in more death.

He was good, but some of us knew the truth. And the truth was Crawford Laing could have killed for a long time to come had the investigation been conducted as Darroch demanded. I switched the television off in disgust and went to bed.

*

The next morning I woke up feeling like I'd been drinking heavily. My movements were sluggish and clumsy and my brain felt little better. I sloped into the kitchen and took a couple of co-codamol – relieved and surprised in equal measure when they stayed down – then stood in the shower for half an hour. When no-one called a vet to come and put me down I decided there was nothing else for it but to face the day.

I was dressed and staring at a cold slice of toast that was proving a tougher mountain to climb than the north face of the Eiger when the news came on the television and I tried to focus on what they were saying. Unlike last night when it had been the DCI Darroch show, today the press seemed only too happy to put the boot in. Difficult questions were being raised over why the existence of a serial killer had been kept from the public for so long, as well as the handling of the investigation in general, and in particular how the killer had managed to so-narrowly evade justice. I smiled with satisfaction, sure that Darroch was now second-guessing his decision to become the public face of the investigation.

The smile stalled on my lips as something snagged in my fog-bound brain. After a second it came to me. I may not have been a psychologist, but Laing was clearly insane, and he may well have been capable of suicide, particularly if the police were closing in. But the police weren't. It was only us, and there was no way he could have known we were onto him.

Or could he?

I thought about the cases I had worked, with and without Laing, and I remembered him as being a terrible investigator, as inept with people as he was with technology. I now knew that I had fallen for his ruse. He was obviously better at moving unnoticed amongst people than he had led us to believe, and I guessed that he was similarly better with technology than any of us had known.

Technology such as listening devices.

I used such devices only sparingly, but I knew that Ogilvie, Laing & Drummond had plenty of them. So many that no-one would miss a few. Jessica, Mack and I had discussed the connection between the victims several times in different locations. If Laing had heard any one of those conversations he would have known the countdown had begun.

Another thought struck me. Drew Nolan hadn't had a bunch of men waiting in his pub on the off-chance we would show up. His lack of surprise when we arrived told me he had been expecting us. Had Laing heard Mack and I arrange to go to Nolan's pub and then tipped him off? If so, he'd almost killed us without lifting a finger.

That conversation had taken place in my office and I was now convinced that he had planted bugs there. And, of course, if he was willing to bug my office, why not my home too? I suddenly became very paranoid and began glancing around my living room as though I may suddenly spot a spy hiding under the rug or posing as a lampshade. It was ridiculous, and it made no difference – Laing was still dead – but I needed to know.

I had equipment for finding listening devices, but they were expensive pieces of kit and I normally kept them locked away in a cupboard in my office, only taking them out when I thought I'd need them. I would have to do this the old-fashioned way.

I guessed Laing would want to pick up any phone conversations so I started with the phone and took it apart, found nothing and put it back together before concentrating on the area around it.

It took a while, but eventually I found it. He had unscrewed the bottom of the lamp and placed the bug inside it. I extended my search to the rest of the flat and by the time I'd finished a thorough sweep of each room I had worked up a sweat and an appetite and was feeling energised once more. I'd also found two more bugs; one inside the lining of the curtain in my bedroom, near the telephone, and the other taped to the bottom of the kitchen table.

It was time to check my office. I left the flat with purpose and jumped into the Honda before stopping abruptly. I had the key in the ignition and was about to turn it when a thought came to me. If Laing had bugged my home and my office, why not my car? I had to check. Twenty minutes later I'd turned the car inside out and I'd found a small, flat rectangular device tucked inside the upholstery on the side of the passenger seat. I knew what this was too, having used ones like it many times for Ogilvie, Laing & Drummond. This wasn't just a listening device, it was a tracker. All it took was a phone call to the device and not only could you hear anything being said in the vicinity, but it also replied with a text message confirming its coordinates. Put those in a Google map and you had your target's location, right down to the street.

That explained why I had never been able to see anyone

following me; Laing had simply stayed out of sight and used this device to track me down. Used his bugs to listen to my conversations about him. It made sense; I was the one he seemed obsessed with killing.

When I finally reached my office I unlocked the cupboard and took out a small device that would pinpoint the location of anything transmitting a signal. Within a few seconds the device began to vibrate and emit a beeping noise, leading me to a bug taped to the back of my top drawer where I would never see it. The device found nothing else, though I did a quick manual check as well, just to be sure. Laing had obviously decided anything of any importance would be discussed around my desk.

I took a seat at my desk and put my feet up to think. The five bugs lay side by side on my desk and I stared at them as I thought about these violations. There was little I could have done to prevent a determined intruder gaining access to my home, particularly one who had access to high-tech equipment, but I still felt somehow responsible, as though I should have known that Laing had been there.

I lifted the phone then paused and replaced it without dialling. I was unsure why, but alarm bells were ringing and I wasn't going to ignore them. Instead I put my coat back on and left the office. I stood for a second and let the harsh wind buffet me, then walked downhill to the turning circle that overlooked the M8 and Charing Cross. I turned my back to the railing and looked back up the hill, some paranoid part of me checking that no-one had followed me, before I finally dialled.

'Stewart.'

'It's Harper.'

'Don't worry, Darroch hasn't mentioned you lot.' There was a smile in his voice. 'He's got bigger fish to fry now that the media's on his back.'

'I don't give a rat's arse about Darroch. I need to check something with you.'

'What? This isn't bloody directory enquiries you know.'

'Have you found any traces of the victims in his house?'

There was a grudging sigh. 'Not yet. I don't believe they were ever there. He's got another property somewhere; we just need to find it.'

'Pity he killed himself before we got to him,' I said, leading the conversation.

'Yes, I think he'd have talked, if only to crow over us.'

'That's what I thought too. So why did he top himself when he did?'

'Brandon says he was on a downward spiral, accelerating at an unusual rate. Either he would have killed himself or begun killing a number of victims very quickly.'

I thought about that and wondered why he chose suicide. 'But still, it seems almost like he knew we were coming.'

'What are you saying?'

'I'm only asking because of his job,' I said. 'Have you looked for any listening devices, anything like that?'

Stewart was quiet for a moment. His voice fizzed when he finally spoke. 'We're not stupid, Harper. We know the man is a PI, so yes, we checked.'

'And?'

'And nothing. There was nothing in his home. There were some in a cupboard at his office, but that's all.'

I was quiet while I thought about that and what it meant. I knew Stewart was still speaking as I took the phone from my ear and cut the call but I was too preoccupied by my own thoughts. Moments later the phone rang in my hand and I saw Stewart's number on the display. I didn't answer. I rejected the call and dialled Jessica instead.

'Fancy lunch?' I said without preamble.

She agreed and I told her to meet me in a small café on Byres Road in half an hour. I walked back up the hill to my car and climbed in. I sat there with my hands on the wheel and my forehead resting on them. I told myself it didn't matter; that Laing was dead and it was over. But I didn't believe myself.

If it didn't matter anymore, why had a feeling of utter dread wrapped around my shoulders like a shroud? And why did I feel like everyone else was standing on their heads and I was the only one who realised the world was upside down?

Thirty-Nine

'What exactly are you saying?' Jessica asked.
'Don't you think it's weird?' I pushed my plate away, the untouched pasta now cold and rubbery.
'Of course it's weird. He was a psychopath. So he bugged you, what difference does that make? He wanted to kill you, remember? Makes sense that he'd be checking up on you.'

I sat for a second and watched Jessica lift the last of her pasta into her mouth. A small blob of sauce landed by the side of her mouth and her tongue flicked out to lick it away. On another day my mind would have wandered, but today it was too heavily laden to travel far.

'But why,' I said, exasperated, 'did the police find no evidence of any listening devices?'

Jessica shrugged. 'Maybe he kept them elsewhere. He didn't kill his victims in his house, remember. And there's still a lot of body parts unaccounted for. He obviously has another place we don't know about. They must be there.'

'If that's somewhere he has peace to torture and kill people over several hours it must be pretty remote. He wouldn't want to traipse all the way out there every time he felt like checking up on me, would he? So the listening devices should be near to hand.'

Jessica was losing her patience. 'How the hell would I know? Maybe he did go all the way out there, wherever it is. Or maybe he's got another wee place; somewhere he can sit and yank his plank while he listens to his tapes. I don't know, but you're thinking about this too much. You're trying to apply too much logic to someone who was clearly insane.'

A few heads turned to look at us and I lowered my voice. 'This guy was an extremely careful, organised killer. He identified his victims at least six months before he killed them. Presumably he stalked them during that time, watched them, learned their habits. Then, when he kills them, he leaves no evidence and no witnesses. Yet now, all of a sudden, he begins to fall apart so rapidly that he leaves incriminating evidence before topping himself.' I spread my hands in a gesture that asked for help. 'You know the psychology better than I do. Explain it to me.'

Jessica looked at me, a hard look that said she didn't want to do this.

'What are you saying?' she asked again, her voice cold.

I paused, not liking this any more than she did. Then I blurted it out, quickly, like ripping off a scab.

'I'm not sure Crawford did it.'

Jessica placed her elbows on the table, either side of her empty plate, and placed her fingers against her forehead, massaging the skin. It was a while before she looked up at me, and when she did her eyes damned me for resurrecting our nightmare.

'He did it. He was crazy and he fucking did it. And he killed himself because he was going even more fucking crazy.' Her eyes scorched me. 'Why can't you accept that?'

'Because if we're wrong, we're still in danger.'

'You're just pissed because he killed himself before we got to him. But that doesn't mean it wasn't him. Do you think he just sat there quietly while someone strung him up by the neck? Then whoever it was stuck a note on him and planted Keith Lamont's cock in his basement?'

I stared at her in disgust.

The shame came in seconds. 'Sorry,' she said. 'That was callous.'

'Think about the evidence, Jessica. There's nothing except the body and a freezer bag of human remains that could easily have been planted.'

'Why would they be?'

'In case we got too close. The killer murders Crawford and leaves him for us to find. The bible reference found on his body links him immediately to the killings and guarantees a thorough search of his house. The cops find what's in the freezer it's a done deal, everyone can go home and sleep easy.'

'Then what?' Jessica asked, though she knew the answer.

'Either he does a runner and escapes for good, or...' I paused, reluctant to say it, 'he finishes what he started.'

'Us.'

'Yeah. Us.'

'So, what you're saying is Crawford Laing was framed by the real killer?'

'It's a possibility. And as long as it remains a possibility I need to follow it up. I can't sit around and hope that it's wrong.'

'God damn you, Harper.' Jessica shook her head. 'You can't just sit at peace, can you?'

'You don't need to get involved.'

'Look,' she said. 'I can accept that the... remains... could have been planted. But how could someone hang him and make it look like a suicide? The post mortem would have found any evidence that it was strangulation rather than hanging, and they'd have found traces of any drugs or restraints. I mean, look at your wrists, they're still ripped to bits after being tied up by Volta's goons.'

I looked down at my wrists and saw that they were indeed still deeply marked from where the rope had bitten into my skin as I struggled to free myself.

'There wasn't a mark on him, and no-one is going to be hung without putting up a fight. You show me how that could be done... maybe I'll believe it.'

I tried to come up with something, but there was nothing. Jessica stood and threw some money on the table. 'I'm sorry, Harper. I can't listen to this. This last week has been the worst of my life and I can't put myself back there just because you can't accept this. You didn't see him for what he was – none of us did – but he still did it.' For the first time I could remember Jessica seemed close to tears. 'Give me a call when you're ready to let it go.'

And she left.

*

I turned up at Mack's gym and moped in through the front door. The student on reception glanced up long enough to recognise me before returning to his books. I made my way past him and into the gym just as a class finished. Everyone lined up facing Mack and bowed to him before being dismissed. They trooped past me towards the changing rooms, a few of them casting curious glances at the cuts and bruises I sported. In this environment at least no-one judged me or thought badly of me for having these injuries. The most thought they might give to it would be to wonder who I had been in the ring with.

Mack sensed immediately that something was bothering me and he gave me a questioning look. I held up two fingers to indicate I would be with him in a couple of minutes then took the scanner from my pocket and began to sweep the room. Most people would have looked a little curiously at me: Mack's face registered nothing and he began to shadow box.

It took only five minutes to satisfy myself that there were no listening devices in this part of the gym. I didn't bother searching the rest; that would definitely get some strange looks from Mack's students. When I had finished I took a seat on the edge of the ring as Mack began to work a heavy bag. He never once stopped his workout while I explained what I had found, never stopped moving, never asked a question. My words were interspersed with the staccato thump of flesh and bone on the leather punch bag. He appeared to be completely ignoring me, but I was used to it; I knew he was taking in every word.

Mack carried on hitting the bag for at least a minute after I stopped talking, his bare knuckles red and angry from the impacts. I was used to this too, and I knew he was allowing himself to absorb what I had told him. He wasn't thinking it through, not consciously, but he would let it seep into his subconscious before he spoke.

Finally he stopped and turned to me as the bag jerked and slowed to a stop.

'You really think it wasn't him?' he asked.

'I'm not convinced,' I said. 'But I need to check it out. Jessica thinks Crawford's as guilty as sin. If I could convince her that his death could be a murder staged to look like a suicide then she might come round.'

'That's easy. Wait here a second,' Mack said, before leaving the room and heading down the corridor.

No, he hasn't... surely?

Mack returned quickly with a large towel in one hand and a sock in the other. 'It's not ideal, but it'll do. You want to see how it's done?'

I nodded and Mack gestured for me to stand in front of him. I jumped down from the edge of the ring and stood a few feet from him.

'Okay,' Mack said. 'You're at home, the doorbell goes, so you answer it. I'm standing there with a knife. I tell you to stay quiet or I'll cut you open, tell you to step back into your house, which you do, because right now you're confused. You don't know what to think, but you don't think you're going to die, so you do it, you step back inside. Now you're alone with a killer.'

'Then what?' I asked, foolishly

Mack launched himself at me and threw the towel around my body, grabbing both ends behind me and fastening them tightly, trapping my arms at my sides, my hands exposed but unable to do anything. He spun me round to face him and crammed the sock into my mouth.

'Don't worry, it's clean,' he said. 'Relatively.'

My eyes were wide with amazement as I tried in vain to move my arms.

'That's not going to leave any marks,' Mack said. He looked at me as though calculating something. 'What are you? Fifteen stone?'

Cheeky sod, I thought, and tried to say, 'Fourteen, fourteen and a half,' but the sock smothered my words.

Mack stooped and picked me up – effortlessly – so I was lying sideways across his shoulders. 'Laing was maybe two and a half, three stones heavier. Someone strong enough could have lifted him up into the loft, tied the noose, pushed him off the edge. Then he jumps down, removes the sock – Laing isn't going to be screaming for help now – waits a few minutes and unties him when he's not going to be able to use his hands anymore anyway.'

I gave a very muffled shout and gestured with my eyes to the gag in my mouth. Mack looked surprised to see it still there, as though it should have removed itself. Or maybe he was expecting me to pull some sort of Houdini trick. He grabbed the sock and yanked it out.

'How the hell do you know how to do that?' I gasped as he untied the towel and threw it onto the edge of the ring.

Mack looked me in the eye. 'I've had thirteen years to think what I'm going to do when I find the man who killed Katie. That's number twelve.'

I swallowed hard. 'So it can be done,' I said.

'Sure. I wondered at the time why his neck wasn't broken.'

'What do you mean?' I asked.

'The way most hanging executions are carried out now,' he explained, 'is using what they call the long drop. They're trying to snap the person's neck instantly so it's more humane. Too short a drop, they slowly strangle and it can take anything up to twenty minutes. Too long, the head can pop off.'

'You're a mine of morbid information,' I said, clearing fluff from my tongue. 'Was the drop from the loft enough to break his neck?'

'With his weight? Yeah, it should have been.'

'But he definitely died form the noose rather than the drop?'

'Definitely. His tongue, his face... dead giveaway.'

'So why didn't his neck break?'

'Someone could have used the rope like a pulley and hoisted him up there.'

That seemed far more likely, especially if it saved having to lug a seventeen stone Laing up a step ladder and into the loft.

'The police would have checked for that though,' I said.

'Depends how badly they wanted to believe he was the killer. Darroch was in charge that night and he wants cases cleared. Whether they're solved is irrelevant.'

That was true.

'You said the towel wasn't ideal,' I reminded him.

'Yeah, you'd want something bigger. A bedsheet maybe.'

A firework ignited in my brain with a red flash. Like the red flashing light in Crawford Laing's kitchen.

'There were bedsheets in his washing machine,' I said, my heart accelerating. 'The killer must have thought there was a chance he'd left traces of himself on it.'

'He'd have been better folding it up and putting it at the bottom of a cupboard. No-one would have noticed that.'

'Trying to be too clever.'

'So we're back to square one,' Mack said.

'No,' I said. 'The link between the victims was real. We just followed it to the wrong person.'

'Remind me,' Mack said. 'Why were you so sure it was Laing?'

I explained how Laing did all of the initial client interviews and that these clients were never taken on, meaning they would have never spoken to anyone else.

'Is that it?' Mack asked in surprise. 'What about when he was out of the office?'

'He never left the office when I worked there, and Jessica said it was still the same. The guy was a crap investigator, he stayed well away from any actual work.'

'So he never had any holidays?'

I felt a plunging sensation and my stomach dropped. We'd never considered this. Laing had been our prime suspect and then he'd very obligingly killed himself and left enough evidence to convince everyone of his guilt.

'Who interviews the clients in Laing's absence?' Mack asked.

'I don't know. I never did it when I was there,' I said. 'And I'm sure Jessica would have mentioned it if she had.'

'So it's Phil or Tim.'

'Yes. But which one?'

'Phil,' Mack said.

'Why?'

'He's far too good-looking. Makes me suspicious.'

I laughed. 'Maybe we should check them both out, just to be on the safe side.'

'Aye well, you're the detective.'

'Not so's you'd notice,' I said despondently.

'I didn't like to say.'

I ignored that and thought about which of my former colleagues was most likely to be a deranged killer. There was no way of knowing. Obviously neither of them had done anything to make me believe them capable of anything like this. There would be no shortcuts, I would have to investigate both of them and hope I found something incriminating.

'Why did he frame Laing?' Mack asked suddenly.

I looked at him as though it was obvious. 'To avoid a life sentence.'

Mack responded by looking at me as though I was a bit slow. 'He's been playing this game for a while now, no-one's ever got close to him, and the first time someone does he hits the road? You really think so?'

'Not when you put it like that.'

'For some reason he wants to kill you. As well as anyone else who catches his eye. If he knew you were closing in on him why didn't he just kill you? If he takes you out, he's still in the shadows, so why go to the bother of faking a suicide?'

The answer came easily, and yet it hurt to contemplate. 'He didn't want to rush it. He had a plan and he's sticking to it.'

'Ten points,' Mack said. 'For a bonus point, what's his plan?'

I thought of what he had done so far. How he had contacted me, dragged me into his game, and forced the police to involve me by presenting me with Keith Lamont's ear. I thought of Charlotte and how she had been killed purely because she had become close to me. And suddenly I knew his plan.

'He never intended to kill me next. He wants to destroy my life first.'

Mack nodded. 'You better warn Jessica.'

I tore my phone from my pocket and hit the speed dial. There was no answer; the call went straight to her answerphone. Was her phone switched off? Or was she somewhere without a signal? Or had something else happened to her? I tried her home phone and it rang out before being picked up by another answering machine. I dialled both numbers a second time, got the same results, and began to worry.

Mack said calmly. 'Don't panic. She could be anywhere.'

'That's the fucking problem,' I said too loudly.

'Then we find her. You go to her flat, I'll…'

'No,' I cut him off, already heading for the door. 'If she was at home she'd answer. If he's got her she's already running out of time. We need to find out who we're after, then maybe we find Jessica. He's been in my home, I'm going to his.'

'We'll take one each. Give me Phil's address,' Mack said as we reached our cars.

I gave Mack Phil's address then looked over the roof of my car at him. 'If he's got her, don't hold back. Do whatever it takes.'

'They'll be picking up bits of him for months.' Mack slammed his door and roared out of the car park.

I was only seconds behind him. All the while wondering if we were already too late.

Forty

I raced along the M8 at a pace that threatened to strip the paintwork from the car, and still it wasn't fast enough. As the rest of the traffic blurred around me the images in my mind became sharper and more grotesque; vivid images of the things I had seen and the things I hoped never to see, and I had to fight the terror that threatened to paralyse me.

I had picked Tim Leach up several times in the past and I knew he lived in Barmulloch, a post-war housing estate a couple of miles outside the city centre. As I slammed on the brakes outside his small semi-detached I noticed his car wasn't there. Then I was out of the Honda and sprinting up the driveway. There was no time to be subtle now. If he had Jessica he wouldn't have brought her to his home; I needed to find where he had taken her.

I went straight to the back door, rather than risk some concerned neighbour calling the police. It was locked, of course. I looked around and found a small rock sitting snugly in an unkempt flower bed. I took a pair of black leather gloves form my coat pocket and slipped them on before lifting the rock free of the soil and tapping it against the glass panel in the back door. The glass broke with a quiet tinkle and fell to the kitchen floor. I reached through, turned the latch, and let myself in.

I stood there for the briefest of seconds and listened to the house, listening for the sound of another presence. There was nothing. I looked around and pulled a knife from a wooden block on the worktop, gripped it tightly and moved through the doorway.

I was in a dining room and could see clearly into the lounge; there was nowhere for anyone to hide on the ground floor. I moved to the stairs and began to ascend, my steps measured, my muscles tense, beads of sweat gathering in my hairline as I climbed. I reached the landing and still there was nothing. There were four doors leading off the landing, all of them closed. I took a deep breath and flung open the nearest one, knife poised in front of me.

There was nothing behind the door but a small bathroom; white, sterile and empty. I opened the remaining doors and found two bedrooms and a cupboard, all of which were empty. I was alone in the house.

Now I had to find something that would help me locate Leach, and possibly Jessica.

If she was still alive.

And all the time I wondered if I was in completely the wrong place; searching the house of an innocent man while Phil Biggart was already playing his sick game. I shook off the thought. Mack was checking on Phil; I needed to concentrate on Tim.

I searched as quickly as I could while still being thorough. I started in the main bedroom and found nothing unusual. There was a bible in the drawer of his bedside table and I checked each of the references that had been left with the victims. Unsurprisingly, none of them, or any of the rest of the book, had been marked in any way. The bible fit with the killer's profile but it was purely circumstantial; there was nothing incriminating in Leach having one in his possession. I returned it to the drawer and moved on.

The next room I entered was obviously intended to be a home office, but had become home to dozens of framed photographs. There were some on the walls, on shelves, the desk and a few on a tall chest of drawers, giving the room the appearance of a shrine. And all of them contained what I thought were pictures of the same dark-haired woman, though the vicious slashes through each picture did nothing to aid identification. I tried to remember if Leach had been married but I had no idea; we hadn't worked together for very long and he'd never been very talkative.

I opened each of the desk drawers and discovered that Leach used the bottom one to store his files and records. I searched through them as quickly as I could, praying for a reference to another property, but again I found nothing. The records seemed to be complete, or at least there were no obvious gaps, and his bank statements and credit card bills showed nothing out of the ordinary. I shoved everything back in the drawer in frustration before pressing the power button on Leach's computer and moving into the bathroom. As I expected there was nothing to be found there.

I checked the downstairs rooms and again found nothing. I even checked the fridge and freezer – just in case – and was relieved to find no body parts lurking between the frozen pizzas. Back upstairs the computer had finally powered up and I was surprised to see there was no password needed. That suggested I would find nothing incriminating, but I had to check. I removed my gloves and laid them beside the keyboard before I began.

Most of the files seemed to be work-related; reports, expenses spreadsheets, and other minutiae. After a time though, I found a folder buried within layer after layer of sub-folders. The folder was labelled simply *Voices* and I opened it with no more expectations than I had anything else. When the folder opened though my eyes locked on the sub-folder with my name on it. Beside it were other folders, labelled *Brodie*, *Laing*, and *Biggart*. I opened the folder marked *Harper* and found numerous files, labelled only with dates and initials I thought for a second then opened one labelled *28.02 – KH,JM*.

The file began to play and my jaw tightened as the words flowed from the speakers. Words spoken between Mack and I mere days ago.

'Yeah?'
'I'm going to see Drew Nolan again.'
'Count me in. Fiver says he pisses himself again.'

I tuned out the rest. I now knew Leach was the man I was hunting, but that didn't bring me any closer to finding him or Jessica. I spent another twenty minutes searching the computer but found nothing more of interest. I shut down the computer, put my gloves back on then took a sock from a drawer and wiped the entire computer down to erase my fingerprints. I stepped into the hallway and looked to the cupboard at the opposite end; my last hope.

The cupboard was crammed full. A rail of clothes hung at eye level; jackets and coats fighting for space with trousers and shirts. The floor of the cupboard was awash with shoes and I had to fight my way past them to search to the back, behind the clothes. There was nothing there. I straightened up and looked above the rail of clothes to where two large shelves stretched the width of the cupboard. The lower one seemed to contain nothing but old videos, half-empty tins of paint, a few dusty tools and a torch. The upper shelf was too high to see its contents and I went in search of something to stand on.

I took the swivel chair from Leach's office and kicked aside a pile of shoes to make space for it. I climbed up gingerly, the old chair rotating creakily. Once upright the upper shelf was at eye level and I could see dusty old boxes stored wall to wall. I lifted the nearest one and had a look inside, finding only old photographs. Two more boxes contained the same, and the fourth contained a wedding album. A quick flick through confirmed the identity of the woman in the slashed pictures. Leach had indeed been married, which – given the absence of anything even remotely feminine in this house, including clothes and shoes – begged the question: where was Mrs Leach now?

I closed the wedding album, returned it to the box and put that that back on the shelf. I pushed the box back and it slid past the others, pushing against something soft at the back of the shelf. I pulled the box back towards me and lifted it down, realising that it was a good deal shorter than the rest, and also that it wasn't coated with the same thick dust. I jammed the box onto the lower shelf and reached a hand into the darkness at the back of the top shelf. I leaned forward and my gloved fingers closed around fabric.

I withdrew my hand and saw it clutched a small, navy blue holdall. I unfastened the zip and looked inside, my eyes widening as I saw a pair of dark blue overalls on top of a folded piece of polythene sheeting. I unzipped the internal pocket and nearly fell off the chair. Inside were a half-used roll of duct tape and a hypodermic syringe.

I thought about taking the holdall with me, but decided to leave it in its hiding place. I was running the risk that he may use it on another victim, but I was certain that Tim Leach had a sufficient supply of ketamine to replace anything I took from his home. I would rather ensure the police had all the evidence they needed to be convinced of his guilt. If the police became involved. That was still up for debate.

I was about to climb down from the chair when my phone rang, the fright almost knocking me from my wobbly perch. I grabbed the shelf and answered the phone without checking the display.

'Harper? It's Jessica.'

'Oh, thank God. Are you alright? Where are you?'

'I'm fine, why? What's wrong?'

'I've been trying to get a hold of you. I thought he had you.' I was too relieved to be angry, but couldn't help thinking *why didn't you answer your damn phone?*

'I'm fine,' Jessica repeated. 'I've been busy, doing a little digging.'

'Into what?' I climbed down from the chair and returned it to Leach's office.

'You're right,' she said softly. 'It wasn't Crawford. I'm sorry I walked out on you, but I think I know who it is. It's Tim. Tim Leach.'

'How do you know?'

'His bank account was emptied last night, Harper. And he was married. His wife ran out on him nearly two years ago. He was so quiet I didn't even know he was married. But she left in April, just before Gemma Sinclair came to OLD. That's the trigger. His wife left and he flips.'

'How do you know she left him?'

'He filed a missing persons report,' Jessica replied. 'But it seems to have been common knowledge that she had affairs and that she kept threatening to leave him. Nobody knows who she ran off with though.'

'She didn't run off with anyone.'

'Police report says she withdrew the maximum from her bank card over the next few days. Manchester, Liverpool, London. Sounds like she was trying to get away from him.

I shook my head even though Jessica could not see it. 'He killed her before she ran off, Jess. I'd bet he withdrew that cash himself, setting it up to look like she'd left. Not much the police could do if she was known for having affairs and no-one said anything against Tim. Maybe he was fed up with her cheating on him. Who knows, but I doubt she's still alive.'

Jessica was silent for a moment, then, 'Maybe Gemma looked like his wife. That could be why he killed her.'

'No. Gemma was short and blonde. Mrs Leach was tall with dark hair.'

'Did you know her?' There was surprise in Jessica's voice.

'No, but I'm looking at a lot of photos of her.'

I told Jessica what Mack and I had realised, then I explained where I was and what I had discovered. When she found her voice it was shrill and panicked.

'Are you crazy?' she shouted. 'Get the hell out of there! Now! He could come back anytime.'

'He's not coming back,' I said, suddenly sure.

'Are you going to take that chance? You shouldn't have gone there in the first place.'

'I had to. I thought he had you.'

'We need to bring Stewart in on this. We can't take the chance of Tim getting away. He could be out of the country already.'

'He's not. Unfinished business.'

'Get out of there and call Stewart,' Jessica snapped.

'I'm on my way. Call Mack and tell him you're alright, he's looking for you too. Tell him we'll all meet up at his gym.'

Jessica hung up and I left in a hurry. There was no point in trying to hide the fact I'd been here, not with a smashed pane of glass in the kitchen door. I called Stewart as I walked to the car, my eyes scanning the street surroundings for anyone watching me. I saw no-one. When Stewart answered I barked down the phone at him. 'Mack's gym. Half an hour.'

I heard a muffled shout before I cut the call, but I didn't care. He would come, if only to read me the riot act. I quickly checked my surroundings again and once more saw nothing. I put the Honda in gear and drove off.

I thought I'd checked carefully. But I hadn't.

I thought I'd been alone. But I hadn't.

The Worst of Evils

As I pulled away I didn't see the eyes that lurked behind me.
I didn't see the eyes that burned with fire and hatred.
But the eyes saw me.

Forty-One

An accident had slowed the motorway to a crawl and I was the last to arrive. As I walked into Mack's office Stewart gave me a look that, on another day, would have made me feel like an especially badly-behaved and disappointing child, while Taylor fixed me with one of her trademark glares. I was long past the point of caring.

The two police officers stood against one wall, while Mack sat behind his desk with his fingers linked behind his head. Jessica perched on the edge of the desk beside him, her eyes showing how relieved she was to see me. Taylor opened her mouth to tear a strip off me, but before she could find the words she wanted I cut her off with enough venom in my voice to penetrate her anger. She stopped and I asked them both to give me just five minutes to explain. Stewart reluctantly nodded his agreement and took a seat, gesturing for Taylor to do the same.

I laid it all out, with occasional input from Jessica, while they listened. When I told them what I had found in Leach's cupboard only Mack's face remained impassive.

When I finished Stewart thought it through for a while before he finally spoke. 'Do you know how unlikely it is that someone has convincingly passed off a hanging as a suicide?'

'Which is exactly why Tim chose hanging,' I argued. 'If it had been pills or gas or even slit wrists you'd have looked harder at it. Hanging automatically prejudices everyone to think suicide.'

'So you think that Tim Leach is the killer. And that he found out from listening in on your conversations that you had discovered a connection between the victims and a private investigator – him. He then went to Laing's home, subdued him, tied him up in bedsheets, hanged him and planted the evidence for us to find. Is that right?'

'Yes,' I said. 'There were bedsheets in the washing machine, weren't there?'

'There was one, yes,' Stewart confirmed. 'But that proves nothing.'

'Who does laundry before they kill themselves?' Jessica argued.

'It might be strange, but it doesn't prove anything.'

'The position of the step ladder proves he didn't kick it away while he was standing on it. He would have had to lean down and move it against the wall, then step out of the loft. And from that height his neck should have snapped.'

'How do we know one of you idiots didn't move the damn ladder?' Taylor countered.

'Get your forensic guys to check the rope against the beam it was tied around,' Jessica said. 'The rope will be frayed and the beam will have rope fibres caught on it, proving that he was hoisted up like a pulley, rather than him tying the rope around the beam himself.'

'While you're at it,' I added, thinking of Mack's demonstration, 'check Laing's mouth for fibres. He must have been gagged.'

'That's all standard practice,' Stewart said.

'Really? With Darroch breathing down their necks demanding an answer – the answer he wanted – as soon as possible?' Jessica folded her arms and looked at Stewart and Taylor. They looked at each other as they realised that Jessica's scenario was all too plausible.

Stewart thought for a second, sighed as though he had been presented with something unpalatable, and made his decision.

'Nothing you've told me proves anything. But it's too much to ignore.' He turned to Taylor. 'Sam, get a unit to Leach's home. Tell them to secure it till we get there. We'll put out an alert for him and see if we can bring him in.'

Taylor left the room to make the necessary phone calls.

'How will you explain this to Darroch?' I asked.

'I got another one of those anonymous tip-offs that I sometimes get. Very annoying because we have to follow up on these things.' His face was the picture of innocence. 'Can't take any chances, you know.'

Then he gave us a stern look, like a rather cross headmaster. 'In the meantime, I want you three to lie low. Stay out of the way and let us deal with this. If it turns out you're right, we'll find Tim Leach and we'll bring him in.'

'Yeah, you've really got him looking over his shoulder so far,' Mack said.

'We might have been a little slow in this case, but we'll get there,' Stewart told us.

'You want to borrow a map?' Mack asked.

Stewart looked at the three of us and knew he couldn't win us over. He turned and left without another word.

Mack tipped his chair back and put his feet up. Jessica took the seat Stewart had vacated, slouching down in it with her legs stretched out and began drumming her hand on her thigh. I stood up and began to pace, trying to work off the nervous energy.

'They won't find him,' Jessica said. 'Unless they get lucky.'

Mack brought his feet down from his desk and let his chair fall forwards onto four legs again. 'I don't want them to find him. I want us to find him.'

'He's killed five people, Mack,' I said. 'That we know of.'

'And?' he asked.

'And I'm shitting myself,' I said, too loudly. 'I thought he had you this morning, Jess. I don't think I could cope if he got either of you.'

'He's not going to get any of us,' Mack said.

'Well sorry for not sharing your confidence, Mack. He's been killing for God knows how long and the cops have got absolutely nowhere. Why do you think we can get him now?'

'Because you two are better than the cops,' he said simply. 'You'll find him.'

'Harper,' Jessica said gently. 'I'm scared too. I don't want to lose you. Either of you. But Mack's right, we can find him. We can't sit around and wait for the cops to find him; we've got further in a week than they have in a year. But we need to do it now, before we get tired and let our guard down. If we wait he can bide his time. We need to take the advantage from him. We need to find him now.'

They both looked at me expectantly. I stared back and relived the pain that had threatened to consume me that morning when I thought I'd lost Jessica for good. These were the closest friends I had, closer than most families are, and the loyalty and love I felt toward them was overwhelming. Blood may well be thicker than water, but some bonds are thicker than blood, and the bond I felt with these two people gave me strength I thought I was incapable of.

I couldn't put them in danger. And yet, if I didn't end this, they would never be safe.

'Then let's go find him,' I said.

Jessica smiled and I felt a new surge of energy run through me.

'Brownstone was doing a background check on Tim,' I said. 'I'll get her to send it to my office. We might get a break.'

Jessica jumped to her feet. 'Let's go get him, boys.'

'I'm sure you're both just full of ideas,' Mack said. 'But I'll wait here and keep myself busy till you've got a lead. Call me when you know what the plan is.'

Jessica looked surprised, but I knew Mack would be too agitated to help with slogging through piles of paperwork. He was happy to let us find Tim, as long as he got to be there when we confronted him. Like I would do it without him by my side.

'Don't worry,' I told him. 'You'll get your shot.'

*

By the time we reached my office and I had logged into the computer the email from Brownstone was waiting to be read. I opened the file and my face fell when I saw the size of it. I pressed the button to print the pages and watched Jessica's reaction as they began to churn out. By the time I had refilled the paper tray twice Jessica was looking dismayed. 'This is going to take ages,' she said.

'You never know. What we're looking for might be right there on the first page.'

'And is it?' she asked sarcastically.

I checked the first page and made an expression of mock amazement. 'My god, here it is. Tim Leach attended St Columba's High School in Perth. That's that solved, then. What are the chances?'

'Very amusing.'

'It's not too bad,' I said. 'Once I take out the stuff on Phil there'll be a lot less.'

'We should warn Phil,' Jessica said. 'He's got no reason to suspect there's still a killer out there. And he certainly doesn't know it's Tim. He could be a target.'

'Shit, you're right. Give him a call.'

'Maybe he can help us work our way through all this,' she said as she dialled.

'Good idea,' I said absently as I began leafing through the pages before me, taking out anything that related to Phil. I placed these sheets on the floor behind my desk rather than explain to him that we'd thought him capable of multiple murder.

'Phil? Hi, it's Jessica... Yeah, I'm fine, thanks... Oh, I'll find something... Listen, are you free just now? There's something I need a wee hand with. Could you come up to Harper's office?... Yeah... Look, Phil, Crawford's innocent. It's Tim... No, I'm serious... How soon can you get here...? Alright, thanks, we'll see you then. Watch yourself.'

Jessica hung up the phone. 'He'll be here in an hour.'

I nodded and carried on reading. Jessica picked up more pages from the printer and took out anything relating to Phil, passing it to me to stash behind the desk. There was silence for a while after that, save for the occasional curse of exasperation from one of us. Silence between us, that is. The students upstairs had their instruments out again and seemed determined to bore through the walls using only their amplifiers.

By the time the buzzer sounded I knew more about Tim Leach than I'd ever wanted to know – from his primary school to his job history to his mortgage payments – and I had heard enough

Nu-Metal to last me a lifetime. We were both grateful for the interruption and Jessica rubbed her eyes and stretched her back while I went to open the door.

I pressed the button to unlock the front door and turned the key in the interior door, pulling it open just as Phil shut the outside door behind him. He was wrapped up against the cold outside; gloves, scarf, and long black coat with a thick jumper and an old pair of jeans.

'Still cold out there,' he said, smiling, his cheeks pink from the wind. He looked at me with concern. 'Damn, that looks sore. How's the other guy?'

'Dead.'

'Oh. Right... Good.' He pushed the door closed behind him and followed me into my office. I took my seat behind the desk and Phil took the chair beside Jessica. They exchanged hellos – friendlier hellos than I was comfortable with – and Jessica began to explain exactly how we'd discovered Laing was innocent and Leach was the killer.

I tuned it out and returned to my reading, hoping something would jump out at me soon. Phil was nodding and listening to Jessica's tale, his eyes bulging and his jaw dropping at the appropriate moments.

My phone rang part way through the story and I answered it absently.

'It's Brownstone. Just checking you got everything alright.'

I looked over at the printer which had stopped churning out pages. 'Yeah. Looks like we've got it all. We know who we're after now, we just need a lead. There's got to be one in this lot somewhere. Thanks, I owe you one. Another one, that is.'

'You don't owe me anything, Harper. Ever.' She paused for a few seconds and I wondered if she had hung up. Then she came back and her voice was quiet, sadder, less confident; the voice she had used in the months after I had brought her back from Manchester. 'Do you think people are born like that? These psychopaths, I mean. Or does something happen to them to make them like that?'

Jessica was still talking to Phil, his attention focused completely on her.

'I don't know,' I said, sighing. 'Smarter men than me have tried to figure that one out.'

'I just wonder if he'd have turned out like that no matter what, or if it was going to that school that did it.'

'School?' I said stupidly. 'Do you know St Columba's?'

'St Columba's? What are you talking about?' Brownstone sounded genuinely confused. 'Oh, wait. That was the other guy. No, I'm talking about St Mary's. You know, the one where the priests were supposed to be abusing the boys? The one that burned down years back.'

The one where Gemma Sinclair's body had been dumped...
Oh fuck.

I looked up and met Phil's eyes. The pretence had been dropped and his mask had slipped. For a split second I saw the madness and the hatred, and then he moved.

He moved faster than I thought possible and with the assurance of a man who had been merely awaiting his opportunity. He smashed his elbow into Jessica's nose, knocking her to the floor, and used the impact to propel himself up and out of his seat. I was clambering to my feet too, the phone still in my hand, when his left hand darted into his coat pocket and brought out a knife. He thrust it into my face, the point sticking in the skin just below my eye socket and I stopped moving.

'Hang up the phone, Harper,' Phil said quietly.

Jessica was climbing to her feet, stunned from the blow. When she saw Phil had a knife to my face the shock visibly rocked her.

'Nice theory, Jess. Just a little off-target,' Phil said with a smile, his finger and thumb held up an inch apart. 'Hang up the phone, Harper.'

He pushed the point of the knife a little harder against my skin and I felt a bead of blood rise to meet the knife point. I cut the call and dropped the phone on the desk, hoping that Brownstone would have realised by now that something was wrong.

Phil rolled his shoulders and tilted his neck, his eyes never leaving mine. 'You've finally found your Redemption, Harper. How does it feel?'

'It's not everything it's cracked up to be,' I replied.

'Don't get lippy, Keir. Or I'll pluck your eye out. Same for you Jess. Behave yourself or Harpo's going to need an eye-patch.'

'You burned down St Mary's, didn't you?' I said.

'Well, duh!'

'So that's what this whole religious thing's about?' Jessica said. 'You were abused, so that makes it okay to kill people?'

'It's not a choice, Jessica. It's a calling. I *have* to.'

'Why?' I asked. And besides trying to stall him, I genuinely had to know. What could have pushed him this far?

'Why?' he raged. 'Because we were sent there for nothing! They locked us up in that fucking hell hole and left us to rot. We'd done nothing – all we needed were families who'd give us a chance. But they didn't. Someone decided we were sinners and we were punished every day for it.'

'That was the priests, Phil,' Jessica said. 'You killed them years ago.'

'And what about the ones who should have been there instead of us? The real sinners. The ones who deserved it! What about them? They should have been punished, not us.'

Phil was becoming even more unhinged. His ranting was gaining volume and emotion and small flecks of spittle were landing on my face as he raged at the world that had failed him.

'I learned that sinners must be punished,' he continued. 'And that's what I'm doing – restoring the balance. Something went wrong and the innocent were punished and the guilty went free. No more. I shall show them Redemption. They shall repent their ways and seek salvation and I shall bring them to their judgement on a wing of steel.'

'Why us?' I asked.

He looked at me through eyes clouded with madness. 'Because you tried to stop me. You tried to help the sinners.' He laughed manically. 'You thought you could stop me. You thought you were better than me. Here's a fucking newsflash, Harper – I'm the best. Not you – me. You took me on and you've lost everything.'

'It's not over yet,' I said.

'No, but we're in injury time.'

Phil reached into his pocket and took out a syringe. Just like the one he had planted in Leach's home. The one I had so readily fallen for.

'Jessica. Inject yourself with this.'

He held out the syringe and Jessica looked at it with eyes wide with fear.

She shook her head, unable to form words.

'That's a shame,' Phil said calmly. 'I guess I'll have to blind poor old Harper then.'

'Wait!' Jessica cried. 'Please. Don't.'

'John, 15:13, boys and girls.' Phil's eyes had taken on a feverish gleam. '*Greater love hath no man than this, that a man lay down his life for his friends.*' He paused momentarily, then smiled. 'Or woman, of course.'

'Jessica, don't do it. Just go, get out...'

I stopped as Phil gave the knife another little push. I tilted my head back as far as I could while still keeping an eye on him. A line of blood now ran freely down my face and the point of the knife was pushing against my eyeball through the flesh.

'Inject yourself in the next five seconds, Jess, or you can forget the blinding. I'll just push it right through his eye into his brain instead.'

'Jessica, please,' I begged as she took the syringe from his hand.

'One.' Phil had regained his calm now that he was no longer talking about his background and his motivations.

I begged Jessica with eyes filled with tears. Hers too were moist with fear and I prayed she'd do the sensible thing and run for the door.

'Two.'

'He'll kill us both anyway, Jess.'

'Three.'

'Get out of here and get Mack. Get Stewart. McKenzie, even. Get everyone after this fucking lunatic.'

'You're really starting to annoy me, Harper... Four.'

Jessica looked at the syringe and placed her thumb on the plunger. Tears flowed from her eyes as she lifted her t-shirt.

'God, Jessica, no,' I pleaded.

Phil's eyes were alive with pleasure as they swivelled from me to Jessica and back again, his face hungry as he savoured every second of our torment.

Jessica stuck the needle into her side and pressed the plunger.

My knees buckled and I felt the world slip away beneath me. Something within me howled with grief.

'Take a seat, Jess,' Phil said, pointing towards the sofa against the wall. 'You're going to need one in a minute.' He turned his attention to me. 'You. Round here where I can keep an eye on you both.'

The knife didn't leave my eye, merely pivoted slightly to guide me around the desk. Phil turned on the spot, letting me pass him, till I stood with my back to Jessica on the sofa.

'You're not going to meet your salvation today,' Phil said to me. 'Jessica is, of course. And you're going to live with it. You're going to live with knowing she died slowly and painfully. And you'll never see me again. Until the day you decide life is worth living again. That's when you'll see me again – when I bring Redemption to you once more.'

'I'll find you, Phil. You can't hide from me. I'll track you down and you'll wish you'd killed me today.'

'But she'll still be dead, whatever happens.'

I glanced at Jessica where she had slumped into the sofa, defeated. She looked up at me through dull eyes.

'Come and get me, Harper,' she said, her voice already thickening with the effects of the ketamine. 'I'll be waiting.'

'I'll be there,' I told her. 'Just hang on.'

'Yeah, yeah. Sure you will,' Phil said in a bored tone. 'Very touching.'

I looked at Phil, and for the first time since I had seen his true face, I felt no sense of danger to myself. My only concern was for Jessica.

'You're going to die, Phil. And I don't mean someday. Today. Before this day is finished, I'm going to watch you fucking bleed.'

Phil's eyes burned into mine. 'You'll have to find us.'

He pulled his arm away quickly. The knife made a small

popping noise as it left the skin and a floorboard creaked behind me as someone else entered the room. Before I could turn, something hard and heavy smashed into the back of my head and I pitched forward, stumbling to my knees.

'Enjoy the pain,' said a voice through the sparks. 'For only pain can bring Redemption.'

And I was hit again, the blow sending me to the floor on my face.

Jessica, I thought desperately, as black fireworks exploded in my brain.

Forty-Two

I came to with a start, jerking back to consciousness as though I'd been plugged into the mains. My eyes darted round the room from where I lay outstretched on the floor and I knew I was alone. The clock on the wall told me I had only been out for a few minutes, though the fuzziness in my brain made it seem like hours and my head ached like it had been split in two.

I tried to sit up and discovered that my hands were above my head, bound together with rough rope and tied to the radiator's downflow pipe. I glanced around desperately and saw my mobile, lying in pieces on the floor by the wall. The phone on the desk was useless too; its wire hanging loose where it had been severed. Even the computer had been smashed to prevent me from contacting anyone. There was no point in shouting for help either; I'd be wasting my time trying to compete against the band upstairs who still seemed determined to avoid anything sounding remotely like a chord.

I fought to control the panic rising in my chest. I had no way of contacting anyone and no-one was likely to wonder where I was for some time. Even if Brownstone thought something was amiss she knew none of my friends. Would she contact the police? And even if she did, how long would it take them to arrive? It was time Jessica didn't have. She had placed herself in the hands of a serial killer to save me and now I was the only person who could save her.

I looked at the rope that bound my hands; the knot was fastened too securely to untie and the rope itself was too strong to break. Phil had cleared the floor around me and there was nothing sharp nearby. There was only one chance.

I studied the radiator and tried to remember which way it moved. I clambered to my knees, then to my feet, my back hunched as my hands were prevented from lifting higher than my knees. I braced my back and laced my fingers together for as much leverage as I could manage. I took a breath and heaved as hard as I could, pulling my hands up towards my chest.

I strained for as long as I could, with no movement at all. I relaxed my hands and felt the burns the rope had left on my already damaged wrists. I adjusted my stance to face the door and yanked again. Sweat bloomed on my forehead as the muscles in my arms threatened to tear. The second hand swept round the clock, each circuit taking Jessica another minute nearer her death.

And still no movement.

My fingers were slick with the blood running from my torn wrists. I turned to face the window and this time as I pulled, the radiator shifted, sagging away from the wall. Hope blossomed in my chest: if it could come loose, it could come off. I gritted my teeth and pulled as hard as I could, ignoring the burning in my wrists, my forearms, my biceps, my back. I pulled harder still and my hopes rose further as I heard a metallic creak.

Images flashed through my head. I saw Phil's victims, each and every one, in life and in death, in life and in torture, in life and in pain. And I saw Jessica, naked and terrified, and I saw Phil, looming above her with a smile as sharp as his knife.

And the beast within me roared with fury and rage. The rope cut deeper into my skin, but I felt nothing. I pulled and I heaved and suddenly there was a screech of metal and a final bang as the radiator tore free from the pipe and I fell to the floor.

Water spewed forth and mingled with my spilled blood to create a watery-red puddle around my feet. The puddle began to spread and by the time I had regained my feet the room was an inch deep in water. I splashed into the hall and came face to face with Mack, his face cold with vengeance, his hand grasping a knife that was every bit the equal of the one Phil had held to my face.

'Where is he?'

'It's not Tim,' I gasped. 'It's Phil. He's got Jessica. He made her inject herself with ketamine.'

'How long?'

'Ten minutes.'

'Shit,' Mack spat. 'They could be anywhere.'

'And he's not alone.' I told him about the second voice.

'Did you recognise it?'

'No. I feel like I should know it, but it was different somehow.'

Mack cut the rope from my wrists. 'How do these fuckers meet each other?'

'I don't know, but his partner's the key. We find him, we find Phil, we find Jessica.'

'How do we find him? We had no idea there were two of them this whole time.'

'The school,' I said. 'Phil kept saying *we* when he talked about the place. I thought he was talking about himself and all the other kids there, but he was talking about himself and his partner.'

'That's where he's killing them?'

'No. The cops would have searched the place when Gemma was found. But there's a man there I want to speak to.'

Mack nodded, trusting me. 'I'll drive. Your tyres have been slashed. Jessica's too.'

I looked for the pile of info Brownstone had collected on Phil and realised it was gone. The question was; did it contain anything useful, or did he take it and destroy the computer purely as a precaution?

'Give me your phone,' I said as we ran from the office and into Mack's Navara. He handed the phone over and I dialled as the pickup roared away from the kerb.

'Cops?' Mack asked.

'No way. They come in now we'll be answering questions till Jessica gets posted back to us in pieces. This time, we do things properly.'

'And we see it through.'

He was right. Now that my darkest fear had been brought screaming into the daylight I had no doubt what had to be done. 'All the way,' I said.

Brownstone answered the call, her words pouring forth in a rush. 'Harper? Thank God. Are you okay? I called Mack, told him something was wrong.'

'You were right, it's Phil Biggart.' My voice was wavering with fear. 'He's got Jessica. And he's not alone.'

'Who else?'

'I don't know. He took all the stuff you sent me, there might be something there. I need you to go through it and see if you can find anything – a second property, another car, close friends – anything.'

'I'll call you as soon as I find anything.'

I hung up and dropped the phone in my lap. 'How did she find you?' I asked Mack. 'I can't have mentioned you more than a couple of times.'

'You said she was good.'

There was silence for a few minutes, broken only by the roar of the engine and the hoot of outraged horns as Mack muscled the pickup through gaps barely wider than the paintwork.

I thought about the bad luck, the timing, the fact that we'd fallen so easily for Phil's misdirection. If only I'd seen Brownstone's file on Phil before I had gone to Tim's house; before I discovered the evidence he had so carefully placed there; before we invited a killer into our midst.

'Ketamine doesn't last very long, does it?' I asked quietly.

Mack didn't respond for a time, and when he did it merely confirmed my fears. 'No. It doesn't.'

'They'll start on her as soon as it wears off.'

'But not before.' He paused, and when he spoke again his words pained us both. 'They'll want her to feel it.'

'That doesn't give us long,' I said as my heart tore.

'Then we better get it right this time.'

*

The sun was setting as Mack turned onto the tarmac path leading to St Mary's church. The sky had turned a fiery orange and red behind the ruined shell of the school, as though Phil's revenge had finally returned to claim what remained. Mack stopped the Navara just shy of the church and jammed on the handbrake. I was out of the car and throwing open the church door before he'd even turned off the engine.

There was a startled exclamation as I burst into the church. A figure got to its feet in the front pew and started down the aisle towards me. I was backlit by the setting sun and he squinted to get a better look at me.

'Can I help you, my son?' Father Flanagan asked with a note of caution in his voice.

'We need you to answer some questions, *Father*,' I said aggressively.

'I'm not sure I like your tone of voice,' the priest said pompously. 'Why should I answer your questions?'

I said nothing as Father Flanagan approached, and recognition dawned in his eyes as he saw me. He was wary at first, then his eyes positively bulged as they took in the blood that streaked my face. As his gaze dropped to the blood beginning to congeal around my wounded wrists, I was reminded of the damage they had suffered and I became aware of a tingling sensation in my fingers that I realised had been there for some time.

'You'll answer the fucking questions,' Mack said as he appeared behind me.

'How dare you,' Flanagan blustered. 'In the Lord's house…'

'This isn't the Lord's house, you prick. The Lord doesn't condone butt-fucking wee boys, so cut the crap.'

Flanagan stumbled back as though he'd been physically struck. He turned away but I grabbed his arm and pushed him down into the nearest pew. 'What… what do you want?' His eyes strayed from my face to my blood-stained hands.

I glanced around the church, at the sunset streaming through stained glass windows like multicoloured flames. I was reminded of my youth, when I still came to church, before the hypocrisy and casual cruelty of the Catholic Church drove me away. I remained Catholic – in my own way – and as I felt the familiar twinge of hushed respect in this building I wondered how far I would be able to push Flanagan.

I looked at the altar, at the cross behind it, and the figure borne upon that cross. I thought about the idea behind this church, and the school it was attached to, and I thought of the men who had corrupted that idea to suit their own evil ends. Men who had been entrusted with the protection of the most vulnerable among us, and who had violated that trust as completely as they had those in their care.

All of that flashed through my mind in less time than it takes to be damned, and I knew how far I was willing to go.

'Do you remember what I said the last time I was here? That hope was the worst of evils.'

Flanagan nodded without looking up.

'Well we found something worse.' I stared at Flanagan until he pulled his eyes up to meet mine. 'And he's going to kill my friend unless we find him first.'

'I don't really see how...'

'You told me you were here for four years before the school burned down. So you started here around twenty years ago.' I waited for him to nod his confirmation. 'Then you'll remember a boy named Phil Biggart?'

Flanagan's eyes bulged once more before he recovered and quickly said, 'No, it doesn't ring a bell. There were a lot of boys here of course. I don't remember them all.'

Mack loomed over the priest threateningly. 'Why don't you remember him, Father? Was he not cute enough for you? Didn't he swing your incense?'

'How dare you! There has never been any evidence of anything like that happening at St Mary's It was a tough regime, yes, and there were many, many punishments given to the boys, but it was done with love. Tough love. The kind that turns volatile boys into sold, faithful men.'

Mack's face pulsed with anger. 'What would you bastards know about love?'

'Phil Biggart came here,' I said. 'He was abused by the priests and that warped him and he's killed at least five people because of that abuse. Don't insult their memories by pretending this never happened. You recognised his name, now tell me why.'

Flanagan voice was soft as he spoke. 'Not all victims become killers.'

'This one did. And he's got a friend. We need to know who he was close to when he was here. Anyone he might have kept in touch with.'

'There was nothing like that,' Flanagan said. 'You have to understand, the boys were not encouraged to forge friendships. Friendships only led to misbehaviour in a place like St Mary's.'

'You mean friendship might have given these boys more confidence and self-assurance,' I said. 'It might have helped them stand up to you lot.'

'You listen to me,' Flanagan said, standing up to assert his authority. 'These boys had problems – some of them were wild – we had to focus on healing them rather than letting them lead each other astray.'

There was a throb in my temple – my usual response to self-serving bullshit. I shoved him back into the pew. Hard. 'Who was he friends with?'

'No-one. The boy was always very insular. Lonely, even.'

'But you remember him,' Mack said. 'Why?'

Flanagan looked away. 'He was a troubled child.'

'You should see him these days,' Mack said.

'But he became extremely well-behaved. He was one of our proudest achievements. We turned him from a boy who constantly picked fights and caused trouble, into a quiet introspective boy who studied hard and spent long spells in prayer. A court had ordered him to see a psychologist a few years earlier, which seemed to help him.'

'But he burnt down the school, didn't he?' I said

'There was no evidence. He only became a suspect because he'd started a small fire behind the school the previous year.'

'He sounds impeccably behaved,' Mack commented.

'He wasn't even in the school that night. He couldn't have started the fire.'

'Where was he?'

Flanagan sighed dramatically to show how much our questions were inconveniencing him. 'He ran away that day. There was some problem in one of his classes and he never turned up for the next one. We alerted the police, of course, and they found him in a neighbouring town a few hours later.'

'Why didn't they bring him back?' I asked.

'He was very distressed. The police spoke to the court-appointed psychologist who recommended they find alternative accommodation for the boy that night, and bring him back the following day when he had calmed down. He managed to find him a space in a group home for the night.'

'The school burnt down the night before he was due to return? And that doesn't strike you as a wee bit too convenient?'

Flanagan was completely nonplussed. 'Don't be ridiculous. The boy's story was corroborated by a very respected professional.'

'He could have sneaked away, made his way back to the school. Who knows, but he did it somehow.'

Flanagan gave me a condescending look. 'Believe me; this man knew how to handle troublesome boys. He does a lot of work consulting with the police these days.'

The penny finally dropped and it landed with the weight of all my mistakes. Pain stabbed through my brain as I realised I had been looking at this the wrong way. I had believed Phil's accomplice was a fellow pupil. Once again, I was wrong.

'What was the psychologist's name?' I asked, already knowing the answer.

Flanagan looked puzzled. 'Brandon,' he said. 'Eric Brandon. He's quite successful. Very well thought of in the police. He might be able to tell you something about this Biggart lad.'

'Oh, I bet he could,' I said as I made for the door. 'I bet he could tell us a whole lot.'

Forty-Three

I was dialling Brownstone before the church door had closed behind us. We leapt into Mack's car as she answered.

'Forget Biggart,' I told her. 'We know who his partner is. Get me anything you can on a psychologist named Eric Brandon.'

'On it.'

Brownstone hung up and I resigned myself to waiting. There was nothing else to do; we had no idea where they might have Jessica. My hopes now lay with Brownstone. She would move heaven and earth and everything in between to find what we needed. And still I didn't know if it would be enough.

We sat in silence for ten tortured minutes before Brownstone called back. I answered the call and put her on speakerphone. 'What have you got?'

'Nothing concrete yet, but there's something worth checking,' she said. 'I figured this guy was too smart to have anything listed under his own name, so I got his parents names and checked them first. They're both dead, but there's a property in Renfrewshire still registered to his dad, Robert Brandon. Eric Brandon's an only child, so it's odds on he's the owner.'

'Where is it?'

'It's an old farm, though most of it's been sold off. It's up the Gleniffer Braes, near the old Mossmuir Quarry.'

'That's it,' I said with conviction. 'It's got to be.'

Mack already had the pickup screaming into the road as Brownstone read off directions and I memorised them. It would take about thirty minutes to get there. 'Give it forty-five minutes,' I told her. 'If you don't hear from me call Detective Inspector Stewart and tell him everything.' I gave her Stewart's number.

'Why don't you call him now?' she asked.

'If the cops get there first Jessica will die. Biggart and Brandon need to feel there's a way out or they'll kill her. I'm not taking that chance. But we need backup... just in case.'

Brownstone knew what I meant and I heard a catch in her voice as she ended the call. 'I'll keep looking in case we're wrong.' We both knew we weren't, but she needed to feel she was doing something useful.

We were silent as Mack pushed the Navara through a gap in traffic, narrowly missing a bus. I gripped the Jesus handle above the window and held on tight as the light ahead turned red. Mack leant on the horn as we rocketed towards it, his foot never straying towards the brake, only pressing harder on the accelerator.

We powered through the junction, swerving as traffic began to cross. I held my breath as the front of a Peugeot came close to my door, its driver standing on the brake at the last second. Mack took his hand off the horn at the same time half a dozen other drivers furiously battered their fists on theirs.

I looked at Mack's profile and saw no expression; just the same focused determination to reach Jessica before it was too late. The question was; even if we got there in time, were we good enough to save her? Should I call Stewart and tell him what we had found? Would Jessica have a better chance of survival if we sent in the police?

I looked at Mack's phone and my fingers hovered over the buttons.

*

Gleniffer Braes is a small range of hills to the south of Paisley, forming the border between Renfrewshire and Ayrshire. The Braes are home to acres of farmland, hills, reservoirs and nothing more exciting than a major electricity sub-station, a radio transmitter, and of course, Mossmuir Quarry. The quarry was well-known locally, having lain disused for nearly twenty years after a lack of funding combined with local protests to ensure it was no longer financially viable. Drainage had always been a problem, no doubt affecting the decision to keep the quarry open, and in the years since it had been abandoned the quarry had filled steadily with rainwater, some draining away over the pitifully short Scottish summer, but returning quickly in autumn and remaining precariously deep all through winter and long into spring. The loose silt dredged up from the bottom of the quarry, combined with the occasional landslide from its steep sides, gave the water an impenetrable thickness. Over the years a number of people had fallen or jumped or dived in, only to discover how treacherous the depths were. Plenty of them had lost their lives, and a number had never resurfaced, their bodies settling out of reach of even the police divers.

There were no streetlights out in the Braes, and little ambient light now that daylight had long since retreated. As we hurtled towards the quarry the rain began to fall heavily, rattling off the car like iron rods and obscuring what little vision we had. I could picture the quarry; its reservoir of water swollen with the recent rains, its surface roiling with the steely raindrops hammering into it, and I pictured holding Phil and Brandon's heads beneath its volatile surface.

We found the turning and Mack spun the Navara onto a slick, muddy path. A few minutes later he stopped beside a thick hedge and turned off the engine.

'We need to walk the rest or they'll know we're coming,' he said.

Mack was right; the quarry was only a few minutes walk from this spot and Brandon's property must be nearby. We got out and jogged along the path, our feet slipping on the churned mud. We rounded a corner in the hedge and slid to a stop as a building came into view a hundred yards ahead, lurking in the middle of a copse of trees. It was sheer luck that we had seen it in the light of the moon as it made a brief, yet fortunate, appearance from beneath its cloudy blankets.

This was it. We left the path, winding our way through the trees as quietly as possible, grateful for the noise of the heavy rain. I stumbled twice in the darkness left behind when the moon retreated once more. Mack was more sure-footed and made the edge of the treeline without mishap. He waited there for me, crouched and alert, until I dropped down beside him, both of us silent as we studied the building that lay twenty feet ahead of us.

It appeared to be an old derelict farm building, and I suspected it dated back long before the quarry had been first opened. Presumably there had been more structures which had been sold off as the quarry expanded. Had the quarry remained active this building would probably have been sold off and torn down too.

It was the height of a barn, and seemed to have only one floor. The walls were made of large stone blocks, with small windows high up that would have let in little light even if they weren't covered with steel plates. The one door we could see was also covered with steel plates. The roof, too high to see clearly, appeared to be made of wood, with yet more sheet metal patching the large areas where the timber had rotted through. The building looked like it had been blocked up to prevent anyone wandering in and injuring themselves. Or finding something they shouldn't.

Beyond the far corner of the building I glimpsed a small edge of bumper, with the curve of a wheel below it. I pointed towards it and Mack nodded. He went first, dashing across the open ground and throwing himself flat against the stone wall of the building. We remained still for a moment, listening for a sound that would tell us he had been spotted, but when none came, I ran to join him.

We waited another few moments to ensure our presence remained undetected, then we crept past the blocked up door and around to the far side, where we found a red van. Mack risked a quick look in the cab, found it was empty, then came back and eased open the back door, the slight clicking noise muffled by the torrential rain. As the door opened we looked inside and saw polythene sheets taped to every surface. They'd kill Jessica, dispose of her body, then destroy the plastic sheeting and there would be no forensic evidence to link her body to this van.

Mack closed the door silently, then walked swiftly round the van, stabbing his knife into all four tyres, each deflating with a short wheeze. Now there would be no quick escapes. For them or us. Though, looking at the determination on Mack's face I knew there was no question of escape. One way or another, this would end tonight.

We crept round the building, looking for another way in and found it on the far side. The doorway on this side appeared to be blocked up with sheets of steel as well, but on closer inspection I realised it was simply a metal door, disguised to look like the doorway was boarded up. There was a loop for a padlock to be hooked through, but no padlock. I looked at Mack and he nodded agreement. They were still in there.

'There's no way to see in,' I whispered in Mack's ear. 'We're going in blind.'

Mack's voice was barely audible as he whispered back. 'I'm going to find another way in. Give me exactly sixty seconds before you go through that door.'

He held out his knife for me to take, but I shook my head. 'They'll see me straight away and they'll make me give it up. Keep it. And make sure you use it.'

Mack looked at me for a few seconds before slipping around the corner of the building. I stood up and took a deep breath. My knees seemed to be made of sand, my arms stiff and heavy as though they would not have the strength to open this door. I closed my eyes briefly and saw Jessica, needle in hand, injecting herself with a death sentence to spare my life. For sixty seconds I thought again about the bond between us, a bond thicker than any blood that Biggart and Brandon may spill when I faced them.

My eyes snapped open.

I opened the door and stepped into darkness.

Forty-Four

The door swung open silently and I eased it closed behind me, though I doubted anyone would have heard me over the din of the rain rattling down onto the steel patches in the roof. The inside of the building consisted entirely of one large room, lit from the centre by a single bare bulb in a wire cage, hanging from a cable looped over one of the exposed roof beams. The bulb lit only the middle of the room and left deep shadows around the edges, but still its brightness obliterated my vision, accustomed as it had been to the darkness outside.

When I was finally able to see I gasped as my heart split in two.

Behind the bulb Jessica hung from another beam by her wrists which were tied together above her head, her bound feet barely touching the flagstones beneath her. She was naked and her head hung forward on her chest. I had no idea if she was still alive. I could see no marks on her body however and I prayed that they had not yet begun to hurt her.

Before her sat a long low table, covered with a cloth to give it the appearance of an altar. On it lay the body of a short fat man, one arm hanging off the edge nearest me, his bald head lolling of the top end where his neck had been almost severed. His torso had been ripped open and his intestines torn forth and draped across him. There was blood on the table and the floor; a lot of it his, a lot of it much older.

Tim Leach had been displayed for Jessica to see when she opened her eyes; a torturous preview of what awaited her.

Jessica's head moved slightly to one side as a low moan escaped her lips. She was still alive, though groggy from the ketamine. She raised her head and her eyes tried to focus. I stepped towards her and into the pool of light; involuntarily, instinctively, foolishly.

There was a rush of movement in the shadows behind Jessica and Phil Biggart emerged from the darkness he belonged to. He was behind her in a second, his knife against her throat as his crazed eyes burned into me. He was dressed in a white suit identical to the ones worn by crime scene technicians.

'You took your time,' Phil said. I could barely hear him over the noise in the roof.

'I got a little tied up,' I called back.

Jessica's eyes remained cloudy, though terror lurked in their depths. I tried to reassure her with a look; a useless gesture even if she had been able to focus on me.

'Give up your weapons, Harper.' Phil fidgeted from one foot to the other, excited by the prospect of pain and torture.

'I don't have any.'

'Liar!' Phil screeched.

'I knew you'd make me give them up, so what would be the point? I'm not giving you more weapons to use against us.'

'Put them on the ground now or I'll skin her!'

'I don't have any! Come down here and frisk me if you want.'

'No,' said a voice. 'I think I'll do that.'

Before I could react Brandon had pressed the point of a knife into the hollow at the base of my skull. 'Congratulations, Harper. You finally fell over the truth.'

Brandon ran his hands quickly over me and discovered that I was telling the truth. 'Well, well,' he said, surprised. 'You weren't lying. Now, why would you come here unarmed?' His words were a sibilant hiss in my right ear, small flecks of moisture landing on my flesh and making it crawl. 'Perhaps because your sidekick is out there somewhere armed to the teeth?'

I had to convince him that Mack wasn't around. If I could keep them focused on me Mack might just be able to save Jessica.

'He'll be here any second. If you let Jessica and I go he won't blow you both to hell.'

'Really?' Brandon mulled that over. 'Now why would you tell

me that? Why not lie and say he's not here; you weren't able to find him in time? Why indeed? Could it be that you were actually foolish enough to come here both unarmed and without your attack dog?'

'You fucking *love* the sound of your own voice, don't you?' I said.

'After you've played a part for a long time, it can become difficult to step out of character. You get so used to showing off, telling your after-dinner *I help the police stories.*' Brandon's tone was almost conversational. 'How did you find me?'

'You gave Phil his alibi when he burned down St Mary's.'

There was silence behind me. I looked at Jessica and saw she was slowly coming round. Her eyes were clearer now, her body less flaccid as she tried to take her weight on her toes.

Phil was still behind her, knife still pressed tightly against her throat, his eyes on Brandon and I, narrowed as though that might help him hear our words over the thundering noise above us.

'I had to look after my protégé,' Brandon said. 'The court presented me with a damaged, angry, resentful boy and I turned him into the sword of the Lord. An avenging angel who would smite down all those sinners who had so far escaped their deserved end.'

I heard the smirk in Brandon's voice and knew he didn't believe in those things, that he had used them purely to gain control over Phil and mould him into another monster.

'What's the matter, can't do it yourself? Too messy for you?' I was pushing my luck but I needed to keep their attention on me and away from wherever Mack chose to strike.

The knife pressed harder. I felt the skin break.

'Don't fool yourself. I claimed my first victim before I started shaving. There are far more notches on my belt than that of my young apprentice.'

'So why let him do it?'

'We all need challenges in our careers. Something to stretch us. And I wanted a legacy. Something that will mark this earth long after I die. Who are we if we leave no mark on the world? When the court referred Philip to me, well, I knew it was a gift. Perhaps

The Worst of Evils

even from this God I hear so much about.' Brandon laughed then leaned forward and whispered in my ear. 'I am God where Philip is concerned. I own his soul. When I persuaded him to burn down that school and kill those priests... well, you can't appreciate the power. It's truly exquisite.'

'Those priests made him exactly what you needed, didn't they?'

'Those fools have no idea the damage they do. The number of youngsters they send into the world damaged beyond repair is astounding. They filled him with resentment and bitterness. I simply used his confliction over religion to take him round that final corner. I convinced him he was doing God's work, and in the process I created Redemption and gave it teeth.'

'How many did he kill before Gemma Sinclair?'

Brandon's response was careless and offhand. 'Oh, I don't know. Who counts prostitutes? Practice swings, as it were.'

'Because they're sinners, right?'

'That's what I told Philip. Of course, I chose prostitutes for his lessons because the police are less than diligent with a victim who works on the street and is addicted to heroin. Somehow they seem to be worth less.'

'You were supposed to help him,' I said. 'You could have made him better.'

Brandon scoffed. 'Do you think that's why I became a psychologist? To help people? Oh come on. Yes, I wanted contact with damaged and fragile minds, but not to mend them. Where would be the fun in that?'

'You're a monster.'

'Very original,' Brandon replied dryly.

'Why did you focus on me?'

'Well, that was Philip at first. You see, I got him the job with that fool Crawford Laing as a cover. I knew he'd never recognise what was in front of his nose. And of course, being a private detective is the perfect excuse for sitting outside people's homes at all hours of the day and night.'

'And that's where he was to find victims.'

'Actually, no. His cover and his calling were to remain separate. But then he met the Sinclair girl and she told him how she abandoned her son. Just like Philip's parents had abandoned him to the abuse he suffered at St Mary's. Frankly I was surprised she didn't leave the room in pieces. But, I'd trained him well, and he reined in his darker instincts.'

'So why kill her?'

'The desire to kill her was there now, and it was overwhelming. I persuaded him to wait a few months, during which time we would watch her. He thought we were giving her a chance to repent her sins and redeem herself. Of course, she was going to die, regardless of what she did. My concern was creating enough of a gap between her death and her visit to the agency.

'Over time Philip met other clients who had committed some minor transgression that he interpreted as a sin. What was it, now? One made dirty movies and screwed everything with a pulse… one was a queer… Any right-minded Christian would have done the decent thing and slaughtered the heathens.'

'How did you know they wouldn't be traced back to the agency?'

'Six months is a long time in the brain span of most of the walking dead that inhabit this city, Harper. In the unlikely event that one of them had told anyone they had gone to a detective, and in the unlikelier event that they had also mentioned the name of the firm to them, that person would then have to store that information in their brain and then attach the relevant significance to it after their beloved was found with their belly turned inside out.' I could sense him shaking his head in smug amusement. 'It was very unlikely that even one of these morons could manage something so complex, never mind enough of them to show a connection.'

'I found the connection,' I reminded him. 'With the help of these people.'

'Well yes, then you showed up; someone Philip had always detested for thinking you were better than he was.'

'That's not true,' I said. 'Seems a bit stupid now, but I always liked Phil.'

I looked at Phil then, but he could not have heard my words, and I doubted they would have registered anyway. His eyes were glazed with madness, but he stood perfectly still, as though waiting only for the order to slit Jessica's throat.

'Regardless, Philip wanted you dead. And as soon as we drew you into the investigation we had the perfect scenario; you'd annoyed the serial killer and the police would chalk you up as another one of his victims. Of course, when I called you and you tried to taunt me… well, you simply had to die.'

'Are you sure? I won't insist on it…' I joked. Keep looking at me.

'Shut up,' Brandon hissed, before finding his train of thought and continuing. 'But when you found the link between the victims, we had to improvise. It was time to kill our scapegoat. Unfortunately for you, you guessed that Laing was innocent.'

'Doesn't matter, does it? You'd have come back for me.'

Yes, we would have come back. But not for you. We were going to kill Miss Brodie and leave you alive with the guilt.'

'That's what you did to Tim, isn't it? You killed his wife and made him think she'd run off with someone else. There was never any affair, was there?'

'Oh, Mrs Leach had a few. Unfortunately for her, she embarked on one with Philip. Obviously having an affair is a sin, so young Philip did the needful. After that, yes, you're right, we let poor Tim suffer. He really did think she'd run off and left him. You've no idea the hours he spent trying to track her down. Well, perhaps they'll be together now.' There was a hint of amusement in Brandon's voice, as though the idea was absurd.

'You were going to do that to Jessica and I?' My blood began to thrum with anger at this monster's casual attitude to the carnage he had wreaked across so many lives.

'A slight variation perhaps, but the same general theme. You know, horrible, slow, painful death of a thousand cuts for the lady; lifetime of tortured mental and emotional agony for the chap.' I could hear the smile carve its way into his voice. 'But, since you're here, we'll just have to kill you both.'

I'd been happy to let Brandon talk for as long as he liked to give Mack time to make his move, but it sounded as though he'd finished boasting. And Phil was still too close to Jessica.

Time to roll the dice.

'Hey, Phil!' I called. 'How come you didn't go after the rest of the priests? You know, the ones who butt-fucked you.'

Phil's face turned a cold grey over Jessica's shoulder. If he remained calm enough to think clearly he'd take it out on her. I needed to bring him to boiling point.

'Guess you'll always be their bitch,' I shouted.

Brandon chuckled behind me, oblivious to my intention. 'You really do have a death wish, don't you, Harper?'

I ignored him and tried again. 'Unless you enjoyed it of course...'

That one landed. The colour rushed back to Phil's face as though it was about to explode and he stepped around Jessica and came towards me. As he did so Brandon's knife pressed harder against my neck and pushed my head downwards. Even as my head dipped I saw Jessica suddenly rise into the air, pulled by the rope that tied her wrists to the roof beam. Phil and Brandon's attention both turned to the sight of Jessica levitating and I dipped further forward, dropping and rolling away from the knife. Brandon slashed wildly as I ducked and I felt his knife kiss the back of my neck.

Everything moved in slow motion for a few seconds as Mack, hidden in the shadows above, heaved on the thick rope and hoisted Jessica into the roof. Phil ran back towards her, reaching out to pull her down, but Jessica was recovering from the drugs now and I saw the fury on her face as she lifted her knees and drove both heels into Phil's face. The blow stopped him cold and sent him stumbling backwards as Jessica disappeared from his reach.

'Get her out off here!' I yelled.

There was a screech of metal and a rush of wind and rain as a section of the roof was ripped free. I prayed to God that Mack didn't try to come back for me; that he took Jessica and ran for the car.

I turned to face Brandon, still crouched, and saw him advancing on me, knife in one hand, hypodermic syringe in the other. He gave the plunger of the syringe a theatrical squeeze, sending a jet of liquid into the air towards me.

'Looks like it's just us now, Harper,' he said in a voice thick with pestilence. He threw a glance towards the altar where Tim's intestines had been torn from his body. 'You think you're tough? Well, let's see if you've got guts.'

Forty-Five

Brandon moved towards me, covered head to toe in the same white suit as Phil, giving him, in the dim light, the appearance of a malevolent ghost. This was the first time I had seen his true face and the transformation stunned me. Gone were the glasses; the vague, unfocused professorial look now replaced with something dark with true evil. His eyes glittered as his tongue slithered out from the corner of his mouth and flicked lightly at the edge of his beard.

I circled away from him, looking for a weapon. My eyes jumped back and forth between the floor and Brandon's face, watching him as he came towards me. Phil had given up on Jessica and was advancing on me too.

I backed up and felt my foot thump against something solid. Glancing down I saw a pile of the metal sheets that had been used to block the windows and doors. I picked one up and held it in front of me. At three feet by two feet it was heavy and cumbersome and little use as a weapon, but at least it would give me some protection.

Brandon feinted towards me with the syringe and I blocked it with my shield. He swung the knife at my exposed fingers, the metal clanging as he narrowly missed. I thrust the shield towards him, pushing him backwards and quickly circled to my left before Phil could get behind me. Phil swung his knife overhead and I stepped sideways out of its arc and snapped a kick into the side of his leg. I was off-balance and the kick had little power but it slowed him momentarily. I regained my balance as Brandon came at me again. I tilted the metal and stabbed at him with its rusted edge. I missed and he came round the side, slashing my bicep. I howled and dropped the sheet of metal. It clanged to the floor, the noise bringing a smile to their faces as though they were hungry dogs hearing meat hit their bowls.

I darted forward, lunging between the two of them. They made no effort to attack me as I passed, confident that I was heading away from the only exit and had effectively trapped myself. I backed up and slid around the makeshift altar, trying not to look at the wreckage of Tim's body as I passed.

Phil came from my left, Brandon from my right; both of them smiling like hyenas with a weaker animal cornered and alone.

What they hadn't realised was that I was not a weaker animal. And I was pretty sure I wouldn't be alone for long.

On cue the door banged open and a blur launched through it, borne on the wind and rain like nature's fury. Two heads turned instinctively towards the noise and I took advantage of the distraction, throwing a low kick at Brandon's knee. It took the legs from him and he went down, still holding the knife and the syringe.

Phil lunged at Mack with the knife, aiming for his head. Phil was unbelievably fast, his shoulders moving with a speed that belied their size. But Mack was quicker. He pushed Phil's knife hand aside and rammed his own knife into Phil's stomach. Phil grunted and the knife fell from his hands. He tilted forward and Mack thrust the knife again, the blade disappearing up to the hilt. He stepped aside and removed the knife, letting Phil fall face down on the flagstones.

Brandon saw his apprentice fall and let out a bellow of rage. He swung the knife at my legs and I jumped back out of range. Brandon clambered to his feet with the agility of a much younger man. He came at me wildly, swinging the knife in front of his face. I backed up and chose my moment. When he paused between swings I powered a kick into his midriff and drove him backwards. He banged into the altar where Mack came up behind him and drove a punch between his shoulder blades. Brandon's head snapped back and the knife fell from his hand. Mack hit him again and knocked him to his knees.

Brandon crawled away from him, but Mack came round the

altar in pursuit, kicking him in the side and turning him onto his back. Brandon cried out with the impact and his hand flew to his side.

As Mack moved in, his face contorted in fury, Brandon gasped the only words that could possibly stop him.

'I know who killed her!'

Mack stopped dead – we both did – and we looked at Brandon in shock.

'I know who killed Katie Jarvie,' he said.

As we looked at him his face twisted into a smile and I realised too late that it was a lie. Suddenly Mack roared in pain and surprise and my head snapped round to see Phil had somehow got to his feet and stabbed Mack in the back. Mack spun away, the knife still embedded in his back, pulling it from Phil's grasp. Brandon sprang forward and stabbed the needle into Mack's thigh, giving him the full shot of ketamine as he staggered.

Mack was falling now, and he clubbed a fist into Brandon's head as he went down, knocking Brandon back towards me. Mack landed on his side with a thud like a judge's gavel. Phil stumbled forward and fell on top of him, his hands grasping for the knife in Mack's back.

I dashed forward, trying to get to Phil. Brandon grabbed at my foot, tripping me to the floor where he began to pummel me with punches. I absorbed the blows on my arms and kicked out at him, catching him on the jaw. There was a crack and he slumped away from me. I turned, my eyes wide as Phil's hand reached the knife.

He pulled it from Mack's back, blood dripping from its blade, and reared upright, his face a mask of triumph as I watched in horror. I was too far away and I knew I could never reach him in time.

The door banged open again and a fresh blast of wind and rain howled into the building. Mack lifted a weak arm and pushed at Phil, trying to knock him off. Phil brushed the arm aside and lifted the knife again, ready to plunge it into Mack's chest.

I had clambered to my feet, already knowing it was too late, when Jessica appeared behind Phil. She was soaked to the skin and dressed only in Mack's coat, but the fire in her eyes defied anything they had tried to do to her. A rain-soaked rock was clutched in her hand and she swung it overhand at Phil's head, smashing it into the back of his skull.

Phil's face went blank and he pitched forward, the knife still clutched in his hand. He hit the stone floor and rolled onto his back, ready to attack again. But Jessica was on him with a fury. She swooped down with the rock and smashed his fingers, sending the knife spinning away. He swung his other hand and Jessica batted it away, screaming with rage, before smashing the rock into his face. Then a second time, a third, a fourth. She pounded away with the rock as though she were driving a nail to the centre of the earth.

Phil's face caved in completely after the third or fourth blow. I heard the bones shatter as Jessica kept driving the rock home. There was a wet squelch and I saw a splatter of something soft and pink and knew this time Phil wasn't getting back up.

I ran past Jessica and slid to the floor beside Mack. He was on his side, his mouth slightly open, eyes clouded and face pale. He was still breathing as I pulled off my coat and threw it to the ground. I stripped off my t-shirt and pressed it against the wound in his back. Within seconds of touching his body it was sodden with blood. I held it in place with one hand and took Mack's phone from my pocket with the other. My fingers were shaking so badly I could barely press the keys.

I glanced up as I realised Jessica had ceased pounding the rock into Phil's skull. She stood before me, hair plastered to her head, sprays of Phil's blood coating her face and upper body, looking tiny in Mack's coat. Beyond her Brandon was on his feet and heading for the door. His feet were unsteady but he was almost at the door and once outside he could disappear.

Jessica grabbed the phone from me and shoved her other hand against the soaked t-shirt, holding it firmly in place. 'I've got him,' she said. 'Don't let that fucker get away.'

I scooped up Phil's knife and sprinted for the door. I yanked it open and barrelled into the night, eyes searching for any sign of Brandon. I saw him immediately, his ghostly white suit betraying him even through the driving rain. He was ten yards from the treeline, his stride still unsteady, the churned mud slippery underfoot. Once inside the thick canopy of trees though, the ground would be more solid and he could escape. The quarry was nearby and it would be dangerous to pursue him too quickly when he knew the area better than I did; a fall into its waters on a night like this could be fatal.

I took off, my feet slipping and slithering on the slick mud as I hurtled across it in pursuit of Brandon. I somehow held my balance, my eyes focused solely on the white phantom ahead of me.

Brandon had reached the trees and was pushing his way into the foliage when I smashed into him from behind, sending us both tumbling to the ground. He kicked out at me as he tried to get to his feet, but I was quicker. I stood above him and stamped on his body, his legs, his head. I stamped and kicked until I heard ribs crunch, then I bent forward and pulled him to his feet by the collar. I grabbed the back of his head in both hands and drove my forehead into his nose. Cartilage broke and blood spewed forth as it shattered.

I dragged him back through the gap in the trees and threw him onto the grass where he sprawled in a puddle three inches deep.

I was on top of him in an instant, the knife sliding under his chin. I knelt there, bare-chested yet immune to the cold, and looked at Brandon's face, the rain washing the blood from his broken nose, taking it back to the earth, and a whisper within told me to push the knife. A single muscle contraction and it would be over.

Brandon read the thoughts that were written across my face. 'Be a man and do it! Your bitch did it. She crushed Philip like an insect and you can't do the same to protect her? You're weaker than I thought.'

Brandon's face was a twisted sneer and I saw an evil in his eyes so dark it hurt to look at. There was nothing human in those eyes; no hint of a soul, no beating heart. Nothing but the darkness that threatened to draw me down into it.

I wanted to thrust the knife so badly it was a physical ache.

My arm tensed and the muscles readied themselves to take his life, as though my body was so certain this act was necessary that it was prepared to override my brain.

The knife began to move, and I felt myself slide towards something dark and nameless that opened its arms to greet me.

Then I realised what I would become and I caught myself before I fell. And at the last instant I pulled myself back from darkness.

I stood up as the sound of vehicles penetrated the curtain of rain. I stepped away from Brandon but kept the knife pointed at him. A few seconds later the first set of headlights rounded the trees and washed across us. Then a second, and a third, casting long jagged shadows as they swept over us.

Brandon smirked. 'I'll get out, Harper. I'm a psychologist, remember? I know how to play the game. They'll think I'm insane and they'll send me to a secure hospital. You want to know something funny?' He got to his feet, wiped a splash of mud from his beard, and looked at me conspiratorially. 'They're not all that secure.'

I stared back at him, silent, immobile.

'You'll never sleep another night in your life. You'll always wonder if it's the night I'm going to escape and come for you. And believe me – one day, soon, I'm going to peel your face off.'

I laughed.

Brandon stared at me, incensed. He screamed at me in rage. 'Will you laugh when I pull your slut's intestines through her fucking nose?'

The engines died and doors opened and feet squelched into the mud. Silhouettes walked toward us, flitting across the headlight beams.

'*You* want to know something funny?' I asked him. 'That's not the police.'

Brandon's face creased in confusion.

'Didn't you wonder where the sirens were? The flashing lights?'

A man's voice spoke from the darkness, colder than the rain that fell all around us. 'Is that him?'

'Yes,' I replied. And Innes McKenzie stepped into the pool of light with Mason a step behind. 'That's the man who killed your daughter.'

I glanced around and saw that McKenzie's men had spread out around us, blocking any escape. Brandon had recovered his confidence though and he sneered at McKenzie. 'A vengeful parent? How very dramatic.' The headlights shone in Brandon's eyes and he couldn't see McKenzie's face as he stepped forward to stand in front of him. 'You don't know what you're dealing with.'

Most men would have been intimidated. But most men hadn't lived their whole lives steeped in violence. 'Don't I?' McKenzie asked quietly.

The movement was so quick that I didn't see the razor rise from McKenzie's side and it had sliced through the flesh on Brandon's cheek before he could blink. A stream of blood ran from the wound and Brandon raised a hand to it in shock.

McKenzie's voice crawled its way into my spine like a parasite. 'You think you're scary because you've killed a few people? Because you sneak up behind young lassies and drug them? You've no idea how many men I've killed. Hard men, at that. I've headbutted a man to death. I've pushed my thumbs so deep into a man's eyes I've felt his brain. I've forced men to kill their own wives to stay alive. Believe me – I'm the scariest fucker you're ever going to meet.'

Brandon's knees buckled slightly and McKenzie caught him under the chin with his fire-ravaged hand. He turned to me with dead eyes. 'How long did he keep Siobhan alive?'

'Twenty-four hours.'

McKenzie turned back to Brandon. 'Oh, you'll beat that. You'll beat that by days.'

Brandon made a noise in his throat that sounded like justice.

Mason gripped Brandon's arms and forced them behind his back, fastening them together with thin wire that bit into his wrists. Brandon looked at me, his eyes wide as he finally realised what I was capable of. He had thought I couldn't kill him, and so had I. Until now.

I had called McKenzie on the way here, and I had told myself it was to ensure there was someone to stop Phil and Brandon escaping if Mack and I were to die. Now though, I realised I had known all along that I would hand them to the one man who could deliver true justice.

And I knew that I had not completely escaped the reach of darkness.

I stepped aside and watched as Brandon was lifted by four men and carried to the back of the third vehicle. The doors of the van opened and I heard the thump as his body was dumped inside. The suspension creaked as the men climbed in with him and then the doors were closed. The rest of the men climbed into the other vehicles and all three engines came to life while Mason stood by the door of the last car, his eyes telling me that no matter what had happened here tonight, there was still a bill to be paid.

Then he got into the car, leaving McKenzie and I alone, and I wondered if I would ever feel clean again. He looked around and seemed to sniff the air as the sound of distant sirens came to us on the wind. 'It's definitely him?'

'Yes. There were two of them, but the other one's dead. Self defence. Brandon's the one who killed Siobhan though. He told me.' The beast within me smiled as I sealed Brandon's fate.

McKenzie looked at me with the eyes of a lizard; eyes that told me Eric Brandon was already dead, it would simply be a few days before his body realised it.

He turned away from me and walked towards his car. Then he stopped and spoke over his shoulder, his mouth stumbling over unfamiliar words. 'You need something, you let me know.'

He didn't wait for a response, and I didn't wait to see his car leave. I ran back to the stone building that had witnessed so much pain and death and I knelt beside my friends. I held my wadded t-shirt against Mack's back and watched him fight, his body torn and weakened. Jessica turned away, her head held in her hands as she sobbed and I felt salt tears carve a path through the wetness on my face.

The sirens came closer and I heard the sound of engines, then doors, and running feet and raised voices. I was numb when they pulled me away from Mack and the paramedics went to work. I was numb when Stewart asked me questions, and numb as I saw other paramedics attend to Jessica.

I was numb through it all until I heard them say his heart had stopped. Then it hit me with the force of all the water in Mossmuir Quarry, and I fell sobbing to the flagstone floor. I wept with guilt and pain and sorrow and I wept with fury for the last victim.

Forty-Six

Mack lived, of course. Apparently, it took more than a couple of sociopathic serial killers, a knife in the back and a syringe-full of dangerous sedatives to take him out.

He had died as the paramedics worked on him, but only for ninety seconds. *Only*. The paramedics brought him back, stabilised him enough to get him into an ambulance and took him to the Royal Alexandra Hospital in Paisley and straight into emergency surgery.

I knew none of this at the time of course; only that they'd restarted his heart. There were two dead bodies to account for after all, and I was the only person in a fit state to answer questions. DI Stewart had arrived at the same time as the paramedics, along with DS Taylor and half of Strathclyde Police. My debt of gratitude to Brownstone was larger than I could ever repay. Had she not had the cavalry already saddled up by the time Phil knifed Mack, I'm not sure even he could have held on long enough.

A paramedic patched me up before the police took me away, assuring me that the cuts on my neck and bicep would heal completely and leave no scarring. There were no such assurances about the damage to my wrists.

I gave Stewart a quick rundown of events at the scene, and then I was taken to the nearest large police station, Mill Street in Paisley. To Stewart's credit, he kept me, and Andrea, as updated as he could during our hours in the interview room. By the time I had finished the first run through of my story we knew only that Mack was in surgery; still alive, but very much in the danger zone. After the second telling we discovered he had survived the surgery and was now listed as that old standby – critical but stable. I shook with relief when Stewart told us.

There was no doubt that Phil and Brandon were the serial killers we had been hunting. There was sufficient blood and tissue spread around their killing house that the police felt confident about matching all of the victims. They had also found a trap door leading to a basement where the missing body parts were discovered in a generator-powered fridge, which also contained a supply of ketamine. Although Janet's hands had yet to be located, Stewart was confident they would be uncovered at some point in the search. Had either Brandon or Biggart still been alive they'd have needed Perry Mason to get them off.

There was one part of the story however, that neither the evidence, nor anyone else, could corroborate, and that was what happened after Brandon ran from the killing house.

'So,' Stewart said for the umpteenth time, 'Brandon ran outside and you chased after him?'

'We've been over this, Detective,' Andrea said.

'One last time, if you don't mind.'

Andrea rolled her eyes and gestured to me to answer.

'He ran,' I said. 'I chased him.'

'And he ran into the trees?'

'Yes.'

'You pursued him until he reached the quarry, and you were just in time to see him slip and fall over the edge into the water where he disappeared from sight. Is that right?'

'Yes. Just like every other time I've told you.'

'You don't seem concerned,' Stewart carried on. 'Why?'

'Brandon tried to kill me and my friends. I'm hardly going to lose any sleep over his death.'

'I meant, you don't seem concerned that he may still be alive.'

'I doubt he'd survive in that water. Not tonight.'

'Still, given everything he has done, I would have thought you'd want to see a body before you could relax.'

'I expect you'll be sending divers in as soon as the weather clears. I'll get a look at him then. Mind you, he wouldn't be the first who didn't come back out. But I'm not going to spend the rest of my life looking over my shoulder just because his corpse is trapped under a rock at the bottom of a flooded quarry.' I felt a little guilty about the time and resources the police would waste searching the waters of the quarry, but it was necessary. Self-defence is one-thing in the eyes of the law. Handing someone over to a notorious underworld figure to be tortured and killed is quite another.

'We will. However, they haven't managed to find the exact location where Brandon fell into the water. I would have thought the ground would be quite visibly marked.' He fixed me with a beady eye.

I said nothing.

'Any thoughts on why that is?' he tried again.

'Maybe the rain washed the marks away,' Andrea said. 'Or maybe your crime scene people just aren't very good.'

Stewart ignored her. 'You'd be able to lead us to the spot though, wouldn't you?'

'No!' I laughed in amazement. 'It was pitch black, two of my friends had almost been killed, and I was chasing a serial killer through thick woods. Do you think I laid a trail of breadcrumbs?'

'You found your way back.'

'Fortunately.'

Stewart wanted me to say more, wanted me to explain how I'd found my way back, but I didn't need to. I wasn't on trial here, and despite Stewart's instincts, there was no evidence against me, and nothing to be gained by pursuing it. Andrea wasn't worried so neither was I.

My one concern had been DCI Darroch being unable to resist the idea of pinning something on his two favourite targets, but he seemed to be keeping a very low profile this morning. It made sense. He had, after all, been the one who told the press that Crawford Laing was a serial killer. And as Mack and I had found previously, Darroch didn't do retractions.

Not to mention the fact that Eric Brandon had been his pet project.

Stewart looked at me in silence for a long time, hoping I would feel the need to fill the void by talking. It didn't work. If he thought I was unused to awkward silences he should see me on a date.

Eventually he sighed and said, 'Interview suspended, 09:21.'

The other officer, who had remained silent throughout, stood up and left the room, while Stewart hesitated at the door. He looked back at me with sad eyes and said quietly, 'I told you, Harper. I can't condone vigilantism.'

'I never asked you to.'

He looked at me a moment longer then nodded to himself as though I had confirmed something he had feared. He rapped his knuckles absently on the door frame then left, closing the door behind him.

*

They let me go a little later. Stewart was on his way to discuss the case with the Procurator Fiscal and Andrea had invited herself along. Before I left I asked Stewart if Jessica would face any charges – she had killed a man after all, and the forensic evidence would make that an indisputable fact.

'No,' Stewart had assured me. 'The Fiscal doesn't prosecute victims. Bad PR.'

Andrea said nothing but the faintest of smiles on her lips told me how quickly she would have destroyed any such case had the Fiscal decided to pursue it.

I walked briskly through Paisley town centre to the taxi rank at Gilmour Street train station. There was no queue and I clambered into the first taxi, flopping into the big rear seat of the hackney. 'RAH please, mate.'

The driver looked at me in the rear view mirror then turned and took a better look. 'Not before time, pal. Eh… there's a fifty quid charge if you bleed in the cab.'

'Don't worry, I'm just about empty.'

I laughed quietly to myself, a discordant, tired note that bordered on hysteria. He looked at me as though I'd come straight from Dykebar before reluctantly turning his back on me and driving off. My mouth split open in a grin as the cab lurched forward. After what I'd been through, you'd have to be crazy to be sane.

*

I had to fight with the nurses to get in to see Mack. They were protective of their patient, pointing out the trauma he had been through and how vital rest was for his recovery. I refused to leave without seeing him though and one of them eventually took pity on me and took me to him, showing me inside and closing the door softly behind me. When I saw him and felt the emotion hit me I was grateful for the privacy.

Mack lay in a bed, swathed in bandages and surrounded by tubes and wires and machines whose soft whirrs and beeps were the only sound in the room. Until his eyes fluttered open and he saw me.

'About time. Where's my grapes and Lucozade?' His voice was ragged and hoarse, slurred with drugs, but there was life there still. I smiled in relief.

'That's strange, I sent some up earlier. Bloody nurses must have nicked them' I shook my head in mock disgust. 'Can't trust anyone these days.'

I pulled up a chair and sat beside the bed. 'How you doing?'

'Just peachy.'

'They told me you needed three pints of blood.'

Mack waved a weak hand. 'Just an oil change, isn't it?'

I wanted to ask him more about his health, but he cared about only one thing. 'Did you get him?'

He had still been conscious when Jessica had visited her terrible fury on Phil Biggart; it was Brandon he wanted to know about. I nodded. 'He's in good hands.'

'McKenzie?'

'Some men will do anything for their daughters.'

I saw a light bloom in Mack's eyes; a light ignited by real justice. He smiled and raised a fist. I bumped my knuckles against it.

He dropped his hand to the bed and drifted into a drug-induced sleep. I stood and walked to the door, where I turned back to look at my friend. I was unsure how to say what needed to be said. Mack had come back for me when he could have left; when he should have left; when I would have happily let him take Jessica to safety and leave me. And he had almost died because of that. *Had* died.

There were no words to acknowledge that debt. God knows I tried to think of them, but nothing came.

For the moment, all I said was, 'Thanks.'

*

I walked into Jessica's room and my breath caught. She looked small and vulnerable; a tiny mound wrapped tightly in hospital issue bedsheets, her eyes closed tightly against the world. A nurse had told me she'd be sleeping for a while yet, but it didn't matter.

I sat down on a chair beside the bed and stretched out a hand, letting it burrow under the sheets until it found her hand. She flinched at first and tried to pull it away, then she seemed to recognise it, or something in the gesture, and her fingers curled around it, pulling it to her chest. She hunkered down in the sheets and her eyelids flickered briefly.

She didn't wake up though, not then, and in a way I was glad. At that moment it was enough to simply sit there and watch over her. I had almost lost her once; lost her because she was willing to sacrifice her own life for mine. I sat for a long time, and yet it would never be enough to explain what I felt, or even to begin. We had all been close to death, but Jessica had stared into its eyes longest, had felt its breath on her neck, and yet she had still returned to save Mack from Phil's knife. True, pure, distilled evil had roared in her face. And she had roared back.

I felt humbled and small, and in awe of her strength.

There was a squeeze on my hand and I realised that I had fallen asleep. I opened my eyes and saw Jessica looking back at me. She cast her eyes down to where my arm disappeared under her covers.

'Pervert,' she whispered.

And then she smiled. And I forgot the aches and pains and the horrific things I had seen and done. Nothing else mattered but that smile and I let myself sink into its beauty. Everything else – every*one* else – could wait.

Forty-Seven

I managed an hour or so with Jessica before the nurses returned to chase me away, adamant that she wouldn't get better if I didn't give her peace. Then they turned their attention on me, casting a collective clinical eye over my various cuts and bruises. I backed off and left them to it. Jessica and Mack were both out for the count anyway, loaded to the gunnels with enough drugs to tranquilise half of Paisley. Even the half that had built up a tolerance.

I left the hospital to find a taxi. My car was still sitting outside my office, tyres slashed to ribbons, and, along with the office itself, probably crawling with crime scene technicians by now. And Mack's was still up in the Braes, part of the extensive crime scene search instigated by DI Stewart. I didn't expect either vehicle to be released anytime soon.

When I finally found a taxi I got the driver to drop me at one of the car rental places near Glasgow Airport and twenty minutes later I drove off in a silver Ford Focus.

I arrived home and trudged wearily up the stairs to my flat where I raided the fridge for a couple of cans of Irn-Bru before collapsing onto my sofa. I popped the top on the first can and drained it in three long swallows. I crushed the can and dropped it on the floor beside me. I rested its pal against my forehead, enjoying the cold feeling against my skin.

I lay like that for a while, unable to summon up the energy to do anything. I knew I should call Archie Bell and let him know what had happened – he was my client after all – but I couldn't rouse myself. *Later*, I told myself, *later's fine*. Instead I sat staring into space and thought about the way things had ended.

I eventually called Brownstone to thank her and to let her know we were okay; something she already knew from listening in on the police frequencies and hacking the RAH records. I was amazed. Not at her; at a hospital having their records up to date so quickly. She waved off the thanks and, wary of making her uncomfortable, I didn't push it. There would be other times.

I switched on the television and caught a news update. The house in the Braes was big news already, hidden in the trees some way behind the windswept reporter talking to the camera. There was a lot of speculation, but none of it mentioned the serial killer; apparently the media hadn't been tipped off that Crawford Laing was no longer guilty. The report droned on with more and more speculation, none of it accurate. I switched it off and my thoughts drifted back to Jessica and Mack. I wished I had some work to occupy my mind, something to distract me from the worry and guilt and I decided to see if there was any business brewing. I picked up the phone to call my office and entered the code to retrieve my messages.

'You have two new messages,' the machine informed me.

Promising. I pressed a button and the first message played. It had been left the previous day by Stewart after I had demanded he meet us at Mack's gym. I heard the beginning of a vague threat before I deleted the message.

The second message had been left last night while we were playing tig in the Braes with a couple of knife-wielding maniacs. It began to play and there was a pause before anyone spoke. I figured it was a telemarketer and had my finger poised to delete it when a young woman's voice finally spoke.

'Eh, hi... this is a message for Mr Harper... My name's Rebecca Davidson... I think you wanted to speak to me... about Janet Bell... My mum told me to call you.'

It took me a second to place the name, then I remembered it was Janet's friend who had been on holiday. It didn't matter now, and my finger returned to the delete button.

'Anyway... I've seen the news... I know they found the man who killed her so... well, I guess you don't need me anymore... I just thought I should call. Well, I wasn't going to... I don't have anything to say about her... but my mum made me. So, anyway... yeah... that's it, I suppose.'

There was another pause before Rebecca Davidson hung up, then a click and the machine told me it had reached the end of my messages. I didn't delete that one though. I played it again as a crease developed between my eyebrows. And I played it again, and again.

I finally ended the call and placed the phone beside me on the sofa, chewing my lip as I thought it over.

*

The door was opened by a girl of about twenty, with black hair and a round face, a little overweight and self-conscious about it. She wore jeans and a thick, cosy looking jumper to hide her shape. It took a second before she noticed the various lumps and bumps that populated my face and head and recoiled slightly.

'Rebecca? My name is Keir Harper. You left a message for me yesterday.'

'Oh, right... yeah.' Still looking at me like I've fallen out of the sky. That didn't feel too far wide of the mark.

'I was hoping we could have a wee chat. About Janet.'

She hesitated and I was wondering how to convince her when another person appeared behind her. The door opened wider and a young man stood there appraising me. He was tall and thin, dressed in a black long-sleeve polo neck sweater, his hair black and spiky, with long sideburns leading to an impressively thick beard.

'Can we help you?' he asked. Not aggressive, but not exactly welcoming either.

'I wanted to speak to Rebecca about her friend Janet.'

As I spoke I watched his eyes, set deep in his thin, almost gaunt face. They were piercing and fierce, yet quite suddenly filled with turmoil as I spoke. I saw something there that was halfway between anger and pain and I knew I was right to have come here.

'Then I think you should come in,' he said finally.

Rebecca turned and gave him a quick, worried look, but his eyes were soft now, reassuring her. They both stepped inside and I followed.

The boyfriend hung back behind me while Rebecca led the way into a living room that was so neat it was almost sterile. I took a seat on a hideously floral sofa that looked as though it was kept purely for show. Rebecca's boyfriend sat down on the sofa opposite me, pulling Rebecca close to him. 'I'm Colin Drysdale,' he said politely.

I introduced myself to him and asked again what they could tell me about Janet Bell.

'Like I said on the phone, I don't have anything to say about her.' Rebecca's voice was verging on strident.

I thought about her reaction for a moment, then took the plunge. 'I came to see you because you were a close friend of Janet's. Closer than most – you lived together. I thought you might be able to help me.'

'We weren't close.'

'Maybe not anymore, but you were once.'

'What difference does it make now? She's dead and they caught the guy who did it.'

'The thing is, you don't sound very upset that she's dead. The message you left – even now – you don't sound as though it bothers you.'

'I told you, we weren't close anymore.'

Colin remained silent, but I got the feeling he was itching to speak.

'You said in your message that you didn't have anything to say about *her*. Funny thing is, Rebecca, it almost sounds like your glad she's dead.'

I sat back and let them stew in that for a while. It may be nothing, it may be some minor argument that had got out of hand, but if this was the reaction Rebecca Davidson had to the news that a once close friend had died, I would hate to see what she did if it was a mortal enemy.

Neither of them spoke for a minute or two, intent only on one another's faces, an entire conversation taking place in their eyes.

'It's a shame,' I said, pushing it. 'Janet was just a nice quiet girl who never hurt anyone. She didn't deserve this.'

'Never hurt anyone?' Rebecca hissed, her eyes sparking. 'The bitch got what she deserved!'

My gamble had paid off, but now I spoke softly. 'Tell me.'

'She was wicked,' Rebecca spat. 'Absolutely wicked and spiteful.'

That seemed overly dramatic, given what I had previously heard about Janet. Nevertheless, I kept a poker face and let her continue.

'I've known her since we were eleven, when we started high school together. Or I thought I knew her. We were close, like you said, so close we got a flat together. We moved in and things were fine.'

'Until I turned up,' Colin said bitterly.

'I met Colin a few months after me and Janet moved in together.' She turned and gave him a smile that came right from the heart. 'We just clicked, you know? So we were pretty intense at first. I didn't see much of Janet; I was either at Colin's or he was at our place and I was too busy with him.'

'Janet didn't like that,' Colin added.

'She was jealous. She'd always been the prettier one. She was the one who met boys while I sat in the corner. I think she liked it that way.'

I thought of Leeann Munro and silently agreed. Janet did seem to choose friends who made her look more attractive.

'She was determined to ruin our relationship,' Colin said. 'Hell bent on it. She couldn't stand to see Rebecca happy when she wasn't.'

'She'd never be happy,' Rebecca sneered. 'She was always looking for something else.'

I sighed inwardly and figured I was wasting my time here after all. This was beginning to look like another case of best-friends-forever falling out as soon as one of them finds a boyfriend.

'What did she do?' I asked, resigned to a recitation of over-inflated squabbles and misinterpreted slights.

'She told me Rebecca was cheating on me,' Colin said in a flat tone. 'Then she got me drunk and... seduced me.'

I raised an eyebrow. I had been Colin's age not too long ago and I knew how unlikely it was that he had needed much persuasion. Telling him his girlfriend was cheating on him was low, but at least it gave him an excuse to salve his conscience with.

'And she told you?' I said to Rebecca. 'Trying to drive you apart.'

'No. Then she'd have been equally to blame.' Rebecca ran her hand over her mouth before she forced the words out. 'She told me that he raped her.'

Oh.

'I didn't believe her at first,' she added quickly. 'But she was my best friend... and he looked guilty.'

Colin's face burned red with embarrassment and anger. Of course he had looked guilty; he'd screwed his girlfriend's best pal. I was beginning to understand why Rebecca and Janet had fallen out and why there was no love lost. If this was the truth of course. It was perfectly possible that Colin Drysdale was the liar and had conned his girlfriend into believing his version of events, something that would have inevitably driven Janet away.

'She didn't leave it there though. Oh no, she wasn't finished.' Colin's voice throbbed with a deep-rooted anger.

Rebecca sobbed now, tears strolling down her cheeks. 'She kept telling me that he shouldn't get away with it. She kept on and on about it. I was a wreck, I listened to her.' The shame in her voice was palpable. 'I wanted to tell the police but she said they wouldn't believe us. It was her word against his. She said we had to confront him together – make him tell the truth to both of us, admit what he'd done wrong.'

'Did you?' I asked.

'I thought it was a chance for Rebecca and I to sit down and talk about this,' Colin interrupted, a bitter laugh escaping his lips. 'To sort out our relationship. I didn't know then what Janet had accused me of. I still thought Rebecca was mad because I'd slept with her pal.'

'What happened?'

Rebecca sobbed, her head in her hands, as Colin spoke. 'They were both there. As soon as I walked in Janet started hitting me, screaming at me – a whole load of things that weren't true. That's when I found out she'd said I raped her. I was stunned, I just stood there while they both laid into me. I didn't hit them back – I can't hit a woman. I tried to fend them off, hoping they'd calm down.'

'They didn't,' I said.

Colin shook his head stiffly. 'No. Janet ran into the kitchen and came back with a pot of boiling water which she threw over me.'

A fresh moan of anguish came from between Rebecca's hands, her face still hidden in shame.

I stared at Colin in shock. He stood up and pulled off his polo neck. 'This is what she did.'

His torso was a mess; burns spreading in a shiny, rubbery mass from one side of his chest to another, splashing his upper arms and reaching up his neck until they disappeared into the beard he'd grown to hide his scars.

'That's what your nice quiet girl was capable of, Mr Harper. All because her friend was happy. Did she deserve what happened to her? You're damn right she did. If the man who killed her was still alive I'd shake his hand.

This was no fabricated tale; the venom in Colin's voice was unmistakeable and the scars he bore backed up their story. I fumbled around for a minute, trying to find the right question.

'Had she been drinking?' I asked feebly. 'Taking anything?'

'Janet didn't take drugs, and she didn't drink much either. She couldn't stand to hand control over to anyone – or anything. She looked right down her nose at anyone who was wasted.'

He looked away from me, his eyes focused on a night in the past; the night he had got drunk and made a mistake that had scarred the rest of his life.

'Why would Janet do something like that?' I asked quietly.

'Because she's evil!' Rebecca cried. She pulled a tissue from inside her sleeve and began wiping her nose.

'Maybe she just wanted to hurt someone else for a change,' Colin said.

'Who hurt her?'

Colin sneered. 'No, she hurt *herself*.'

'Physically?'

'Oh aye, she had scars all up her arms and thighs from where she cut herself.'

Rebecca looked at him in surprise. Then her face clouded as

she realised how he knew about Janet's scars. Colin looked ashamed and stared at the carpet.

'Did you know about this?' I asked Rebecca.

Her head bobbed up and down a couple of times. 'At first I was really worried about her, then I realised she was trying to get attention.'

'It's not usually about that when people self-harm,' I said. 'It's a coping mechanism. Generally they're very self-conscious about it and try to hide it from others.'

'Well that wasn't Janet,' Rebecca said angrily. 'I walked in on her cutting herself plenty of times. I know now it was deliberate. She wanted me to see, and she used it to manipulate me, make me feel sorry for her so I would worry about her and try to look after her. She just wanted the rest of us to dance to her tune.'

'Who else knew about her self-harming?' I asked.

'I'm not sure. She wasn't very close with many people. Her dad would have known, she'd have used it to wrap him even further round her little finger.'

'He didn't mention it,' I said thoughtfully.

'Figures,' Colin said. 'He wouldn't say anything that might be construed as a negative remark about his precious daughter.'

'He's right,' Rebecca agreed. 'Janet's dad would do anything for her. She's still got him fooled. I'd been hoping some day she'd push him too far and he'd throw her out, but I doubt that would ever have happened.'

I didn't respond for a minute, so engrossed was I in that comment. Eventually I realised they were both staring at me expectantly. I thanked them for their time and Colin followed me to the door, leaving Rebecca in the living room, wiping her reddened nose and blotting her teary eyes with the same tissue.

'I hope you two can get past this,' I said as I opened the front door.

Colin's chin jutted out in defiance. 'We will. We're not going to let her ruin our lives.'

I didn't share his confidence, but I nodded and told him I was sorry for reopening old wounds.

'And I'm sorry you wasted your time looking for someone who

was better off missing,' Colin replied. 'She wasn't what you thought she was, was she?'

'No.' I stopped at the bottom of the small flight of steps and looked back up at him. 'She wasn't.'

'Ah well, she's still dead,' he said with a degree of satisfaction. 'So it didn't matter. It didn't change anything.'

I heard the door close behind me as I swung open the garden gate. I got into the Focus, closed the door behind me and sat for a moment with the key in my hand. I let my mind go where it needed to; where it should have long before now.

He was wrong. It did matter.

And it changed everything.

Forty-Eight

Archie answered the door and smiled sadly at me through the security chain. He closed the door and opened it again, stepping back and inviting me inside. I pushed past him without speaking and stood in the middle of his living room. There was an open holdall on the end of the armchair with a neatly folded pile of clothes inside.

Archie closed the door and came back inside, still smiling. I nodded at the bag. 'Going away?'

Archie followed my gaze. 'I'm not sure I can stay here without Janet. The memories... you know? I'll take a week or two away somewhere and think things over. I might sell up, find something smaller.'

I nodded understandingly.

'I still can't thank you properly,' Archie said, shaking his head and wringing his hands. 'You've given me closure – something I never thought I'd get.'

'Closure is a term used by psychologists and people who've never lost anything that mattered to them,' I told him. 'It doesn't make it easier. The dead are still dead. Knowing who, where and why just means you have specific nightmares instead of vague ones.'

'Well, eh, yes, of course,' Archie stammered. 'Obviously nothing can bring Janet back, but I appreciate the effort you put into finding that man Laing. And I thank God you did. At least no more families will go through this.'

Archie slid into his armchair. I remained standing and moved to the cabinet where the framed photographs were displayed. I picked one up and looked at it, searching for a face I recognised. I replaced the picture on the shelf and turned back to Archie, making sure I could see his eyes as I spoke.

'Crawford Laing didn't kill anyone, Archie.'

He was stunned. 'But the police said... you said...'

'We got it wrong. All of us.'

'Then who killed all these people?'

'Two men, named Phil Biggart and Eric Brandon. They've been caught now and they're in police custody at the moment. They'll be going away for a long time.'

Archie's eyes bulged and he took a moment to gather himself. 'But... well... you still found her killer. It was them, wasn't it?'

I shook my head and looked at another picture on display, saw the similarities, and felt the last piece slide into place.

'No. They didn't kill Janet. They killed the others. But not Janet.'

'I don't understand? They must have.'

'I spoke to one of them before he was caught. He told me about the other victims and why they had been chosen.' The words rang in my mind – *she abandoned her son... one made dirty movies and screwed everything with a pulse... one was a queer...* 'He never mentioned Janet.'

Archie looked at me for a moment, waiting for more. Then he gave a snort of disbelief. 'Oh, come on. You can't listen to people like that. They're not even people. They're evil; they play mind games with you. They want to manipulate you even after they've been caught.'

'When he told me this he had a knife pressed against the back of my neck. He was very much in charge and he had no intention of being caught. There was no reason for him not to mention it – he was proud of his scalps.'

Archie stood up, looking indignant. 'I think you should show some respect. One of those *scalps* was my daughter.'

I sat on the sofa, taking the wind out of Archie's sails by leaving him standing alone. 'Thing is, Archie, I began looking for Janet and before I even had a chance to form an opinion on what might have happened I found out she'd been killed by a serial killer. After that the case was no longer about Janet Bell; it was about a serial killer.'

'Isn't that the same thing?' Archie asked, a confused half smile on his face.

'No, not exactly. You see, I once knew a girl who was murdered. Brutally murdered, just like Janet. I've never forgotten her – never want to – but I went after this guy like it was her killer I was hunting. I lost my focus and started chasing the ghosts from my past.'

'But you found the killer, so... does it matter?'

'I found him alright. And I'm going to make sure he goes to jail for a long, long time.'

'Maybe the police will have charged them by now?'

I gave him a cold look. 'They didn't kill Janet, Archie. You did.'

His mouth dropped open, revealing unsightly yellowish teeth. He stared at me as he collapsed into his armchair again. I stood up and crossed the room, looming over him as I spoke.

'Here are the facts, Archie.' I reeled them off and slapped each one down in front of him like I was dealing cards. 'The killers didn't mention Janet. Conclusion? They didn't kill her. There was no trace of Janet found at their killing house. Conclusion? She was never there. Janet's hands were the only missing body parts of any victim not recovered from that house. Conclusion? They didn't remove them. The biblical reference carved into Janet's chest was the only one that didn't refer to a specific sin. Conclusion? Her killer didn't understand their significance. Janet was the only victim who can't be definitively linked to the firm of private investigators that all of the other victims consulted. Conclusion? She was never there. Conclusion? She never met the serial killers. Conclusion? Someone else killed her. Conclusion? *You* killed her, Archie. You murdered your own daughter.'

Archie sat and shook while I glared into his eyes and saw what I had expected to see. It was several seconds before he could calm himself enough to speak.

'You... you're mad... I didn't... I couldn't. It must have been someone else. Maybe it was her boyfriend, the one who beat her up.'

'There's no way Johnny D'Arienzo could have killed your daughter without leaving evidence that he was the killer. He's not that smart. And there's no way he could have passed the killing off as the work of the serial killer.'

'Then who could have?'

I stalked across the room and lifted the picture I had been looking at; the one I had noticed the first time I came here; the one that showed Archie and his university colleagues seated around a dinner table, wine glasses in hand.

'Only someone who knew enough about the killings.' I pointed to the back corner of the photograph, to where Eric Brandon sat tucked between two women, glass raised in a toast to the camera. 'Brandon played a part, and he played it to perfection; the part of a loudmouth blowhard, someone who was too much of a pompous buffoon to be taken seriously. The kind of man you'd never suspect. He was happy to spill the details of all the cases he worked on with the police. He told his tales at dinner parties and you lapped them up, waiting for one you could use to get rid of your daughter.'

'That's absolutely ridiculous! I never listened to Brandon. The man's an arrogant imbecile. You've lost your mind – I could never hurt my daughter.'

'I'm getting used to the evil that people can do to each other.

'But why would I kill her? Tell me that. I adored her – why on earth would I murder her?'

I stopped then, clenching my fingers in frustration. 'That's the one thing I've not figured out yet. Who knows? Maybe you were sick of running around after her. Maybe she was going to run away with Johnny and you'd rather kill her than have her leave you. Maybe there was something a little more intimate going on between you and she wanted to call it off, or she threatened to tell the cops.'

Archie rose to his feet in a rage. 'How dare you!' he screamed. 'Who the *fuck* do you think you are? Get out of my house!'

I looked at him in satisfaction; again seeing what I had been looking for. I smiled inwardly and stepped towards the door.

'I know you killed her, Archie. And as soon as I find something I can nail you with I'll be back here to drag you to the cops myself.' I nodded at the holdall. 'You might want to pack more; you'll be away for about thirty years.'

I closed the door behind me and walked back down the path to the Focus. I smiled in grim satisfaction as I got into the car. I had done what I came here to do.

I had rattled the cage.

Now I had to wait for the bird to fly.

There wasn't long to wait. Less than an hour later Archie panicked. He left his house with barely a glance up or down the street, jumped into the Volvo and sped off.

I started the car and followed.

Forty-Nine

And here I was; standing in a hotel corridor – one of a thousand featureless, unremarkable ones like it in the city – with blood pounding in my ears and a dark, cold determination in my muscles as I stared at the door to room 134.

People had died – some I had known and some I hadn't, scars had been inflicted and received, and people I loved had been to the verge of hell. The wickedness within this room hadn't caused all of it, but in this place, in this moment, it had become impossible to differentiate: like two strains of the same malignant virus. I had faced evil. I had seen its teeth and heard its howls, and I knew it well.

And I knew it lay behind this door.

The sounds inside the room stopped. I stepped forward and drove my heel into the lock.

The door smashed open, and I went in.

Archie spun and stared at me in shock as I slammed the door behind me, its ruined lock preventing it closing fully.

'Knock... *fucking*... knock.'

'What... what are you doing?' Archie stammered. 'You can't just barge in here.'

'Why are you in a hotel, Archie?'

'Because you're harassing me! Why won't you let me grieve in peace?'

'Not bad,' I admitted grudgingly. 'Not bad at all for on-the-spot-bullshit. But you're still a lying sack of shit.'

'How dare you!' Archie stood by the window with his arms crossed, his eyes flitting beyond me to the only exit.

'Drop the act, Archie. I know exactly what happened.'

'For God's sake! I did NOT kill my daughter!'
'I know.'

Archie looked at me in confusion. Then his expression changed to horror as I took two steps and threw open the bathroom door.

'Nobody did.'

Janet Bell looked back at me with eyes that could have skinned a rhino. She stood in the centre of the bathroom, her arms crossed inside long black sleeves. Her now-brown hair hung to her shoulders, her mouth was thin and pinched, and the eyes that had been light and sparkling in photographs were dark and malevolent.

'You're looking pretty healthy for a dead girl,' I told her.

Janet stepped towards me as I backed towards the door to the corridor. She stopped at the bathroom door and leant on the frame, looking me up and down as though measuring me for a plot. 'I don't have the first clue what you're talking about,' she replied quietly. 'My name's Sarah Brown.'

'Well, that's the name you checked in under. They told me that downstairs.' I reached into my coat pocket and took out a piece of paper, unfolded it and held it up. 'They also identified you from this photo. Funny, you look happier as a blonde.'

'I'm happier when I don't have lunatics breaking into my room.'

'So how do you know Archie?' I asked conversationally.

'I don't need to answer to you. I don't even know who you are. Now leave my room or I'll call security.'

'You can drop the act, Janet. The scars gave you away.'

I looked at Archie and saw his jaw tremble. Once I would have sympathised with his weakness. Now I felt only revulsion.

'Rebecca and Colin told me about you, Janet. Told me who you really are, and about your manipulative cutting and the scars it left you with. They thought you really were dead, but Janet Bell's post mortem report only mentioned one old scar; the one on the forearm.' I grabbed Janet's arm and pushed up her sleeve, revealing several pale scars running across her arm below the elbow. 'It didn't mention these.'

'Don't you dare touch her!' Archie bellowed. This was the Archie I knew existed, the one that had shown his face when I'd accused him of screwing his daughter; the one that had told me I was right.

The Worst of Evils

He rushed across the room towards me and I fired a short jab into his nose. He stumbled back and I followed up with a straight right, putting him on his arse.

'Nice poker face, Archie. I guess this is your daughter then.'

I turned to Janet who hadn't moved other than to roll her sleeve back down, covering her scars once again. 'How much was all this for then? What was it you took from Johnny? Twenty-three grand?'

'Who's Johnny?' Janet sneered.

I walked over to the small wardrobe built into the room and opened the door. On the floor was a pale blue holdall. I lifted it out, unzipped it and tipped it out onto the bed. The contents spilled out; clothes and shoes, toiletries and make up. And a wad of banknotes.

Archie's eyes widened as he saw the money. Apparently this was a part of the plan he hadn't been aware of.

I picked up the money and waved it at Janet. 'It wasn't really about the money though, was it? You took it because you wanted it and you're used to taking what you want. Johnny died because you stole that money.'

A smile teased the corners of her mouth.

'You know your problem, Janet?'

'Do tell.'

'Your life sucks.' Anger flashed in her eyes and I pressed on. 'You hate your life because you're a nobody and you think you should be somebody. So you decided to steal the money and move on, hoping you wouldn't balls it up this time.'

'You think twenty-three grand is enough to start a new life?' She looked at me pityingly. 'That says a lot about your life.'

'No, I don't. And neither do you. That's why you were waiting for your dad; the grief-stricken father who couldn't live in the same city that had robbed him of his daughter. He packs up, sells the house, puts the money straight into an account while you both decide where to live, then wakes up one morning to find you've buggered off with his money too.'

A dark glimmer in her eyes told me I was right. Archie would do anything for his daughter – had performed unspeakable acts – but this was no two-way street. The only reason she would hang around and wait for him was if she had something to gain. And the only thing Archie had of any value was his home. Add that to Johnny's money and Janet would have well over a hundred grand to start afresh somewhere no-one knew she was supposed to be dead.

'How'd she talk you into it, Archie? Was it the old *my-boyfriend-beats-me-up-I'm-scared-for-my-life* routine?'

'What would you have done?' Archie growled through the tissue he held against his nose.

'I'd have put him in the fucking hospital!' I shouted. 'And if you'd done that I'd have shaken your hand and walked away. But you didn't have the balls to face him.'

'He'd have killed me and taken it out on Janet.'

'He never laid a hand on her, Archie. Not once.'

'One punch. That's all. Just one punch and she could have lost her child.'

'Is that what she told you?' I shook my head at her manipulation. 'She's not pregnant. Never has been. She's too selfish to have a baby. She only told you she was so you'd think you had two generations of your family to protect.'

'What are you, a fucking gynaecologist?' Janet seethed.

Someone's getting rattled. Good.

'So you told Archie you were pregnant, terrified that Johnny would kill you and your fictional child, and desperate to escape. You convinced your dad that he would never let you leave, but it was the money Johnny couldn't let go. Not when it belonged to Ruby Volta.

'And you knew exactly how to stop Johnny coming after you.' I reached into my coat pocket again and pulled out another folded picture. I opened it out and held it up. 'Recognise her?'

Janet shook her head, acting bored, while Archie's jaw sagged a little.

'You should. She's the woman you killed; the one you identified as your daughter, Archie. Her name's Diane Hill.'

I held the two photos side by side; two young women; a victim and her killer. 'Johnny followed you after Janet went missing. He wasn't impressed at you checking out hookers while your daughter was supposedly missing. You weren't though, were you? You were trying to find a look-alike. Johnny saw you finally pick one up, one he said could've been your daughter. I missed it at the time – I thought he was talking about her age – but he actually meant she looked like Janet. Same height, build, hair. All you had to do was choose a vaguely threatening biblical reference, bash her face in till it was unrecognisable, cut off her hands in case she'd ever been fingerprinted – possible, since she was a hooker – and tell anyone investigating that Janet had been into drugs and casual sex with anyone she could find.'

I turned to Janet's frosty face. 'You see, I thought all your friends were reluctant to bad mouth you, but even Rebecca and Colin – who have plenty of reasons to despise you – said you didn't do drink or drugs. Guess you were just worried about your stunt double being a junkie.'

'What is this?' Janet exploded. 'Agatha fucking Christie? You come in here and give us this shite and expect us to, what, confess? Not a shred of evidence, but we'll suddenly dissolve into floods of tears and admit everything we've done? Aye, right. Don't hold your breath, Poirot.'

'And where exactly are we supposed to have killed this girl?' Archie asked, emboldened by Janet's outburst.

'Don't know,' I admitted. 'But it's not my concern. The police will find it. You're not good enough to have erased all your tracks.'

'This doesn't make any sense,' Archie argued. 'If I killed someone, why would I hire a private investigator?'

'Because you needed the body to be identified as your daughter. The police can't do much when adults go missing and there are no suspicious circumstances. That meant someone else could report Diane Hill missing and identify the body before you, sending you back to square one. You needed to claim the body first, so you used me to present the police with a ready-made identification; their dead body, my missing client. All you had to do was plant some of Diane's hair in Janet's bedroom and at the hotel. The DNA then links your home, the hotel, and the victim, who everyone now believes is Janet.

'You screwed up though, Archie. When I first told you Janet had been murdered by a serial killer I never told you how many victims there were, but you told me he'd killed Janet plus two other girls.

And then you tried to force a link between Janet and the rest of the victims, phoning me to tell me that you'd *suddenly remembered* Janet had talked about tracing her mother. Do you think I'm stupid?'

Resignation stole across Archie's face. He knew the end was here and he decided to face it the only way he knew how.

'You're right.' He removed the blood-stained tissue from his face and clambered to his feet. 'I killed her to protect my daughter. I found that prostitute and decided I'd rather she died than my daughter. Janet knew nothing about it.'

I cursed inwardly at his misplaced honour. 'Then why is she hiding out in a hotel room?'

Suddenly Janet was a different person. Gone was the hard-faced bitch that had been willing me to burst into flames, and here in her place was a scared, confused little girl, lip trembling as she looked at her dad like she'd never seen him before.

'Dad, tell me you didn't? Tell me you didn't hurt someone?'

And at that moment, that precise moment that his daughter sold him out to save herself, I saw Archie's heart break and his life end. His chin dropped to the floor and a tear trickled down his face. His voice was choked and cracking as he spoke. 'I'm sorry, darling. I just wanted to protect you.'

'Oh, Dad,' Janet sobbed. 'You shouldn't have hurt anyone. Why did you do it?'

'You're my daughter. I had to protect you.'

'By murdering an innocent woman?' I asked.

'She was a hooker,' Archie spat. 'Don't ask me to measure my daughter's life against that of a prostitute. There's no comparison.'

Janet's hands flew to her face in shock, laying it on thick. 'Dad, you can't mean that,' she said, shocked. 'She was a person, just like the rest of us.'

'Your mum would be glad to hear you say that,' I said offhand.

'What?' Janet's face had hardened once more while Archie looked at me in confusion.

'Your dad said you'd talked about finding your mum. After you were found dead I tracked her down, felt it was my duty to tell her what had happened to you.' I shrugged as though it was the least I could do. 'Turns out she's a prostitute now...'

Janet's eyes blazed and the little lost girl disappeared into hard darkness. 'You're a liar.'

'...And not your high-class hooker either, we're talking tenner blow-job stuff...'

'Don't you dare!'

'...Don't know how she gets any punters to be honest, she's got track marks like tram lines...'

'Shut your mouth!'

'...Seriously, who knows where she's been. You could be stirring anyone's porridge...'

'You bastard!' Janet screamed. 'I'll fucking kill you too!'

Her hand went to the back pocket of her jeans and came out with a razor blade. She swung her arm in a wide arc, the blade missing my face by inches as I leant backwards. I pushed her hand as it passed, turning her sideways, and punched her on the arm. The muscle deadened and her fingers opened, the blade tumbling to the carpet.

Janet looked at me with the same eyes Eric Brandon had; eyes that swam with pure malevolent hatred. I saw those eyes and her features blurred before me until I saw only the shape of evil. And I lashed out to make it go away, my fist knocking her back against the bathroom door, where she crumpled to her knees.

There was a roar behind me and I turned in time to dodge Archie's wild punch. I knocked his hand away and drove my knee into his gut. He staggered back and I smashed an elbow into his face. He fell like a stone, his arms splayed wide as he hit the carpet.

The door opened and heavy footsteps pounded into the room. 'Police!' shouted two voices simultaneously.

I raised my hands in a gesture of compliance as two burly uniformed constables barrelled into the room. I needn't have bothered; they made a beeline for Archie, hauling him to his feet and pushing him face first into the wall. He groaned as his nose smeared a streak of blood on the magnolia wallpaper.

'Oh, thank God,' moaned Janet. She pointed at Archie. 'You have to stop him, he's killed someone, he's crazy!'

DI Stewart stepped into the room and looked around. 'Read him his rights,' he said to the uniforms.

Janet scrambled to her feet and went to Stewart, her face once more bearing the expression of the innocent girl lost in a world she couldn't understand. Tears bubbled to the surface and she tried to throw her arms round Stewart in gratitude.

'Her too,' Stewart said, his words falling like broken icicles.

Janet's mouth opened in surprise. She looked around wildly then pushed past Stewart to get to the door. He let her go, only for her to be stopped in her tracks by DS Taylor's palm slapping hard against her chest as the policewoman entered the room.

'What's the rush, darling? Can't wait to get to Cornton Vale to see all the big hairy rug-munchers?'

'Fuck off, dyke,' Janet said, pushing forward again.

The next thing she said was ayafuckingbitch as Taylor wrenched her arm up her back and pinned her against the wall.

DI Stewart wore a small smile on his face as he surveyed the scene. He glanced down and saw the razor blade where Janet had dropped it, bright against the dark blue carpet like a new star in the night sky.

Stewart raised an eyebrow at me and asked, 'Do you ever do anything the easy way?'

I said nothing, just watched as Taylor and the two uniforms huckled Janet and Archie Bell into the corridor. Archie shuffled from the room like a man with no reason to live. He had committed heinous acts to protect the daughter he adored, and now she had burned him to save herself. I almost felt sorry for him. Then I pictured Diane Hill's face

I reached into my pocket, removed the transmitter and placed it in Stewart's palm.

'Is it enough?' I asked.

'It will be,' he replied. 'Archie was screwed anyway, but now we've got a confession. And Janet's only chance was to play the scared little girl card, act like she had no idea what her dad had done. That'll fool no-one now she's come at you with a razor blade.'

'Archie will try to take the blame. It's all he knows.'

'We'll get her.' Stewart paused for a second then said, 'She helped with the killing, didn't she?'

'Definitely. Archie did what he felt he had to, but she would have enjoyed it. You can see it in her eyes.'

'We'll get her,' he repeated. He paused again, then asked, 'Did you really find her mother?'

'What do you think?'

Stewart nodded softly. 'That's what I thought. Pity, we could have charged her with bringing motherhood into disrepute after giving birth to that psycho.'

'I'll settle for seeing the two of them locked up. That'll do.'

It would have to. It wasn't enough – not really, not for all the pain they had caused – but it was as good as we could hope for. Sometimes you have to take what you can get and find a way to live with it.

It wasn't closure, and it never would be.

And I wasn't sure that it was justice, or ever could be.

Maybe all it amounted to was retribution.

In the end, I could live with that.

Epilogue

Ruby Volta lay back on the sun-lounger and stretched his arms as far above his head as he could before the huge rolls of flesh bunched around his shoulders. It was eleven o'clock; the night was dark outside the skylight windows of his custom-built indoor swimming pool, the room lit only by a soft amber glow from the hidden lights around the pool.

He lowered his arms and folded the towelling bathrobe around himself once more as he tried to relax. He was loathe to admit it, but the war with Innes McKenzie was not going well. Things would change – he had too much confidence in himself to doubt that – but for the moment his home was the one place where he was untouchable. And this room was special. The only people allowed to venture beyond the doors were the young girls he ordered like takeaway. Even his bodyguards did not cross the threshold unless a clean-up was required.

This was his sanctuary, his private place; a room that fluctuated between quiet solace and cries of pain and terror.

Volta closed his eyes and smiled to himself as he thought of the last young girl he had brought here. Lithuanian, no more than twelve, with a voice that almost scarred the walls when she screamed. His hand strayed to the front of his trunks as he felt a stirring within.

Suddenly Volta became aware of another presence and his eyes snapped open. A figure in black stood over him, a gun in his hand, pointed directly at Volta's crotch.

'Hands off the worm, fat boy,' said the man.

'Who the fuck...' Volta's words died as the man smashed a fist into his face.

The Worst of Evils

Volta groaned as a thousand starbursts exploded in unison behind his eyes. The man wasn't particularly big, but the force he had hit him with was unbelievable. Volta blinked several times to clear the last of the dying embers. 'You'll never make it out of here alive,' he hissed.

'I got in, I can get out. But thanks for your concern.'

'What do you want?' Volta's eyes widened as he realised the gun sported a silencer.

'Your head. On a big fucking stick.'

'I have money. How much will it take for you to walk away?'

'Bill Gates doesn't have that much money.'

Volta swallowed hard. 'Who are you?'

'You tried to kill me, *Ruby*. Me and my friend, and that hacks me off. I wasn't going to wait around for you to try again, so I decided to kill you first.'

Volta tried to stand, his huge bulk making it difficult enough, the second punch in the face making it impossible. He fell back against the sun-lounger, his robe splaying open and exposing his swollen, hairy belly.

'But I've changed my mind. I'm not a petty man. I can forget that you tried to kill us.

Volta's chest rose and fell in relief as he thought about how he would kill this fool.

'Problem is, Ruby, I checked you out before I came for you. And now I know too much. I know what you get up to, especially in here. I know about the children you've raped and tortured and killed.'

Volta tried again to stand but his legs were kicked from beneath him and he fell to the tiled floor like a sick elephant. He tried to roll onto his back, but the man stood over him with his foot pressed into the flabby folds, keeping him pinned to the tiles.

A hand snaked down and wrenched the cord from Volta's bathrobe. Before he could fight it, his hands had been pulled behind his back and tied tightly together. A moment later the man was using a large towel to do the same to his ankles.

'Please,' Volta begged. 'Please don't.'

'I reckon that's what the kids said too.'

Volta screamed for help, his lungs almost tearing with the effort.

'Wishing you hadn't soundproofed the room now?' the man asked.

The man stood up and rolled Volta onto his back. He crouched down, his face close to Volta's, his eyes flat and cold as slate.

'What do you want? Volta asked again, fear leaking from his pores.

'All I want you to do is think of the kids,' said the man. 'I want you to think of them as you die.'

He stood up and used his foot to roll Volta over and into the pool. He entered the water with an enormous splash then bobbed around for a few seconds. His mouth was barely above the water and he spluttered as he craned his neck for air. It wouldn't be long before he sank beneath the surface – not with his arms and legs immobilised – then it would be over. Then, the kids would be safe.

Mack sat down carefully on the end of the sun-lounger, his body still stiff and painful from the knife wound and the weeks in hospital. He placed the gun on the tiles between his feet and watched Ruby Volta struggle to remain afloat.

No-one would disturb them. No-one would hear his coughs and splutters and cries for help.

Mack leaned back in the sun-lounger and relaxed. Evil was dying and he had all the time in the world to watch.

THE END

Printed in Great Britain
by Amazon.co.uk, Ltd.,
Marston Gate.